HIS MORNING KISS

BOOKS BY JAN THOMPSON

CITY/COASTAL/BEACH ROMANCE

Seaside Chapel (7 Books)

JanThompson.com/seaside

Savannah Sweethearts (12 Books)

JanThompson.com/savannah

Vacation Sweethearts (8 Books)

JanThompson.com/vacation

ROMANTIC SUSPENSE/THRILLERS

Protector Sweethearts (6 Books)

JanThompson.com/protector

Defender Sweethearts (6 Books)

JanThompson.com/defender

Binary Hackers (4 Books)

JanThompson.com/binary

JanThompson.com/books

HIS MORNING KISS

SEASIDE CHAPEL
BOOK THREE

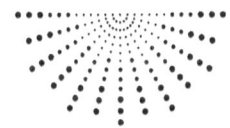

JAN THOMPSON

GEORGIA
PRESS

HIS MORNING KISS (SEASIDE CHAPEL BOOK 3)

Published by Georgia Press LLC
Author Website: JanThompson.com
Book List: JanThompson.com/books
Book News: JanThompson.com/newsletter

Book Cover by Carpe Librum Book Design

The lyrics for the "His Eye Is on the Sparrow" hymn penned by Civilla D. Martin in 1905 are in the public domain.

The lyrics for the "And Can It Be" hymn penned by Charles Wesley in 1738 are in the public domain.

Second Edition eBook ISBN: 978-1-944188-72-6
Second Edition Paperback ISBN: 978-1-944188-77-1

To my Lord and Savior, Jesus Christ, who died on the cross to save me from my sins and rose again from the grave to give me eternal life in heaven.

For God so loved the world that He gave His only begotten Son, that whoever believes in Him should not perish but have everlasting life.
—John 3:16

READ A FREE EBOOK IN THE SAME STORY WORLD

Set in Georgia, South Carolina, and Tennessee, this clean and wholesome Christian romance tells the story of art gallery archivist Sheryl Breckenridge and world-famous sculptor Winton Pace. Read this ebook for free!

Time for Me (A Vacation Sweethearts Prequel)
JanThompson.com/time-free

ABOUT THE SEASIDE CHAPEL
SERIES

Welcome to *USA Today* bestselling author Jan Thompson's **Seaside Chapel** Christian beach romance series. These novels are set on real-life St. Simon's Island, Georgia—a beach town where history is all around and the future is a moment away—and the neighboring fictitious Seaside Island, where the rich and famous in Jan's story world live.

Savor the small-town atmosphere and the warm southern beaches of St. Simon's Island and the idyllic Golden Isles along the Atlantic Ocean. Enjoy the music of the orchestra and hymns of the church, and hang out with our Christian friends who attend Seaside Chapel, a little church by the sea known for its beach weddings and fair share of love and life.

As these Christians grow in their knowledge and understanding of God, they are tested in their spiritual maturity, their love lives, and their relationships with others. Share their heartaches and healing, and cheer them on as they celebrate faith, family, and friends.

JanThompson.com/seaside

- Book 1: His Longing Heart
- Book 2: His Wake-Up Call
- Book 3: His Morning Kiss
- Book 4: His Quiet Serenade
- Book 5: His Waiting Love
- Book 6: His Beach Retreat

While Seaside Chapel novels can be read as standalone stories, you can see a bigger picture of the Seaside Chapel community and get a glimpse of the futures of previous characters if you read Books 1-6 in order.

A FREE EBOOK FOR YOU!

A Christian beach romance novel, *Ask You Later* is the story of artist Leon Watts, who returns to Tybee Island and Savannah to jump-start his fledgling career. This novel is a part of the Savannah Sweethearts collection, and happens one year before the Seaside Chapel series begins.

Download this FREE novel now:
JanThompson.com/ask-seaside

YOU ARE READING HIS MORNING KISS

SEASIDE CHAPEL BOOK 3

**A singing chef.
A widowed billionaire.
A cottage by the sea.**

A father of two, widowed billionaire Diehl Brooks returns home to St. Simon's Island and falls in love with his sister's personal chef. Will complications from his unfulfilled first marriage threaten his chance for love a second time around?

A SELFLESS PERSONAL CHEF...

Chef Skye Langston cooks for local residents and visitors to the Golden Isles. When her friend and client, Brinley Brooks, asks her to cook for her older brother, who will be in town for the summer, Skye is wary. Although they move in different social circles, she has heard a lot about Diehl Brooks, once the most eligible bachelor on the island. Now their worlds intersect in his sister's beach house. Seeing him almost every day changes Skye's opinion of him, but she tells herself that she is only being kind to the widower, as the Bible asks Christians to be kind to others.

A SINGLE-AGAIN BILLIONAIRE...

Having drifted away from God, almost-forty-year-old Diehl doesn't know how to come home. After being tragically widowed, he works himself aground, leaving his two school-aged children with their nanny and grandparents. Diehl burns out at work, and is forced to take a sabbatical before he destroys the multi-billion-dollar family business. On St. Simon's Island and the neighboring Seaside Island, his casual friendship with his sister's personal chef quickly turns into something romantic, but his past shows up to collect yet another pound of flesh.

A SPLINTERED FAMILY...

Diehl might be newly single again, but his first marriage has long tentacles. When secrets from his marriage-of-convenience threaten his present-day happiness, Diehl is convinced he is not good enough for Skye. Why would God bless him with love a second time around when he failed the first time?

In the middle of his emotional angst, Diehl's children throw his life into a tailspin. Even as Skye's presence soothes his soul, Diehl has a hard time believing in happy endings. How can God give him sweet promises of a better tomorrow when his life is so bitter right now?

His Morning Kiss is the third novel in *USA Today* bestselling author Jan Thompson's **Seaside Chapel** Christian small-town beach romance series. This book was previously published as *Sing with Me*.

His Morning Kiss (Seaside Chapel Book 3)
JanThompson.com/morning

Seaside Chapel
JanThompson.com/seaside

Sign up for Jan Thompson's mailing list:
JanThompson.com/newsletter

HIS MORNING KISS

CHAPTER ONE

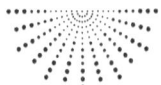

 iehl Brooks woke up to the flapping of wings where the sun shone into his bedroom through the open French doors. Thin white curtains fluttered on both doors leading to the balcony, beyond which he could see clear blue skies above St. Simon's Island, and hear the constant waves of the Atlantic Ocean. It had been music to his ears since his childhood summer days with his three siblings, back when Parker had been alive and their youngest sister, Zoe, had been a scrawny thing. And as for his middle sister, Brinley, she was always Brinley.

To this day, Brinley cared for the rest of the family more than they cared for themselves. Diehl hadn't planned on taking a sabbatical until Brinley had stepped in. Being the level-headed sister that she was, Brinley saw Diehl's soul and knew he needed a time-out. Dad agreed, and they made Diehl stay home. Only Diehl couldn't stay home. He had to work. So

Dad decided to come out of his semi-retirement and run Brooks Investments for the entire summer—right out of Diehl's Atlanta office.

Dad had said he had to save the company.

From his own son?

Diehl closed his eyes to hear the ocean again, a balm of Gilead for the pain in his soul. If he could just hear the ocean, it would smooth out the wrinkles from the one year of woes he had undergone, for which he could blame no one but himself.

And Isobel.

He could always blame his dead wife.

The crashing of the waves on the sands of the Georgia coast always put him at ease, beckoning sleep to come again. Sleep, sweet sleep.

To sleep away his sorrow...

Flap! Flap!

What on earth?

Diehl's eyes popped open again.

There, circling the fan above him, was a lone sparrow. A little brown bird with nowhere to go.

"That way, little one!" Diehl pointed to the French doors beyond his Californian king-sized bed and the oak floor. "Go back to your family."

And for good measure, he added, "Out there."

Not in here, where there were wounds in his heart at the perpetual roil of crisis after crisis in his life, as though God was trying to get his attention.

God, whom Diehl had ignored for years.

What had God done for him? Could anyone tell him? Where was God when Isobel drove her car over the cliff on the Amalfi Coast between Sorrento and Positano? Why hadn't God prevented Isobel's 800-horsepower Pagani Huayra BC Roadster from hitting the rails and going airborne?

Better yet, why hadn't God stopped her from speeding on the winding road on a rainy day?

God could have done all that and more.

Sometimes Diehl wondered why he had married the same woman twice when they hadn't gotten along since day one. Their first marriage had somehow lasted nine years. Their four-year divorce lasted longer than their second marriage to each other.

Six months after their second wedding, Isobel was dead.

Could God have prevented them from being divorced from each other in the first place? He could have kept the family together from the beginning for the sake of their two children, Elisa and Ethan. After all, wasn't God pro-family?

Well, to be honest, Diehl knew that Isobel always had a wandering heart. Diehl couldn't keep her in the house, even though it had been her own decision to give up a high-paying corporate job to stay at home with the kids so she wouldn't miss Elisa's first words and Ethan's first walk.

She had made the decision herself to stop working.

Low maintenance, she was not, although Diehl hadn't cared that she had spent millions renovating their twelve-bedroom family home near the Chatta-hoochee River in the ritzy Buckhead part of Atlanta just so they could have grand Christmas parties with friends Diehl didn't know they had.

As long as it had made Isobel happy.

He had to make her happy. He had no choice. After all, she had threatened to take the kids to Italy and never return.

Perhaps he should have let her.

So many years and two kids later, they were done with each other. They went through a bitter divorce and custody battle. Isobel's lawyer dragged their family dirt all over court. She had recorded everything he had ever said about Brooks Investments and the transactions and mergers, and threatened to make them public.

Diehl had told her what he did because he wanted her to see how hard he worked to provide for the family, his billions in inheritance from Grandpa Brooks notwithstanding. He still put in the effort to keep the money in the family.

It was all for the future of their children, he had told her.

She hadn't cared, had she?

All Isobel had wanted was to be free. And Diehl alone knew that. To the rest of the Brooks family, Isobel had painted herself as a victim, especially when she talked to Diehl's sister. Consequently, to Brinley, Diehl was to blame for the failed marriage. It took a few years for Diehl to explain his side of the story to her.

Their prenuptial agreement had all sorts of clauses in it, and at the end of the day, Isobel won. Diehl bought her a cliff house in Positano and another in Sorrento, as if one wasn't enough.

And he bought her an Aston Martin Valkyrie.

And she bought herself a Huayra.

Yep, Isobel liked her fast cars. And one took her over the cliff.

Flap! Flap!

"Go!" Diehl yelled at the sparrow. "Go already! I told you to fly out on your own, stupid bird!"

He watched the sparrow. Maybe it was afraid of something.

Somewhere at the back of his mind, a Bible verse wanted to pop up. But he had been away from the church for so long that he couldn't remember much. Still, surely there was a verse about sparrows.

He felt an urge to google the verse, but he didn't. He had left his Bible in Atlanta, but truth be told, he hadn't opened that Bible in years. He had kept it only because Grandpa Brooks had gifted it to him when he graduated from high school years ago. It was one of the precious things that reminded him of Grandpa.

Like this entire island. Whenever he was here, he felt an urge to change his life, be a better person, improve his perspective, and seek a higher learning.

And return to God?

Perhaps.

Brinley expected him to go to church with her family. Maybe he would. Maybe not.

Diehl had rarely been back to the small hundred-year-old church by the sea since Grandpa Brooks passed away. He could recall the few times he went to

Seaside Chapel in the last twenty years. Once was for the wedding of his now-deceased older brother, Parker. The second time, it was for Parker's funeral. Brinley's wedding was the last time he stepped foot in that church. That ceremony brought back a lot of memories about Parker, who had told Brinley he wanted to dance with her at her wedding.

How ridiculous it was for Parker to drown in a boating accident at sea, leaving behind a loving wife and two kids.

Same as him.

Diehl made himself a mental note to call his sister-in-law. Maybe Riley had some tips for him on parenting two kids after losing a spouse. What was the probability of both of them being widowed within ten years of each other?

Diehl had always liked Riley. She still had shares of Brooks Investments—whatever Parker left for her. But Riley never went to the Brooks building in downtown Atlanta. In fact, she rarely left her house, as far as Diehl knew.

At least Diehl made himself carry on and work after...after...

Why had God allowed this to happen?

Why?

Flap! Flap!

Diehl sighed. "I'm sorry, little sparrow. You're not a stupid bird."

Diehl crawled out of bed. He could see now that the whitewashed room with a few mirrors here and there to make the space look bigger, the curtains that framed the French doors, and whatever else Brinley put in the room, had confused the poor bird.

"Come here!" He said softly to the sparrow as he padded to the French doors. "Showing you the exit."

The bird flew in circles and then out to freedom.

A realization hit Diehl. He had left the French doors open. "Really, Brin should put a screen here so that the mosquitoes don't fly in."

The open door meant he hadn't set the alarm in the middle of the night when he arrived. He had driven all the way from Atlanta instead of flying in their family jet because Mom wanted to use it to pick up the kids from Hawaii, where they had been staying with their maternal grandparents for the school year.

It was summer now, and the two sets of grandparents were negotiating how to share their grandchildren between Hawaii and Georgia.

Diehl opted to stay out of it.

Anyway, he drove to St. Simon's the night before in his Ram 1500—just in case Brooks Renovation had any work for him to do while he was in town—and fell asleep without showering or unpacking or setting the house alarm.

Nobody had broken in—he hoped. He had slept through it all, in any case.

Diehl climbed back into bed. It was a big bed, too big for one person, but in many ways, it was better to be alone than to have a bickering wife.

Bickering?

Diehl stared at the ceiling.

He could not recall many moments of bliss with

Isobel. They always fought. They fought so much that his sister Brinley had to break up their quarrels. Mostly words, which Diehl could have won hands down.

To his credit, he had never lifted a fist at Isobel.

Or the children, who had to put up with their mom and dad arguing every time they were together. It was always the little things, like which restaurant to eat out at or whether Elisa should be allowed to wear short skirts and put on makeup before she reached puberty. Family stuff.

Isobel had always complained about everything. She hated their neighbors—who were almost never there. She hated Atlanta, with its humid summers. She hated the Georgia coast—too plain compared to Amalfi. She hated everything.

Diehl found peace at the office. He loved working. Work was life to him, and life was work.

Ironically, not for the rest of the summer this year.

Banished to the Georgia coast to rest his brain and heal his heart, Diehl had opted not to stay in the Brooks family home on Seaside Island. Not with Mom constantly nagging about how he was *not* raising his two children.

Wasn't having a full-time bilingual nanny with a bachelor's degree in sociology enough?

Maybe Dad should put Mom to work. Then she would stop harassing Diehl about the kids.

Then again, poor Mom. She hardly saw her grandchildren.

Every Christmas for years, Isobel had taken the kids to Hawaii, where her parents lived, running that pineapple plantation of theirs. It was warm in Hawaii in December, and the kids loved it. However, it meant that Diehl's own parents hadn't been able to spend Christmas with the kids for years.

So he could see why Mom was all agitated with her sudden role as mother figure now that Isobel was...

Dead.

Gone.

Diehl found himself sobbing softly into the down pillows.

The mother of his children. The woman he had married in his twenties, divorced when Elisa was only seven years old, and remarried when their daughter was eleven and their son turned eight.

"Why did I remarry her?" Diehl couldn't pin down a reason.

Somewhere in the noise, he'd found out that Isobel's bank account was dry. All those millions she had gotten from the divorce proceedings were gone very quickly.

Did he feel sorry for her? Isobel needed him. He liked being needed.

So he had remarried her.

Several months into their second marriage, Isobel flew to her vacation home in Positano and bought that Huayra. She called from Italy, asking if she could stay for a few months there—alone. No husband, no kids. To catch her breath, she said. Their second time around had been a whirlwind to her.

A whirlwind? What on earth did that mean?

And she never returned to the States.

Within a month of their last conversation, she was gone.

Since then, Diehl had been at the bottom of an emotional well that affected everything in his life until now.

I have to get out of this funk.

"Where have I gone wrong, God? Help me. Help me."

CHAPTER TWO

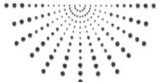

$\mathcal{I}$t wasn't Skye Langston's job to fill the bird feeder in the side garden outside the kitchen window, but standing at the farmhouse-style kitchen sink, rinsing out the dishes for her assistant to put into the dishwasher, she could clearly see that the feeder was empty and that someone ought to feed the birds.

The birdbath next to the feeder under the shady live oak trees looked like it needed to be refilled as well. The water had all but evaporated from the tiled top on this hot June day.

Where did Brinley get that bath?

Seven months pregnant, Brinley Brooks-McMillan spent more of her time indoors at her other house. She hadn't been to this beach house in a while and had mentioned that someday she might sell it. The cleaning lady had aired out the place before Skye came the day before to fill the refrigerator and pantry.

However, no one had filled the bird feeder or bird-bath. Probably in days.

Skye didn't recall if it had rained in a few days.

Her feet felt tired. She had been working non-stop for the last two weeks driving from house to house on St. Simon's and also Seaside Island, cooking for vacationers. They came in droves about now, and their summer life was easier if they didn't have to cook for themselves.

Most of the time they ate out in the local area restaurants, but Skye was glad to accommodate some of their special preferences and dietary requirements. Some people had food allergies, and if not them, their kids.

She often planned the menus after consultation with her clients, but not this one. Brinley simply told her that Diehl ate "anything" but was partial to peach cobblers. Brinley asked her to cook some mushroom risotto, which Skye had made for their Seaside Chapel women's Bible study group on some Tuesday nights.

Last night, Skye made a peach cobbler as a welcome present.

She and her assistant, Marlo, had been here since ten o'clock in the morning. Brinley had told her that Diehl liked to eat his lunch at noon, but that he might be late.

Well, his truck was parked outside. He was probably still upstairs somewhere. She hadn't heard anything.

When Skye and Marlo had arrived, the door was not only unlocked but the alarm wasn't set. In retrospect, she should have called Brinley and asked if Diehl was here, but Skye had so many containers to haul into the house to cook lunch and prepare for dinner that she had forgotten all about calling anyone.

Besides, it was relatively safe on the island, as everyone knew. And most importantly, Brinley had given Skye a key to the beach house so she could come and go any time. Apparently, Diehl had signed off on that too.

In fact, Brinley had said to walk right in. She said her brother wouldn't mind because Skye was like family.

Am I like family?

Skye wasn't sure she wanted to have much to do with Diehl. She had heard things about him that unsettled her.

Skye and Marlo made quick work of the prepared ingredients—Skye liked to get everything ready before she arrived at the client's house—and the mushroom risotto was soon in the oven. Then it was out of the oven.

And still no sign of Diehl.

Skye glanced at the clock on the wall. It was past noon. She had to leave soon because she had a final rehearsal that afternoon with Brinley and their friend from church, Avery Chung. Avery usually played the trumpet, but she was singing a duet with Skye this time, while Brinley played the piano accompaniment.

Skye dried her hands, and messaged Brinley and Avery in their group chat, while Marlo finished loading the dishwasher.

Other than mushroom risotto, they had made cucumber sandwiches for the afternoon. Skye had no idea whether Diehl liked that or not, but since he hadn't returned her calls when she tried to find out what he wanted to eat, she decided that he was going to have cucumber sandwiches with his tea this afternoon.

Skye chuckled. He probably wasn't the tea and finger sandwich sort of guy—considering the giant gas-guzzling charcoal-colored Ford pickup truck in the driveway—but it was his fault for not returning her call or replying to her email. She even attached a link to the menu software she had paid a lot of money for to simplify her life as a personal chef.

If the client wouldn't discuss with her what he wanted to eat, then every day would be full of surprises.

Of course, now that Diehl had arrived in town, she'd finally get a chance to speak with him in person and ask for a meeting to make sure the next three months would go smoothly for both Diehl and her chefs.

After all, she was too busy to chase after clients. She had a personal chef business to run and a restaurant to manage. If she wasn't cooking at clients' homes, she'd be at Saffron on Jekyll Island, looking after her forty-nine percent share of the award-winning restaurant, which had been her brother's.

Sebastian and his ex-girlfriend, Talia, had co-owned the place once upon a time. To help her brother out in his messy relationship back then, Skye bought his minority share of the company. Unfortunately, majority partner Talia lived in London and didn't care much about the day-to-day operations. Skye ran the restaurant and did all the work, but only received the profit as a minority partner.

Skye had sold her million-dollar oceanfront house on St. Simon's Island to buy out Sebastian's share, and now she lived in a rental condo by the river where she could see the sunset from her screened-in porch, although she didn't have much time to enjoy the scenery.

Skye didn't want to sell her land on Seaside Island to buy Talia's shares. Nor did she want to downsize Skye's the Limit and fire any of her twelve personal chefs. And she did not want to dip into her savings and stocks any more than she needed to.

It would be unwise to cash out everything Uncle Miller and Aunt Irma had left her, which had formed the seed of her businesses now and kept her out of financial debt. In fact, she had multiplied her fortune by wisely investing in her business.

She might consider investing in her brother's future ventures in Atlanta, but there was still time to think about that. Sebastian now lived in Athens, Georgia, where his wife, Emmeline, was finishing up her master's degree in harp performance at the University of Georgia. His goal was to start a new flagship restaurant in Atlanta after Emmeline was done with graduate school.

"What did she say?" Marlo asked, wiping down the countertop and island.

Marlo had been a godsend to Skye. He worked hard, had no family obligations, and was available at any time. He was attending Brunswick College to get a degree in culinary science. He was such a good cook that Skye almost suggested he aim for a chef's hat. But then again, who was she to tell him what to do?

"I'm waiting for her to text me." Skye put her phone back into her apron pocket. "I kid you not, Brinley told me to come right in."

"What if her brother walks around in his underwear?" Marlo laughed.

"I know, right. My brother wore boxers at home all the time—and probably still does even though he's married."

"No comments about myself."

Skye washed her hands. "We don't know where he wants to eat. Dining room or kitchen table."

Marlo shook his head.

"Let's set the dining table. We can always move either way."

"Right."

"Thank you for working with me today and adjusting to our client's schedule." Skye looked for silverware to set the table. "I would normally tell you to leave if you want, since we've been here half an hour past our time, but I'd rather not be alone, so thank you for staying."

"No problem."

Obviously, Skye didn't want to be alone with Brinley's older brother, who was all by himself in this beautiful house, although he was single again.

Not only did she have a professional reputation to keep, she was also concerned that the guys at church she might be interested in would change their view of her if she were found alone with a backsliding Christian—possibly even an unsaved person—such as Diehl, who had once cussed out Pastor Gonzalez when the latter asked him if he had ever accepted Jesus as his personal Lord and Savior.

Diehl had insisted that he was a believer.

Who had fallen away from the faith?

Was it because he was a gazillionaire? The verse from 1 Timothy 6:9 came to Skye's mind.

But they that will be rich fall into temptation and a snare, and into many foolish and hurtful lusts, which drown men in destruction and perdition.

What did the verse mean? Skye had been pondering it for a while. She and her brother had worked their way up from nothing. Now they were successful business people. Would they someday fall into "temptation and a snare" or would they be able to stay on the straight and narrow path of serving God with their successes?

What about Diehl? Diehl was successful too. But he had received a shoo-in job at his father's company. Not that he wasn't working as hard as everyone else. However, he probably had it easier.

Maybe?

Skye felt bad for being judgmental—

Or jealous of his immense wealth?

She shook it off.

The women at church who had grown up with Diehl in their childhood summer days—some of whom he had dated in years past—all warned Skye to stay away from him. He had a reputation for being a trap—although he had only been married twice, to the same woman.

A trap?

And here I am in this house, cooking for the next three months.

"I'm yours if you want me to stay all day," Marlo said.

"I have a rehearsal at two and then we'll be over at Mrs. Morton's at three, and then back here at five." Skye read off her schedule for the day as she walked toward the refrigerator with her phone.

There was little for Marlo to do, really. However, Skye liked having someone to talk to. She touched the side of the baking dish on the counter. It was still warm.

She found a thick mitten and used that to line the refrigerator shelf. She put the mushroom risotto on the mitten, closed the door—

And shrieked.

Diehl Brooks stood there, grinning at her. "Do I look that bad?"

He seemed to have just stepped out of the shower. His hair was damp. His five o'clock shadow was untrimmed. His T-shirt had designer holes in it, yesteryear's style where five-hundred-dollar shirts came ripped here and there.

A rag. Skye wouldn't use it to wipe the kitchen floor.

"You must be Chef Langston," Diehl said.

"Skye."

"Pretty name. I believe I've seen you before—at various dinners at my parents' cottage, for example." Diehl extended his hand.

Ah. He remembers me.

Skye hesitated. She had just done the dishes. Her palms were rough. She was going to apply some lotion to her fingers. She did not want his first impression of her to be that she didn't have soft hands.

Why would it matter?

"Would you like your lunch now?" Skye asked instead.

"You can call me Diehl." His voice was cold. He retracted his hand.

"I'm sorry. We're not answering each other's questions." Skye drew a deep breath. "Let me start over. I can't shake your hands right now because my hands are rough. I've been doing dishes, and I left my hand cream at home."

"I have the best lotion ever. Let me get it." And he dashed upstairs.

"That was unexpected." Skye glanced at Marlo, who shrugged.

Skye opened the cabinets until she found dinner plates. She put a plate on the island counter and waited. She had no idea if Diehl wanted to eat or not.

She glanced at her phone. Text message from Brinley.

"Yes, I know he's here," Skye said to no one.

Diehl was back, not even huffing. He looked athletic and fit. Muscles everywhere, even on his thighs and calves. Maybe he worked out a lot. Cycled some, maybe.

But why did she care?

Skye stared at the bottle and laughed. "Coconut oil."

"The best. Put your palms out," Diehl said. He poured a couple of drops on them.

Skye rubbed her palms together. "My coconut oil is in a jar. How do you get yours out of that bottle in the winter when it solidifies?"

"I just put it in a warm tub of water." He placed the bottle on the island counter. "Now can you shake my hand?"

"Is it important?" Skye asked.

"I don't suppose it is. But I went to a lot of trouble to get you the lotion."

"You ran up and down the stairs and got some exercise. You're welcome." Skye opened the refrigerator again. "Mushroom risotto for lunch?"

Diehl made a face. "Could you cook me some breakfast?"

"Breakfast wasn't on the menu today. Your sister said that you'd be here for lunch."

"I arrived last night—two in the morning, in fact."

"We did see your truck outside when we got here at ten."

"Ten? I didn't hear you come in."

"You left the front door unlocked and the alarm off."

"Did I? I must've been tired after a long day at work. I had to drive five hours to get here."

Skye nodded. She pointed to the labels on the glass containers in the refrigerator. "We labeled everything. Reheat according to the instructions."

"Could you add breakfast for today, please?"

"Chef Joseph will be in tomorrow morning at eight for breakfast—unless you want to adjust that time."

"Adjust it to now."

"Well, if you had answered the emails I sent you, we might have known you'd want breakfast today at lunchtime."

"Sorry. I was busy."

"Starting tomorrow, we'll prepare three meals a day for you—except on days when you eat out. However, before we can go forward, we do need to meet and figure out what you want us to cook for you all summer. I have some sample menus we can look at. We usually do that *before* we show up to cook."

Diehl nodded. "Any time. I have all day."

Skye pointed to a pretty clock on the wall. "I have to go to a prescheduled activity. For today, we will be back at five to cook you dinner—unless you want to eat the risotto for dinner as well."

"I don't like risotto."

"Your sister said..."

Diehl made a face. "I used to like it. Not anymore."

"Peach cobbler?" Skye asked.

"I love peach cobbler."

Skye pointed to the pie on the table. "I'll put that in the fridge in a minute."

"I still want breakfast."

Are you a kid? "We don't have time to cook you breakfast now at such a late notice."

"He can cook." Diehl pointed to Marlo.

"Marlo's my assistant. He's not a chef. At Skye's the Limit, only chefs cook."

"Skye's the Limit?" Diehl grinned. "But no breakfast."

"If we'd had that meeting, you could have told me, right?"

"Are you rubbing it in?"

Well, yes. "No, sir."

"Don't *sir* me. It's Diehl."

"Well, Diehl, for today, your lunch and dinner are on me. I didn't want you to pay for what you won't eat, although your sister said you'd eat anything."

"Including breakfast." Diehl stood his ground.

Marlo made a sound.

Skye glanced at the clock again.

Under her breath, she prayed for mercy as she thought about walking out and never returning to this client.

A verse popped into her head, stopping her from doing anything really bad, like opening the refrigerator again, taking out the risotto, and throwing it in his face. Well, she had never done that before, but there was always a first time—although she'd have to clean up the floor afterward.

Also, she might ruin her reputation and that of

Skye's the Limit personal chef service, not to mention taint her testimony as a Christian.

Okay. Let's not throw food at new clients.

She tried to remember a verse.

But love your enemies, do good, and lend, hoping for nothing in return; and your reward will be great, and you will be sons of the Most High. For He is kind to the unthankful and evil.

Luke 6:35. The words of the Lord Jesus Himself.

Is Diehl my enemy?

Maybe the verse meant that if she had to be kind to her enemies, how much more to someone in between friend and enemy—say, a friend's older brother she hardly knew.

Skye drew a deep breath. She leaned against the kitchen island and checked the schedule on her phone. "I mentioned that Chef Joseph will be here at eight tomorrow morning. Do you prefer another time?"

"Wait. I'm connecting the dots. You're not cooking for me tomorrow?"

"Didn't I tell say that Chef Joseph will be here?"

"I wasn't paying attention."

"I don't work on weekends or on Wednesday nights," Skye explained. "Saturday is my day off and Sunday is church day."

"My sister says you're the best. I'm not sure I want anyone else cooking for me."

Skye began to realize that Diehl was looking for familiarity, for things that were not constantly or unexpectedly changing. She had tried to prepare him for how she managed her business, but he had apparently not read that email either.

"The details of the contract were in the email," Skye said. "One of many emails I sent you."

"Frankly, I just assumed Brin took care of everything. She knows what I like to eat, but I can see that a few things fell through the holes. Breakfast, for example."

"And risotto?"

"Yeah."

"She signed the contract on your behalf since this is her house, but it looks like we need to clarify something here. She hired a personal chef who rotates among clients, and not a private chef who works exclusively for you," Skye said. "I have twelve personal chefs working for me, and a bevy of assistants who shop and help us prepare the meals for our clients."

"I thought Brin hired me a private chef. After all, she gave you the key to the house and the security code to come in and cook for me, so I don't have to get up and unlock the door for you."

"She did that because she trusts me. We're friends."

"Are we friends?" Diehl asked.

"Well..."

"Friends don't let friends skip breakfast."

"Is that right?"

"Uh-huh."

Skye didn't know whether to laugh or cry. She had to do what the client wanted—within reason, of course

—because he was paying the bills. If he wanted breakfast for lunch, who was she to deny him the special meal?

"Also, can you be my private chef? I don't want to share." He looked serious.

Skye tried not to read too much into that, but she didn't know what he meant. For now, she would take it literally.

"Frankly, I don't know if you need a dedicated chef who works in this kitchen only. You're on vacation and you'll be more flexible if you can eat at The Priory or at your sister's home or out in restaurants."

"If I hadn't let my private chef go, he'd be with me today. He traveled with my family to our vacation homes, and he also handled all my dinner parties, which Isobel..."

His voice trailed off.

Skye knew exactly who Isobel was. Her heart sank.

He cleared his throat. "No worries. I'll eat the risotto."

Skye did everything she could not to give the poor widower a hug. She felt sorry for him, although he was going to make her late for her rehearsal at church. She couldn't miss that, could she? After all, the whole point of the rehearsal was so that she could better minister to others—

Ah, especially the unchurched.

From all that she knew about Diehl through his sister, this man needed to be ministered to. How could Skye not see that? He had gone through so much after getting his wife back and losing her again. Skye remembered how everyone had cheered in Sunday school that Brinley's older brother had finally reconciled with his wife.

Within months, she was tragically killed in a car wreck, leaving behind a husband and two elementary-school-aged children.

Skye's heart melted.

She turned to Marlo. "Let's cook some breakfast."

CHAPTER THREE

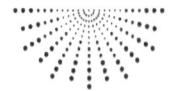

When Diehl told Skye he wanted eggs, sausage, bacon, toast, and a side of pancakes, she didn't flinch. And miracle of miracles, she had all the ingredients in Brinley's refrigerator or pantry. This woman came prepared.

Diehl didn't leave the kitchen, but tried to get out of the way by moving to the other side of the island. He watched Skye cook sausage patties and bacon while Marlo prepared the pancake batter.

He wasn't sure if he could eat all of that, but he hadn't eaten anything since a quick dinner on the road the night before. It had been over twelve hours since he'd eaten anything substantial.

"I can help," he said.

"Huh?" Skye almost didn't hear him. She had her back turned to him.

Her hair was tied up in a bun, but it looked

caramel colored. She was tall, maybe five feet nine or ten. Her assistant was even taller, at least six feet.

"I can make coffee," Diehl offered.

"Feel free." Skye flipped the sausage patties.

"Must be hard to cook for one," Diehl said.

"It can be."

"How about if you cook extra, and I'll microwave them tomorrow morning so you don't have to send anyone until lunch?"

Skye didn't answer right away. "I guess we can cook more sausage and bacon, but Chef Joseph will be here tomorrow morning."

"I should've said that sooner." Diehl found the coffee maker. It wasn't much of one, but he knew that Brinley didn't drink much coffee—especially now while she was carrying her first child.

"What about pancakes?" Marlo asked.

Diehl shook his head. "I'm not sure I want pancakes every day, you know."

"Yeah."

"Where are the coffee beans?" Diehl asked.

"I saw some in the pantry," Skye said. "The grinder is in there too."

Marlo stepped over to the coffee maker. "I'll take care of it, sir."

Diehl nodded. "Now I have nothing to do."

"You can go fill the bird feeder and pour clean water into the birdbath," Skye suggested.

"Where are they?" Diehl asked.

Skye pointed toward the window above the farmhouse kitchen sink. "In the side garden. You might ask your sister where she keeps the birdseed."

Diehl made his way through the kitchen and breakfast area to the back door. There was a low deck that led off to a side garden.

But first, the view.

He thought the view from the upstairs master bedroom was spectacular, but it was here too, on the ground level. Beyond the deck was a well-mowed back-yard, leading to a boardwalk over some dunes and sea oats, and then it was the beach and sea and sky.

He thought he might go for a swim in the ocean, though he'd rather not go alone. Ever since Parker drowned out there, Diehl had been loath to step into the ocean.

It was irrational, he knew, but he felt the weight of his brother's responsibilities on top of his. With Parker gone, Diehl was the first child now. He felt that he had to make sure his parents lived out their retirement years without any needs or wants.

Ironically, Dad had gone to Atlanta to bat for him, to cover for him, and to fix the five-billion-dollar errors he had made in the last two months. At least Dad didn't yell at him over it. Diehl was sure that Dad could salvage the deal. Either the merger would not go through or they would walk away with great investments.

It could go either way.

But he wasn't going to think about that now. His job was to rest for three months until he healed from this pain in his heart. And then he'd be raring to go back to work.

What pain, exactly?

He walked around the house toward the garage—which was closed. Of course. Sigh.

Before he returned to the house to open the garage door, he texted Brinley to find out where the birdseed was.

She called him immediately. "How's lunch?"

"I'm sure the risotto is good, but they're making me breakfast."

"What?" Brinley's voice sounded concerned. "Please don't push my dear friend around."

"Skye or Marlo?" Diehl asked.

"You know it's Skye. She tried to contact you for days. You never replied."

"That's what she said too."

"You really didn't get back to her, so you made her work more difficult."

"I didn't have time."

"Now you have time. Please apologize to Skye and work out your meal plan ASAP."

Diehl chuckled. "You sure are pushy."

"Just trying to keep food on your table for the summer. Skye has a very kind heart, but I don't want to see her taken advantage of. She works hard and I don't want you to drive her to the ground like you drive yourself."

"I don't. What does she know about Isobel?" Diehl asked.

"Our entire church knows about the tragic accident in Italy, although it's been a year." Brinley's voice was quiet. "Why do you ask about Skye?"

"I just want to know. She dropped everything and cooked me breakfast. I felt like a spoiled child."

"You can be, Diehl."

"But I'm still your brother."

"Right. And I'm praying for you that you'll come back to the Lord or meet the Lord, whichever is your case."

That was her way of saying that Diehl had strayed and probably needed a divine spanking. "God still loves me, no matter what."

"Yes, but does He want you to stay stuck that way? He wants the best for you, not the worst in life."

"All I'm getting is the worst right now." Diehl laughed. "Is God punishing me?"

"I don't know."

"Anyway, where's your birdseed?" Diehl stepped onto the grass barefoot. The noonday sun shone on him, making him sweat a little.

"None left. I have a fifty-pound bag here at my house you can get the next time you come over for dinner."

"That's too late. The birds are hungry now."

"Are they?" Brinley chuckled. "Then it's your job to feed them."

"I will. But I'm only here for three months. You need to send someone over to do it the rest of the time."

"Maybe the new owner will."

"You're thinking of selling this beach house?"

Diehl looked around the yard and small garden and the live oak trees. "How big is this property?"

"One acre. Very rare on this small island, but we razed the house next door to extend the yard."

"Good move. How much do you think a house like this will go for?"

Brinley named the price.

Chump change for him. "Don't sell it yet. Let me stay here for three months. I might want it."

"Why? You have a house in Atlanta."

"Well, I might want to come to the coast from time to time, and I don't want to stay with Mom and Dad."

"It will be nice to see you more often," Brinley said. "You're the only brother I have left."

"Why is life so tragic, Brin? I mean, Parker left behind two kids. I have two motherless kids now."

"God is still sovereign. That is all I know."

"If He is sovereign, why didn't He stop the tragedies?"

"Do we know the mind of God? Did we make the universe?" Brinley asked. "Do you remember what Job said when he lost his sons and daughters?"

"I don't know, Brin. I know you've been catching up on the Bible ever since you became a Christian, but I'm not sure if I'm a believer or not, you know? Sometimes I think I am, and sometimes I think I'm not."

He felt that he had wandered so far away from God that maybe he was at a point of no return.

Would God take him in?

"Job 1:21 says, 'Naked I came from my mother's womb, And naked shall I return there. The Lord gave, and the Lord has taken away; Blessed be the name of the Lord.' Job 1:22 says, 'In all this Job did not sin nor charge God with wrong.' The last thing we want to do in a tragedy is to blame God."

Diehl considered himself sufficiently lectured and he didn't want to talk about it anymore. "When did you become so religious, Brin?"

"It's not about religion, and you know that. It's about my relationship with God through Jesus Christ. When I accepted Him as my Lord and Savior, that was a one-time event called salvation. After that comes sanctification, which is a lifelong process."

Diehl was almost sure he had believed in Jesus Christ—back in college. Then again, had he really? If he had, he hadn't grown as a Christian.

It was too hard.

Much too hard.

He thanked Brinley and then hung up. He found the garden hose. The leftover water still inside the pipe was warm. He hosed down the birdbath and let the water run until it cooled down. He wanted the birds to have cool water.

He looked around for the sparrow who had flown into his bedroom that morning, but he didn't see any birds. They were probably cooling off in the massive oak trees in the area.

If left to anyone else, they might cut down these trees and build another beach house. Brinley wouldn't. However, if she sold the house, there was no telling what the new owners would do. And where would the sparrows go?

He tried again to recall the verse in the Bible about the sparrow. He couldn't remember. And there was his younger sister, Brinley, who remembered verses. He wondered if their youngest sister, Zoe, recalled any of their old times at church. Perhaps not, since Zoe would have been too young to remember much.

Diehl felt that he wanted to return to the days when he had been much closer to God's heart. Back to the brief period in college when he studied his Bible and attended church.

In the days before Isobel...

No one dared to tell him to his face, and it was too late now since Isobel was dead, but Diehl had stopped going to church after he met Isobel.

Back when he and Brinley were in high school, they went to church with Grandpa Brooks, who had been a Christian. Oddly enough, no one else was saved —until Diehl went to college. An evangelical student witnessed to him, and he believed in Jesus.

Or at least he thought he had.

After college, he went to graduate school to get his MBA, met Isobel, and the rest of his married life revolved around her—even during those years of separation and divorce.

It was all about what Isobel wanted.

Not about what God wanted.

If Isobel didn't want to go to church, they'd skip. If Isobel didn't want to tithe, they didn't.

After a while, Diehl had wondered if Isobel was a Christian. She had insisted she was, and that she believed God would be fine with whatever they did.

Whether they went to church or not, she believed that God would let them choose.

Would He, really?

Perhaps Diehl knew better, but he had been so besotted with Isobel that there was no way out for him. Had he been trapped in a snare that he wasn't even aware of it?

Once Diehl and Isobel became an item, he pushed God out of the picture, along with church and the Bible. From then on, Diehl worshipped Isobel and lived like her. Drinking, cussing, partying up a storm every weekend. How could he attend church when he was passed out on Sunday morning after partying all Saturday night?

Yet there was the fundamental question that he had been unable to answer. Had he loved Isobel, or had it all been lust?

"There you are!"

Diehl spun around, hose in hand, thumb still on the sprayer.

Skye shrieked and screamed as the water sprayed all over her.

"Oops." Diehl dropped the hose, but it was too late.

Skye was soaked from head to shoes. Her apron stuck to her shirt.

She laughed. "This is one way to cool off on a hot day."

"I'm so sorry." Diehl picked up the hose.

"I have to go home to change. I'm going to be so late to my rehearsal." Skye wiped water off her arms.

"Well, I came to tell you that your breakfast is ready."

"I'm sorry I was being difficult. I should have shut up and eaten the risotto."

"Speaking of which, you haven't eaten anything all morning, have you?"

"And all night."

"It's time to eat." Skye motioned for him to go indoors. "I'll put away the hose. Did you find the birdseed?"

"Brin said she's out."

"I can pick up some on the way back this afternoon."

"Would you? That's nice of you."

"If you don't mind, I'd like to go over some assessments and sample menus with you after dinner." Skye dragged the hose to where it had come from, in a little shed.

"Any time."

"Thanks. That will give us time to shop tonight for your lunch and dinner tomorrow."

"How did you know where the hose goes?" Diehl asked. "Have you been here before?"

"Yes, our trio sometimes rehearses in this house. There's a piano in the living room."

"I saw the baby grand when I arrived last night."

"Brin plays accompaniment for us. I usually sing, though Avery has started to sing with me. Sometimes she plays her trumpet."

Diehl helped Skye with the hose.

"You should go inside," Skye said. "Your breakfast is getting cold."

"It's okay. We're almost done here. Do you play an instrument?"

"Guitar." Skye closed the shed door. There was no lock. "You?"

"I am learning to play the guitar too. I used to play the piano—but it's been a while. Brin and I sometimes played piano duets at Christmas at church when we were kids so long ago."

"You went to church when you were little?" Skye walked with Diehl toward the oceanfront porch leading back to the kitchen.

Diehl nodded.

"You don't go to church anymore?" Skye asked.

"Brin asked me to go with her, so I might while I'm in town."

"I can't imagine not being in church. That's why it's called a sanctuary—although we know that Jesus is our sanctuary."

Diehl didn't say anything.

Is Jesus my sanctuary?

At the top of the stairs to the deck, Diehl asked Skye a question. "Do you think that a person can be saved and then lost again?"

"I think that once you are saved in Jesus, you are forever saved, but it's also possible for you—speaking in general terms—to not have been saved in the first place if you fell away from Jesus or reject Him."

"I don't reject Him."

"I meant *you* as in the general public, not you specifically." Skye stopped at the kitchen door.

The weather was warm, the sun was hot, and Skye was still wet. Her hair was matted, but her face was bright and shining, like it was sunny inside.

She smiled a little bit just as the sun moved. Her eyes had specks of gold, and made Diehl want to see how far he could look into her eyes. What was she thinking right now? Assessing his prodigal state of mind?

"Next Wednesday night, our trio is singing at the Fire Pit Service on the beach by the pavilion at church. Would you like to go?"

"What is your trio called?"

"Treble Trio."

"Interesting."

"Most of the time, we just call ourselves the trio." Skye turned her attention back to the Fire Pit Service. "If it rains, we meet in the wedding chapel. Either way, Pastor Gonzalez brings a short sermonette. We don't call it a sermon because he keeps it to fifteen minutes."

"Ah...I can't go." Diehl remembered his last encounter with Pastor Gonzalez.

Skye reached for his arm. "No one remembers. Besides, Pastor Gonzalez doesn't always preach on Wednesday nights. He just is this time."

"No one remembers what?" Diehl's eyes widened. How much did everyone at church know about him?

"We've been praying for you since your wife passed away." Skye's eyes glistened. "It's all going to be okay. God will take care of you, just like He takes care of the sparrows out there."

Sparrows.

The theme of the day, it seemed. What was God trying to say to him?

"You might recall the sparrow verses in the Bible," Skye said. "For example, Luke 12: 6-7 says, 'Are not five sparrows sold for two copper coins? And not one of them is forgotten before God. But the very hairs of your head are all numbered. Do not fear therefore; you are of more value than many sparrows.' God will take care of you and your kids."

"Why is everyone quoting Scripture to me?" Diehl asked. He started out genuinely wondering, but as he stood there with Skye, he started to feel less than everyone else, as though he had fallen short of every standard he ever knew.

"I would love it if someone shared a Bible verse with me," Skye said.

"Well, I don't. And for the record, I don't need God." Diehl sidestepped her and disappeared into the house, leaving her standing on the deck alone.

CHAPTER FOUR

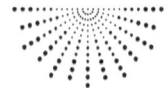

"*H*ow was your rehearsal?" Diehl asked as he invited Skye and Marlo into the house several hours later.

"I missed it totally," Skye said. "I had barely enough time to go over to Mrs. Morton's house to cook her dinner and then rush back here."

Skye tried to sound polite but inside, her heart broke for Diehl.

He had told her earlier today that he didn't need God.

He might think so in his mind, but Skye didn't know anyone who didn't need God, especially in times of grief. There seemed to be a bigger spiritual problem here.

Was he a prodigal son who had wandered away from the faith? Or did he ever know the Lord at all?

Skye decided the best thing she could do was pray for Diehl.

He seemed acutely unaware of what he was missing. Right now, his concern seemed to be the tangible. Obviously, he walked by sight, not by faith.

"I'm sorry. That's my fault. I hosed you." Diehl stopped her and offered to carry the basket in her hand.

She let him. "I should've brought spare clothes in my van. I was unprepared."

It hadn't been entirely Diehl's fault.

"So what are you going to do?" Diehl walked with her to the kitchen.

Marlo was already there, unpacking the groceries.

Before they had left Diehl with the afternoon breakfast, Skye asked him what he wanted to eat for dinner. He said salmon, spinach, and any sides she wanted to cook for him. No salad tonight. He wanted more peach cobbler.

"We'll rehearse later tonight without Brinley since she turns in early. Also her ankles are swollen and the baby is heavy. She needs a lot of rest," Skye said. "We'll use accompaniment tracks."

"Will that work?"

"Sure. We've used them before."

"What are you singing?"

"Two hymns for Sunday and then two more for Wednesday night." Skye found a colander to wash the spinach.

Marlo cleaned the salmon, removing bones as he went along.

"Didn't you say that on Wednesday night, you're outdoors on the beach?" Diehl asked.

Skye nodded. "We use a portable keyboard. Or accompaniment tracks."

"Live music is always better."

"I agree. I'll play my guitar, so it's halfway live." Skye put away perishables in the refrigerator.

She checked her menu and put a pot of water on the stove to boil.

"Feel free to take it easy and we'll text you when dinner is ready," Skye told Diehl.

He didn't move. "Is there something I can do?"

"You paid us to cook for you."

"I have to do something." He tapped the countertop.

"I think we're good." Skye turned to Marlo. He nodded.

"I have an idea," Diehl said.

"Good or bad?"

Diehl looked intently at her. Under the kitchen light, Skye could not tell what color his eyes were, but they were intense.

"I know my piano skills are rusty, but if I had the music sheets, I could practice while you cook, and then maybe you can rehearse here this evening."

Skye was surprised at the offer. "Say again?"

He did.

Skye took the colander of Brussels sprouts and carrots from Marlo, and found a chopping board.

"I don't know what to say." Skye retrieved a knife from her own backpack.

"That knife looks sharp." Diehl pointed.

"Sharp knives are safe knives. Accidents happen when knives are blunt."

"That so?"

Skye nodded. "You were saying... You know you don't have to do this. The hose was an accident. I was late for the rehearsal because I was unprepared."

"No. You made me lunch. I refused it. I wanted breakfast. You cooked it for me. You ended up being late—so late that the rehearsal was over."

"Don't mention it." Meaning she did not want him to rehash over and over again what he had done wrong. "You need to learn to forgive yourself."

"So let me pay my penance."

"Penance? No. You're forgiven. Go take it easy, and let us cook."

Diehl still didn't move. "I hope you didn't misconstrue, but I really am available to play the piano for the next three months as a backup for my sister. She's going to have a baby in a month."

"That's true. After that, she's on maternity leave."

"You still need an accompanist."

"Well..." Skye portioned out enough couscous for two people and poured it into the boiling pot. She figured that Diehl could have leftovers since she had bought him a big salmon filet.

"If you need someone to vouch for me, ask my sister and mother. My mom can tell you how many years I played the piano, and probably how much she paid for our music lessons."

"You did say earlier that you might be rusty at the piano."

43

"As long as it's not Tchaikovsky, I can manage. So let me try? You'll rehearse tonight without Brin. Let me fill in for her. I offer you the piano in the living room. I'm sure Brin will be happy it gets played. In fact, I'll ask her if she'd like to rehearse here this summer."

"You can ask me." Skye smiled. "I'm actually in charge of the trio."

"Oh, you are? Good. Please think about it and let me know." He remained standing.

"What? Right now?"

"I have to practice before the rehearsal and we don't have much time," Diehl said.

Skye figured he wasn't thinking about all the implications of such an offer. She was going to meet Avery at eight o'clock in the evening, after dinner. Skye would have to leave Diehl's house, drive back to her new house off Frederica Drive, and then drive back here for the rehearsal.

It was easier for Avery since she lived about five or six streets away from here. Avery also had a piano in her house, but she couldn't sing and play the piano at the same time. She said it had to be either this or that.

"Let me talk to my trio and see what they say, okay?" Skye started cutting the Brussels sprouts into halves.

Diehl nodded. "Hope I'm not too pushy."

"No. It's a very generous offer. You're volunteering without pay, right?"

"Of course."

"Because you have nothing better to do."

"Nothing whatsoever."

After Diehl left the kitchen, Skye wasn't sure how to pray or think about it.

"What do you think?" she asked Marlo.

"You're asking me?"

"Uh-huh. Take up his offer or not?"

"Let the man pay his penance." Marlo laughed.

"There are complications," Skye said.

"Like what?"

"I don't want his sister to not feel needed, you know? I'll call Brinley and Avery and talk to them." Skye stirred the couscous.

She heated up a frying pan while Marlo finished cutting up the Brussels sprouts and carrots. She sliced up some butter and looked for her bottle of olive oil.

Salmon tonight was going to be simple. All she wanted to do was sauté the filet in a wash of basil in melted butter. "Could you melt down the butter for me?"

Marlo nodded.

The butter in the measuring cup seemed too little for the size of the salmon filet, so Skye added more butter. "Melt that in the microwave for about thirty seconds, and then stir in two tablespoons of chopped basil."

"Yes, ma'am."

Meanwhile, Skye heated up the olive oil in a stainless-steel pan. She prayed the pan would work fine. She had been in such a hurry to leave her house that she had forgotten to pack her own favorite pan.

It would take ten minutes to drive back to her

house, and another ten or fifteen—depending on traffic—to get back here. She wanted to serve dinner at five o'clock so that they could do some menu planning at six o'clock, while Marlo cleaned up the kitchen.

After that, Skye and Marlo would need to leave. Skye planned to have a light dinner tonight at home before the rehearsal at eight.

After putting the salmon filet, skin down, in the frying pan, Skye called Brinley and Avery on Face-Time and told them about Diehl's offer.

"I can't believe it." Brinley looked stunned. "I can't imagine my brother playing hymns at all, let alone offering to take my place for the next three months."

"If needed."

"I don't know when I'll get back after the baby's born."

"So you like his offer?" Skye asked.

"I love it, but..."

"But what?" Skye couldn't think of anything except that they still might need a second backup person just in case. "We can always ask someone in the women's group if Diehl doesn't work out."

Avery nodded. She was munching on something. Salad, maybe. "I'm okay with whatever you decide. I have to go now. A student is waiting for me in my studio. So how is this going to work?"

"Can we rehearse at your house?" Skye asked Avery.

"No. I don't want strangers coming to my house and playing my piano." Avery was as blunt as ever.

"Okay."

"Since you're already there in his house, I think it's safe."

"Safe?"

"You might know Brin's brother, but he's still a stranger to us," Avery said. "He doesn't attend our church—or any church—so frankly, I don't know how someone like that could help us minister to our congregation."

"You brought up an important point," Brinley said. "He's my brother, so I'm leaning toward letting him help us. He said that he accepted Jesus in college, though I have no recollection of it. All I know is that he's been hostile toward the Gospel, but since Isobel died, he has softened a bit. When I found out he had some sort of encounter with Jesus in college, I was floored."

"You know the tree by its fruit," Avery said.

Another good verse, Skye thought. She wondered if Matthew 7:17-18 was something she had to bear in mind every time she came to Diehl's beach house.

Even so every good tree bringeth forth good fruit; but a corrupt tree bringeth forth evil fruit. A good tree cannot bring forth evil fruit, neither can a corrupt tree bring forth good fruit.

"That too," Brinley agreed. "As far as I know, he has attended Seaside Chapel all of three times—two weddings and one funeral."

"And now he wants to play hymns. Maybe God is calling the prodigal son home." Skye doused the salmon with the mix of butter and basil. She ground some pepper over it. Sprinkled the salmon with Himalayan sea salt.

As she heated up the next frying pan to sauté the Brussels sprouts and carrots, she wondered if it was wise of them to have this discussion on speaker phone and FaceTime, live in the kitchen.

Marlo was a Christian too, so he didn't mind the salvation thought.

However, could Diehl hear their conversation from wherever he was in the house?

"I'm open to the idea," Brinley said. "I'm biased toward my brother. I want him in church. So if this takes him back to church, then maybe God has something in mind."

"Avery wants proof in the pudding." Skye sautéed the Brussels sprouts and carrots. She kept the heat on high.

"I don't know," Avery said. "At the same time, I don't want to get in the way of what God might be doing in his life."

"Neither do I." Skye poured some water into the pan and quickly covered it. The steam threatened to burst out of the frying pan. She kept the lid down. "How about you pray for us right now?"

Avery did. She knew that Skye was cooking, so she kept the prayer short.

"All in favor of Diehl playing piano for us, say aye," Skye said.

Surprisingly, Avery voted for it.

"It's unanimous then," Skye announced. "To be

sure, this is not the first time we've had instrumental help from others. Remember when we needed extra strings, and Matt helped out with his guitar?"

The ladies nodded.

"Also remember when musicians visited our church and we sometimes sang with them?" Skye reminded them. "We didn't know what denomination —if at all—they were in. But we recognized that the gift of music comes from God."

"Indeed," Brinley said. "I'll send Diehl the link to the music sheets. He has an iPad, I think, or he can put his laptop on top of the grand."

"Thank you, Brin." Skye ended their conversation.

She felt pretty good about how they worked well together as a trio, but at the back of her mind, she wasn't sure how Diehl would affect their ministry to God's people.

After all, he had told her point blank only hours before that he did not need God.

And here they were, accepting his offer to play accompaniment for them? Would he think that God *needed* him? Heaven forbid he should think that way.

Then again, Avery had reminded them about casting stones. Skye knew that passage from John 8:7 well.

So when they continued asking Him, He raised Himself up and said to them, "He who is without sin among you, let him throw a stone at her first."

Skye felt that she had to be extra careful about viewing immature Christians—if Diehl was such a one

—through the sometimes critical lenses of pious church life.

God worked in each person's heart differently from another.

To some Christians, Diehl might be lost and unsaved. To some, he might be a baby Christian without enough spiritual knowledge. Either way, he had such an enormous pride as to declare that he didn't need God.

Perhaps he was angry at God for taking his wife and leaving his two children motherless.

Perhaps he wanted to be self-sufficient after making such a mess of his life.

Yes, a mess. Brinley had confided in Skye about the strange marriage of Diehl and his wife, Isobel, about all the things that those two had put each other through. If two people had such intense dislike of each other, why had they married—not once, but twice?

Skye shook her head as the sounds of piano scales filled the small cottage.

Then arpeggios.

Then scales again, in a different key this time.

Skye wondered if Brinley had sent over the music sheets to Diehl. He was clearly warming up on the Steinway.

She was glad to hear the piano.

It was such a shame that an expensive piano would be left unused in the living room.

If she had the money, Skye would buy this house from Brinley—if she would sell it. However, all her money was going into buying out Talia's majority shares of Saffron on Jekyll.

After that, she hoped to sell the restaurant back to her brother, Sebastian, if he wanted it. He had started the flagship restaurant some years ago with Talia, although their relationship didn't work out.

If Sebastian didn't want the restaurant back, Skye would run it alone. She wasn't sure how, since her plate was full to the brim, but taking over the restaurant sure beat having to deal with an absentee—and voting—business partner who had moved to London, with no plans to return to the States.

So. Skye would have no money left to buy a beach house such as this one.

Her rental condo across the island was small. She wanted a bigger kitchen. If she could find the time to look for a house to buy, she could renovate the kitchen. Oh, to have a dream kitchen once again.

Someday.

She had done what she had to when she needed the funds to invest in her brother's restaurant. She bailed him out and freed him to pursue the love of his life. A noble cause at a great cost to herself.

Sigh.

And then she heard it.

A slow, jazzy, harrowing "His Eye Is on the Sparrow" came forth from the piano in the living room, filling the air in the small kitchen and dining area.

Full of sadness and sorrow, the instrumental tune spoke of love and lost love. And hope in Christ.

Skye knew the words well. The poem had first

been penned in 1905, long before anyone put it to music.

> *I sing because I'm happy, I sing*
> *because I'm free,*
> *For His eye is on the sparrow, and I*
> *know He watches me.*

Skye turned down the stove, and left Marlo to watch it. She hummed the tune as she walked toward the living room.

Diehl looked up from the piano and smiled at her as he continued playing an arrangement she had never heard before.

She waited until he reached the next stanza, and she began to sing.

His eyes widened. He almost lost his place on the piano, and Skye could tell he'd skipped a couple of notes. He resumed playing.

She continued singing, her voice soaring.

Yes, singing was a stress relief for her. She realized that she hadn't sung all day. No wonder she felt uptight and all stressed out about her challenges.

All washing away with the therapy of singing hymns of praise to God.

The windows were closed and the air conditioner was on, so she couldn't hear the ocean waves. All she could hear were the piano and her own voice.

When the song finished, a tiny tear rolled down her face. She reached up to wipe it, but someone else got there first.

A soft thumb, firm yet gentle, wiped away the single tear from her cheek.

Blue eyes stared at her. Or maybe they were gray. She couldn't tell in the indoor light.

"You have a beautiful voice," Diehl said quietly.

"God gave me this voice to sing for Him."

"You only sing hymns?"

"Yes."

"Why?"

"It's all I have time for."

"You're very busy."

Skye nodded.

"And yet you look so calm and at peace," Diehl said.

"Thank you. God's peace is indescribable."

"That's what I'm missing. Peace."

"Not just any peace. God's peace." Skye didn't want to correct him, but she did.

CHAPTER FIVE

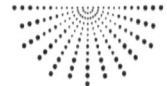

S ight-reading had never been Diehl's forte but he worked hard to impress the ladies, especially Skye. Something about Skye's voice still lingered in his ears three hours later when Mom called from Hawaii just as he was brushing his teeth, getting ready for bed.

He called Mom back after he flossed, mentally preparing himself to hear more complaints from her. Truly, her concerns were mostly valid, but he was still tired of hearing her shrill voice. If it were anything like Skye's smooth, crooning voice, Diehl could listen to it all day long.

Diehl propped a pillow behind his head on the bed.

Across from the foot of the bed, the sheer curtains were drawn. He couldn't hear the ocean now, but at least he wouldn't have creatures from the great outdoors flying in at night.

"Did you know that Isobel had a boyfriend in every port?" Mom looked horrified on the phone.

"I think that's an exaggeration. Who said it?" Diehl didn't admit that he had been in denial all this time. Surely Isobel had taken her marriage vows seriously—twice with him.

"Zeta."

"Why would she tell you that?" Was Isobel's mom trying to cast aspersions on his children's parentage?

"To make you jealous?"

"Mom, she's dead. Leave her alone." Diehl hated to say it, but it was true, although he felt like a hypocrite. While he told his mom to move on, he himself was still at the tail end of his grief.

How long was this going to last?

He had accepted that Isobel had passed away and that perhaps she hadn't been a faithful wife. What did it matter now?

"The repercussions," Mom said.

Somewhere off camera, Dad's voice came through. "What repercussions, dear?"

"What I said. Repercussions."

"Mom, make sure the kids are not around when you talk like that," Diehl warned her.

"Don't worry. They're with their other grandparents for one last night. We fly home tomorrow."

Frankly, Diehl had no idea how long this sort of arrangement was going to last. How could two school-aged children live in both Hawaii and Georgia?

Up until the year before, they had attended school in Atlanta. Diehl worked all the time, so he hired a full-time nanny to take the kids to school and back.

After Isobel died, her parents suggested that Elisa and Ethan stay with them for the next school year. They could learn more about where Isobel came from, her heritage, and that might keep her memory alive.

Diehl wasn't sure why he had agreed to it.

He missed his children too.

He thought they might grieve together. However, those merger-and-acquisition talks at work kept him busy and away from the house. Instead of Elisa and Ethan only seeing a non-family nanny for the entire school year, Diehl thought it might be better for them to stay with their grandparents.

Now he had a hard time getting them back to Georgia.

"How did you get Elisa and Ethan to come back with you for the summer?" Diehl asked.

"Well, it took a lot of work," Mom said.

Off camera, Dad yelled, "And bribes!"

"Bribes to whom?" Diehl asked. "My kids or the other grandparents?"

"Both," Mom replied. "But we got the kids."

"Mission accomplished, I guess." Diehl wondered how much correction he would have to make when he saw his kids again.

It wasn't the time to tell his parents that he wanted the kids to stay with him in this house and not in the Brooks family home on Seaside Island. He would wait until they arrived in town.

"Yeah," Dad said. "I can't wait for us to go home because I have to get back to work."

"You work too much," Mom said. "Diehl, what did you do today?"

"I bought birdseed for the bird feeder, and refilled the bird bath."

"And?"

What did she mean? Diehl waited to see if Mom would explain herself.

"How's the chef situation working out?"

"Nice not to have to cook on my own," Diehl said.

"Skye's a delight to be with."

"She is."

"What did you talk about?"

"Food." They were professional all the way, except for the moment he wiped a tear from her cheek. She had soft skin.

"Told you to marry a nice girl," Mom said. "Why couldn't you marry a nice girl?"

Nice girl? "What would be a nice girl to you, Mom?"

Mom seemed taken aback by the question, even though he wanted to know what she was thinking.

"Well, for one thing, a nice girl wouldn't be living with her boyfriend in Positano while her husband worked in Atlanta."

"What? That was a long time ago. She confessed."

"Nope. Two weeks before she drove off the cliff, she met him again. Apparently, they had revived their friendship—or shall I say, relationship."

That got Diehl's attention. "Did you say two weeks?"

"Zeta told me that the man's wife has a fortune. Isobel was only his mistress. He was never going to marry her."

"You said girlfriend. Now you say mistress." Diehl was glad he was sitting down.

"He was estranged from his wife. When she found out about Isobel, she was livid and threatened a divorce—which meant he would get nothing due to their prenup."

"Is all this information just now surfacing?" Diehl had stopped paying attention to news about Isobel because none of it mattered. Isobel was still dead.

"Zeta said the Italian police are not letting up. By the way, they think the brakes to the Huayra didn't work that day."

Diehl was too stunned to speak. "It's been a year."

"Well, new information can always surface over time."

"True."

"She's suing the man," Mom added. She refused to say his name.

"Luigi?" Luigi Bellini, the other man whom Isobel couldn't let go of. They had met in college about the same time as she had met Diehl. However, he had gone home to Italy shortly after graduation, which led Diehl to believe it was over between Isobel and Luigi when she married Diehl.

She nodded.

"Mom, suing won't bring Isobel back."

"Now Zeta wants paternity tests for Elisa and Ethan."

Paternity tests.

Mom's words rang in Diehl's head and kept him up all night. He hardly slept a wink.

He got up in the middle of the night and went downstairs to get something to drink from the refrigerator. On the countertop was a printed menu of the next day's breakfast, lunch, and dinner. On top of the page, it said, "Skye's the Limit Personal Chefs."

Diehl drank some milk as he read the menu. Read and not read. He stared at the menu, yes, but all he saw was Skye's face. Why?

He was sure he wasn't falling in love with a sort-of stranger the first time he had a day of interaction with her. Or was he?

To be fair to Skye, she was more of a stranger to him than he was to her. According to Brinley, Skye attended the same women's Bible study, and they both went to the same church. Brinley trusted Skye. One proof: Skye had the key to the beach house.

Trust had been an issue for Diehl. As messed up as it had been, he hadn't trusted any other woman beside Isobel. Look how she let him down!

Diehl wasn't certain he could trust another woman again.

Perhaps his sister's trust of Skye was only professional. Skye had to stock the refrigerator ahead of his arrival. Since getting here, he had been keeping odd hours. He attributed that to being in instant vacation mode. Sleep until noon. Eat breakfast at lunch and whatever.

Diehl went back upstairs to try to sleep.

Sleep did not come.

And there was no one to call.

Usually, if he worked too hard at the office, he didn't crash. He'd go home and stay awake for hours more. His mind would go a mile a minute and not calm down. It mattered not if he had coffee or other forms of caffeine. His mind was wired to go, go, go.

If Isobel was in Italy, Diehl would call her to talk on the phone. She was usually on audio only—for reasons he was beginning to understand—but it would be morning on the Amalfi Coast, and she would give him her listening ear.

Right now, Diehl badly needed someone to listen to him hash out his life's worries.

How could he move on?

CHAPTER SIX

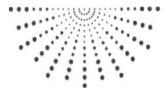

*A*fter sleeping fitfully through the night, Diehl woke up again when dawn broke. He pulled aside the sheer curtains, opened the French doors, and stepped onto the wooden balcony.

The rush of waves onto the shore was at a consistent time signature. Back and forth, back and forth. He watched as the sky lightened up.

"God is turning on the light," Grandpa Brooks used to say.

Diehl closed his eyes and let the morning breeze wash over his face and through his hair. He could feel Grandpa pat his head and say, "Diehl, I pray that someday you will serve God."

He had never forgotten those words. Why would Grandpa say such a thing to a then ten-year-old boy who could hardly differentiate Jesus from Santa?

I pray that someday you will serve God.

Oh, if only Grandpa knew how far away Diehl

was from that prayer. Granted, some nine or ten years after Grandpa said that, Diehl accepted Jesus while he was in college.

Accepted.

That was almost twenty years ago. Like old news.

Today he felt that he had unaccepted Jesus. He felt so distant from God.

He looked up at the brightening sky. The clouds stretched across the sky, wispy clouds here and puffy clouds there. He couldn't remember all their names, but Grandpa had known. He had studied the clouds in the sky—back in school, he said—and could name them all. Cirrus this and altocumulus that.

Diehl hadn't paid too much attention to all that Grandpa said as the four grandchildren walked about the beaches of Seaside Island minutes from St. Simon's Island, shoveling up more sand than seashells.

All he had remembered were those words.

I pray that someday you will serve God.

Diehl couldn't see how. After college, he and Isobel went to graduate school. Both earned their MBA degrees. Both worked at his father's company. They partied a lot, to say the least. They had many friends. Sometimes Isobel hosted dinner parties on her own without Diehl. It seemed that her daily life consisted of going from party to party.

To be honest with himself, Diehl couldn't recall whether Isobel changed at all. She had always been an extrovert. As for Diehl, he'd rather keep to himself and come home to a quiet house after work. He had friends, but not all over his house every Friday night.

Then the kids came, and Diehl thought the partying would stop. Nope. Isobel carried on. The parties moved from Atlanta to Hawaii and the Amalfi Coast. Destination parties and all that.

Diehl stopped keeping up.

Perhaps that was when his marriage died.

To this day, he wondered if he and Isobel ever loved each other at all—or whether they were simply using each other to fill in their own lonely spaces.

He couldn't pin down a reason he had married her. Was it because she was the life of the party?

She played hard, and then she died.

By the time eight o'clock rolled around, Diehl could barely keep his eyes opened. He had to get dressed and let Chef Joseph in to cook breakfast. He hadn't showered because he wanted to go back to bed as soon as he let the chef in.

See, that was why he had asked Skye to cook extra breakfast on Friday. That way, he could sleep in on Saturday morning. However, Skye did not end up making extra pancakes at all. She told him that Chef Joseph would cook him a fresh batch.

Unfortunately, Chef Joseph did not have a key to the house. Only Skye did. Truth be told, Diehl would rather eat leftover pancakes than get his sleep interrupted.

Diehl came downstairs just as he heard someone turning the lock on the front door. He rushed to the security keypad and turned it off—before he checked who it was. He figured that whoever had the key had permission to enter the house. It couldn't be Chef Joseph, could it?

The door opened and there was Skye. Her hair was tied up in a bun and her face was scrubbed fresh. No makeup at all. Diehl recalled touching that smooth skin even though it was only for seconds.

"Oh, hey Diehl. Good morning." She pulled the key from the lock. "I wasn't sure what time you'd be awake, so I decided to let Joe in."

She stepped aside to let a burly man with a chef's hat in. "Chef Joseph, meet Diehl Brooks."

They shook hands.

Behind him, someone carried a basket.

"His assistant, Chuck." Skye closed the door behind them.

She showed Chef Joseph and Chuck the kitchen. Diehl followed them.

"From time to time, Chef Joseph will fill in for me," Skye said.

Diehl's heart dropped. He wanted to see Skye every day.

"I guess I'll see you Monday morning." Skye left the kitchen. "Or tomorrow, if you decide to go to church with us."

Diehl followed her to the front door. "Us who?"

"My friends and I. Brinley, Ivan, and others. Would you like to come to my Sunday school class to meet everyone? Most of them are in town for the summer."

"Are you saying I don't have friends in town?"

"No." Skye looked perplexed. "I was suggesting that maybe you'd like to meet new friends."

"Do I need to expand my circle of friends?"

Skye appeared calm, regardless of how he replied to her. Such a contrast from Isobel, who had flown off the handle every single time Diehl disagreed with her —especially on the millions of dollars of frivolous spending over the years of hard partying.

"You're testy this morning." Skye lowered her voice. "Did you get any sleep last night?"

How did she know? "Uh, not really."

"Figured. After breakfast, you might consider going back to bed."

"Then who will let the chef in to cook lunch?"

"We brought all your lunch and dinner ingredients," Skye said. "They could cook your lunch and put it away in the fridge with instructions for reheating the dishes when you get up."

"Sounds like a plan. Did you all shop before you came here this morning?" Diehl wondered what time they got up.

"No, I bought all the groceries last night."

"Last night? After rehearsal?"

Skye nodded. "Yeah, it was a long day."

"And it's my fault. I shouldn't have ignored your emails, text messages, voicemail. I am so sorry." Diehl searched Skye's eyes.

"I forgive you."

"Just like that?" Diehl was surprised. Too often, people held grudges. Isobel could hold grudges for years.

Isobel? Why was he thinking of her? She had been dead for a whole year.

Why can't I move on?

"If God forgives me when I confess my sins to Him, why would I hold back forgiveness to anyone who has wronged me? Not that you wronged me personally. I was running a tight shift in my business, and there's a chain reaction whenever one moving part is not in place."

"I'm that part. I'm not moving. I'm stuck." Diehl wondered if that was the metaphor of his mental state right now.

Perhaps his sister was right. He needed counseling. However, he did not want to see Pastor Gonzalez. They hadn't gotten along well the last time they met.

"I'm not saying that at all," Skye said. "Please don't misread my words."

Diehl rubbed his forehead. "I'm sorry. I'm listening and superimposing what people say to me in my own life—for good or bad."

Skye smiled. "You know, only God's Word matters. Only His Word doesn't return void. You can listen to the world and its frequencies of white noise, but all that will pass away. Only God's Word remains."

She swiped her phone. "Listen to this verse from 1 Peter 1:24-25. 'All flesh is as grass, and all the glory of man as the flower of the grass. The grass withers, and its flower falls away, but the Word of the Lord endures forever.' Isn't that good that God's Word is permanent? So many things today don't last."

That voice again. If Skye narrated the Bible, he would listen to it.

He caught himself.

Here she was, trying to impart truth to him, to speak a blessing into his soul, and there he was, focusing on the wrong thing. Yes, she had a wonderful voice, but she had just read a verse from the Holy Word of God.

Diehl reminded himself to have some respect for God's Word. He might have wandered far away from God, but God hadn't moved, had He? According to this verse, God remained.

And this is the word which by the gospel is preached unto you.

That sentence reminded him of Grandpa Brooks. "You know, my grandpa was a religious man. He took us to church every Sunday in the summer when we were kids."

"Yes, Brinley told me. Seaside Chapel, in fact." She stood there in the foyer as though she had all the time in the world, but Diehl knew she had other plans for the day. "Perhaps attending church tomorrow is like a homecoming for you. It's the same church—with a new paint job, a different pastor. But we still have the choir and orchestra."

"There's so much going on in my life right now..."

"All the more reason to... You know, I can't tell you what to do." Skye stepped toward the door. "I have to go."

"I'm sorry."

"About what?" Skye's eyes widened.

She truly had beautiful eyes. They were peaceful.

Diehl shrugged. "Being antagonistic and all."

"Are you? I haven't noticed."

"No? I countered every suggestion you gave me. And yesterday, I argued with you about breakfast at lunch."

"Brunch. You had brunch. No worries."

Yeah, worries. Diehl started to get concerned about this newfound perspective he was staring at. Was this what people meant when they said the glass was half full?

"Look on the bright side," Skye said. "If you're sorting out things in your life, then you might be emerging from the valley of the shadow of death."

"Am I?"

"I don't know. Think about it. God has brought you here to St. Simon's Island, a place where you spent your childhood. You said that your grandpa took you to church back then, and that church is still here. Your sister and brother-in-law and their friends attend the church."

"Am I among friends?" Diehl asked, searching, wondering.

"I'm just a chef." It was all she said.

CHAPTER SEVEN

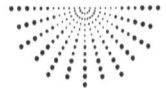

*S*kye was floored when she saw Diehl in Sunday school class the next day, sitting beside his brother-in-law, Ivan.

She had arrived at the church parking lot at the same time as Matt Garnett, who helped carry her tray of food from the church entrance to the classroom.

Skye was telling Matt about how much she liked the new reading lamp she'd bought from Matt's antique shop, when she spotted Diehl talking to his brother-in-law.

Brinley was nowhere to be found.

"Where do you want this?" Matt asked as he headed to the side table where other breakfast items went.

"Anywhere." Skye thanked him and then opened up the cover of the large rectangular tray. She had brought thirty eggs-in-a-basket, and they all looked lovely, if she did say so herself.

In fact, she had already eaten two at home, saving four more for her own Monday morning on-the-go breakfast.

Skye tidied up the table, making sure the food trays all lined up. Someone had brought mini muffins.

Yummy.

Skye thought she'd try one of those. She was looking for a paper plate when she heard a voice beside her.

"Good morning." Diehl's voice was low key, almost like a whisper in her ear.

"Good morning. Glad you're here." Skye offered him a paper plate.

He took it. "What did you bring?"

"Eggs in a basket." She handed him a serving spoon. "One egg in a nest of hash browns. This side of the tray is over medium, and that side is over well."

"Good. Glad there are choices. I don't like runny eggs." Diehl made his selection.

"Neither do I, but many of my clients do."

"Let's not talk about work." Diehl offered her coffee.

She declined. "I drank some before I left the house. I try not to drink more than one cup a day."

"Why?"

"Too much caffeine. I much prefer mineral water." Skye looked around. "Is your sister here?"

He shook his head. "She's not feeling well. Her feet are still swollen. She decided to watch the livestream of the service instead."

"Oh dear." Skye hadn't gotten a text message from

Brinley. Really, it wasn't necessary because they weren't singing in the service until this evening.

"Last minute. I went to pick them up, but only Ivan came out of the house."

"I'll be praying for her." She wondered if Brinley could make it tonight. If not, they had Diehl.

"Thanks. She had a smooth first and second trimester. She said she hardly threw up. One last mile and the baby will be here soon."

Skye had nothing to say about it. She had no personal experience of carrying a baby.

"Ivan's an excited dad-to-be. Now I'll be an uncle again."

"How's your niece doing?" Skye asked.

"You mean Zoe's daughter?"

Skye nodded. Brinley had mentioned that Zoe was still living in Paris with her husband and child.

"I haven't seen them since Christmas. I guess she's fine. She's a precocious toddler," Diehl said in between eating the egg. "This is good. Will you make this for me?"

"Sure. We can cook anything you want," Skye said.

"I'm sorry. Didn't I say not to talk about work?" Diehl grinned.

Speaking of work, Skye remembered that Diehl's name wasn't on the couple's baby shower invitation list. She made a mental note to ask Brinley if she wanted to invite her brother. Regardless, she had planned to make extra food in case there were last-minute guests. Also, some might not be able to make it.

The Sunday school class started with Matt filling

in for Benicio Ketteridge, who was out of town visiting his family. Skye chose to sit in the back with Avery Chung, who walked in just as Matt took the lectern.

When it wasn't her turn to bring breakfast to Sunday school, Skye would sit somewhere else, but the back seat was closest to the food table. That way she could get up every now and then to tidy up the table without interrupting the class.

The seats were in a semicircle facing the board, so Skye couldn't see Diehl's face. Just as well. She told herself to keep him in the professional compartment—the work zone. She tried to be friendly with him to make him feel at ease in Brinley's beach house. From what she had heard, he wasn't one to talk to strangers much. Skye considered herself and Marlo as strangers in Diehl's vacation home.

It made her wonder why he had wiped a tear from her face on Friday afternoon. Why had he done that?

Matt was talking! Skye scolded herself for letting her mind wander.

"Today, we're going to talk about praying for one another," Matt said. "The Bible says in 1 Thessalonians 5:17 that we are to 'pray without ceasing.' There's time involved in that. But what kind of time? As you turn to our text for the day in 2 Timothy 1:3, I'm going to tell you a story."

A chorus of "Uh-oh!" rose up the room.

Skye liked listening to Matt teach. He was funny and kept everyone awake with his tales of woe on the road, searching for lost pieces of Americana that he might add to his antique store. Somehow, he always found a biblical lesson in his interesting everyday life.

It made Skye wonder if her life was interesting enough to make Bible lessons out of it. Hopefully good lessons and not tragic ones.

However, back to Matt, one never knew what story he was going to bring up. It seemed like no one at church was immune to being the subject of Matt's stories. And he knew almost everyone at church.

"I don't want to pick on her but..." Matt stepped to the side of the lectern. "We go way back, so I don't think she minds."

She.

Skye waited for the victim—uh, subject.

"I've known Skye Langston since kindergarten."

Oh no! Don't pick on me.

Not today. Not with Diehl in the room.

Skye held her breath. She wanted to impress her new client. She hadn't burned his dinner yet.

"I knew she was going to be a chef someday because at five years old, she challenged me to eat fried ants." Matt couldn't contain his laughter.

Not that story!

Skye rolled her eyes.

Diehl glanced back at her, a grin on his face.

He was cute from this distance.

Exactly. If she kept her distance, all would be well.

"Let's just say that her grand idea was to barbecue an ant in the sun under a magnifying glass and feed it to me, the tester."

"You mean taster," someone said.

"Well, tester, taster." Matt chuckled. "At the very last minute, holding the magnifier in her hands, she started to cry."

Skye looked down at her Bible. It had been so long ago that she hardly remembered the episode. Mom and Dad were still alive then. The wreck that had taken their lives happened years later when she and Sebastian were in high school.

She drew a deep breath, trying not to recall that awful night.

"You know what she did?" Matt asked. "She decided to set the ant free. And she fed me her PBJ lunch instead."

"Generous," someone said.

"That's right. Skye is someone I know who is very generous. She goes out of her way to help everyone, and if you let her, she will cook for the whole town. But we won't let her do that, will we? We all need to chip in." Matt looked around the room. "As a community, when we share the burden of helping one another, being extra kind to one another, we are doing good work as unto the Lord. Likewise, when we all pray for one another, the blessings of God flow to all."

Many people nodded.

"Now let's turn to 2 Timothy 1:3. Will someone please read it aloud?" Matt asked.

Ivan raised his hand. As he read it, Skye followed along, her head still down. She blinked away the emotions of many years, telling herself to pull it together. She was at church in public, not at home in private.

I thank God, whom I serve with a pure conscience, as
my forefathers did, as without ceasing I remember you
in my prayers night and day,

"Did you catch that?" Matt tapped his Bible. "Imagine praying for others 'night and day.' Let's go around the room and hear some suggestions on how we can do that. I admit that I forget to pray sometimes, just as I forget to eat."

Pray for me now.

Skye prayed she wouldn't lose it in class.

She wondered how long a person could grieve. Decades? It seemed that she had been grieving the loss of her parents for so many years that it was part of her now.

Of course, Matt couldn't have known that his story about their kindergarten days would trigger a dark memory of her high school years.

Sitting next to her, Avery patted her knee.

Instantly, Skye knew that her friend was praying for her.

It might seem insignificant to some people, but to Skye, even where she sat, this morning had been ordained. God knew that she needed prayer.

Avery, Brinley, and Skye prayed before their rehearsals, that their songs would touch many who heard them sing.

Songs of joy and encouragement.

Skye recalled their last rehearsal the night before at Brinley's beach house. It only lasted forty-five minutes, but that was plenty of time to sing four songs.

Diehl was a trooper and he sight-read the piano sheet music better than some of their past accompanists.

In fact, he played "His Eye Is on the Sparrow" on the piano quite flawlessly. Skye might suggest they sing that hymn this summer when their turn came up again on the offertory roster.

Sparrows.

Do not fear therefore; you are of more value than many sparrows.

And just like that, God had comforted Skye with His Word from Matthew 10:31.

"We can tape reminders around the house," someone said.

"Good idea. My mother tapes scripture to the inside of cabinet doors so that when she opens the cupboards, she sees a word of encouragement from God." Matt pointed to another raised hand.

"Tie in prayer time to what goes on during the day," Ivan said. "For example, when I get to the studio to teach, I pray each time before the student arrives."

"Good one."

Skye thought so too. She made plans to incorporate that idea into her daily routine. Maybe pray for the people her chefs cooked for according to their sched-ule. It wouldn't take too long to pray if she was praying all day. It wasn't like she had to pray for everyone in one sitting.

Had to?

No. Skye knew that wasn't what she meant. She

wanted to pray for everyone, including Diehl. A lot was going on in that man.

If Skye was still grieving for her parents who had been gone for almost twenty years, then how much more grief was Diehl experiencing within a year of his wife's passing.

Unless what Brinley had told her was true. Even though Brinley felt sorry for Isobel, who had to raise the children herself—albeit with a nanny—while workaholic Diehl was at the office all the time, it turned out that the couple had mentally and emotionally lived apart for a very long time.

Still, it was sad that Isobel had died when her children were still not quite in middle school.

Skye wondered how the kids were doing.

She added them to her ever-growing prayer list.

CHAPTER EIGHT

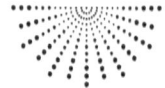

Skye, Avery, and Diehl arrived at church an hour early for soundcheck in the main sanctuary. It wasn't the biggest church that Diehl had been in, but he usually sat in the pews. Tonight, he was playing accompaniment at the piano in front of everyone—for the first time in his life.

"Don't be nervous." Skye was adjusting her guitar strap. "The evening service has fewer people attending. You're playing to extended family. Think casual."

"That's comforting." Diehl wiped his palms on his jeans before he adjusted the piano bench height.

The grand piano was a Yamaha, not a Steinway. They each played differently. He sat down and warmed up with scales.

He could hear Skye playing the guitar and talking to Avery at the same time. How did she do that?

Avery suddenly laughed out loud. "Look at us. Skye, Avery, and Diehl. Our new band is SAD."

Diehl chuckled. Never had he imagined that he'd be taking a sabbatical from work and taking up piano again after decades of not playing it.

That was why he felt inadequate.

He was outside his corporate comfort zone where he had a solution for every problem. Seriously.

Now he was at the mercy of things that could go out of control. He could miss notes again. Truth be told, the music was elementary to him. Mostly single notes. Mostly harmony. The ladies would sing the melody, and Skye's guitar would fill in the rest of the music bars.

Also, he had practiced all afternoon for hours and hours. Well, three hours. Non-stop. It felt like forever. It was a good thing that Mom and Dad had decided to stay another day in Hawaii. Otherwise, he'd have to manage his kids and practice the piano at the same time. Perhaps Mom could keep the kids—if they agreed to stay with her.

Not that he hadn't missed his kids, but he felt an obligation to follow through with this project to which he had agreed. If he made a promise, he would keep it.

There were only two hymns. How hard could it be?

In fact, having an ability to memorize helped tremendously.

Diehl was glad that the sheet music was in front of him. He had gone to the Scrolls bookstore in downtown St. Simon's Island to print the two hymns on thicker paper so that they didn't fall off the music rack and he didn't have to turn the pages.

Additionally, having printed music sheets meant he could make annotations on them, which he couldn't do when the music was on his iPad.

Details mattered.

"Ready?" Skye asked, a guitar pick in her hand.

They sang through "His Robes For Mine" twice. And then "I Run to Christ" three times because Diehl asked for it.

The modern hymn reminded him of something he was missing in his life. Something lost.

When they finished, someone clapped.

Pastor Gonzalez.

Diehl collected his music sheets as the pastor talked to the ladies. They'd had a guest speaker that morning for their summer sermon series, so Diehl hadn't gotten to hear Pastor Gonzalez preach.

Right after church, Diehl and Ivan had picked up some takeout barbecue from Southern Soul, and then had gone straight to Ivan's house to devour pork and beef brisket and jugs of iced tea.

Then Diehl had gone home to practice his piano.

He'd forgotten all about his tiff with Pastor Gonzalez until now.

The pastor walked toward him, his arm extended. "Diehl Brooks. So glad to see you today."

They shook hands. "Thank you, Pastor."

"How are your parents?"

Diehl told him about their delayed flight. "They should be arriving Monday afternoon."

"I'll pray for travel mercies."

"Thank you."

"How may I pray for you?" Pastor Gonzalez asked. His voice showed care and concern.

Diehl wondered if anyone knew what he was doing—or not doing—here on the island. Then again, surely Ivan and Brinley had put him on the Sunday school class prayer list, which the church leadership no doubt knew about.

Then again, he wasn't that important.

"Well, praying for the safety of my parents and kids flying home is plenty," Diehl said.

"How old are your kids?"

"My daughter is twelve and my son is turning nine." As Diehl said it, he watched Skye pick up her guitar case. He wondered whether she'd heard him, and whether his having kids made any difference in her view of him.

View of him as what?

Diehl wasn't sure where he was going with his thought process.

"We have some summer camps for those age groups," Pastor Gonzalez said. "In fact, they start next week, if you're interested."

"I think it's a great idea." From the corner of his eye, Diehl saw Matt come up to Skye. He wondered if there was something going on between those two. They had entered the Sunday school classroom together this morning, for example, although they could have easily run into each other in the hallway. "Frankly, I haven't thought about summer much, and here it is."

"I know. And we started planning for the fall

semester way back in the spring."

Diehl nodded. "Man, the church runs like a corporation."

"Well, in some logistical ways, yes, but not exactly. We have to answer to God for all our failures and successes. No boards."

Failures and successes.

Might as well get it out now.

"Pastor, the last time we talked, I said some things..."

"All forgotten. All forgiven." Pastor Gonzalez placed a palm on Diehl's shoulder. "If you heard what I said to my wife in anger... Whew. Who am I to cast the first stone?"

In anger.

Diehl tried to recall how many times he had been angry with Isobel in their years of marriage. It seemed that they had ticked each other off almost every day and every time they were together. In the last years of their first marriage, they had slept in separate bedrooms. And then Isobel was gone half the time—to Hawaii or the Amalfi Coast.

For all practical purposes, their marriage was broken long before they were divorced.

So why had he remarried Isobel?

If they had remained divorced, would he be called a widower today?

The word "widower" made him feel old. Like he wasn't supposed to be one at his age.

Someone came to talk to Pastor Gonzalez. One of

the deacons that Ivan had pointed out to Diehl this morning.

He let the pastor go and then he couldn't see Skye or Avery anymore. He was standing alone on the platform.

He looked for them, and there in the distant pews by the wall, Skye waved to him. She pointed to the edge of a pew where she had placed her guitar case.

Diehl assumed that was where they were sitting. He nodded.

He took his music sheets and walked toward her, wondering how he had ended up this way.

When Isobel had been alive, they wouldn't step foot in a church. Neither of his kids had grown up in a church. Summer in church would be strange to them. Isobel had sent them to summer camps, but they were mostly secular. This time things would be different.

Different how?

Diehl didn't know.

Avery walked up to Skye just as Diehl was making his way around the pews.

"Are we eating somewhere after church?" Avery asked.

Diehl pretended not to hear. Skye glanced his way.

"We could grab a bite," she said. "Diehl, would you like to join us?"

"For what?" Diehl asked nonchalantly.

"Dinner after the service."

"I don't know. I might be tired." It was the truth. Having stayed away from church for years, today was quite an avalanche. He had attended Sunday school, the morning service, played hymns all afternoon, and now he was back at church. How much church could he take?

Then again, he felt refreshed even as the day drew to a close.

In fact, he felt more refreshed than he had ever been coming off the golf course on Sundays. As for that, he might beg off playing golf on Sundays anymore. Dad would be disappointed, but strangely enough, Diehl was looking forward to church next week.

"I'm tired too," Skye said. "I have to get up super early in the morning."

To cook breakfast for me, Diehl didn't say.

"But food is food..." Skye said.

"Maybe a quick to-go?" Avery asked. "As long as I'm not cooking, I'm happy."

"I bet it's the opposite for Skye," Diehl said.

Skye almost nodded.

Diehl didn't know what that meant. Was she trying not to agree with him?

He had thought they were starting to be friends. There was still a wall between them, and he didn't know what it was.

There was nothing for them to talk about except food.

People trickled into the sanctuary, almost all wearing casual clothes. Skye glanced at her watch.

"Okay, so what we're going to do is this," Skye said to Diehl. "I'll give the cue—about two songs and a prayer away—and we'll make our way out the back door over there, and find our way to the doors outside the platform. When the pastor prays for the offering, we take our positions."

"You've done this before," Diehl said.

"Many times. I've been attending this church since I was in kindergarten."

"Wow. When Matt talked about you in Sunday school, it never dawned on me that it also meant you two were attending this church when you were kids."

"Actually, Matt didn't get saved until he was an adult. We just went to the same school and lived in the same neighborhood."

"Ah, sorry. I shouldn't have assumed."

"There you go again, saying sorry." Skye grinned.

"I was. Anyway, that was a cute story this morning." Diehl didn't have to remind her about the ant. "So you're a native islander."

Skye chuckled.

"How come we never met when we were in high school?"

"Well, you're older than I am by several years, and you were in college before I made it to high school," Skye said. "When I finished college and decided to go to culinary school, you were wherever you were— somewhere else—running your dad's business."

"Atlanta."

"I go there occasionally, but mostly I stay here on the Georgia coast."

"You know my parents though."

Skye nodded. "My brother catered your sister Zoe's birthday party some time ago."

"Are your own parents still in town?" He wondered if they attended the same church.

Skye's lips started to tremble. Were those tears pooling in her eyes?

"Did I say something wrong?" Diehl was alarmed.

She shook her head. Drew a deep breath. "My parents died many years ago in a car wreck on the railroad tracks."

"Oh, I'm sorry." That story with the ant... Had it triggered a bad memory for Skye? Everyone in class had laughed, but had she? Sitting in front, Diehl hadn't paid attention.

Skye shook her head. "Excuse me."

She turned and walked away briskly, leaving Diehl standing there at the edge of the pew all by himself.

CHAPTER NINE

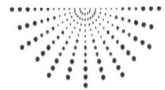

*A*t six o'clock on Monday morning, Marlo called in sick. Said he ate something bad the night before and now he couldn't make it. It was too late to call anyone else to fill in for him because Skye had assigned everyone. At STL, nobody sat idly without any work to do.

Skye stopped at the local organic grocery store to pick up some turkey bacon on the way to Diehl's house. She had forgotten it the night before during her quick shopping trip after the evening service.

The church service had gone well, all things considered. She wished she wouldn't be so easily triggered by the memories of her parents, but from time to time, it happened. Sebastian told her repeatedly to focus on God and not her own loss. She had been thirteen years old when her drunk parents drove in front of an oncoming train on their way home from a bar in the middle of the night.

Twenty years ago.

Lord Jesus, ease my pain.

Skye pulled up in the driveway of Brinley's beach house. With her car windows down, she could hear the morning waves. How she would love to walk on that beach. But she was here to work, not frolic in the sun.

Before she could roll up the windows, the front door opened, and out ambled Diehl. He wore a T-shirt, shorts, and flip-flops.

"You didn't bring your van today." He opened the car door for her.

"No grocery haul today. I just have a couple of bags."

"Let me help you carry them." He waited for her to show him where the bags were.

Skye popped the trunk. While he went to the back of her car, Skye retrieved her purse and tote bag from the back seat.

"I got them." One bag in each hand, Diehl carried the bags into the house.

Skye closed the trunk and followed him in.

"What did you buy?" Diehl made his way to the kitchen.

"What we're cooking for lunch and dinner today— plus the bacon you wanted for breakfast." Skye put away her car keys and donned her apron.

"Where's Marlo?"

"He called in sick this morning and it was too late to replace him." Skye washed her hands at the sink and started to take things out of the grocery bags.

"Then may I assist?" Diehl asked.

His eyes were earnest.

A wispy wind ruffled his hair. Skye turned toward the direction of the wind and saw the windows above the breakfast nook open. The screen prevented insects from coming in.

"You don't have to pay me." Diehl waited.

"Ah, well... You'd be the first client who offered to help cook."

"It's just breakfast."

"Right. I'll have an assistant with me at lunch."

"I can do breakfast. In fact, I've cooked breakfast for..." His voice trailed off into silence.

"Your wife." Skye put the cookie mix in the pantry. She had thrown that in as an extra because she knew from their conversation at church the day before that Diehl's kids were coming to town today. "Again, I'm sorry for your loss. I'm sure you loved her very much."

"Love?"

Skye was surprised by the answer.

"She was pregnant, and her parents didn't want the child to be born out of wedlock."

"Oh."

"So it was a marriage of convenience. We decided we'd raise the child together but we didn't have to live together, necessarily. However, after we married, we lost our first child. Stillborn."

"I'm sorry."

"I think the episode drew us closer to each other as husband and wife. We started to grow on each other."

"That's good, isn't it? A husband and wife should have feelings for each other."

"She wanted stability, and I wanted all her business contacts."

"Are you serious? My personal life doesn't revolve around my professional life."

"Ours did. Isobel needed money and a place to stay, and I needed her to keep up my appearances among my peers. It was a transactional marriage."

"I cannot believe I'm hearing that, especially from a Christian." Skye put away fresh produce in the refrigerator, leaving out potatoes on the island counter.

"Well, in retrospect, I wasn't a practicing Christian."

"You don't *practice* being a Christian, Diehl. Either you are, or you're not."

"Then I was backsliding. Or was I even a Christian at all?" Before Skye could respond, Diehl kept going. "I'm saying that Isobel and I made a decision. Do you think everyone marries for love?"

"Isn't marrying for love the best kind of marriage?"

"Yes, but that wasn't what we had." Diehl hadn't touched the groceries since he helped bring them in. He simply stood on the other side of the island.

Skye sensed his need to explain his marriage. She began to feel sorry for him. Had his marriage been unfulfilling? "Your arrangement is odd to me, considering this is the twenty-first century."

"We both came from wealthy families, so our circle of friends is small. I'm not sure if there was anyone else I could have married except her."

"Wow. No one else?"

Diehl shook his head. "Unless I let Mom be the matchmaker. There was no way I'd do that."

"I feel like I've been transported to the nineteenth century here." Truth be told, she wasn't sure if she should care. What he had—or hadn't—with his deceased wife was none of her business.

"Like I said, she was pregnant. My child, my responsibility," Diehl said. "Besides, I've always wanted to be a father."

Skye simply listened while she rearranged a few things in the refrigerator to make it easier to find them later. She took out the carton of organic eggs.

"After we lost our baby, I wanted to try again. I was in my twenties and she was in her early thirties, so I figured we were young and in that childbearing age."

"I don't need to know more," Skye said. "I really don't."

"I wanted to tell you that a year later, she conceived Elisa. I was overjoyed."

"Congratulations."

"And then Ethan came two years later. So God gave us two more children after we lost our firstborn."

"God? I thought you said you don't need Him." Skye cringed. She hoped her words didn't shut him down just when he was opening up. If he mentioned God at all, perhaps he was returning to Him. "I'm sorry. I shouldn't have said that."

"Your turn to say sorry?" Diehl grinned. "I've got thick skin. That's how I got to be where I am in the company. Words are not going to hurt me."

"What will?" Skye folded the two grocery bags for use later.

"A lack of loyalty, unfaithfulness, that sort of thing."

Skye washed her hands again, and looked for a pan to cook those bacon strips. "Those are important moral elements."

"Okay. Great. What can I do to help?" Diehl asked.

"Wash your hands first. Then you can choose. Do you want to watch the bacon or peel the potatoes?"

"Bacon." Diehl washed his hands at the sink and dried them on a kitchen towel.

Standing that close to him in the kitchen gave Skye some kind of feeling she couldn't define. He looked domestic, though she hardly knew him.

Well, she knew a lot about him from the many prayer requests that his sister had asked for in the last few years. Most of them related to stress at work and his difficulty with being a single father who had to be at the office all the time. The prayer requests had extended to his live-in nanny, and then the children's grandparents on both sides—none of whom were saved. And then they circled back to Diehl, who had been far away from God.

Skye knew all that, but confidentially, of course. No one divulged those prayer requests from the women's Bible study group at church.

"Just want to be sure we're on the same page," Skye said. "Yesterday morning at church, you told me that you want eggs-in-a-nest for breakfast today."

Diehl nodded. "What I said."

"Okay. Just want to be sure because it's not on our original menu."

"It's perfectly fine to deviate from it." Diehl reached for the bacon.

"Let me start it for you and you can flip it." Skye pushed the bacon away from Diehl.

"You don't trust me to cook bacon."

"I don't want you to give me a bad rating at the evaluation."

"I don't think I can give you a bad rating at all. In fact, you've been top-notch. Flexible. Accommodating. And an excellent cook—I mean, chef."

Skye smiled as she heated up a stainless-steel pan on the stove. "Please put all that in my evaluation."

"You own the company, don't you?" Diehl asked.

"Yes, STL has a single owner." Skye poured a thin layer of olive oil in the pan. She swirled it until it coated the entire pan.

"Why do you need an evaluation?"

"Well, I'm a chef too."

"How many chefs do you have working for you?"

"Twelve, and going on a few more if I need more." Skye placed the turkey bacon strips in the heated pan. She handed Diehl a pair of steel tongs. "I'm assuming you know what to do."

"Yes, ma'am. Shall I sprinkle some black pepper on top?"

"Whatever you want." Skye washed the potatoes in the sink and started peeling the skin.

"This is a pretty good-sized kitchen," Diehl said.

Skye nodded. "I like this kitchen. If I build a house, I want this kitchen in my house."

"You could buy this house."

"Say again?" Skye stopped peeling for a second.

"Brin told me she's selling the house."

Skye went quiet for a minute, trying to process the news. "I love this house, but..."

"But what's not to like? Look at the view alone. Oceanfront with a side yard for kids to play in."

Kids? "I wasn't thinking about kids. I was only thinking about this kitchen." Skye continued peeling the potatoes. "I helped Brinley and her team design this kitchen."

"Really? No wonder it's functional. Next time I need a new kitchen, I'll call upon Chef Langston to give me some advice."

"Sure. Any day." Skye rinsed the potatoes under cold running water. "This kitchen do-over was easy because the whole place was gutted. They basically kept the frame and redid the entire interior."

"I remember Brin mentioning it. She loves renovation work."

"And you? What do you do in Atlanta?" Should she have asked the question? Wasn't this man on a sabbatical from work?

"I run Brooks Investments." It was all he said initially, but then he added more layers to it. "My dad semi-retired to the golf course, so Brin and I were running the company. She traveled most of the time while I stayed put in Atlanta. Then she got tired of traveling. She sold me her share of the company so she could focus on renovation projects here."

"That's a load on you."

Diehl nodded. "If my brother, Parker, were still alive today, I'd be happy just to shadow him. He was the genius that expanded the company."

Skye had heard about the drowning. "I am so sorry."

"My family is full of tragedy." His voice was low, as if he regretted something.

"God is sovereign." Skye cut up the potato into julienne strips. There would be enough for four eggs. Diehl would get two, with two to spare. She'd give him the best ones now and he could eat the rest later. Or she could take them home. However the client wanted the leftovers disposed of.

Diehl looked at her intently. "You always bring God into our conversation."

"God is all I have, Diehl. Without Christ, I can do nothing. Remember that verse?"

"I have a feeling you're about to quote it for me. But I'm ahead of you. I do remember the verse, and I will read it to you. It's in John 15 somewhere." He put the tongs down on the counter and reached into his pocket. "Ah, my phone is upstairs."

"Mine's in my purse over there." Skye pointed to her purse on a chair at the breakfast nook. "Side pocket."

Diehl retrieved her phone. She pressed her left thumb on the button and the screen cleared. "See the Bible app? Pick your translation."

He nodded and tapped in the verse reference. "Here we go. I'll read the verse before it also. 'Abide in Me, and I in you. As the branch cannot bear fruit of itself, unless it abides in the vine, neither can you, unless you abide in Me. I am the vine, you are the branches. He who abides in Me, and I in him, bears much fruit; for without Me you can do nothing.' John 15:4-5."

"Good verses."

Diehl put the phone back in Skye's purse. "I'd forgotten how refreshing God's Word is until yesterday. It was good to be back in church. It's been a while."

Skye heated a new pan on the stove. She turned down the other burner and flipped the bacon. "I've been in church all my life, so I can't imagine being away."

Diehl took the tongs from her, and the base of his palm brushed against her fingers.

Skye felt it.

Sometimes she wondered what it would be like to have someone special in her life other than her own family. Sebastian was great and gave her a lot of hugs, but he was no longer living on St. Simon's. When his wife finished school, they wouldn't move back here. Without other relatives in town, Skye was the only Langston left.

To be sure, she'd had boyfriends in years past. In the last couple of years, she had been so busy splitting her time between the chef business and the restaurant, that she hardly had time to go out at all. All her dates had been pre-restaurant.

Sigh.

CHAPTER TEN

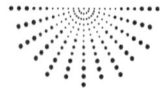

"*A* penny for your thoughts?" Diehl asked.

"Nothing." Skye sautéed the potatoes. Now they were standing next to each other at the stove.

She had cooked with numerous people before in her life, but this was the first time she felt nervous.

"Something was on your mind," Diehl pressed.

"And then it was gone. Don't burn the bacon."

They cooked quietly for a minute or so. Skye heated up the oven. She retrieved her muffin pan from her tote bag.

She buttered the muffin pan and then dished the cooked potatoes into them, making little nests.

"Those were delicious yesterday," Diehl said. "I hope you make it often."

"Well, you're here all summer, so there'll be plenty of time."

"Seemed like a long time when I arrived on

Friday." Diehl turned off the stove and transferred the bacon to a platter lined with a paper towel. "Now I'm looking forward to the entire summer."

"Because your kids are arriving today?"

Diehl stepped closer to Skye. "Because of you."

"Me?"

"I'd like to think we struck up a friendship. We get along well."

"It's only been a few days." Skye laughed. "Give it time. Our true colors will seep through."

"I was actually thinking that we knew each other a little bit before now, so it helped."

Skye nodded.

"And I'm sorry I made you cry last night," Diehl said quietly.

"What?" Skye had moved on.

"Last night at church, I asked about your parents. I'm sorry I did."

Skye blinked. "It was a memory. That's all."

"Parents are never just memories. They'll always be with us, no matter where they are, and no matter if they're gone." Diehl lifted Skye's chin with a gentle finger.

His eyes seemed to be on her lips.

Then the moment passed.

He dropped his finger.

Skye was glad he did. It wasn't the right time.

"Seb—my brother—handled it better than I did, but my parents died needlessly that night." Skye felt that Diehl should know. "They were drinking and driving across a railroad track. Their car was split into two by a train."

"I'm sorry." His face changed. "I'm so sorry."

"Twenty years ago." Skye cracked four eggs into the potato nests she had made. "Then again, God worked it out. We went to live with an uncle here in town. He owned a restaurant. We discovered we loved to cook and we ended up in cooking school."

"I'm glad."

Skye sprinkled some salt on the eggs, and into the oven the muffin pan went. She washed her hands. "I'm afraid the bacon will get cold."

"No, it won't." Diehl walked over to the breakfast nook with his platter of bacon. "Let's eat it."

Skye washed her hands and dried them on a clean kitchen towel she found in a drawer. "You eat it. I'm here to cook only."

"No, Skye. Sit down with me." He moved her purse and tote bag to the floor. "We're waiting for the eggs to cook, and I want mine well done. I don't want anything jiggly in the eggs."

"Then you need to wash your hands," Skye said.

"Again?" Diehl complied.

Skye looked for forks and knives, plates, and napkins. There were paper napkins, but she could not find any cloth ones.

"Paper is fine," Diehl said. "Would you like to say a blessing?"

Skye nodded. She kept her hands on her lap when she prayed. "Dear Lord Jesus, thank You for yet another beautiful week. Thank You for the morning sun and sea breeze coming in, for the warmth of Your unending love, and for Your sovereignty over our lives. I pray that You will keep Diehl's family safe as they fly in today. Give him a wonderful time with his two children. Give the Brooks family a special blessing today that only You can give. And now for this breakfast, thank You for the food we're about to eat. You are the provider of all things. I pray that You will cause the food to be nutritious to our bodies. Keep us healthy, Lord. In Your most holy name, I pray. Amen."

"Amen." And Diehl reached for the bacon with his fingers. "I washed my hands."

"You remind me of my brother. He likes to eat bacon with his fingers too. Like snacks."

"Why not?" Diehl waved the bacon around in the air. "We should cook more."

"Not everyone likes turkey bacon," Skye said. "You do."

"That's all I eat. It's less oily than pork bacon."

"For sure. I try to eat healthy too. That's why we source all our ingredients locally if at all possible, or at least from organic farms."

"I appreciate that."

"When did you start eating organics?" Skye munched on the crispy bacon. It was cooked just right. Was Diehl a secret cook himself?

"Since I was little. Cara made sure the family chef only cooked the healthiest food—which didn't always make my siblings and me happy, especially when our friends from school could eat anything they wanted."

"Cara?"

"Yes. She's in charge of the housekeeping staff at my parents' house now, but back then she was also our nanny and menu planner. Sometimes she also cooks."

"Multitasker."

"She was. To top it off, after she took care of four rambunctious kids during the day, cooked and cleaned for us, she went home to her own family. She has three kids of her own."

"Supermom." Skye wanted more bacon, but she decided not to. She could always cook more at home. She didn't want to eat her client's food.

Diehl picked up another strip of bacon and put it in front of her. "Take a bite."

"What?"

"Come on. You want to."

"No."

"Liar."

Skye made a face.

"I know you wanted to compliment me on the great job I did with the bacon," Diehl said. "Here I am, not a real chef, and I did not burn the bacon one bit."

"I turned down the stove for you." The bacon came closer to her mouth.

"I see you're not going to give me credit. Try this and give me a rating." Diehl waited.

"All right. I'll bite." She did. It tasted the same as the other strips. Delicious. "I'll give you an A."

"A plus?"

"An A is huge."

"A plus plus?" Diehl smiled.

He had a charming smile, Skye thought. How

could this man be so easy to talk with? "Are you this easygoing back home?"

He raised an eyebrow. "You mean back home in Atlanta? At work?"

"I wasn't going to bring up work since you're on vacation."

"Vacation?" Diehl sat back. "Well, it's turning into a vacation. But I'm supposed to be taking a mental health break. Dad didn't want me to think about work at all for three months. I don't know why he's telling me what to do. I'm turning forty this fall."

"It's good to take some time off."

"I don't know. If you didn't let me play accompaniment in your Treble Trio, I might be bored to tears."

"Maybe you could learn a new skill?" Skye suggested.

"You mean like cooking?"

Skye hadn't expected him to say that. "I was thinking along the lines of learning a new musical instrument or taking an art class. There are plenty of adult programs at the local college and in the Village shops."

"Music can be therapeutic."

Skye nodded.

"I might learn to play the guitar."

"There you go."

"Or I can hang around you and Marlo when you cook. Teach me some knife skills?"

Did she want him that close in proximity in the kitchen?

The oven chimed. Skye donned mittens before she

opened the oven door. Her eggs-in-a-nest looked perfect. She still felt awkward that Diehl had asked her to sit with him at the breakfast table to eat the bacon. She could not assume it meant the rest of breakfast too.

The pan was hot. She placed it on the island counter on top of a trivet. "Would you like to use the same plate?"

"Yes." Diehl brought his and her plates over to the island. "Eat with me?"

"I was going to save you the rest of the eggs for later."

"I don't think it's a good idea to reheat them. They'd only taste rubbery, right?"

"Not if you don't overheat them. Besides, I need to do the dishes and leave."

"Go after breakfast. I can tell we enjoy each other's company."

True. Skye nodded.

"We get along very well."

Skye nodded again.

"It's only breakfast."

"Right."

"It's just us, two friends who are here at this moment in time," Diehl added. "Who knows what's in store for us? Maybe we'll be friends after this summer. Maybe not. For now, let's enjoy the day while it lasts."

Friends.

That wasn't so bad.

He was only a friend, not a new romance.

CHAPTER ELEVEN

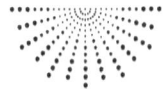

*D*iehl's kids arrived in town exhausted and cranky, and he didn't know how to deal with their emotions. It had been a year since their mother passed away, although they hardly saw her in the six months prior to her death. No one here in the States saw her, not even her own parents in Hawaii. Isobel had spent her last months in Italy on her own —supposedly.

Adult problems aside, Diehl now had a problem with his twelve-year-old. Elisa refused to speak to him. No "Hi, Dad!" and no hugs. To think, she was his hugger. And talker. Every time she had been away from him, they'd talk at least once a day on the phone about everything.

Now his daughter wouldn't look at him in the eyes.

Oddly enough, a couple of years before, Elisa had been Daddy's little girl. At that time, Ethan had the tantrums. The only way Diehl could speak to him was to ply him with gifts. Bribes. Today, the situation was reversed.

"What's going on, Elisa?" Diehl asked point-blank as Elisa walked past him, ignoring him almost, and dragged her hot pink rolling carry-on behind her, following Cara.

"Cara, stop a minute." Diehl remained in the foyer.

The housekeeper—and once Diehl's childhood nanny—turned around and brought Elisa back to him. They left her carry-on in the hallway.

"Elisa, are you okay?" Diehl asked.

She stared at him with steely eyes. He could see so much of Isobel in their curly-haired daughter. When Elisa smiled, it was Isobel's smile. Right now, that smile was non-existent.

Even that looked like Isobel's frown when she couldn't get her way. Like the day they had discovered they were expecting Elisa thirteen years ago. Diehl wanted to name her Elizabeth, but Isobel had insisted on the name Elisa. She had been listening to Beethoven's "Für Elise," and that was the name she had latched on to.

So, Elisa she was, although they ended up pronouncing her name as though it was the first part of Elizabeth.

"Tired?" Diehl tried again.

"I'm tired of life," Elisa snapped.

She speaks.

A breakthrough. At the office, if he could get information on the problem, he could begin to solve it. Yet, this was his daughter, not some corporate employee he could fire if things didn't work out. He could never get rid of his daughter.

"I'm tired too," Diehl said, thinking quickly about how to identify with her problem.

She remained in her frowning posture.

"Grandpa Ned banished me to this island—well, the island next door—to get some rest. Did you know?"

Elisa's big gray eyes widened. "Banished?"

Diehl nodded. "I'm not allowed to do any work related to the office."

"No work?"

"I know, right. It's terrible. I can hardly stand it. I don't even have chores."

"No chores?" Elisa's face changed into one of surprise. Utter surprise. "Grandma Zeta made us do a lot of chores."

"Well, I hope you enjoyed it because you're not getting any of it for the next three months." Or however long the kids were going to hang out on these islands.

"No chores. Are we still getting allowances?" Elisa started to open up.

Diehl thanked God for small victories.

"What are we going to do for three months?" Elisa asked.

Diehl shrugged. "Sleep a lot. Play a lot. I hope we don't ruin our lives."

Elisa placed a hand on Diehl's shoulder. "Dad, we're not going to ruin our lives."

"Do you promise?" Diehl hoped Elisa would grow up to be a better adult than he and Isobel had been.

Perhaps God would take a hold of Elisa and protect her from all the bad things in the world. It would certainly be a matter of prayer for him as a father. How could he pray for a daughter who was still innocent and pure? Maybe he could ask Skye.

Skye?

How did she pop into his head?

Somehow, he had thought of her when he considered who was still pure. Skye seemed like a nice woman in her early thirties, unmarried, with a good set of moral values, church-going, God-fearing. Maybe she might be able to impart some good influence on Elisa.

"We can play in the yard and have a picnic on the beach." It sounded so carefree that Diehl himself warmed up to the idea of a laid-back, idyllic summer.

He made a mental note to ask Skye to prepare a picnic lunch—wait. She wasn't his private chef. Well, he could request for her to turn one of their lunches into a picnic on the beach. Then he could take the kids to the beach behind Brinley's beach house.

If it was on a Saturday, and if she was free on her day off, perhaps she could join them.

It was odd, but his tension had dissipated the moment he had arrived on the Georgia coast. The sounds of the ocean and waves and seabirds took away the stress he had carried with him for one year. In retrospect, he should have taken an immediate break after he found out his wife had died.

If he had done that, would he have met Skye too soon?

She might think he was sending feelers out to her on the rebound.

Sending feelers?

What was he talking about?

Diehl wondered if his heart leapfrogged ahead of his head. Skye was lovely, and he had met her in passing. She and her brother Sebastian had catered for Brinley's wedding reception three years ago. Diehl remembered briefly talking to her about the finger food. He had no idea then that Skye was such a talented chef.

A hidden gem in the Golden Isles. If she were discovered by the food channels, would she be gone from the Georgia coast? Would he see her again?

His mind went back to their breakfast alone this morning at the beach house. She had seemed hesitant to eat with him. Yes, they were alone in the house, but they respected each other's space, didn't they? Although they cooked at the stove standing next to each other, Diehl hadn't taken advantage of their time together.

Why would he?

Skye was so beautiful, so pure, that he wanted to protect her from himself.

For the last twelve years, his personal life had revolved around Isobel and the kids. Now that Isobel was gone, he could move on to a new beginning. What would he like to do? Who would he like to be with?

All he could think of now was Skye.

Was it possible for someone to fall in love again a second time around this quickly?

"Dad?" Elisa's voice brought his wandering mind back to his present reality.

A single dad with two preteens to raise without their mother.

"Yes?" Diehl replied.

"Don't be sad." Elisa placed both palms on his cheeks. "Mom is in a better place."

Is she?

Did anyone ever think about what a "better place" meant? Where was that place that everyone went that was better than on earth? Christians believed in a heaven and hell, but that only believers in Jesus went to heaven.

So. Where did Isobel go after death?

Diehl knew that was a question for God Himself.

"Promise me something, Dad?" Elisa asked.

"What, honey?"

"No work for the summer."

"For me or you?"

"Both of us."

"Unless it's something we want to do."

"Can work be fun?" Elisa scrunched her nose.

"Sure it can." Diehl told her about playing the piano again. "I practiced a lot, but it was fun."

"Dad, practicing piano is never fun."

"Unless you have a goal you're working toward. My goal was to play the piano well at church for my team."

Someone gasped.

Diehl turned around to find Mom and Dad standing there, holding Ethan's hand. Ethan seemed to have grown a couple of inches taller since Diehl last saw him.

"You played piano at church?" Mom's voice rose several notches.

"Since when do you go to church?" Dad laughed.

Ethan broke off from their grips and walked toward Diehl, like he was all grown up at nine years old. "Dad!"

Never the hugger, he was one now. "Did you buy me something, Dad?"

"Like what, Ethan?"

"Like a sports car!" Ethan was loud. "Grandpa said he bought himself a new car. Did you buy me a new car?"

"No, I drove my old pickup truck." It was only two years old, but whatever.

Diehl turned to Dad. "Hey, Dad. Thanks for flying all the way to Hawaii to pick up the kids. Appreciate it. Mom, you too."

"It's the least we can do."

Mom didn't directly respond to Diehl. "We have a lot to talk about later."

Diehl nodded. He suspected she referred to the paternity test that the Bishops had asked for. Or perhaps a new development.

"But first, I need to take a nap," Mom said. "I didn't sleep well last night."

"I'll go with you." Dad motioned for Cara to

handle their luggage. "Take the kids upstairs to their rooms, please."

"Yes, sir."

Ethan returned to his small rolling carry-on. It had Iron Man decals all over it. "Where's your room, Dad?"

"I'm staying in Aunt Brin's beach house," Diehl said.

"Auntie Bling?" Ethan looked surprised.

That had been Ethan's moniker for Brinley when he had been a little boy, unable to curl his tongue. He could now, but he still sometimes called her Auntie Bling.

"You're not upstairs with us?" Elisa sounded disappointed.

"My room is still upstairs." Diehl could not give up his childhood memories. "However, your aunt's house is empty and rent-free."

"That's the good kind." Dad laughed.

"The house is small, but there are two rooms there ready for you if you want to stay there sometime." Now wasn't the time to ask the kids to go to church with him on Sunday, but he had all week to sort that out. Maybe they could stay with him on weekends and spend their weekdays here in this big old Brooks Cottage.

"I want to stay with Grandma," Elisa said.

Mom beamed. "That's fine. We can all get together during the day. At night, we all sleep, so does it matter where?"

"Only if the bed is not warm and comfortable." Dad reached for Mom, and they held hands.

"You warm up the bed and we'll see," Mom said unabashedly.

All those decades of marriage and they still looked at each other with longing.

Diehl wished he had a great marriage like that. Sure, Mom and Dad fought and argued a lot in their lives. However, they rarely went to bed angry, no matter what happened during the day.

As for Diehl, he could only recall a handful of times when he and Isobel had gone to bed happy. Sometimes she even woke him up in the middle of the night, griping about something or other. Why couldn't it wait until morning?

If he didn't stay up with her, she would find someone else who did.

Why hadn't Diehl seen the warning signs? Why had he ignored them all?

Had he been that gullible?

Isobel had stepped all over him. Their marriage had been anything but fulfilling.

And yet, he remained faithful and loyal to her, regardless of her own potential promiscuity—which he had suspected, but never bothered to investigate.

What Mom had told him over FaceTime on Friday night bothered him now.

Had Isobel been sleeping around during their marriage?

Sure, she flirted with people at parties, but...she was married!

Diehl watched his parents and kids disappear down the hallway. The grandfather clock struck eleven, reminding him that Skye was cooking lunch at the beach house.

He texted her, saying that he wouldn't be home the rest of the day, but she could leave the covered dishes in the refrigerator for him to eat the next day.

Which meant that Skye didn't have to cook for him on Tuesday.

He had no problem eating leftovers, but he sensed his own disappointment that he wouldn't see Skye until Wednesday.

Wednesday would be interesting. Brinley was still not feeling well, so Diehl had suggested that they sing "His Eye Is on the Sparrow" for the Fire Pit Service at church—because he could play that song on the piano or keyboard. Skye already knew the words. Avery could sit out if she wanted to.

He didn't mean to take over the Treble Trio and tell the members what to do, but the ladies were fine with the change of plans as long as it suited their commitment and schedule. It wasn't like he had suggested they play a wedding repertoire no one could practice for at such a short notice.

Diehl found himself excited about going to church. Maybe he needed a place to belong. Something to do to while away his time.

Or maybe it was because of Skye.

He recalled their breakfast this morning. He had enjoyed every moment of it. He found Skye easy on the eyes and pleasurable to chat with. She let him talk about whatever he wanted, and didn't interrupt him like Isobel had always done. In fact, he told her about his marriage to Isobel, their first stillborn child, and their unusual marital arrangement.

Something Skye had said hit him now.

Isn't marrying for love the best kind of marriage?

Perhaps that sort of marriage could last a lifetime.

Was that something he could find? He was almost forty now. Half his life was over.

CHAPTER TWELVE

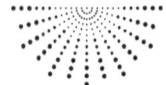

$\mathcal{T}$he Wednesday evening sky over the beach pavilion looked cloudier than the weather forecast. Skye worried about the keyboard she had borrowed from the Yun McMillan Music Studio for this evening's outdoor offertory. The keyboard was in the trunk of her car, waiting to be transported to the beach. If it rained, the expensive keyboard would be destroyed.

Half an hour early to the service, Skye took her time getting out of the car and walking the length of the boardwalk to the pavilion. To be on the safe side, she brought an umbrella with her. It was flimsy, but she had left her bigger golf umbrella in her work van parked at home.

Someone called her name, and she turned and waved. She didn't know why she was happy to see Diehl, happy to hear him call her name in public. They were friends now.

Still, she was concerned.

With Brinley on bedrest, Skye and Avery had no choice but to accept that Diehl might be their main accompanist for the entire summer. Usually, during holidays and school breaks, Seaside Chapel let their main vocals and ensembles take a break from performing, thereby allowing other talents in the church some opportunities to shine on center stage. That meant more opportunities for the Treble Trio.

Their trio used to be listed on the church bulletin as "Skye, Avery, Brinley." Now they were "Skye, Avery, Diehl."

There was a problem about where Diehl stood spiritually. Was he really saved in the Lord but only fell away as a prodigal son? Or had he never been saved at all and only going through the motions of church life?

Skye was afraid to ask, to judge. After all, only God could read and know the human heart fully.

Only God knew if Diehl was truly saved.

Then again, the Matthew 7:18 verse that Avery had reminded them of was still true.

A good tree cannot bring forth evil fruit, neither can a corrupt tree bring forth good fruit.

So far, Diehl had not shown himself evil. He had been friendly to her at the beach house. He had not been a foe.

So far.

"Hello." Diehl met her halfway on the boardwalk.

He was wearing a color-block polo shirt and a pair of matching blue shorts. "Looks like it's going to rain."

"I hope we don't get hit by lightning."

"Surely they'll cancel."

Skye nodded. "If there aren't too many people here tonight, we might just stay in the pavilion."

Diehl glanced back. "Looks big enough for maybe twenty people."

"At most. It'll be standing room only."

They walked back together to her car. Skye popped the trunk.

"When do you have to return the keyboard?" Diehl lifted the heavy case.

Skye reached for the lighter stand. "Tomorrow."

"Give me the address, and I'll return it for you. Save you a trip."

"You will?" Skye was moved.

"Sure. I have time. Besides, I'm a member of the trio now." He grinned.

For a man of almost forty years, he had a cute boyish grin. Skye wondered if his children looked like him. She hoped to meet them someday. Maybe she could cook for them.

"You like to do things for people, don't you?" Skye asked.

"I don't mind."

Perhaps his love language was to serve others, Skye wondered. Some people showed their love for others by doing things for them. So far, Diehl had volunteered to fill in for Brinley at the piano, he had assisted her in cooking breakfast for him on Monday morning, and now he was carrying the quite-heavy keyboard for her.

"Are you free Saturday?" Diehl asked as Skye closed and locked the trunk.

"It's my day off."

"My kids and I are going to have a picnic lunch on the beach," Diehl said quietly. "I was wondering if you'd like to join us."

"Will your parents be there?"

"No. They've got other plans. It's just the kids and I behind Brin's beach house."

"Oh, I see. Ask Chef Joseph to prepare you a picnic basket. He's good with that." Skye said hello to other church members coming and going on the board-walk toward the pavilion. Some were carrying covered dishes and some were carrying drinks.

"You didn't answer my question," Diehl said.

"Let me think about it? When do you need to know?" Really, she had no plans for Saturday before two in the afternoon, when she would head over to Saffron on Jekyll Island. It was important for her to show up once a week as the part-owner of the restau-rant to make sure that Chef Onada had everything he needed.

She could FaceTime him from afar, but it was only half an hour of driving from her house. She could have dinner at Saffron and not have to cook.

"Any time before Saturday is fine," Diehl said.

"Okay."

"One more thing. Mom wants us to eat out on Friday night, so you don't have to make dinner that night. However, I don't want you to take it off the cost."

"You want to pay me for not cooking?"

"I don't want to put your chefs out of work because of our constant change of meal plans."

"It happens," Skye said. "You're on vacation."

"How do you get paid when people cancel their plans?"

"We get paid. God always provides." Skye shrugged. "We have corporate customers who sometimes pick up the slack. Otherwise, I just cook the dishes for myself or to give them away to the women's shelter in town."

They placed the keyboard and stand near the microphone, and started to set it up. They had maybe twenty minutes left for soundcheck.

Hayden Hartley, one of the Sunday school teachers at Seaside Chapel, ambled over. He introduced himself to Diehl. "I heard you play on Sunday night, but I had to leave right after the service and didn't get a chance to meet you."

They made small talk while Skye texted Avery to ask if she was coming to the service even though she wasn't singing. Avery said she was running late, but she'd do her best to make it.

Skye made a note on her phone to bake Avery something as a surprise. That girl worked hard. She was not only the principal trumpet in the Sea Islands Symphony Orchestra here in town, but she also had a trumpet studio at home where she taught brass instruments to students. That was in addition to being an assistant editor, telecommuting for a small press out of state.

"Skye and I go way back." Hayden put his arm across Skye's shoulders. "Though not as far back as Matt."

Were Skye's eyes deceiving her or was that a slight frown on Diehl's face?

She saw that brief irritation.

"He's trying to say that I never left town—that I was born here, I live here, and I will probably die here." She tried to make light of Hayden's words because there was no reason for her to explain that she and Hayden dated briefly a long time ago.

"You forgot the rest of it." Hayden laughed. "You might also marry and have kids here."

Diehl looked at Skye.

No, stared.

Stop staring, Diehl.

A light rain fell all around the pavilion in the waning light. Some people scrambled around them and left the pavilion.

"I don't think we'll be lighting the fire pit tonight," Hayden said, letting go of Skye finally. "I hope you'll stay around for the message. I prepared a long time for it. Months."

"Of course, I'll stay for the entire service, music or no music. It's the Word of God that matters." Skye turned to Diehl. "Let's do our soundcheck."

It went quickly. Everything worked. They left everything as it was, and Skye followed Diehl to get some food at the potluck table. Rain sprinkled on part of the table, but the plastic tablecloth stayed in place.

"Did you bring anything?" Diehl asked.

"Not when I'm singing. I didn't have time to cook and practice before tonight."

Diehl leaned toward Skye to whisper in her ear. "Do we even know the ingredients in these dishes?"

"Even if they're labeled, we don't always know for sure."

Diehl chuckled. He tried what looked like chicken pot pie. "Oooh. This is delicious."

"That's Matt's pie. He only knows how to cook one thing."

"Matt Garnett?" Diehl's face changed slightly. "The guy who walked into class with you on Sunday morning?"

"You don't miss a thing, do you?" Skye was surprised he had noticed them.

"Not when it comes to you."

"Why me?" She put some jello on her plate. It was a mess. The jello dessert was next to a small slice of pecan pie, which was sitting on top of Matt's chicken pot pie.

"You're different from all the women I've ever known."

"Inside our church, I'm quite ordinary. One of many."

"You're being humble, but God made each of us unique. There's only one you in the whole world." Diehl offered to carry her plate. "Where would you like to sit?"

"I'm assuming that means we're sitting together."

"Is that okay with you?"

"Yes."

"Glad to hear that. I like sitting with you too."

What was he saying? "Are you trying to tell me something, Diehl?"

"I'm trying to persuade you to come to my family picnic on Saturday. I'd like you to meet my twelve-year-old daughter, who doesn't yet know what to do with her life, and my nine-year-old son, who thinks he knows everything about his life.'"

"They sound like how I was at those ages." Skye led Diehl to two empty seats to one side of the pavilion. Sitting down, they could see the ocean and the keyboard at the same time.

"For the record, you're the first woman outside of my mom and my sisters whom I've invited to a family picnic on the beach," Diehl said.

"You forgot Isobel."

Diehl's eyes met hers. "No, I didn't. Isobel hated the beach. She liked the coastal atmosphere, but preferred rocky shores."

"Wow. How could anyone hate the beach?" It baffled Skye.

"To each her own."

"Didn't she grow up in Hawaii?" Skye asked.

"Yes, she did. Never sunbathed. Never went surfing. She was on the island, but she wasn't an island girl. As soon as she could leave, she did."

Skye didn't like where the conversation was going. Where was Diehl in his grief recovery? She would have to pray for him more, that perhaps he would get some grief counseling to overcome his past. From what he had told her on Monday morning and now, Skye had the impression that he had a complicated relationship with his deceased wife.

There was an underlying unforgiveness there.

Maybe he had to let go of the past—

She caught herself.

Throw the first stone, why don't you?

Skye shouldn't be talking—thinking—about Diehl's life issues. She herself had a hard time letting go of her own past. The painful memories of having lost her parents at the tender age of thirteen had affected her entire life until this very day.

Hadn't she been triggered on Sunday evening when Diehl asked about her parents?

She had yet to accept that her parents were gone forever, and that she had to move on with her life. Until then, she suspected she would have a hard time making her own love relationships permanent. At the back of her mind, she feared losing the one she loved.

As such, she had never made a real commitment to anyone.

Sure, she had gone out to dinner with guys, even dated a few of them—Hayden, for example.

Diehl asked for Skye's empty plate. He tossed them out in the trash can and returned with two bottles of water. "That's all they have."

"Thank you."

His calf brushed past Skye's knees as he took his seat in the now crowded pavilion. "Sorry."

"No worries." She glanced at her watch. "Time to take our place."

Diehl followed Skye to the keyboard. The sound guy gave Skye a cordless microphone. She stepped back and leaned against the pavilion railing when Hayden stepped forward with his own microphone.

"Welcome, everyone, to our No Fire Pit Service tonight," Hayden said.

The talking ceased a bit.

"I'd like to think that those people who left earlier and didn't return did so because of the rain and not because I'm teaching tonight," Hayden continued.

"It's probably you," someone shouted.

"See there? No respect for his own Sunday school teacher." Hayden laughed and everyone else did too. "Okay, now that we're all relaxed, let's get on to business. Tonight's mini-sermon is on Philippians 4:13. 'I can do all things through Christ who strengthens me.' Feel free to find that verse on your phone or tablet or Bible as we begin our midweek meeting with prayer and song."

Skye placed her hand on Diehl's shoulder to assure him that they were going to be fine. He put his palm on top of her hand, turned to her, and gave her the warmest smile she had ever seen.

The smile broke through the rainy night.

Skye didn't want to let go, but let go she must.

Hayden prayed, asking God for protection, and then he nodded to Skye, who then nodded to Diehl.

When Diehl started to play "His Eye Is on the Sparrow," Skye almost wept as she sang the old hymn.

All the many sorrowful years of having lost her parents at an early age whooshed through her and washed away in the rain. It was as though God had pulled her through the darkest nights of her entire lifetime, and she had come out on the other side of the valley of the shadow of death.

> *"Let not your heart be troubled," His*
> *tender word I hear,*
> *And resting on His goodness, I lose my*
> *doubts and fears...*

When she finished singing the refrain for the last time that evening, Skye knew she had to accept Diehl's invitation to his family picnic in three days. His daughter had lost her mother when she was eleven years old. Skye had been motherless since she was thirteen.

She remembered a New Testament verse she had read and that had been read to her in years past. II Corinthians 1:3-4 had always been true since the day Paul had written it.

> *Blessed be the God and Father of our Lord Jesus*
> *Christ, the Father of mercies and God of all comfort,*
> *who comforts us in all our tribulation, that we may be*
> *able to comfort those who are in any trouble, with the*
> *comfort with which we ourselves are comforted*
> *by God.*

Perhaps God had comforted Skye so that she could

now comfort Diehl's daughter who had no Christian around her—except for her grandpa, her aunt, and her aunt's husband. If Diehl was a Christian, he had a long way to go toward spiritual maturity. Besides, he was also grieving himself.

Perhaps for such a time as this, Skye had to be here.

CHAPTER THIRTEEN

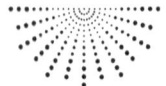

hey had renovated Saffron on Jekyll since the last time Diehl was here. He liked the new decor, which seemed to be a mix of the old and new. He could spot a great interior designer any day. At work, he regularly updated his list of interior designers, decorators, and architects for the numerous building projects that Brooks Investments were involved in.

"Who designed the interior?" Diehl asked when they were seated at the rectangular dinner table, with Mom and Dad on one side, and Elisa and Ethan on the other side.

The kids knew to be polite at this place, and they had dressed up for dinner. Elisa went all out with flowers in her hair. She looked like a girl plucked out of the Hawaiian Islands with her floral dress and matching floral purse and Mary Janes.

Ethan was Ethan. He wore anything Grandma put

on him. Today, his striped button-down shirt matched Grandpa's.

The two of them were poring over the menu together, with Dad pointing out his favorite desserts.

"I heard that Skye did, together with Meg Zimmerman," Mom said. "You remember Meg? She works for Brooks Renovations."

Wait a minute. "Did you say Skye? As in Skye Langston?"

"Uh-huh. She's part owner of this restaurant. She bought out her brother's shares back when he had a tiff with his business partner, who happened to be his ex-fiancée, Talia. You remember Talia?"

"I had no idea Sebastian sold his share to Skye. When was this?"

"About a year or so ago."

Diehl wouldn't have paid attention to the outside world at that time. He had been busy transporting Isobel's ashes from Italy to Hawaii, making funeral arrangements, dealing with Isobel's will and estate, sending his children to grief counseling, and all the other things involved in the death of a spouse.

"What happened to Talia?" Diehl tried to recall what happened between Sebastian Langston and Talia. Talia was something else. She would flirt with every guy in sight—the wealthier, the better. Whether they were married or not was a minor detail.

"As far as I know, Talia still owns fifty-one percent of Saffron. She lives in London now, you know, raising a child on her own."

"Is she?" Talia with a baby. Diehl didn't ask whose baby. It was none of his business.

"Jared Urquhart's baby, if you want to know." Mom put down her menu. Somehow, she had been able to chat with him while reading the menu.

"Jared's in London too?" Truth be told, Diehl hadn't kept up with the Urquharts either. They were also in the real estate investment business, but the primary thing he recalled was how Jared wanted Brinley badly.

No, he didn't get the girl.

"Jared's here," Dad finally said. "He's Talia's proxy and he likes to hang out some nights at this restaurant. You might see him tonight."

"I don't care," Diehl replied.

Famous last words.

The server came to take their orders, and when he left, out of the corner of Diehl's eyes, he saw something that made him suddenly care.

There, by the bar, Jared Urquhart stood next to a tall woman in a paisley dress that reached all the way down to her ankles. She did not look too familiar to him, except that she was as tall as...

The woman turned her face, her long and shimmering wavy hair swept her shoulders, and Diehl nearly fell off his chair.

Skye Langston.

Diehl had never seen her hair down. He had no idea it was that shiny or wavy. She had put on very light makeup. But the lipstick made her lips look...

Kissable.

Was this the other side of Skye? Diehl didn't know she was now running her brother's restaurant. Correction: her restaurant.

Diehl resisted the urge to walk up to the two of them to see what they could be talking about. Jared didn't own a part of this restaurant, did he?

The idea that Skye and Jared could be business partners bothered Diehl when their lobster and filet mignon dinner arrived.

Diehl cringed at the memory that Jared had also tried to romance his sister Brinley a few years ago.

Call him old fashioned, but Diehl thought that if Jared had any decency, he would marry the mother of his child—just as Diehl had.

On the other hand, Diehl had been trapped in a loveless marriage for ten years, although in their last year together, he thought they had turned a corner.

Only, it had ended their marriage forever.

Diehl prayed, as much as he could muster the words, that God would protect Skye from Jared and his ilk.

He felt compelled to run over there to shield Skye, but at the same time he didn't want to look stupid.

He glanced over, and saw that Jared and Skye were walking away from the bar. Jared's hand was on the small of her back. Fortunately, there was fabric there. To Skye's credit, her long dress was modest.

"Excuse me." In a huff, Diehl placed his napkin on the table, got out of his chair, and was off to rescue the lady from the villain.

He called her name even before he reached them. He liked hearing himself call her name.

Skye stopped and looked in his direction. "Diehl."

"Diehl," Jared said. "Man, haven't seen you in a while."

He let go of Skye and shook Diehl's hand.

The entire time, Diehl's eyes were on Skye. "You look lovely tonight."

"Nice jacket," Skye said. "Are you here with your family?"

Diehl nodded. "It was between Saffron and The Priory. We let the kids choose, and Elisa wanted to eat here tonight."

"I'd love to meet your kids." Skye smiled. "If I had known you'd be here tonight, I would have saved the chef's table for you."

Jared cleared his throat. "We're heading upstairs for a business meeting."

"On a Friday night?" Diehl raised an eyebrow.

"I work all the time. It will be a good meeting. I just bought half of Talia's shares, so that makes me a co-owner of this fine establishment."

Oh. It gets worse, doesn't it?

Diehl's mom had said earlier that Talia owned fifty-one percent of Saffron. If she had sold half of it to Jared, then Talia was now a minority owner, same as Jared. With the split, it meant Skye was now the majority owner of the restaurant. No wonder she was smiling broadly. She must have just received the news very recently.

"Jared, we have time. Let Talia sleep for a few more minutes over there in London. Let's go meet the kids first." Skye asked Diehl to lead the way.

Awkward.

Diehl realized his mistake now. He had been rash. He had forgotten that his parents were with him tonight. That meant Mom would talk about Skye endlessly for the next several weeks, at least—as soon as Mom found out that Skye was also his personal chef.

How did Skye handle the two businesses without burning out? What strength did she have that he didn't?

"Rose, Ned. Nice to see you again." Skye waved even before she reached their table.

Walking alongside her, Diehl smelled a faint floral perfume of some sort. It was very light, but very...

Enticing?

He tried to keep his cool, but he knew that his heart was falling hard for her.

Now, to keep Jared and Hayden and Matt away from her while Diehl sorted out his messy life. How long did he need? How much time would Skye give him?

While Skye and his parents chatted, Diehl found nothing to say to Jared. Back in the days when they had both been young and wild and carefree, they had always been rivals.

Being born into wealthy families had its drawbacks. The stakes kept getting higher and higher, until they were unsustainable. Who bought a more expensive car than the other? Who snagged the better woman? Who went to a better Ivy League school? Who got his MBA first?

It was endless.

As the years wore on, the friends called a truce.

And now they were standing on both sides of the same woman—who hadn't expressed her feelings either way.

"Are you married?" Ethan suddenly asked.

The whole table was silent.

Diehl looked at Skye.

Skye smiled. "No, I'm not married."

"Never been married?" Ethan asked again.

Dad cleared his throat.

Mom and Jared laughed.

Diehl was aghast. He had failed in his parenting.

"Never been married," Skye replied.

"Good to know." Ethan nodded.

What on earth?

"Diehl, your steak is getting cold," Skye said. "I'll have them send you a new filet."

"No, no, I'm fine." Diehl sat down. "I wasn't hungry. I'll take it to go."

"Make a sandwich maybe?" Skye asked.

"That's an idea," Jared said. "A very expensive sandwich."

"If it's delicious, it's worth it," Skye said.

"You know your food. I'll defer to your expertise, Chef Langston," Jared replied.

"I'll ask the kitchen to turn it into a sandwich for

you before you leave," Skye said to Diehl. "Or I'll make the sandwich for you in the morning. Or make you a salad so you can put the beef slices on top."

"Whatever you think is best." Diehl glanced at Mom.

Mom seemed to pretend she hadn't heard.

And Diehl wished the entire conversation hadn't happened, and that he had left Skye alone with Jared. He didn't know why he'd had a knee-jerk reaction to seeing them together. He experienced the same angst on Wednesday night when Hayden put his arm over Skye's shoulders. And perhaps on a smaller scale, on Sunday morning, when Matt walked into Sunday school with Skye.

Something inside made him want to protect her from all those men.

Protect her for what? For whom? For himself?

Diehl wasn't sure whether he was seriously interested in Skye. Could he be? She was sweet and kind. Her voice comforted his heart in ways no one else on earth could. She was interesting in many ways he couldn't describe. Now he found out she ran a multi-million-dollar restaurant on top of her personal chef business.

Diehl suspected that Skye was a personal chef simply because she liked to cook for people. Look how easily she had offered to dress up his soon-to-be left-over filet mignon.

He dared not consider the possibility that Skye was only nice to him because he paid Skye's the Limit for the daily meals. Maybe she was kind to all her clients.

The whole situation bothered Diehl to no end on the drive home to Brinley's beach house, where Dad dropped him off before they took the kids to their home on Seaside Island.

CHAPTER FOURTEEN

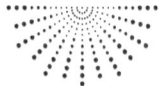

*A*lone in the beach house and resting on his bed with the fan spinning above him, Diehl asked God to show him the way through life. He had tried to manage and balance everything himself. He realized now that even on his best days, his own thoughts were no match for God's.

On his tablet, he bought and downloaded a Bible app. It looked similar to what Skye had on her phone the other day.

He searched for the verse that talked about God's thoughts being so much higher than his own. He found it in Isaiah 55:9.

> *For as the heavens are higher than the earth, so are my ways higher than your ways, and my thoughts than your thoughts.*

Recognizing that God was greater than his own

mind, Diehl thanked God for the reminder and asked God to forgive him for going his own way for so many years. Thirteen or fourteen years now?

So much time wasted wandering through the wilderness or through dry and weary deserts with no water.

He copied the verse and texted it to Skye.

It was too late before he realized what he had just done. He cringed. Who was he to send verses to Skye, who had been in church her entire life and hadn't strayed from God?

He was the prodigal son, wasn't he? Even when he had been wandering away from the faith, he knew he had sinned against God. He knew that God hadn't been pleased with him, living a decadent lifestyle with Isobel. However, after they married, he kept his marriage vows and remained faithful to Isobel. Could it be possible that his withdrawal from their once exciting nightlife had caused her to stray from their marriage?

He wished he could ask Isobel if she realized that when his older brother had died suddenly, he lost all interest in their partying days, their opulent lifestyle, and temporal things?

Diehl spent the next number of years filling Parker's shoes at Brooks Investments. Diehl soon discovered how much work Parker had done with Dad in the company, taking it from millions to billions. Between Diehl and Brinley, they carried on Parker's legacy.

However, Diehl's marriage fell apart in the interim. He and Isobel grew distant. They had once married for money and convenience, to make sure that their children had two parents, and that was the extent of their connection with each other.

He should never have remarried her after the divorce.

Still, she was the mother of their children, and had custody of them. Once remarried, the children would be in the same household again.

Had Diehl remarried Isobel for the children's sake?

Why had he taken such serious matters so lightly? If marriage was ordained by God, then it wasn't a frivolous business transaction that could be terminated at any time. Wasn't marriage for life?

Ironically, Isobel had passed away.

Their marriage had ended.

Was he now free to marry again? Perhaps for love this time?

Isn't marrying for love the best kind of marriage?

Skye's words. A statement wrapped up in a question. Her convictions?

His phone chimed. He checked the notifications. A text message from Skye.

Thank you for the verse.

Diehl debated on whether to call her or text back. Before he knew it, he called her. Audio only. "Hi. Still awake?"

"Getting ready for bed. You?" Skye asked.

"Same. Hey, I want to apologize for interrupting your business meeting at Saffron."

"We hadn't started the meeting. We were on our way to the top deck."

"Beautiful night."

"Yes," Skye said. "Next time let me know when you'll be at Saffron."

"It was a last-minute decision." As he had told her at the restaurant.

"How did you get a reservation at such a late notice?"

"Well, you'll have to ask Mom," Diehl said. "She has her ways."

"Enough said. Rose is Rose. She gets her way."

"Yeah. I didn't know you bought your brother's share of Saffron."

"Long story. I was hoping to buy out Talia, but Jared showed up."

Jared. Diehl didn't like to hear Skye say his name. If anyone could seduce a woman and then spit her out, it was Jared. "I would advise you to avoid him at all cost. You know Jared. His reputation precedes him."

"Your reputation also precedes you, Diehl."

"I'm reformed."

"Reformed or transformed?" Skye asked.

"Is there a difference?"

"One word implies that things get remixed into another shape, but the elements are still the same. The other implies an inside-out transformation, where you're a totally new person. Only God can do that in your life—change you from the core of your being, giving you a new heart."

"I want to be transformed." Diehl meant it.

"Then ask Jesus into your heart. He will change your life. You will never be the same again."

"I thought I did accept Jesus in college. I guess my lifestyle didn't match up."

"Whether you once did or not, what matters is whether you are saved *now*."

"I have a lot of head knowledge, but I don't feel Jesus in my heart." Diehl adjusted the pillow behind his head.

"You know that salvation is not a feeling. You walk by faith in Jesus, not by feeling or an idea." Skye paused. "Walk by faith, and your feelings will follow."

"How many times do I need to pray to receive Jesus in my heart?" Diehl remembered only praying about salvation once in college.

"Salvation is once and for all. After that is sanctification, which is a lifelong process."

"Which is which? That's my question." After he had supposedly believed in Jesus, he met Isobel, and he hadn't been a Christian since.

Just because he remembered hymns and how church worked, didn't mean that he was a part of the flock. He knew that.

"That's an easy question to answer, actually," Skye said. "If salvation is an issue, then pray again to ask Jesus into your heart. It's as simple as acknowledging that you are sinful and God is holy. As a result of that, you are separated from God and are unable to have a relationship with Him."

"I know that part."

"Your sin is a debt that you cannot pay on your own. God bridged the chasm between you and Him by sending His only Son, Jesus, to die on the cross to pay the penalty for all of your sins, thereby paying off that debt completely. When He rose again from the grave, He gave Christians a new eternal life. Believe that Jesus has done that for you personally, and ask Him to give you a new life in Christ. Ask Him to forgive you of your sins. And you are thus saved."

Diehl had to process it for a minute. He tried to recall what he had prayed in college, but he couldn't. "I think I believed most of that."

"You know you can't be partially saved. Either you're all saved or you're not. You can't be half-saved."

"I hear you." Diehl searched for "believe" on his Bible app. "I found a verse. 'Believe on the Lord Jesus Christ, and you will be saved, you and your household.' Acts 16:31. Does that mean my entire family?"

"Everyone in your family has the opportunity to individually believe in Jesus." Her voice sounded tired. It must be past her bedtime. "After salvation comes the long process of sanctification, where God prunes you and puts you through the fire to see whether you're gold and silver, or wood and hay."

"Because if I am truly saved, then I would live my life like I am truly saved," Diehl concluded.

"Exactly."

"You have given me much food for thought."

"I suggest you talk to Pastor Gonzalez or to your brother-in-law, Ivan, for more details," Skye said.

"Not to you?"

Instead of answering his question, Skye simply said, "I'll continue to pray for you."

CHAPTER FIFTEEN

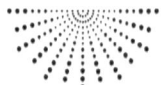

$\mathcal{U}$sually, Skye slept in on Saturday mornings, but today, she rose early to try to look halfway decent for the picnic with Diehl and his kids. Even as she painted new nail polish on her toes and looked for matching flip-flops to go with her summer blouse, she felt out of place.

"Lord, I don't know about this." She hadn't asked Diehl if anyone else would be there.

The last thing she wanted was to give Diehl the wrong idea about where she stood with him.

Which was nowhere.

Skye admitted that she was a little bit attracted to Diehl. He was single, and so was she. However, she knew that some things were never meant to be. Sebastian's catering company had cooked for the Brooks family before in their numerous Christmas functions, and Skye helped whenever she had time.

She had seen what inherited money looked like.

She didn't want to say that the Brooks had it easy, but they certainly didn't have to scrape and make do from scratch all the way up to middle class. They had begun at a different plane than she and Sebastian had.

Then again, Skye wasn't poor. Uncle Miller had paid for chef school for both Skye and her brother. After their uncle died, he left them an established Sage Café, which Sebastian still owned. From there, Sebastian started the highly successful Saffron on Jekyll, which Skye still partly owned.

On top of that, Skye ran her personal chef establishment.

Neither of them was short for money.

On her way to the bathtub, she swiped her iPad to check her bank account. Saffron on Jekyll turned a profit yet again—five years in a row. Her personal chef business was vibrant, although she wasn't sure what the future held. She wanted to start that cooking show, but she wasn't sure if she was up to the task.

"I mean, that's adding one more thing to an already full plate," she said aloud to no one.

The hot bath soothed her muscles and bones. Skye had worked as hard as her brother, but he knew how to relax and have fun too. In fact, he still managed his Sage Café on St. Simon's Island, even though he spent most of his time in Athens and Atlanta now.

He promised to come home to St. Simon's for Christmas, but that wasn't for another six months.

In other words, Skye had to find ways to fill her lonely days since she couldn't hang out with her brother anymore.

Happily married, Sebastian couldn't wait for his wife to finish her graduate school because they were planning to have a baby afterward.

Marriage.

Babies.

Family.

Those things seemed so far away to Skye. Almost unattainable.

She had told herself once before that she had plenty of time. Well, at the age of thirty-four, she hoped she still had plenty of time for marriage and family.

For now, she looked forward to being a doting aunt to her future nieces and nephews.

Speaking of which...

Babies!

She got out of the tub, took a shower, and went straight to her schedule. How could she almost totally forget about it? Brinley's baby shower was in three weeks!

She dried her hair and threw on a cotton T-shirt and shorts—because she wasn't sure what she wanted to wear to the picnic yet.

She texted Avery.

Avery called back on FaceTime. "I'm on it."

Skye felt relieved. "I've been so busy cooking that I forgot all about the prep work."

"Well, it's not like you and I have to organize baby showers all the time. With so many women in our Bible study, it's nice to see everyone taking a turn."

"Right. Thank God."

"We've discussed the theme, so that goes a long way," Avery added. "Brinley seems okay with the rubber ducky theme."

"She's so easygoing, she's okay with everything."

"If you want, we can meet this afternoon for a quick update. It's easier to talk in person. I'm visual, you know."

"What time do you have in mind?"

"How about right after lunch? If you want to come over for lunch, I'm cooking bibimbap, recipe from a friend. You can tell me how it tastes."

"Uh, I can't make it to lunch but I could do dinner?" Skye did not want to tell Avery about her picnic.

But why not?

There was no secret.

It was a simple picnic with a widowed man who seemed to be just as lonely as she was.

"We can do dinner. How about five o'clock?"

"Done." Skye updated the calendar on her iPad.

"Anything I can pray about?" Avery asked.

It was not unusual for them to ask each other that. Since Emmeline moved out of town, Skye had found Avery to be a loyal friend and confidant.

"I don't know how to ask," Skye said.

"About what."

"I don't want people to know."

"Uh-oh."

"Well, it's not a secret, but Diehl asked me to go on a picnic with him and his kids."

"Okay. Are there other adults there?"

"Only him and the kids, as far as I know. Besides, it's just going to be in his backyard—although that's the beach. I mainly agreed to go because his daughter lost her mother at eleven, and I lost mine at thirteen. I thought I might minister to her."

"But you feel like maybe you should have said no." Avery hit the nail in the head.

"Or make sure that there's a crowd."

"It's not a public beach in that area, is it?"

"It is." So what was the problem? Skye still had a gnawing feeling that perhaps she should not be hanging out with her client. If there was a fallout, she might lose the business.

"And you're afraid that someone from church might see you?" Avery asked.

"I don't know." Well, she wasn't as concerned about people seeing her with Diehl as the fact that she wasn't sure if she wanted to be with Diehl. They were starting to know each other and it had only been one week.

"Have you prayed about this?"

"Well, I thought I did. Maybe I did. I don't know if I went on my knees and *prayed* prayed, you know? After all, it's just a picnic."

"Nothing in life is just a picnic, girl," Avery said.

She was right again. The voice of reason.

"I don't know what to do," Skye said.

"You know me. If I'm not sure about something, I don't do it."

"If I did that, I'd never try new dishes." Skye

laughed. Then she turned solemn again. "It's too late to ask someone else to come with me."

"A chaperone? What century are you living in?"

"I don't think it's outdated." Skye had a thought. "I could text Diehl and ask if I could bring a friend."

"Like who is going to go with you at the last minute?" Avery laughed.

"You are!"

CHAPTER SIXTEEN

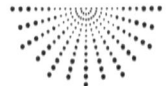

"Whose bright idea was it to have a picnic at noon in the hot southern sun?" Avery laughed.

"It was mine. Thank you for the vote of confidence." Diehl laughed with her as he checked the base of the canopy to make sure the winds didn't topple it over.

"It'll be a few degrees lower in the shade." Skye rolled a cooler toward them. She was wearing aviator sunglasses.

In the sun, her brown hair looked lighter. It was in a ponytail today, and she wore a modest-looking sleeveless blouse and a pair of shorts. Her legs were longer than Diehl remembered, and they were nicely tanned. She had painted her toes a delicate shade of pink.

Walking next to her, Ethan donned his Ray-Bans and wore his Hawaiian shirt like he was ready for a yacht party. He carried something in each arm, trying to puff up his skinny arms. No muscles there, kid.

Diehl watched his son stick to Skye so closely that her elbows were almost always near his face.

"May I help with that?" Ethan asked.

"I'm just going to leave the cooler here. Thanks." Skye seemed amused, but she responded to Ethan kindly.

Diehl appreciated that, even though he worried about a future Ethan going through puberty.

Skye put down her tote bag on the sand in the shade.

"Hello, Skye." Diehl asked her if she wanted some cold water. "Glad you could come."

She stepped around the beach chairs to get the bottled water from him.

"Avery, you want one?" Diehl asked.

"After I finish mine." She lifted her bottle in the air. "Thanks."

Diehl nodded.

Skye opened a picnic basket that Chef Joseph had prepared them. "What have we here?"

"I asked Chef Joe to keep it simple. Reubens, roast beef, chicken. Sandwiches and wraps." Diehl pointed to another basket. "Fruits and cookies in there. He said the cookies are your recipes."

Skye didn't respond.

She closed the basket in front of her and stood up.

She was standing so close to him that he could smell that light floral perfume again.

"What perfume are you wearing?" Diehl asked

quietly. He rattled off a list of name brands. "Oh, I'm sorry. Don't think I know too much about what women spray on themselves."

"There you go again, saying you're sorry." Skye lightly swatted his arm.

He reached up and held her hand.

Someone cleared his throat. Ethan.

Trying to stand tall, he glared at Diehl. "Why are you holding her hand?"

Diehl dropped it immediately.

To Skye, Ethan said, "Are you Dad's girlfriend?"

"No."

One little word disappointed Diehl so much.

"Then will you be mine?" Ethan asked.

"Your what?" Skye raised her eyebrows.

"My girlfriend." He looked serious—as serious as a nine-going-on-nineteen-year-old could be.

Behind them, Avery laughed so hard that Diehl thought their canopy was going to explode.

Throughout the picnic lunch, Diehl didn't know whether to laugh or cry at his own son. There was so much of Isobel in Ethan. He had no fear of talking to strangers and putting himself at the center of attention. He made jokes that everyone tried to laugh at, and he was suddenly loud.

Ethan sat on one side of Skye while Diehl sat on the other side in another beach chair, but Ethan dominated all their conversations. Diehl resigned himself to observing everyone.

Still, Ethan wasn't Diehl's biggest worry.

Since Diehl had picked up his kids from Mom's

house this morning, he had noticed the sullenness in his daughter.

The same daughter who told him on Monday not to be sad about her mom's passing now didn't feel like talking to anyone at the picnic. All week long, Diehl had seen a progression in her behavior. She stopped interacting with the rest of the family— not even with her grandpa, whom she doted on. By the time they had gone to Jekyll Island for dinner on Friday night, Elisa had stopped talking altogether.

Maybe she needed to be with kids her own age.

Diehl tapped Skye's arm. She turned her face, covered with a sheer glisten of sweat. She might want to cool off in the ocean, but she hadn't brought a swimsuit.

"Does Seaside Chapel have summer programs for teens?" Diehl asked quietly.

"Oh, yes. We get a lot of visitors in the summer, and sometimes they drop off their kids at church for day camps and such. The VBS runs to sixth grade, but the teens have their own thing. Half of them went to camp just last week."

Diehl nodded. "Maybe there's something for my kids."

"Of course. Let me ask Hayden." She reached for her phone in her pocket. "He works with the teens during the summer, so he'll know."

Hayden. Her ex-boyfriend.

Diehl tried not to be judgmental, but he couldn't help it. He waited for Skye to text Hayden. In seconds,

Hayden texted back a link to the church website with activities for kids.

Skye handed her phone to Diehl.

He scrolled to see the various teen programs at church he could send his kids to for the next three months. Good. They could meet other kids their age.

While he was reading, a notification popped up. It was right there, so he couldn't help but read it. Jared Urquhart sent a short note saying he was considering buying out the rest of Talia's shares.

"Looks like you have a note from Jared." Diehl handed the phone back to Skye.

"Oh? On a Saturday?" Skye read it.

Her face dropped.

"What?" Diehl asked quietly.

"Nothing...I mean, it's something I'll have to deal with. Nothing of concern to you, though."

Diehl could hear the disappointment in her voice. "Well, I know Jared. I pity anyone who has to deal with him. What are you going to do?"

"What can I do? He's telling me that he and I are competing for the rest of Talia's shares. He's taunting me to give up and bail out of the restaurant. All my brother's hard work went into it. In my mind, I see Seb and myself owning Saffron again someday."

"Where's your brother now?" Diehl had met Sebastian before, but they weren't friends.

"Athens. One more year and Em will graduate."

"Has he said anything about Saffron?"

"Not lately."

"Why not, if the restaurant is so important to him?"

It took a moment for Skye to reply. "It was important to him when he was dating Talia. It was their love project together."

"So you *think* he wants it back."

"I know my brother, but he won't want it back with Talia in it. It would cause trouble for him and his wife." Skye's finger flew to her mouth. "Actually, I don't know. I'm guessing."

"As someone who has been married before, I can tell you that it's best if the husband and wife are on the same page."

"I suppose that's best for any strong relationship." Skye sighed. "Maybe God is telling me to let go of it. It's only a restaurant that Seb isn't a part of any longer."

"Do you think Jared will sell his shares to you?"

"I have no idea," Skye said. "I wonder if I could persuade Talia to sell me the rest of her shares instead."

"So you'll be the majority owner."

"However, if Seb is done with the business, I don't need the trouble, you know? I'd rather build up my personal chef company."

Diehl smiled. "Let me tell you something about Jared."

"What?"

"He texted you his intention, right?"

"Yeah."

"He does that a lot. What you read might not be

what you think it is," Diehl said. "He's extremely competitive."

"Is he only messing with my head?"

"I think he wants to be the majority shareholder. Seems to me that he could buy out Talia or you. Either way, he will be in charge."

"He already has part of Talia's shares."

"But you're in charge."

"I just..."

Diehl waited.

Skye pursed her lips.

"Just what?" he asked.

She shrugged. "Maybe it's just me."

"Just you what?"

She drew a deep breath. "Yeah. It's probably just me. Some people are the super-friendly type, and I'm not."

Anger flared in Diehl's eyes, surprising himself. "Are you saying Jared tried to flirt with you?"

When she didn't say anything, Diehl could put two and two together.

"We all have our idiosyncrasies, you know? While you can avoid people you don't want to be with, what if they're your business partners?"

"Say no more." Diehl knew exactly what she meant.

And right then and there, Diehl knew what he had to do. He hadn't planned to do this, hadn't intended to work this summer, but when the opportunity presented itself, how could he reject it?

He had known Jared a very long time. That man

wasn't into restaurants. He spent more money investing in building projects than anything else. Brinley had told Diehl about the mixed-use properties he tried to buy on the island here and also in Savannah, about an hour's drive north of St. Simon's.

Why the sudden interest in restaurants? For the simple reason that, as long as Diehl had known him, Jared was an opportunist. If he saw a situation in which he could exert control, he would do it, regardless of the consequences. Whatever he needed to do to get his way, he'd do it in a heartbeat.

Diehl determined then and there to do everything in his power to prevent Jared from pushing Skye around. Jared wasn't getting his way this time, not with anyone Diehl knew, and certainly not with anyone Diehl was interested in.

Am I interested in Skye?

He was sure he was, but right now, his son seemed to do better at attracting her than he did.

"Skye, would you like to take a walk on the beach with me?" Ethan asked. His politeness oozed.

Skye glanced at Avery, who tried not to laugh again.

"Why don't we *all* go for a walk?" Diehl said.

"Daaaddd!" Ethan bellowed. "I asked only Skye."

"We're all on this picnic together, son."

Ethan pouted. Now he looked just like his sister...

Diehl scooted forward in his seat, looked around. "Where did Elisa go?"

Isobel's warnings from a few years ago came to his mind. She had insisted that Diehl hire private security for the family. He had always balked at the extra costs involved. He remembered telling her, "That's what 911 is for. We paid our taxes!"

"Elisa?" He sprinted outside the canopy.

Skye followed him, and so did Avery.

Only Ethan remained in his beach chair. His arms crossed his chest.

"She wore a black shirt and long black tight pants," Skye told Avery.

Avery nodded.

"We need to pray that God will help us find her," Skye said.

"You pray." Diehl's eyes swept the crowded beach for a child dressed in all black.

"I am," Skye said as she looked the other way— toward the dunes and boardwalk.

She placed her hand on her forehead above her aviator sunglasses. "I see someone."

She sprinted toward the boardwalk.

Diehl followed her. He stopped suddenly. "Ethan, are you coming?"

Ethan refused to reply.

Diehl grunted. Glanced back at Skye, who was almost at the boardwalk. "Ethan, we have to go find your sister."

Caught between two children. How could his son be this selfish? What had Diehl taught—or not taught —him?

Ethan sighed. "Just trace her cell phone."

Diehl's shoulders sagged. He retrieved his phone and checked. Sure enough, Elisa's phone was near

Brinley's beach house. Still, Diehl didn't trust technology. He wanted to see his daughter face to face. To hold her, make sure she was okay.

"Go, Diehl," Avery said. "I'll stay here with Ethan. I'm sure our handsome gentleman is going to help me eat the rest of the cheesecake right now, and then we'll pack up and see you at the house. Right, Mr. Ethan?"

Ethan made a face. "If we eat the rest of the cheesecake, we'll be so sick."

"Shall we find out?" Avery asked.

"Really?" Ethan didn't even look at Diehl.

Diehl gasped. But he turned to go. "Thanks, Avery. I owe you one."

"You owe me nothing. Go find your daughter."

CHAPTER SEVENTEEN

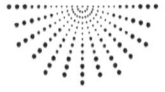

Thank God she's wearing black.

Elisa stood out from the crowd on the boardwalk heading toward the public entrance to the beach.

Skye found it hard to walk fast in her flip-flops. She took them off and carried them as she ran barefoot across the boardwalk.

Ahead of her, Elisa made a sharp left turn and illegally crossed someone's yard. She disappeared somewhere in the front of the house which was next door to Diehl's cottage.

Skye picked up the pace and followed Elisa across the driveway to Brinley's beach house.

When Skye rounded the corner, Elisa stood there, waiting for her.

"Why are you following me?" Elisa snapped.

"Because my mother died when I was thirteen and I never had a chance say goodbye." How all those words tumbled out of her mouth, Skye would never know, but she wasn't going to retract them.

Elisa's jaw dropped. "You too?"

Her words were a confirmation to Skye regarding why she had to come to the picnic today. She had something Elisa needed. She had the comfort that God had given her way back then, as it was written in 2 Corinthians 1:3-4.

"In my darkest time of need, my aunt sat down with me on the back porch and comforted me," Skye said.

"You're not my aunt." Elisa started walking again.

"Does it matter?" Skye went after her.

At the base of an old live oak tree on the other side of the bird feeder and birdbath, Elisa sat down on a protruding root.

"It took me years to heal," Skye said. "However, I believe that it would have taken me longer if my aunt had not talked with me."

"Don't talk to me."

"How about if I listen?" Skye found a patch of green grass within earshot of Elisa. She dropped her flip-flops to the grass and sat down.

She was six or seven feet away from Elisa. "Go on."

"Go on what?"

"Talk to me. I'm here."

Elisa didn't say a word.

Skye checked the grass around her. It was dry. She lay down on the grass, with her face looking up at the canopy of spreading branches.

"You know, this tree has been here for at least a hundred years. It has seen many life cycles in human lives. Maybe deaths, destruction, rebuilding, and so forth. What do you think it has seen?"

Elisa didn't respond.

"I can say that it hasn't seen as much as my God has," Skye continued. "My God has seen everything since before time began."

"Is that possible?" Elisa asked.

A breakthrough.

"Yes. God has always existed. That's what the Bible says."

"You believe everything the Bible says?"

"It is the Word of God. In my darkest hour of need, God comforted me beyond anything anyone in this world could." Skye sat up and brushed off the pieces of grass and dead leaves that had stuck to her. "When my mom and dad died, I didn't understand why God would let them drive their car in front of an oncoming train."

Elisa flinched. "Eeek."

"I know, right. My parents were drunk."

"Does that mean they weren't aware of what they were doing?"

Skye drew a deep breath, holding back her tears. "They were impaired. Their judgment, their thoughts, their response time. They were not at full capacity when they tried to drive home drunk."

"That sounds very bad."

"That's why my brother and I do not drink alcohol,

even though we're chefs and we own restaurants where people do drink."

"Makes sense." Elisa thought for a moment. "Why do you allow them to drink?"

"In the restaurants?"

"Yeah. You could say no drinking here. Like they do for smoking. You know, no smoking."

"Because of free will. It's a free society in which we live, and people are free to do what they want, including drinking themselves to death."

"That sounds bad."

Skye nodded. "For years after my parents died in that fiery wreck, I asked why God would allow them to sin and mess up their lives and ours—my brother's and mine—when He could have stopped it. If God is all powerful, why didn't He stop the train from running over my mom and dad?"

"It's kinda hard to stop when it's going so fast," Elisa asked.

"But I still asked. For years, I asked."

"Did God answer your question?"

"As a matter of fact, He did. However, it took years for me to be ready to hear the answers." Skye remembered that morning in April at least ten years later when the answer had come to her.

"I have my own questions too," Elisa said. "Do you think God will answer me?"

"Yes." Skye was certain of it. "What are your questions? God is listening right now."

"Really?"

Skye nodded. "He's always listening. He's God."

"Why didn't God stop Mom from driving over the cliff?" Elisa asked. "If there is a God, why didn't He save her?"

"Those are very good questions. Difficult questions."

"Not too difficult for your God, are they?"

"Not at all. We live in a complicated world, but God cares and knows what we are going through. He cares so much that He sent Jesus Christ to save us from our sins in this corrupt world. In Christ, we have peace that surpasses all understanding, and in Christ, we have faith that can endure any trial because ultimately, He is with us."

"Why didn't He prevent Mom from dying then?" Elisa seemed eager to hear it now.

"I can tell you that God always answers your prayer, although not in the way you want to hear it. It can take time before you see the answer. In my case, it took ten years." Skye braced herself. She usually did not like to talk about her parents' last moments on earth, but this time, she felt that it was necessary to revisit it for the child's sake.

"I want the answer now."

"I mentioned that I wasn't ready to hear the answer for ten years," Skye repeated.

"I'm ready now."

"Only God knows when you're ready." If at all. Skye decided to keep it simple for the twelve-year-old. "Someday, God may tell you exactly why. Or He may not tell you for a long time. I can say that you look way more mature than I was at your age. So you might be readier than I was at the time to hear big things from God."

Elisa didn't respond.

"In my time of greatest need, God answered my cries with Himself."

"Can He do that?"

"He sure did for me. I felt his presence the entire time we learned about the car wreck. At that time, I had only been a Christian for two years. My brother had been a Christian longer. He prayed with me, and he held my hand through the funeral and graveside burial. By God's mercy, we went to live with my aunt and uncle—down the road from our old house—and they took us to church and comforted us for years."

"Is God going to answer my prayers with Himself?" Elisa asked.

"In times of our greatest grief, God is all we need. Later on, we will learn more and more about the situation. Why this, why that, and so forth. For now, it's best to focus on God and let Him hug us and comfort us."

"I don't feel God right now. He seems distant." Elisa hugged her knees.

"Come here and let me show you something." Skye patted the ground where she was sitting.

Reluctantly, Elisa traipsed over there.

Skye lay down on the grass again. Elisa did the same next to her. Skye pointed up, beyond the canopy of the oak tree.

"How funny that your name is Skye," Elisa said. "Skye pointing to the sky."

Skye smiled. Another breakthrough.

"Look at the big blue sky up there. Who made it?" Skye said.

"It just happens."

"Some people may say that, but the Bible says that God created the sky and moon and stars and the entire universe. Genesis 1:1 declares, 'In the beginning God created the heaven and the earth.' That's the first verse in the entire Bible, you know?"

Elisa didn't respond.

Skye swiped her phone to find the verse she wanted so that she didn't misquote it. "Psalm 33:6 says, 'By the word of the Lord were the heavens made; and all the host of them by the breath of his mouth.' Let me read one more verse from Psalm 97:6. 'The heavens declare his righteousness, and all the people see his glory.' All that to say that God is huge, bigger than the universe He has created."

"If you believe that God created it."

"Right. I do believe, but there is a point I am getting to." Skye took a photo of the blue sky beyond the leaves of the trees. "Even though God is the Creator of all that we see and can't see out there, there is something else that reaches that high. You know what it is?"

Elisa shook her head.

"God's mercy." Skye read Psalm 108:4. "Listen to this. 'For Your mercy is great above the heavens, and Your truth reaches to the clouds.' God, the Creator of the universe, has mercy that goes way above the heavens up there, and has a truth that pierces through all those clouds high in the sky."

"We flew through clouds on the way here," Elsie said. "I can't remember how high up we went, but Grandpa Ned would know."

"Higher than that is God's truth and mercy." Skye turned to Elisa. "Right now, we need God's truth about your mom's situation. The investigators are probably still working on why her car went over the cliff. We will know the truth about that in due time. Meanwhile, God shows His mercy on us because He is helping us go through this grief."

"Us? You're not grieving anymore, are you?"

"I still feel sad whenever I remember my own mom. I know it's been twenty years, but you don't just forget everything, you know? She wasn't there for my high school senior prom, when my brother and I graduated from college and chef school, when he started his award-winning restaurant, when he got married to the woman of his dreams, when I started my own personal chef company, and here now, when I am looking at the sky. I wish Mom were here with me right now."

"I wish my mom were here with me too." A tear trickled down Elisa's face.

"And yet God comforts us with His mercy." Skye wanted to hug the poor child, but she did not. She wasn't a hugger like her brother. "Would you like us to pray for God to show you the answer to your questions and to comfort you at this time?"

Elisa nodded.

"So we close our eyes when we pray."

"Okay."

Skye closed her eyes. "Father God, we know that You are the father to the fatherless and motherless, and that You comfort and care for us in our time of need. My sister Elisa here is very sad right now. Many years ago, You comforted me greatly when I was suffering after my parents passed away suddenly. You walked with me through the valley of the shadow of death. I pray that You will walk with Elisa now through her valley. Let her know that You are with her. Give her the peace of Jesus Christ in her heart." Silently, Skye prayed for Elisa to know the Lord someday soon. "In Jesus' name I pray. Amen."

Elisa didn't say anything.

But another voice did.

"Amen." It was Diehl.

Skye's eyes sprang open. On the other side of Elisa, lying down on the grass like they were, was Diehl.

"What are we looking at?" he asked.

"The universe, Dad." Elisa pointed. "You see the clouds up there?"

"Yeah?"

"God's mercy goes above those clouds. How high did we fly in Grandpa's jet?"

"At least forty thousand feet in the air, but clouds can go way beyond that," Diehl said.

"And all around the world," Skye added. "Like God wrapping the whole world in His mercy."

"Cottony, cotton ball mercy. Soft and comfy," Elisa said. "Skye?"

168

Skye turned her face toward Elisa and smiled. "Yes?"

"What did you do while you waited for God to answer your prayers?"

"I kept praying, kept busy, kept going," Skye said.

"I missed the first part: praying," Diehl said. "I kept so busy—such that I didn't have to think about it—that I shipwrecked."

Elisa chuckled. "That's very bad, Dad."

"I know. How did you keep busy, Skye?" Diehl asked.

"I was in high school then, so I started working in my uncle's kitchen after school. I was also very active in my youth group at church. We were busy all year long with many activities. We did field trips, camps, drama, Christmas plays, charity events, local missions to the nursing homes and homeless shelters in the area. There was always something going on to keep me busy, keep me going."

"Plus school," Elisa said.

"Right. I practically lived at church since Uncle Miller's house was one block from the church. After they passed away, we sold the house before we knew it was going to be razed to build those high-priced condominiums."

"I remember that," Diehl said. "That wasn't us. That was the Urquharts."

Skye didn't want to be distracted by rabbit trails. "But that wasn't all. My aunt sent me to take voice and guitar lessons. At that time, Seaside Chapel had a huge music academy. They still teach music to kids, but it's not as big anymore since there are other music academies in town, like your Aunt Brinley and Uncle Ivan's Yun McMillan Music Studio. If you want to learn a musical instrument this summer, that's a place to check out."

"What do you think, Dad?" Elisa asked.

"Skye has a beautiful singing voice," Diehl replied.

"I'm asking if you think I should play a musical instrument."

"We have a piano in our house in Atlanta, but you were not interested."

Skye decided to say something before Diehl dismissed his own daughter entirely. "You can't carry a piano around."

"You can carry a keyboard," Diehl countered.

"It's not the same," Skye said. "A real piano is acoustic. A keyboard is digital. Besides, it doesn't always have weighted keys."

"Listen to her, Dad," Elisa said. "She knows what she's talking about."

"Maybe you could try several instruments and see which ones you like," Skye said. "I'm sure you can ask your aunt what the options are—what they teach over there."

"As long as it's not drums or the tuba. Too loud. I'm not paying for music lessons for those," Diehl said.

"How about the guitar?" Elisa sat up. Grass cuttings were in her hair.

"Why guitar?" Diehl asked.

Elisa pointed to Skye. "She plays the guitar. It's a start. I might find something else I like."

"Like the violin? Your aunt has a collection of old violins."

"You think she will let me touch those?" Elisa rolled her eyes. "Grandpa Ned says she protects them like a hawk, whatever that means."

"Yeah, you'll have to get your own violin." Diehl sat up.

"It'll take forever to learn violin, I think."

"I don't care what instruments you want to play, Elisa, except those two I listed—plus anything too noisy. Let's call the music studio and see what they have to say."

"Good idea." Skye got up. "Well, I have to go. Thank you for inviting me to the picnic. It was fun."

Elisa tried to help Diehl stand up. He pretended like he was stuck to the ground. "Help me, Skye. Dad's a joker again."

"Joker? I've never seen him joke." Skye laughed. "He's always so serious when I'm around."

Diehl didn't say a word, but he had a silly grin on his face, as Skye pulled one of his hands and Elisa pulled the other. He got up on his feet.

"You have grass cuttings on your hair," he said as he brushed them off Elisa's head and shoulders.

In the distance, Avery and Ethan were heading toward the back porch.

"Look what I found!" Ethan shouted. "A seashell!"

"Show me!" Elisa ran toward them.

They went inside the house.

Skye turned to Diehl, concerned. "You didn't lock your back door?"

"It's safe on the island."

"There's a reason your house has an alarm system."

"Truth be told, I forgot. I'll try to remember next time." Diehl's hand reached for her hair. "You have grass on your hair too."

Gently, he picked it off. Then his fingers wove through her hair and he placed his palm at the base of her neck. His eyelids were half-closed and he tilted his head toward hers.

"Stop me, Skye," he whispered in her ear.

She didn't.

His full lips on hers were warm and inviting, promising more to come that Skye wasn't sure she could handle.

Right now, she knew that their feelings for each other were indeed mutual. He had been showing signs of it, notably his reactions at Saffron on Jekyll the night before, but this was a new confirmation. And she had responded.

Even after the kiss, he held her in his arms. His face was in her hair, and his heartbeat was calm.

Calmer than Skye's own heart.

CHAPTER EIGHTEEN

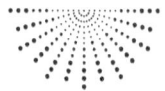

On Sunday morning, after talking with the youth pastor before Sunday school, Diehl was convinced that Seaside Chapel was a safe place for Elisa and Ethan to be this summer. After he picked up his kids from Sunday school, he took a couple of fliers from the front desk for his kids to check off all the activities they wanted to do at the little church by the sea. Each camp lasted a week, and Diehl was willing to pay for them all through the end of July.

August was up in the air. He wasn't sure how long Dad would be able to fill in for him at the Atlanta office. Already, Dad complained about not being able to get enough golf time. Sigh. Diehl figured Dad wouldn't last past August.

He walked into the Seaside Chapel sanctuary, looking for Skye. They had not made any arrangement to sit together, but Diehl remembered which side of the auditorium they had sat on the Sunday before.

To his disappointment, Skye wasn't there.

Well, they had fifteen minutes to spare before the service began. Maybe Skye would come in soon.

He found a section of empty seats in the very last row, and ushered his two kids in. Somehow, he ended up in between them, with Elisa to his left and Ethan to his right. There was an empty seat on the other side of Ethan.

"Do you want to sit with your new friends?" Diehl asked.

"I don't know where they are, Dad," Ethan said.

"I don't have any new friends." Elisa frowned.

Great. Let's make a big fuss in church. "How about we sit here for today? After you go to day camp, you can find out where everyone sits."

Still looking to spot Skye, Diehl saw Avery Chung in the brass section of the orchestra. Skye had mentioned that she played the trumpet.

Somewhere near the piano and the organ, Ivan walked across the platform. Diehl's brother-in-law, and expectant first-time dad, looked happy.

Then Diehl saw her.

Skye chatted away with Matt and a couple of people from Sunday school. She swiped her phone and compared notes with Matt. Matt was a super friendly guy.

Diehl knew that Matt was also divorced. He ran the Garnett Antique Shop that Mom frequented. He also headed up the men's Bible study group to which Ivan had invited Diehl.

Thing was, Diehl didn't like to see Matt being friendly with Skye—

Oh, he is hugging her now. Squeezing her shoulder.

"Dad, I want to go to the music camp, but it's at the same time as the soccer camp." Ethan pointed to the flier with his pen.

Diehl read the paper that Ethan shoved in front of his face. "There's a second music camp. Pick one of each if you want to do them both."

"I can do that?"

"Yes, son. Do them all if you want."

"Wouldn't it be expensive?"

"Don't worry about it." Seriously.

Ethan looked happy as he circled everything, including a sewing class.

When Diehl turned to see what Elisa was doing, she had ripped the flier into shreds. Bits of paper were on the carpeted floor beneath their feet.

"Elisa, pick them up. No littering." Diehl's voice was stern.

Elisa ignored him.

What had gotten into her?

Diehl repeated what he said.

She ignored him still.

Diehl almost stooped down to pick up the shredded trash himself when along came Skye.

"Wow, what a mess," Skye said. "I guess the unpaid volunteers are going to have to work extra hard after church to clean up that mess, while everyone else goes out to lunch. Hope they don't starve."

Diehl almost laughed, but Skye seemed serious.

Ethan touched her arm. "Would you like to sit next to me? I saved you a seat."

Diehl glanced at Skye.

"I usually sit over there." She pointed in the general direction of who knew where. "However, I'll sit here with you today if you want."

Ethan nodded vigorously. "Look at all these day camps Dad said I can attend."

Skye sat down on the other side of Ethan and looked over the list of camps Ethan had checked off.

"Sewing. That's new for this year. What are you sewing? Curtains?" Skye asked.

Diehl chuckled.

"I don't know. Maybe space costumes." Ethan shrugged.

"Looks like your sewing camp is at the same time as your cooking camp," Skye said.

"Is it?" Ethan leaned over—all the way over to the other side of the armrest into Skye's seat.

That little flirt.

Diehl dared not think that Ethan took after his mother, but Isobel had been like that. Flirted with every guy.

Diehl closed his eyes. Asked God to forgive him for that snide thought. Isobel was dead.

Let the dead go.

He felt a warm hand on his right shoulder. He opened his eyes to check whose hand it was. When he saw that it was Skye's hand, he reached up to hold it in place.

His heart did a little jig.

Throughout the entire service, Diehl wished he could switch seats with Ethan, but his son knew he had the better deal and there was nothing Diehl could do about it.

Pastor Gonzalez preached this morning about the prodigal son in Luke 15:11-32, and Diehl couldn't believe what a long passage it was to squeeze into half an hour of sermon. Somehow the pastor managed to get the highlights in.

The last verse caught Diehl's attention and made him wonder about his spiritual condition.

It was right that we should make merry and be glad, for your brother was dead and is alive again, and was lost and is found.

What did Luke 15:32 mean?

Did it apply to Diehl himself?

Once upon a time in college, he had believed in Jesus. However, he hadn't done much about it. Twenty-some years later, here he was, at forty years old, wondering whether he was lost or found.

His daughter had all but tuned out since the first congregational hymn. Diehl wondered if it would be a waste of money to pay for her camps. She might skip some—or all—of them. Perhaps it would be better to pay for her music lessons because she seemed to have shown some sort of interest in music.

"If you're new to Seaside Chapel, know that this is a safe place for your family," Pastor Gonzalez said. "Safety is paramount at our church. However, there is another kind of safety we need to talk about today."

He walked around the pulpit, Bible in hand. "Let me ask you a question, congregation. Are you only physically safe but not spiritually saved?"

Safe versus saved.

"Did you know that you can have everything you need in this world and be totally *safe*, yet at the same time you can be spiritually not *saved* and thus be separated from God forever?" Pastor Gonzalez asked.

Diehl was thinking about that question when he found his daughter fast asleep in her seat.

He suspected then that she might have stayed up all night for some reason and then became cranky at church all morning. No wonder she'd rather stay at Grandma's house. Diehl knew that his mom wouldn't care what Elisa did in her bedroom all night.

Time to enforce an internet curfew?

Diehl didn't want to be rash about it. The poor child had lost her mother. If he was too strict on her, he might lose her too. At the same time, he didn't want to be permissive of everything Elisa wanted, regardless of whether it was good or bad for her.

This was not a child-centered household anymore.

Isobel had run their home that way. Whatever the children wanted, they got. It was the only way to keep them happy and occupied so that Isobel could go get her nails done or meet her friends for lunch or fly to Italy to be with her secret boyfriend.

About that, Diehl realized he had to take it with a grain of salt. Whatever Mom and Zeta thought happened with Zeta's daughter in Italy might be simply speculation. Until the Italian police completed their investigation, nobody knew what happened.

Then again, it had been one year. Wasn't it a terribly long time to investigate a cliff-top death?

When everyone stood up, Diehl realized that his mind had wandered.

Forgive me, Lord.

And now he couldn't cast the first stone at his daughter. There would be no difference between Elisa sleeping through the sermon and Diehl's mind wandering to another place and time. Both had not been paying attention.

The last thing he had heard Pastor Gonzalez say still rang in his head.

Are you safe and are you saved?

Diehl knew he had to think about that for a while.

When church dismissed, Ethan started to talk to Skye. "Would you like to have lunch with us?"

Diehl almost reminded Ethan that they were heading over to Grandma's house. Mom had asked her cook to make some roast beef for lunch. There would be apple pies.

However, Diehl had not talked to Mom about inviting anyone else. Certainly, he did not want Mom to get the idea that he and Skye were an item. It was still too early.

In fact, they hadn't officially dated.

However, Skye's presence could prevent Mom from matchmaking him with those suddenly-single heiresses he'd rather avoid. Most of them had not been his type. And many of them wouldn't want to go on a date in his pickup truck.

Ironically, he hadn't used his pickup truck much for hauling or construction work because Brinley was on bedrest, and thus had cut back on taking new projects. Her general contractor handled most of their renovation jobs right now, and Diehl was not needed.

"I'm sorry," Skye said. "I'm having lunch with my chefs. How about next week then? Are you planning on coming back to church?"

"Yes," Ethan said immediately. "I'm planning on being in church every Sunday that you are."

"How about Sundays when I'm not here?" Skye asked.

"Well..."

"Jesus is always here," Skye said. "How about being in church whenever He is here?"

"Every single Sunday?" Ethan's eyes widened.

"You know that God is not confined to a building, so if Jesus is in your heart, He's always with you." Skye stepped out of the row of seats.

When Diehl passed by her, he reached for her hand.

He didn't care that they had only started to get to know each other. He didn't care that they were in public.

Somewhere in his heart, he felt that he had to claim her now before all those other eligible bachelors asked her out.

But who was he to do so?

Was this the woman he should date? How would he know?

He had made multi-billion-dollar deals, negotiated projects with heads of states, and singlehandedly ran the fifty-billion-dollar Brooks Investments after Parker died, Brinley left the company, and Dad retired to the golf course.

Yet, for the first time in his entire adult life, he was unsure about what to do.

CHAPTER NINETEEN

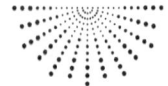

*I*n the middle of listening to Ethan tell his grandma about the various summer camps he'd be attending at Seaside Chapel, Diehl heard the doorbell ring. Moments later, Cara ushered into the large dining room none other than Siobhan, the twenty-something younger cousin of Jared Urquhart.

Diehl didn't even bother to look over in Mom's direction, knowing this was all a set-up.

The Rose Brooks Matchmaking Service was in full bloom again. This time, she must be thinking that Diehl would entertain someone fifteen years his junior. Someone else might, but to him, it was too late. His heart was taken.

Mom had done it before, a long time ago when Parker had been alive. After two years of matchmaking, Parker had found his Riley all by himself without any of the family's help. At first, Mom was livid because Riley wasn't her type of daughter-in-law and they didn't see eye-to-eye on many things.

However, after Parker drowned in a fishing accident at sea some nine years ago now, Riley had been Mom's staunchest supporter and loyal friend, even though for the first five years of her widowhood, she rarely left her house. Eventually, she did go out because her remaining teenage children had become active in their high school.

The kids had moved on sooner than Riley, who still mourned her deceased husband and firstborn daughter. Then again, Riley was a practical woman. She knew she had to raise the two future Brooks heir and heiress well. She put aside her grief and stepped back into her life, and the life of Parker's children.

Speaking of whom, Diehl reminded himself to get the cousins together. Riley and the kids were on a train vacation for the entire summer, but perhaps they'd be able to meet in early August before Elisa and Ethan returned to school—

School.

Where, though?

Diehl wanted the kids to attend school in Atlanta, not in Hawaii. He wished that he hadn't given Isobel's parents an inch the year before during the grieving period. He had agreed—against his better judgment—to let the kids finish the school year in Hawaii. After all, they needed someone at home, and Diehl had been neck-deep in work.

Work that had run him ragged, and eventually caused him to burn out.

However, now that he'd spent a week off, he thought he could return to the office.

Sigh.

He forgot his agreement with Dad. No work for Diehl until August.

What was he going to do? Play piano for the next two months? Not substantial enough. Besides, Skye had told him that the trio wasn't in the rotation to sing again at church until August.

Perhaps he could talk to Brinley about doing some volunteer work at her renovation office. With her baby coming, she could use some help at the helm. Yeah, he'd do that.

Somewhere in the middle of it all, the question raised about his children's paternity bothered him. Isobel's mother had been insistent on all the DNA tests.

Sure, do them. Whatever.

Diehl had confidence that the two kids were his. As far as he knew, Isobel had been faithful in their first marriage. Perhaps their remarriage had been a mistake, but that was another matter altogether.

"Diehl." Siobhan's voice was somewhat pained as she sat down next to him at the dinner table. "Sorry I'm late."

Mom looked annoyed that Dad hadn't joined them for lunch. Dad had to take a phone call in his office because he didn't want anyone to hear the conversation.

Diehl didn't want to know what it was about. Two months before, he would have been curious whenever

Dad had taken a business call on a Sunday. Today, not so much.

He sensed his own shift in focus from work to…

Skye?

There he went again, thinking of Skye. Speaking of her, Siobhan's presence at their lunch table today reminded Diehl of Jared, who had been all over Skye.

I take that back.

Jared had been all over Skye's *business* due to Talia, his ex-girlfriend and mother of his firstborn child. That was all.

He hoped.

"How's your family?" Diehl asked Siobhan.

"Mom's cancer is in its last stages," Siobhan said. "I should be with her right this instant, but she's taking a nap, so here I am. I can't stay too long."

"She's staying with you?"

"Yes. I asked her to move in with me so I can take care of her."

"That's nice of you."

"Time is running out."

"I'm sorry to hear that," Diehl said. "I'll pray for her."

At the other end of the table, Mom made a noise. "Pray? Since when have you become the praying kind?"

Since he met Skye, but he couldn't say. "I went to church this morning. We prayed all the time."

Siobhan's shoulders sagged. "I should pray more. Maybe God would heal my aunt."

It was an interesting choice of word. *Would*

instead of *could*. Diehl wondered where Siobhan stood spiritually.

"Maybe you'd like to come to Seaside Chapel sometimes. I'm in Brin's Sunday school class, and we pray a lot. I will add your aunt to our prayer list. We're praying for Brin right now, for her third trimester."

"Thank you for your prayers." Siobhan sipped water.

She did not look interested in Diehl at all. Just as well. He did not want to mislead her.

He only wanted Skye. In fact, he had never wanted anyone else more than he wanted her at this moment. He wondered where she was having lunch with the chefs. Was it at Saffron? That seemed to be the natural choice. He was curious about what they ate. He wanted to know what Skye said at their luncheon.

He wanted to be a fly on the wall everywhere she went.

It was the first time in his life that he had fallen hard for someone one week after they got to know each other. Granted, he had seen Skye all week long—every single day—more than he had seen Isobel a month into their second marriage.

Maybe if he and Isobel had spent this much time together, they might not have divorced each other in the first place.

"Cara!" Mom called. She was never one to be lady-like and keep her voice down.

"Yes, ma'am?" The family housekeeper came running into the dining room.

When Parker, Diehl, Skye, and Zoe were kids, Cara was their nanny and fill-in cook of midnight snacks whenever the family chef was not available. She had been college-aged when she started working for the Brooks family, and she was in her fifties now. She still worked at Brooks Cottage today, but in more of a supervisory role—and still the cook of midnight snacks—which she'd prepare and leave in the refrigerator before she left the Brooks Cottage to go home to her own family in Brunswick across the river.

"Go see what's taking Ned so long." Mom waved her away.

"You could have texted Dad," Diehl said.

"He's down the hallway in his office."

"Text him. Three words: *lunch getting cold.*" Diehl didn't like the way Mom still pushed Cara around. Everyone else had always been nice to Cara, but Mom still treated her more like a servant than a family member.

"Dad." Across the table, Ethan looked up from his phone. "You forgot *is*. Lunch *is* getting cold."

"Well, looks like my hundred-thousand-dollar-a-year elementary school is paying off," Diehl said.

Ethan grinned. "Just saying."

"Thank you, Ethan. You are right, grammatically." Diehl glanced over at Elisa, who was also on her phone.

She was in her own little world over there, sitting next to her brother. Sometimes Diehl wondered what Elisa did on the phone and internet. He should have insisted on installing a safety filter on her phone, but she was twelve years old. What could a kid that age possibly do on the internet? Also, he did not want to violate her right to privacy—

Wait a minute.

She was twelve years old, and she was his daughter.

Wasn't a dad supposed to protect his own kids? Who could he talk to about internet safety?

At Brooks Investments, all their computer communications had NSA-grade security. Yet at home, Diehl had let his kids just use the internet without any firewall or safety features.

Wow. Did I drop the ball somewhere?

Diehl almost took out his own phone to text Malik and ask him to look into internet security for his two kids. He decided not to touch his phone right now—to make a point. Besides, it was Sunday, and the Director of Security deserved the right to have the day off to spend time with his family.

Diehl decided to talk to Malik on Monday, when he was back at his office. Malik oversaw all the physical security at their properties worldwide, but Diehl wanted to know how much of that included online security as well. One could never be too careful these days.

Diehl's MBA was old school, but the last acquisition at Brooks Investments that had burned him out had been for a majority share of a software company in Atlanta. He knew he was in way over his head because of his lack of knowledge on computers beyond simply being a user.

Dad was even worse. Dad was the pen-and-paper sort of guy. He wouldn't sign an electronic contract. He'd have to drive to the ninth green if he wanted Dad to sign a contract when he was out of the office.

Speaking of whom, here he came.

"Siobhan," Dad said. "So you're the surprise guest and the reason we're having a formal lunch on a Sunday instead of just eating sandwiches on a tray while watching TV."

Mom grunted her disapproval of what Dad had said.

"Thank you for inviting me." Siobhan smiled.

Cara came in. "Lunch is ready. Is there anything else you need?"

Ethan put up his hand. "Are you making me banana pudding, Cara?"

Cara nodded. "Chef Pierre is going to serve it right after lunch, okay?"

"Thank you." Ethan returned to his phone.

"Kids, please put away your phones until after lunch." Diehl watched Elisa.

Sure enough, she made a face. It was her default setting that said she was irritated at the world.

However, Diehl had seen another side of his daughter only the day before at Brinley's beach house, when he found her lying down on the grass with Skye as they talked about God and the universe.

Somehow Skye had been able to reach his daughter.

Thank God for Skye.

Once again, Diehl's thoughts wandered to Skye.

He resisted the urge to get his phone and text her. He didn't want to be a hypocrite in front of his children. Or even behind their backs.

But he was starting to miss seeing Skye.

The tug in his heart scared him.

CHAPTER TWENTY

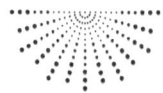

*D*iehl called after lunch asking what she was doing. The next thing Skye knew, he showed up at the vegetable section of the Seaside Organics grocery store on Demere Road.

"May I push your cart?" he asked.

What was Skye supposed to say?

Diehl followed her from the vegetables to the fruits to the nuts and then the seafood. He inspected a container of dry seafood rub. "This has lemongrass in it."

"What do you know about lemongrass?" Skye waited for the fishmonger to scale and debone the grouper for her.

"I know it's used in curry."

"Very good."

"Cara often had our family chef cook curry for us. Brin and I love her curry dish. Don't tell Cara that the chef often did a better job than she."

"Does she cook for you at all?"

"Sometimes. She doesn't like to travel, so Mom hired a backup chef for us when my parents went around the world, taking their chef with them."

Skye's phone pinged but she ignored it. "Have they been to many places?"

"That was their plan, but Dad had a mild stroke a couple of years ago, and that spooked Mom, so now they make short trips to Paris and Europe, and then they're back home again to be closer to Dad's cardiologist and the hospital they like."

Skye thanked the fishmonger, put the filets in her cart, and checked it off her list. This one was for Mrs. Morton. She led Diehl to the dairy section, where she inspected eggs.

"I feel so domestic," Diehl said.

He seemed to mean it as a joke, but Skye didn't get it. "Are you saying that people you know don't shop for their own groceries?"

Diehl looked around. "I don't know. I go to the store sometimes. On my own."

Like a big boy? What was he trying to say? That he could be independent?

"I love the life here on St. Simon's. Casual and unhurried," Diehl added. "It's not overrun with tourists in the summertime, and people are not on top of one another like in a crowded city."

"For sure."

"I understand why my sister left the corporate world to move here permanently."

Skye didn't ask him if that would be something

he'd do. They were still in such an early stage of their relationship that she told herself it might not last. Diehl could have anyone in the world he wanted, and yet he chose her.

Perhaps it was only a summer romance.

Probably short-lived.

Skye warned herself to guard her heart so she would not be disappointed if Diehl went home to Atlanta and found someone else in the fall.

Skye placed three dozen eggs into the cart.

"So many eggs?"

"Yeah. A dozen for you, a dozen for another client, and a dozen for me."

"Client." He made a face. "I don't know if I want to be called a client. I'd rather be your friend."

"Yes, I cook for you and another person, and then I manage everyone else. The other chefs will shop for their own clients."

"Sounds like you have a system."

Skye checked off another item on her list. "Yep. Each chef will have plenty to remember as it is—who eats lunches at three, who goes out for dinner every night, who wants snacks, and so forth."

"A lot to handle."

Skye nodded. "Especially during the summer, when schedules can be erratic. A lot of cancellations."

"They pay though, whether you cook or not."

"Yes, if it's within twenty-four hours. I mean, we can't return the fresh groceries."

Diehl followed Skye to select fresh bread. "Smells good here."

"You said you prefer sourdough."

Diehl nodded.

"Have you tried some other kind of bread?"

"Like what?"

"Here's rye."

Diehl scrunched up his nose. "Let's stick to sourdough."

"I figured you'd say that." Skye picked up a round sourdough bread. It was uncut.

"How did you figure? We've only been with each other for a little more than a week." Diehl then raised a finger. "Wait. You talked to my sister."

Skye wasn't about to divulge her research on her high-profile clients. Not that they required much digging. Those clients often attended luncheons and dinners catered by renowned chefs. And they sometimes gave interviews to food magazines. However, her most important gleanings of what they wanted to eat came from her interview with them—the one that Diehl had skipped and which his sister had filled in the blanks for him.

Still, in between cooking and running around between Friday and Sunday, Skye painted a food art collage for Diehl. And she had pegged him. Comfort food, no surprises.

"We've planned for steak on Tuesday night," Skye said. "But if you want us to grill on Monday night, we could do that."

"Will you be there on Tuesday night?" Diehl asked.

"Yes, and I will leave at six o'clock after we cook the steak. Marlo will stay back to clean up."

"Do you have a date?"

Skye wondered what kind of a question that was. Had Diehl forgotten that he kissed her on Saturday afternoon? It had only been about twenty-four hours.

"A date?" She looked for clarification.

"That might cause you leave my house early on Tuesday nights."

"If I do?"

Diehl blinked. "Uh...I guess..."

Skye felt awkward. It seemed to her that he wanted her, and yet he wasn't showing it. She checked her grocery list and walked toward the butcher.

The cart came along, and then she felt Diehl's arm around her waist.

"I'm hoping I'm your only date," he whispered in her ear.

"We sort of put the cart before the horse," Skye said. "I don't think we ever went out, did we? And yet..."

"And yet I kissed you yesterday. To be fair, you didn't stop me."

A crowd was forming in front of the butcher, and Skye felt they had to hurry along so she could drop off the groceries before evening church tonight.

She broke away from his arm. "Well, where I'm going on Tuesday night, you're not invited unless you're on the roster of the women's Bible study group."

"Oh. That's a relief." Diehl returned to his cart.

"By the way, Ivan invited me to the men's Bible study group on Monday morning."

"Good. You should go." Skye waited in line to get to the beef and chicken. "Matt and Ivan are great teachers. They sometimes fill in for Ben in Sunday school."

Diehl nodded.

"Does that mean you won't need breakfast in the morning?" Skye asked.

"Ah, yes. I forgot to tell you, didn't I?"

"You just did." Skye swiped her phone to check on the calendar and cross out breakfast.

When they reached the cheese section, Diehl headed for the samples. He put a few cubes of various cheeses on a napkin and speared them with a toothpick. He tasted one. Then he used the same toothpick to pick up another cheese and offered it to Skye. "Try this."

"Not with the same toothpick. Nope."

Diehl chuckled. "But we..."

Kissed?

Skye still shook her head.

Diehl found a new and clean toothpick. "Here you go."

Skye opened her mouth, and Diehl fed the cheese to her.

"Hmm." Skye chewed it slowly. "An odd mix of sheep cheese and cow."

"Doesn't the Swiss take away the strong taste in the sheep cheese?" Diehl asked.

"I don't know, but I usually don't like sheep cheese."

"I don't either." He snapped his fingers. "There, we have one more thing in common."

They finished shopping, and Skye picked up a bar of dark chocolate on the way to the checkout.

"You didn't get a lot today." Diehl helped Skye put the groceries on the conveyor belt.

"No, because I'll be back on Wednesday. We want the food fresh for our clients."

"Clients. Maybe you can assign another chef to cook, and you can have meals with me as my invited guest."

Skye gave him a puzzled look. "I need to work also."

"Well, how about I pay double?"

"No. This is not Japan where you can pay a stranger to come to your house and eat dinner with you." Skye kept her voice down.

The checkout lady glanced her way as she scanned another customer's groceries.

"They do that over there?" Diehl asked. "Must be terribly sad to be so lonely that you have to rent a family."

They made quick work of loading Skye's car.

Before Diehl pushed the cart back to the store, he offered to help her unload the groceries wherever she was going.

"Sometimes I will drop them off at the client's house, but today, I will be taking them home. After church tonight, I have some prep work to do."

"I thought you didn't work on weekends."

"Except when the clients ask for certain dishes on Mondays that take time to prepare."

"Is it me?" Diehl asked.

"No. The fishmonger has already scaled and filleted your fish, so all I have to do tomorrow is clean and cook it."

"I saw that you bought a giant piece of fish. I don't eat that much."

"Don't worry about it. You're sharing it with my other client."

"That's smart planning." He still hadn't taken the cart back.

Skye jingled her keys. "Thank you again for helping. Will you be in church tonight?"

"I'm planning on it. May I sit with you?"

"Sure. There are no names on chairs—unlike in the nineteenth century."

Diehl checked his watch. "We have two hours before church."

"You do. I have to take these home and then run back to church for a meeting."

"What about?" Diehl asked.

"Such a curious guy, you are." Skye waited to see if he would let it pass. He didn't so she told him. "Matt asked me to fill in for someone in the upcoming fall festival. We're doing four guitars."

"Wow. I'd like to see that."

"It's in September. Aren't you supposed to be back in Atlanta by then?"

Diehl nodded. "Doesn't mean I can't come back again."

"Just to see us play guitar?"

Diehl reached for her face. "To see you."

He lowered his lips...

Once again, Skye didn't stop him. How could she? She enjoyed their moment as much as he evidently did.

The sun baked down on them, and Skye knew she had to get her groceries home. Fortunately, the fish and steak were in bags of ice, so she might have a few minutes to spare.

"Hello," someone said. A woman's voice.

Skye and Diehl both looked that way.

"Cara," Diehl said. "Have you met Skye?"

"Yes, we've met," Cara replied.

Skye remembered Cara from some of the Brooks parties and luncheons in years past—the same time she had met Diehl. Whenever Skye's brother had catered an event for the Brooks family, Cara hung around, although she wasn't in charge.

"Shopping, I see." Cara wiggled her eyebrows as though she had just found a delicious secret. "That's why you're not staying at your mother's house, huh?"

"I need my own space," Diehl said.

"More privacy. I hear you."

Diehl nodded. "Are you shopping for your own family or mine?"

"The kids—your kids—sent me here. They want cheesecake, all of a sudden. I told them I'd buy them some."

JAN THOMPSON

"Ethan, right?" Diehl asked.

"I'm not giving away names. I'm no tattletale." Cara chuckled. "I'll let you go now."

Skye wasn't sure if it was a good thing for Cara to see them together. She felt nervous.

Diehl held her hand. "It's all good."

"Okay."

"She's not going to say anything to Mom unless it helps us."

"Is this a secret?" Skye frowned.

"No, no. I mean... That came out all wrong. Let me try again." Diehl drew a deep breath. "Cara and my mom don't always get along. However, Cara's always on the side of the kids. I know we're all grown up, but she still defends us."

"Loyal."

"We like that. Well, today I had lunch with my parents, and guess what?"

"What?"

"Mom's playing matchmaker—again—and invited someone to have lunch with us. She thought I might be interested in that someone. Clearly I wasn't."

"Oh?"

"I've already found someone special." Diehl rubbed the back of her hand with his thumb. "And I want to spend more time with her. Walk on the beach with her. Talk with her. Every single day, if at all possible."

Skye enjoyed the nice words until she remembered her schedule. "Not every day, though. One week from Monday, I'll be gone for the week to attend a food festival in Miami Beach with my brother. We go there every year. Chef Joseph will cook for you while I'm out of town."

"I'm going to miss your company," Diehl said.

Your company.

He showed that he appreciated her for more than just her cooking.

"Will you miss me?" Diehl asked.

Would she miss him? She'd find out in one week.

CHAPTER TWENTY-ONE

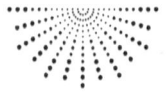

*A*t the bagel breakfast, Ivan told Diehl that the Seaside Chapel men's Bible study group had been recently renamed the Monday Morning Men after having moved from Friday to Monday. That way, they could wear T-shirts and sweatshirts with "Monday Morning" emblazoned on front and back.

At the side table, Diehl slathered more strawberry cream cheese on his raisin bagel. More guys started to trickle into the Garnett Antique Shop. Each face seemed to say that meeting at six o'clock on a Monday morning wasn't a terribly good idea. Matt, who owned the shop, handed out hot coffee to everyone as each found his place in a circle of chairs.

Diehl didn't need coffee to stay awake this morning. Interestingly, after the church service the evening before, he had gone home with happy thoughts of Skye sitting beside him in the service and holding his hand when they prayed. He fell asleep with a smile on his face and slept for eight hours straight.

By now, it was apparent to Skye's friends at church that something had happened between the two of them. It would take time to see what would come next. Looming at the back of Diehl's mind was the grim reminder that he had to go back to Atlanta in August.

Both of them were established where they were: Skye on St. Simon's Island and Diehl in Atlanta. Neither of them could leave their workplace, although if he were to guess, he'd say that Skye was more flexible. Couldn't she run her personal chef business from Atlanta?

Perhaps that would be too much to ask of her.

Ivan gathered everyone together in a circle near the kitchen. Some people sat on old kitchen chairs and some sat on refurbished barstools.

"We have a couple of visitors today," Ivan said. "Adam Garnett is Matt's brother, who is helping him manage the thrift shop next door. And we have my brother-in-law, Diehl Brooks, who is in town for the summer."

"You can't tell Diehl from Adam," Matt added.

Half the group laughed, and the other half tried to stay awake.

Diehl had only seen Matt in Sunday school. This was the first time he had seen Matt outside of church. He seemed like a nice guy, about the same age as Diehl. Certainly older than Skye.

Skye?

Why did I bring her up with thoughts of Matt?

"For the sake of our visitors, who might not know the rest of us, let's go around the room and introduce ourselves, shall we?" Ivan asked. "I'll start. I'm Ivan McMillan. I teach violin at the Yun McMillan Music Studio—which we named in memory of my grandma—and I play in the Seaside Chapel Sanctuary Orchestra. I used to play in the Sea Islands Symphony Orchestra, but after I injured my wrist a couple of years ago, I retired."

"He retired into his music studio, that is," Matt said. "Since I'm sitting next to Ivan, I'll go next. Matt Garnett here. I'm an antique collector. I go around the Southeast and elsewhere—sometimes the country and on occasion, Europe—to find antiques I can sell in this shop. My thrift shop next door does a lot of charity work, and that's why I asked my brother to come help me get organized with how we can use the thrift shop to glorify God."

A chorus of *amen* went around the room.

Adam lifted his cup of coffee in one hand. His other hand held a half-eaten bagel. "Adam Garnett here. Matt and I might be biologically half brothers, but we're spiritually full brothers. I worked at various jobs after I left the Army, and now I'm here for the foreseeable future. I didn't want to just drop in on a church just because my brother attends there, but I think I'm staying at Seaside Chapel for a while."

Matt patted his shoulder. "You're welcome to attend our Sunday school class next week."

"I might do that if I can get up early enough to

make it to class." Adam laughed. "I like to sleep in on weekends. However, I made it to the eleven o'clock service."

"You did. Thank you." Matt turned his attention to the next person. "Dr. Rao?"

"Hello. Tristan Rao here. I'm a physician at Rao Medical Center. This doesn't usually bother me." Tristan touched the top of his hair. "But I just got a haircut at a place I've never been to before, and I hate it, so don't anybody ask me why my hair is so short today."

"Buzzcut. You should go to my hair stylist," Ivan said. "Same one my wife goes to."

Diehl hadn't kept up with his sister, so he didn't know who styled her hair.

"Seriously, does anybody care if you had a haircut?" someone on the other side of the circle said.

"No one would care," Matt said. "Except that Tristan has a date this Friday night and there's no way his hair is going to grow back in four days."

"Now that you mentioned it, we're all looking at your bald head," someone else said.

"It's not bald." Tristan touched the top of his head. "Do they let you wear a hat to church?"

"I don't think they care what you wear on your head as long as you have clothes on your body," Matt replied. "Besides, on Wednesday night, it's dark outside when the Fire Pit Service gets going."

"True." Tristan went to get another cup of coffee.

"Seriously," Matt continued. "Tristan is our local physician, and he's been around forever. I think

Tristan was barely a baby when the Rao family moved here, and his dad opened the practice—which he has now taken over."

Tristan nodded. "If you can, please pray for my dad. He's not doing too well with chemo. He wants to forget it, go home, and die."

"That's tough." Ivan handed a clipboard to Tristan. "Why don't you start our prayer request sheet?"

To everyone, Ivan said, "We're passing around this clipboard, so if you have any prayers, write them down —legibly, please. I'll type them into our prayer logbook and send everyone an email by tomorrow."

Diehl finished his bagel and coffee, and waited for the next person to introduce himself.

"Benicio Ketteridge. Call me Ben," he said. "Former chaplain, now helping with the teen ministry at Seaside Chapel. Summer is super busy with many camps, so please pray for us that we'll be able to minister to the kids and not be weary of doing well."

"Certainly. Interesting you should mention doing well. That's our Scripture this morning, which we'll get to in a minute," Matt said. "For those of you who don't know, our youth pastor is leaving us. His mother is ill on Hilton Head, and as the only child, he feels obligated to go home and take care of her in her last days on earth. Therefore, Seaside Chapel is offering the position to Ben. Ben's been praying about this decision for a couple of months."

A couple of months? Diehl wondered what kind of prayer would be prayed over such a long span of time.

What words would one say to God to stretch a prayer across two months?

Diehl decided he needed to know how to pray like that. It seemed to be a battle.

All attention turned to him now as they waited for Diehl to speak.

"As Ivan has said, I'm Brinley's brother," Diehl said. "I'm spending the summer on St. Simon's, so I thought that I should do something useful, like going to church. My two kids are in town right now. One signed up for every imaginable summer camp at Seaside Chapel, and the other has zero interest in attending anything."

"What are your kids' names?" Benicio asked.

"Elisa and Ethan Brooks."

"Cousins to Petra and Zachary Brooks?" Benicio asked, but he already knew the answer.

Diehl nodded. "Zach is one year older than my Elisa."

If Parker's kids weren't out of town at the moment, Diehl would get them together with Elisa and Ethan. Perhaps the older cousins might provide some Christian influence for his kids.

When he had been single, he hadn't thought about how important it would be for children to be in safe zones, but now that he was a dad to two growing kids, he worried about who might influence them, how their future might look, and whether God would protect them when he wasn't around.

Diehl was convinced more than ever that he made the right decision to take them to church.

Thanks to Skye, once again.

After Ivan finished praying, all the coffee was gone.

Matt began his Bible lesson for the day. "Would someone please read Galatians 6:9 and another person read Galatians 6:10?"

Benicio put up his hand. "Galatians 6:9. 'And let us not be weary in well doing: for in due season we shall reap, if we faint not.' That's what I read this morning. How did you know, Matt?"

Matt shrugged. "It's been on my mind for a while. God worked it out for today, didn't He?"

Everyone nodded.

Diehl wondered how God worked it out. He assumed that because God was all-powerful, He could do anything He wanted.

If so, why...

Why had God let Isobel's car fly over the cliff?

Why had she driven the Pagani so fast?

"What is due season?" Matt asked. "Anyone take a guess?"

"That's in God's timing," Tristan said. "When we do good to others, we know we're going to reap a reward, but we may not know when."

"Exactly," Matt said. "It could be here on earth. It could be in heaven. We don't know when. However, we shall see the reward if we don't faint. What is fainting? Passing out. So let's stay awake, work hard, serve the Lord, and not faint in the day of distress. Comments? Questions?"

No one said anything.

"I have a question for you then," Matt said. "Are you 'weary in well doing'? Are you tired of doing good things for people who may not appreciate all that you do for them? Don't answer that question until we get to the next verse. Will someone read it for us?"

Tristan raised his hand. "I will. 'As we have therefore opportunity, let us do good unto all men, especially unto them who are of the household of faith.' Galatians 6:10."

"Therein is the catch," Matt said. "Now let's go back to my question. The Bible says we need to do good to all people, particularly those in church. What if some of those people are unlovable or even spiteful?"

"It's not conditional," Ivan said. His Bible in one hand and a pen in another, he was in focus. "When God tells us to do good, we do good, regardless of how the recipient behaves. They, in turn, have to answer to God for their own issues."

Diehl remembered the first time he met Ivan, back when Brinley and Ivan became an item. Diehl had opposed the relationship, convinced that the poverty-stricken Ivan was out to get Brinley's money.

The opposite had been true. Ivan had refused to sign the prenuptial agreement that was standard fare in Brooks marriages. However, he had a prenup of his own that made everyone impressed with the way he managed what little money he had. He had turned Yun McMillan Music Studio into a profitable venture. Somewhere in that violinist mind, there was a pocket of business savvy that served him well.

That wasn't all. In fact, Ivan had been such a godly

husband to Brinley, taking care of her in her times of need. In her last trimester of her first pregnancy, Brinley didn't have to lift anything. Ivan did everything for her.

An exemplary husband.

Diehl wondered if he could come close. He dared not compare himself with Ivan.

"Ivan summed it up," Matt said. "There's only one more thing I can add to that. We've discussed doing good to others. What about when they do good to us? Let's be careful not to take advantage of Christians who are kind, benevolent, and selfless."

Everyone nodded.

That made Diehl wonder. Skye had been kind to him and his children, spending a couple of hours of her days off picnicking with them. Had he returned that kindness by taking advantage of her?

On Saturday, an opportunity presented itself in the yard of the beach house. She was standing there, looking kissable. And he wouldn't be one to miss a chance.

Yes, he meant it. Every moment. Every savor.

His heart was in it.

However, had he moved too fast?

Within a week of her being in the beach house practically three times a day, Diehl felt that he had known her for ages. By the time the next Saturday rolled around, he was sure there was something between them.

Something special.

Something he could lose.

His heart told him she was the one. And yet, how could he tell either way? After all, he had failed in his first marriage. He had married poorly and ended up very unfulfilled, in spite of their having two kids.

Could love—true love—come to him a second time around?

CHAPTER TWENTY-TWO

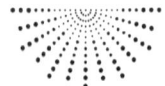

*W*hen Avery gave her a concerned look as soon as she arrived at Olivia Gonzalez's house for the Tuesday night women's Bible study group meeting, Skye knew that something was off. Avery had several levels of concern, and this wrinkled-eyebrow expression with heavy sighs only appeared in a Category 4 hurricane.

It was too hot to take their dinner outside, but fortunately, fewer women were in attendance this evening. It was summer, after all. School was out, and many of the mothers had gone out of town with their families. Also, they were early because it was their turn to set up the buffet table.

Skye and Avery settled near their spot by the microphone. They were both leading the singing that usually opened their Bible study. At the moment, they were the only people on the couch.

Tonight's Bible study was a continuation of last

week's, but Skye admitted that she hadn't spent enough time preparing for it. Usually, she'd read the email that Olivia sent, then the attached verse and notes. This week, she had spent more time making sure she looked decent and presentable whenever she showed up at Diehl's house, and more time shopping for the food that he might like to eat.

Clearly, Skye's heart was elsewhere.

First sign of trouble?

"Doesn't it feel weird to you at all?" Avery asked.

"Feel?" Skye asked. "I thought you, of all people, walked by faith and not feelings."

"Brinley has told us about her brother for a couple of years now, all the way up to a couple of weeks ago before he came to town," Avery began. "Every time we pray for him, it's about his lack of interest in going to church or matters pertaining to God. How many times has Brinley cried because her brother doesn't want to talk about Christ? Which Christian do you know who refuses to talk about their Savior?"

Skye recalled their many prayers for Brinley's brother. However, when he showed up at Brinley's beach house, he seemed like a nice guy.

And very attractive.

"Brinley has told him about our sister church in Atlanta, but did he ever go there? Not even once."

That was true. Skye recalled being excited about Midtown Chapel because her own brother planned to attend that church after his wife finished graduate school.

Not even once.

Those three words bothered Skye. She recalled Brinley saying so. Diehl had not made any effort to go to church in Atlanta. Was it possible for a Christian to never step inside a church's door except for funerals, Easter Sunday, and Christmas?

"Why is he suddenly all over church now?" Avery asked.

"Maybe he realizes how important church is?"

"It's not about the church per se, is it? It's about Jesus Christ. How important is Jesus to him?"

Skye remembered her conversation with Diehl over the phone on Friday night, how she had mentioned salvation in Jesus. When Skye told him that he couldn't be partially saved, he did not say which side of the fence he was on. His question to her was telling.

How many times do I need to pray to receive Jesus in my heart?

Skye ate her salmon salad quietly. Was Diehl truly saved? Or was he a Christian prodigal son who had to find his way home to the Heavenly Father?

It mattered to her because her brother would rather she date a Christian than an unbeliever.

Date?

Skye didn't know what to think. If Diehl was unsaved, then their relationship wouldn't work out because how could he lead the family in the ways of the Lord when he himself had no idea what they were?

Family?

Skye closed her eyes. She needed to step back and assess the whole situation.

Maybe the Lord had sent her good friend to her for such a time as this to wake her up.

I don't want to wake up. I think I'm in love.

Avery drank more tea—her second or third glass this evening—and then she had more to say. She was on a roll tonight.

"Are you two dating?" Avery asked.

Did she read her mind?

Skye couldn't answer her.

"I saw him kiss you on Saturday," Avery whispered. "You two held hands at church on Sunday."

It happened so fast.

Too fast.

"I wonder what Brinley would say," Avery said. "She knows her brother very well."

Brinley? "I don't think we should bring her into this. I'm not dating her. Besides, she's having a difficult third trimester, so the last thing she needs is to be stressed out over her brother."

"She cares for us, for you. We're like the sisters we each never had—I have a cousin around my age, but I'm closer to you and Brinley than I am to her."

Skye knew she was referring to Gillian, who had now decided to find a job in town.

"Thank you for your concern," Skye said. "I am grateful."

Avery nodded. "Pray about it and see what God tells you. I know you're in the thick of it, so you might not see what's going on."

"I wish there was a litmus test." Skye finished her

salad and decided not to go for dessert. "I don't want to judge him, you know."

"You're not judging him, but we're talking about you giving your heart to someone who may not be on the same page with you regarding everything you hold dear—prayer, planning, purpose, just to name a few examples. You want to put God first, but does he? You want God's will for your life, but does he? And then the future comes.... Marriage, children..."

Whoa. "I haven't thought that far out, to be honest. I was thinking this is a summer fling."

"A short and sweet summer romance?" Avery tilted her head. Her ponytail swung out over her shoulder. "When was the last time we took a vacation from God's best for our lives?"

Skye knew that her all-seeing God had no doubt seen her with Diehl and read their thoughts. What was in Diehl's mind and heart?

"Is it possible that he is genuine?" Skye wanted to believe it. So far, Diehl had been nothing but nice to her.

"Sure. My parents have loved each other all their lives and they are still not Christians, both of them," Avery said. "In your case, you have a confirmed Christian—you—and someone who seems to be on the fence —according to all that we know about him."

Was Diehl on the fence?

Avery swiped her phone. "You know 2 Corinthians 6:14. 'Be ye not unequally yoked together with unbelievers: for what fellowship hath righteousness with unrighteousness? and what communion hath light with darkness?' The contrast is clear."

"I know."

"If you know the right thing you need to do, then do it, right?" Avery sighed. "I'm so sorry."

Sorry? It was the thing that Diehl said a lot.

Skye realized at that moment that Diehl had occupied her mind, her headspace, more than God had this whole week. Perhaps it was time for her to step back and evaluate what was happening between her and Diehl.

"What are you sorry about?" Skye asked. "You spoke your heart, sister. I would rather you don't sugarcoat the truth."

"Or my opinion of the truth? You must forgive me for being so assertive." Avery blinked. "I'm sorry. I don't know what overcame me just now. I felt so strongly that I had to protect you from yourself—and that sexy billionaire."

Skye cringed. She had tried to look past the first impressions. "If you get to know him, he's a gentleman. So far, he has respected and honored me. When I go to his house, Marlo is with me—except last Monday when he called in sick. Diehl helped me cook his breakfast that day."

"I'm sure he would want to keep a clean reputation out of respect for the Brooks family name on the island. Everyone knew who his grandfather was. His parents do a lot of charity work in the area. And Brinley even more."

Skye agreed with her. "We all have baggage in our

lives. You reminded me the other day that you don't want to cast the first stone."

"I hope I haven't tonight." Avery's shoulders sagged.

Skye hugged her. "No. You're advising me to assess my situation with...him. That's wise counsel."

"Well, someone had to sound the bullhorn to reach you in your fog of love." Avery laughed so hard she nearly spilled tea all over her shorts.

"Next time you date, I'm going to be all over you, checking off the sin list, and I'll just bash you over your head with the Bible." Skye took the paper plate and cup from Avery to throw them away.

"Please do. Better to know what's going on before marriage than to drag out the mess in divorce court."

"Isn't that the truth?"

Speaking of divorce, Diehl had remarried the same woman twice. Had it been because she was the mother of his children? Because he wanted to keep the family together?

It had been a year since she was killed in Italy. Skye recalled Brinley saying that the investigators were looking into faulty brakes and potential sabotage, but none of that panned out. It seemed that, for whatever reason, Isobel Brooks had simply driven off the cliff in the pouring rain, leaving behind a husband and two beautiful kids.

Skye wondered how much Diehl grieved. Brinley had told them that the first few months were hard, but he had poured himself into his work at the office for the rest of the months, driving everyone crazy at Brooks Investments.

Then the day came when he made a mistake and lost a multi-billion-dollar merger that could have expanded the family business. Instead, a few of their other potential mergers fell through, and Diehl's business acumen could not hold the company together.

Brinley had said that the day she and her dad confronted Diehl about taking a sabbatical was the first day that Diehl looked positively relieved to have the weight of the family fortune lifted off his shoulders.

Perhaps that had been why he was a changed man when he arrived on St. Simon's Island to rest. He was relaxed, easygoing, and helpful in so many ways.

Then again, being helpful in doing good works couldn't get one to heaven.

Skye knew that.

And with that, she realized another reason God had placed her here for such a time as this.

Besides comforting Diehl's grieving daughter, who had lost her mother at about the same age as Skye had lost hers, she now had a second purpose: pray for Diehl's salvation—if he wasn't saved—or for his return to God—if he was a prodigal son.

CHAPTER TWENTY-THREE

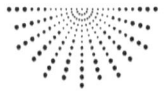

When Mom called Diehl to Brooks Cottage two hours before dinner, he wanted to say no, but Mom always got her way. Diehl texted Skye to ask her to cook the dishes and leave them in the refrigerator. He'd eat them the next day.

More leftovers.

To his own disappointment, he would miss the Fire Pit Service at church tonight. Mom's voice was too urgent to dismiss.

Diehl had no idea what to expect this evening on Seaside Island. Another socialite to meet? Or a single woman in need of company? Mom's matchmaking service knew no bounds.

He hummed a hymn he had heard at church on Sunday as he parked his truck on the circular driveway leading to the front door. Normally, he would park in the porte-cochère, but a limousine he had never seen before had taken up space there.

He locked his truck and made his way to the front door.

Before he reached it, Cara opened the door and stood outside. She looked worried.

"Is everything okay?" Diehl asked.

"You have company." She didn't say more.

"I figured. Thanks for the warning." Diehl handed her the truck keys. "If you need to move my truck."

He walked past her, still humming a medley as he made his way into his parents' house. As he crossed the foyer, he heard somber voices coming from the sunroom, where Mom liked to receive her guests.

Uh-oh. Doesn't sound like a party.

He braced himself as he turned the corner into the sunroom—

And froze at the door.

Zeta and Wilson Bishop in the flesh.

"Missing your grandkids already?" Diehl asked. It had only been two weeks.

"Have your DNA test results arrived?" Zeta asked.

So that's what this is about.

"Nice to see you again too." Diehl decided to remain standing where he was.

Sitting next to Zeta, her ever compliant husband waved. He barely smiled.

Something was up.

Across from the coffee table, Mom wrung her hands.

She did that when she was beyond nervous.

With Dad away in Atlanta solving their company's financial problems, Diehl was glad he was here tonight to lend Mom whatever support she needed. Pushing her mid-seventies, Mom had more lines on her face now than she used to. Maybe it was the sunshine outside or the tanning salon.

"Have they?" Zeta asked again.

"I expect them any day now," Diehl said. "It's been expedited. Maybe Friday. Why?"

"Good. It will only confirm what we already know." Zeta shifted in her seat.

Mom sniffled.

"What is going on?" Diehl asked, arms across his chest.

"You're not the father of either child, Diehl." Zeta drew a deep breath, as though in great relief.

"Come again?" Diehl leaned against the doorframe for support.

He must not be hearing it right.

Zeta waved a piece of paper that had magically appeared in her hand. "Elisa and Ethan belong to Luigi Bellini."

"How could that be?" Mom blurted. "How?"

Diehl didn't know either. "Wait. Elisa was born twelve years ago, which meant she was conceived thirteen years ago, thereabouts. Ethan was born nine years ago. I don't recall Isobel hanging out with someone else other than me ten or thirteen years ago."

"That's the way it goes, sometimes," Wilson said. "We were all blindsided. I never said our daughter was a saint."

"You're saying that after we married, Isobel carried on a multi-year on-and-off affair with Luigi that resulted in two children." As Diehl said it, the reality finally sank in, and he began to feel anger rise in his chest. "The other day, you said that a year ago, Isobel met with her lover in Italy shortly before she died."

Mom wept softly.

Diehl didn't go to her. Shame shrouded him, but he couldn't run from this now. He had to show strength. How could his wife have had an affair under his nose? It was his work, wasn't it? He had been so busy with work that he had neglected Isobel to the point of pushing her into someone else's arms?

How would Grandpa Brooks handle this if he were alive?

Well, Grandpa wouldn't get himself into such a situation.

Diehl felt like a fool. His marriages—both to the same woman—had been one big sham to fund Isobel's Italian tryst. He knew it now, though too late.

If he could help it, he would never marry again.

Marriages are overrated.

"The test is accurate." Wilson made a noise. "I paid too much for it to be faulty."

"Luigi signed an acknowledgment of paternity," Zeta said. "He agreed to let us raise them."

"Let me call my attorney," Diehl said. He texted Mark Gill. The family attorney would know about Diehl's legal rights.

"Where are my kids?" Diehl looked at Mom.

My kids.

It felt natural for him to call them his.

"They're in the indoor pool next door," Mom said. "Too hot outside."

"Who is with them?"

"Malik's men."

Security. Good.

"I invited Zeta and Wilson to stay in our guest cottage tonight instead of in a hotel," Mom added. "I wish your dad were here, but he said he's busy in Atlanta."

Diehl nodded. Dad was trying to save the family business. Diehl wished he could be there with him, but he had burned out trying to do the right thing. He hoped to God that he would get over it so that he could get back to work.

This new development wasn't helping any.

Somehow it felt surreal. Yet at the back of his mind, he had always known that he could not trust Isobel. She had spent entirely too much time and money in Italy for them to say they were happily married.

If Isobel had loved another, why not just say so?

In fact, Diehl remembered how Isobel had complained to his sister that he had no time for her. Was it his fault now? Had he driven his own wife away to her lover's arms?

Two kids!

How could Diehl not know?

Diehl recalled what Mom had told him the week before when she was still in Hawaii. Luigi had money troubles with his estranged wife. So how long had he sponged off Isobel, who in turn had sponged off Diehl?

What a mess.

Diehl had willed his fortune to his two children, but if they were not his, would he have to modify his will?

"They've never been yours," Zeta said. "I wish we had known sooner—like before Elisa was born—but such is life."

"I raised them," Diehl said. "I was there from their births until now."

"Don't you want them to have a good future?" Mom asked.

"Money is not everything, Rose," Zeta said. "Right now, these two kids are all I have left of my Isobel."

Mom blinked.

Diehl went to her. Put his hands on her shuddering shoulders.

"You have to let us have them," Zeta said.

No. Diehl might not know much about child custody law, but he knew that he had been married to Isobel when both children were born. His name was listed on their birth certificates. The court would consider him the legal father of Elisa and Ethan.

In essence, he was the surviving parent—biological or otherwise. No way was he letting these two non-parental third parties get custody of his kids.

"You're holding these two minors against their will," Zeta said.

Against their will? Diehl didn't recall Mom saying anything about the kids not wanting to leave Hawaii when she had gone to pick them up.

Still, Zeta's statement made Diehl second-guess

whether his own kids wanted to be with him. If anyone were to ask his twelve-year-old now, in the bad mood she was in, the answer could be anything.

How would they respond once they found out that Diehl wasn't their biological father? Would Elisa revolt? Would Ethan be devastated?

"Why are you like that?" Diehl couldn't stand this part of Zeta that Isobel had inherited. Tenacious pit bull persistence was one thing, but she was barking up against the wrong wall here.

"I'm sure you want everything done in the best interests of the two children." Mom reached for another tissue.

Diehl had spent a fortune raising the two kids and paying for everything, from their twelve-bedroom family home on West Paces Ferry in Atlanta—which was bigger than Jared's cousin Logan's house down the street—to their education at the most expensive private school in Georgia, and to their many vacations all over the world, flown there and back on the Brooks private jet.

Diehl wondered if the kids would want to stay with him. If the court asked, would they say yes?

"We are their biological grandparents, their closest relatives," Wilson added.

Zeta and Wilson seemed to be in agreement on the matter. Sometimes Diehl found that Zeta would do her own thing and then surprise Wilson later.

Now Isobel kept surprising Diehl long after she had died.

Like mother, like daughter.

Diehl pursed his lips. Mom opened her mouth to say something, but Diehl shook his head slightly. She closed her mouth again. Wiped her nose a bit.

Mom turned to Diehl. "Can Mark come over for dinner tonight?"

"I'll ask." Diehl texted the attorney. Of course, he could come. The Brooks family had him on a retainer, even though most of the time, they called him only to update a will or something benign like that.

"Mark will be here at six thirty. Is that okay?" Diehl asked.

Mom nodded. She looked relieved. "I'm sure we can come up with a win-win solution."

Is there such a thing?

There were no winners here.

The kids had lost their mother. The Bishops had lost their daughter. Diehl had lost his wife—regardless of how she had dishonored their marriage twice.

"Zeta, we're friends," Mom said. "You can have the entire guest cottage next door. The kids can stay in their rooms in this cottage, and we can have dinner together."

When Zeta didn't say anything, Mom continued, "We'd want to wait until Friday when Diehl's DNA results come in. Just for peace of mind."

Wilson glanced at Zeta. "Well, Zeta, what's a couple of days? We had a long flight. At my age, I'd rather not just turn around and fly back."

"I'll have the Gulfstream fueled and waiting for you whenever you go home to Hawaii," Mom sweetened the deal.

"Even better," Wilson said. "I'm tired of waiting at airports to catch a flight."

Something didn't seem right, but Diehl didn't know what it was. Elisa and Ethan would automatically lose over ten billion dollars' worth of inheritance each if they were taken from him—which the Bishops legally could not do. The Bishop name and their pineapple plantation could not come close to Diehl's fortune.

Why were they doing this then?

Why did they want the grandchildren so badly?

"I want to see my grandkids now." Zeta stood up.

Wilson did too, stretching.

"Of course," Mom said. "We can join them in the pool, if you want. Dinner isn't for another hour."

"Could you get someone to bring my luggage from the limo to our rooms?" Zeta asked.

Mom nodded. She waved to Cara.

Cara's eyes were red. Diehl could see them from where he was standing. For as long as he had known his once-nanny, Cara had always had a soft spot for children—especially those left behind in empty houses while their parents frolicked around the world.

For many years, Diehl and his siblings had been left with Cara. She practically raised them. Grandpa Brooks would take them to church, but Cara would feed and clothe them.

Diehl watched them leave, but stayed behind in the sunroom to catch his breath.

CHAPTER TWENTY-FOUR

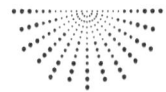

*D*iehl could use some company about now. Maybe a hug from Skye. He couldn't remember the last time he had been attracted to someone this quickly.

Back in graduate school, it had been Isobel who had enticed him to her bed. Once that happened, he was attached to her. Isobel had played on his weakness, his sense of obligation and responsibility, and the rest of their relationship had been based on her playing psychological tricks on him, manipulating his feelings of guilt for having bedded her before they married. To Isobel, she had done something wild and illegal, wrong and secretive: she had slept with a professed Christian and ruined his testimony.

He had thought he could never set foot in church again.

Until now. At Seaside Chapel, he was incognito. Pastor Gonzalez had taken over the church after

Grandpa Brooks passed away, so it was as though all things had been made new at that church. No one at church seemed to care about how much money he had in the bank, or how he had put his MBA to good use, or that he was from the Brooks family. They cared more about the condition of his soul, whether he was truly saved or not, whether he was studying his Bible— hence their encouragement for him to attend church, Sunday school, the Monday morning men's Bible study, and the Fire Pit Service on Wednesday nights.

Truth be told, he wouldn't have gone to any of that if not for Skye. Regardless of how much his sister might have told Skye about his past, Skye had not shown any prejudice against him. In fact, she had tried to differentiate for him what it meant to be saved versus not being saved. Diehl was still thinking about that. In his heart, he could not fathom how God would forgive him after all that he had done, and take him back to His family. How?

Speaking of church, Diehl felt disappointed that he could not go to the Fire Pit Service tonight with Skye. He rather enjoyed her company.

Those kisses were premature, and he hated to have led her on, but in his heart, he knew that he wanted to see her every day, or at least as often as he could. In fact, he couldn't recall anyone else he'd want to spend more time with than Skye—not even Isobel.

While Isobel had been spiteful, Skye was sweet. Isobel had been vengeful, but Skye was kind—as far as he could tell from the last two weeks he had been with her.

He could use her company now to take the edge off this awful news.

Then again, if Skye found out what a mess his first —and technically second—marriage had been, would she trust him with her heart? If he couldn't be in the right relationship, what did that say about his own judgment about personal matters?

There were several good guys at church. Diehl suspected that any one of them didn't have nearly half the problems he had found himself in.

Perhaps he should spare Skye some of his problems.

His phone buzzed. Mark Gill wanted to talk. He had to find a private space. Dad's office was locked. He heard Mom coming down the stairs—her bangles gave her away—in her swimsuit. For a woman in her seventies, she looked great.

She waved to him as she made her way down the hall toward the stairs that took her to the garden outside. There would be a path there to take her next door where the indoor pool was.

Diehl heard people talking in the kitchen across from the large dining room. He could hear pots and pans clanging, people talking, and Chef Pierre talking loudly above everyone, like he was wearing a microphone or something.

Where could he find a quiet place to talk to his attorney?

Diehl made his way downstairs to the terrace level. Dad used to like sitting out there in front of the outdoor fireplace. It was too hot in June to be outside, even with the ceiling fans spinning at full blast.

He stepped into the man cave, and walked by the bar. He should have kept walking, but he glanced over and saw the glass cabinets full of liquor. He knew that behind that wall was his parents' wine cellar.

Dad had stopped drinking after his minor stroke a couple of years before. Mom still drank on occasion, when she visited Zoe and her husband in Paris, or when her friends came over. Brinley had always been a rare drinker, though she had stopped altogether since she became a Christian. Her husband was a teetotaler.

Diehl supposed that Dad hadn't cleared out those liquor cabinets because they still entertained friends who drank.

"You should get rid of them all, Dad," Diehl said. Alone in the room, no one could hear him.

Those days when he used to drink heavily were over. Back when Parker had been his drinking buddy, Diehl and Parker would be wasted every weekend. Sometimes Jared Urquhart joined them—though Diehl figured Jared might be there to glean corporate information he could not have gotten otherwise.

Then again, Brooks Investments and Urquhart Enterprises were not rivals, not in the true sense of the word. Yes, both companies dabbled in constructions and properties, but usually in different regions. Besides, there was plenty of room for both of them to thrive.

Diehl's business association with Jared remained, but they stopped socializing after Parker drowned. No one wanted to bring it up, and it was never mentioned in the obituary, but Parker was drunk when he dove into the ocean to rescue his adopted daughter.

Feeling bad about the whole matter, and wondering if he could have done something to prevent Parker from being an alcoholic, Diehl had avoided talking to Parker's widow for many years. They would see each other casually at Christmas and whenever Riley brought her kids over to Mom's house, but that was it.

What a big mess this family is.

Perhaps a good thing that resulted from Parker's death had been the change in Diehl. He stopped drinking alcohol altogether. There was nothing that could make him go back to those days when he could barely sit up, let alone think and make multi-billion-dollar business deals. A quick thought of Parker's death ended his desire for a strong drink.

Diehl wouldn't lie by saying he wasn't tempted every now and then, but he also knew he should be all here, to have fully functional faculties to deal with this situation. Now, more than ever, he needed to be able to think straight about his two children.

They've never been yours.

Zeta's words stung so much that Diehl felt he needed something to blunt the trauma. He tried to hum another hymn but the words didn't come to him.

God, are You there?

He heard nothing.

However, right in front of him in those liquor cabinets was another type of spirit calling his name.

CHAPTER TWENTY-FIVE

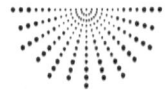

*B*rinley's obstetrician had put her on bedrest for the rest of her pregnancy. That caused the baby shower to be canceled. It wasn't a big deal because Skye and Avery decided to collect all the gifts and bring them over to Brinley's house before the baby was due.

In fact, the situation lightened Skye's load. She had many things on her calendar for this month. Not only were Skye's chefs rather busy cooking for vacationers, Saffron on Jekyll Island also experienced a rise in patrons due to the summer break. Add to that singing at church, agreeing to help her brother at the food festival in Miami Beach, and organizing a baby shower for her good friend, and Skye felt overwhelmed by the time Thursday rolled around.

Fifteen minutes to eight on a cloudy Thursday morning, Skye and Marlo arrived at Diehl's house to find a note taped to the front door.

"What is that, an eviction notice?" Marlo laughed. The paper sack on his arms shook.

Skye read it. "A note from Diehl. He's canceling all meals on Thursday and Friday."

Diehl's truck was not on the driveway—but it didn't mean he hadn't moved it into the garage and closed the door. The carriage house-style garage door had no windows for them to peek in.

"Are we still getting paid?"

"Yep. It's late notice. Policy says we should be paid for today, but tomorrow is still twenty-four hours away, so he has leeway there." Skye put down her basket on the ground.

She texted him for confirmation.

No reply.

"Okay. I'm going to assume this is a valid note." Skye took a photo of the note before she pulled it off the door. "I'm going to keep this note as evidence."

"Good idea."

"I don't want anyone to say we didn't show up. We stand ready to make breakfast."

"We are. So what now?"

"I guess we go home. I'll see you at Mrs. Morton's at three o'clock today."

"Anything you need my help with?" Marlo followed Skye back to the van.

"I'm assuming the note is telling us we can't go inside, so we can't remove the groceries we left in the refrigerator until Saturday when we can come back."

"What a waste of food."

"If they're still good on Saturday, we'll send them

to Parker's Shelter. I'll let Chef Joseph know." Skye rotated leftover food among the various missions and shelters in town—what most area restaurants did—but they would prefer cooked food. That meant Skye would have to take time out of her already busy schedule to cook the dishes when she could get access to the refrigerator—unless Chef Joseph could do it.

Saturday would be tight.

On Sunday, she had a round-trip ticket to Atlanta. "Some days, I might bring you with me to the food festival if I need an extra assistant."

"Are you trying to persuade me to go to chef school?" Marlo chuckled.

"Is it working?"

"Keep trying." He shut the back door of the van. "If I get some form of scholarship, I might do it."

"If you like to cook, it's worth it." Skye thought about what Marlo said.

Scholarship.

She hadn't provided that for her employees. Her finances were stretched thin due to Saffron's expenses. If Sebastian didn't want the restaurant anymore, there was no reason for Skye to try to keep her minority share and hope to buy out Jared and Talia.

If she didn't have the restaurant holding her down, she could potentially provide scholarships for her potential chefs.

"Why don't we pray about scholarships? God can provide anything," Skye said as she put the van in reverse.

Leaving Diehl's house, Skye couldn't help but think about the fact that she wasn't going to see Diehl until the following Monday.

She hadn't seen her brother all year long because they had been busy with work. The Miami Beach food festival was a small opportunity for them to get together again. It would end on Thursday. Then she would fly with Sebastian back to Atlanta. From there, they'd drive to Athens. Skye looked forward to spending a long weekend with Sebastian and her sister-in-law, Emmeline. They had been best friends for a few years.

"God works out all things for our good," Marlo said.

"Indeed."

Not just the situation with Marlo's scholarship to culinary school, but also every situation that Skye found herself in.

Like the one with Diehl.

Perhaps it was a good thing for them to have time apart. The previous two weeks had been different from how Skye normally conducted her relationships, that was, with careful planning and precision. Without planning, there was no way the menus could be executed flawlessly. Likewise, without planning, the relationship would be...

What?

More interesting? Exciting? Unexpected?

Like his kisses?

Had he meant them, though?

Stepping back a little bit to take a deep breath might be a good thing for her emotions.

Traffic was light this Thursday between Diehl's house and Skye's kitchen at Sage Café, where her brother had rented a portion of the refrigerator and freezer to STL. Certainly, the restaurant at The Village was closer to her than Saffron's kitchen on Jekyll Island.

Marlo helped her take the two bags to the walk-in refrigerator, and then he left.

Skye stayed back to eat a late breakfast and check her email. Another message from Jared. He wanted to make sure Skye was going to show up on Saturday night for their meeting. Skye texted him back, suggesting a day meeting instead since she was going out of town Sunday after church, and needed to pack on Saturday. Besides, she had these cancellations from Diehl.

The phone rang. Jared.

Couldn't he just text back? "Hello?"

"Where are you?" Jared asked.

"I'm at Sage, eating breakfast."

"I'm at my house. If you like, we can have our meeting here."

Uh, no. "I think we should meet at Saffron. Are you free at lunch? Say, noon?"

"A working lunch. I guess we can do that since we have to eat."

"I'll let Chef Onada know."

"You sure you don't want to come over?" Jared asked again.

"I'm sure I don't have time. Thanks for the invite. I'll see you at Saffron at noon, but I need to be done at one o'clock. I have another appointment right after that."

"What can we discuss in one hour?"

"Lots of things can be discussed in forty-five minutes. I'll bring a list." On top of the list were Skye's options. She had checked her funds only to realize that she could not afford to buy out Talia's shares at this time, but perhaps Jared could buy Skye's shares instead—or she could sell her shares to someone else. Either way, she did not want to be a business partner to Jared.

It wasn't something that required too much prayer. She knew she did not feel comfortable in Jared's company and she wanted out of it.

Sebastian hadn't said anything to her in a very long time about whether he wanted to get back into Saffron's business. To Skye, it meant her brother was done with it.

How long must she cling to that which she should let go of?

Would it be the right thing to do?

She had thought about it on and off, but hadn't prayed much about it.

Perhaps Chef Onada and other chefs could come together to buy Skye's share of Saffron. The restaurant was profitable, but Skye had lost interest in it since her brother didn't want it back.

She kept reminding herself that if not for Sebastian, she wouldn't have become a co-owner of Saffron.

"I'll see you at noon then," Jared said.

"Please don't be late. The meeting has to end at one o'clock."

"Yes, ma'am."

Skye finished her breakfast. She had two hours before she had to start driving to Saffron for the meeting. If she could get an hour of guitar practice in, she would be much better prepared for the quartet's performance at the Christmas festival in December. She liked to be prepared early and not worry about it—even though December was over five months away.

Her mind was anywhere but on driving when she got into her van. Fortunately, traffic was still light going away from the beaches and pier. She did not turn on the radio because she wanted to think through a few things and pray along the way.

"Most of all, Lord, I want to be in Your perfect will for my life," Skye prayed in the van.

The windows were rolled up, the AC was on, and she was alone with her thoughts and prayers.

"I don't know why Diehl canceled today, but I pray that if he has some unspoken prayers, please answer them. May Your perfect will be done there as well, whatever his problem might be."

Skye turned in to her tree-lined street. As pretty as this road might be, Skye still preferred a beach house any day. She had been keeping an eye on Brinley's beach house for a few years, but there were other houses along the oceanfront too.

If she sold her shares of Saffron, she could buy herself a beach house with a nice kitchen in it, like the one she had helped Brinley design. It would beat renting any day.

Sometimes she would pass by her old house near the pier and wish she hadn't sold it. However, she'd had to do it.

It made her happy to have helped her brother—although now she was stuck with two business partners she'd rather not have anything to do with.

"I know You can do anything, Lord," Skye prayed. "Is there something You can do about my Saffron situation? Soon, please?"

She entered her empty house, kicked off her shoes, and padded across the wood floor to her guitar propped up on its stand in the small living room.

She had pulled back the curtains before she left the house this morning. And now sunshine streamed into the living room, exposing the scratches on the pine floor and the coffee table.

She found her guitar pick.

"His Eye Is on the Sparrow" came to mind, and she recalled how she had almost fallen in love with Diehl after she sang the song with him on the piano, when he wiped tears from her cheek that Friday when he first came to town.

One week and a day later, they had kissed.

Five days after that, Diehl abruptly canceled his meals for two days.

What did it all mean?

Skye reminded herself not to read too much into it. She picked up her guitar and began practicing the first parts of the classical piece she had agreed to play. The difficult piece kept her occupied for a good hour, during which time she did not think of Diehl.

At all.

Her mind switched gears to her upcoming business meeting, and she left Diehl in another mental compartment to be dealt with on another day.

CHAPTER TWENTY-SIX

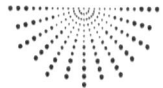

*A*fter his DNA results came early on Thursday evening, the next two days fused together for Diehl since he returned from his parents' house on Seaside Island to his sister's beach house on St. Simon's Island.

It was problematic that he hadn't come home alone. With him were at least several bottles from Dad's cellar, and half a dozen of Mom's assorted finds at auctions she had frequented when she was too bored with nothing better to do. A couple of the bottles looked like they had diamonds on the glass carving, but he'd make sure to return those to Mom, just in case she wanted to leave them in the cabinet for show.

He couldn't recall which bottle he had emptied first, but he saved the most expensive booze for last—in honor of the mother who had birthed him.

"Assuming I'm really her son, and Dad is really my dad."

Diehl slumped over the living room couch, his curtains drawn so that nobody walking around his backyard or on the beach could see him—although the dunes would cover for him.

"I'm a sparrow alone." The bottle slipped from his grip, and hit the rug on the floor. Fortunately, the rug was thick and the bottle didn't shatter.

He wished he could talk to someone about his messed-up life and marriage.

What if he could never have children? All those years with Isobel and no biological kids of his own? What on earth?

"What if Skye wants children? What if I can't give her any?"

He felt that his manhood had been threatened.

If he had known ten or thirteen years ago that he could not have children, he could have done something about it. Now that he was almost forty, was it too late for him? By the time a child born today went to college in eighteen years, he'd be fifty-eight.

Well, to be fair to himself, just because the DNA results said he wasn't the father to his two children, whom he had doted over since they were babies, it didn't necessarily mean that he was unable to have children himself.

"In fact, to have children, Isobel and I had to get together more often than she got together with Luigi, right?" Diehl asked no one.

His body felt hot. He had to turn down the thermostat. It was somewhere in the living room or house, he was sure. He peeled himself off the couch, but didn't make it far before he tripped over the blasted rug on the floor and went down by the coffee table.

He made no attempt to get up. Slowly, he turned over. Lying there on the floor, he looked up at the spinning ceiling fan.

"Oh, God. I need help."

He closed his eyes, and heard guitar playing. Skye's guitar. Then he heard her voice, singing.

> *His eye is on the sparrow, and I know*
> *He watches me...*

"Are you watching me, God? Right now?"

No answer.

Diehl wept quietly.

CHAPTER TWENTY-SEVEN

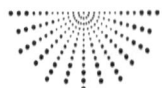

*F*riday, Friday. Skye loved looking at her books toward the end of the week, even though most of the restaurant's weekly income came on weekends. Still, she couldn't help taking a peek at her bank account this Friday night, as she usually did when she didn't have anything else to do.

Skye's the Limit did well so far. No debt. No loans. All rental fees were paid up. Skye was pleased with her finances and the money management skills that her brother had taught her.

Eleven o'clock was too late in the evening to send Sebastian a "thank you" text message. He was probably asleep by now. Instead, she sent an email on her laptop, and then shut it down. She left the laptop charging on her kitchen table as she made her way upstairs to her bedroom.

Her rental house was quiet. There was no party

down the street tonight. As soon as she was able, she would find a house to buy.

She had gotten over her regrets about selling her half-a-million-dollar house to buy up Sebastian's share of Saffron. However, two years later, perhaps it was time for a change.

To begin with, she had never been interested in owning or managing a restaurant. Saffron was a bit far away on Jekyll. With Jared in the ownership mix, Skye didn't feel comfortable about dealing with Saffron anymore.

She had prayed about it, but she wanted to run her plans by Sebastian. He probably didn't care what she did with her shares of Saffron two years after he gave it up. He had kept Sage Café, and added a new location in Athens, Georgia.

Skye washed her face and brushed her teeth. That was pretty much the extent of her nightly routine. Blessed with clear skin, she rarely had to deal with pores or pimples. Eating fresh fruits and vegetables all her life had helped, she was sure.

She loved putting together meal plans and menus, shopping for groceries, and cooking what she bought. That might be why being a personal chef worked out for her.

The job had less pressure and more flexibility compared to cooking in a high-pressure kitchen such as found in a restaurant. Running a personal chef business, she could always hire another chef if she needed more time off. Chef Joseph had filled in her weekends for her so that she could get a break and do other things like rehearse church music and attend church.

While she wished that everyone could have a chance to go to church twice on Sundays and once on Wednesday nights, not everyone was a Christian, and some churches did not meet that many times a week. Somehow her crew worked it out, whatever their personal beliefs might be.

Skye changed into her pajamas, climbed into bed, and read her Bible.

Half an hour later, she nearly dozed off reading Hebrews, but when she turned off the lights and pulled the blanket up to her chin, sleep wouldn't come.

Why?

She tossed and turned this way and that way until it was way past midnight. Should she get up and pad around the house until she felt sleepy? Should she stay in bed until she fell asleep?

"Why am I awake, Lord?" She hadn't drunk any coffee since Friday morning. No chocolate. No caffeine.

She turned on the lights to continue reading her Bible. Her eyelids started to shut, but when she put her head on her pillow, she was wide awake again.

Weird.

Pray.

She recalled Aunt Irma telling her to pray, pray, pray.

Always pray. Never let up.

In the quiet of the night, Skye prayed for Sebastian and Emmeline in Athens. They were all the family she had. Aunt Irma and Uncle Miller did not have any kids in their long lives. They had passed away within months of each other when they were in their nineties.

Church became her extended family. Skye prayed for Avery, her best friend after Emmeline. Avery's cousin Gillian had just moved to town, so they had been busy. Gillian was a Christian too, but she decided to attend a women's Sunday school class instead of their mixed group. Skye hardly saw her.

Brinley had become a good friend. Their friendship had started at work when Sebastian catered some of the Brooks family's past events, especially their Christmas dinners. Now that Sebastian had moved out of town, their private chef decided to take on all that.

Brinley said she wasn't having a difficult pregnancy, but the doctor wanted her on bedrest anyway, just in case. Skye didn't ask for details. Next week, she and Avery—and some of the ladies in their Tuesday night Bible study—would take the baby shower gifts to her house.

Skye prayed for Brinley and Ivan. The lovely couple would make great parents. They were both Christians and would raise their children in the way of the Lord.

As for Skye, she wasn't sure if she would ever marry. Sometimes she wondered. She had gone out with two men at church at separate times in the past: Matt and Hayden.

Hayden might have thought that their one dinner was fun, but Skye felt nothing for him. It wasn't that Hayden was three years younger than she was, but that

Hayden had no interest in food or food preparation or cooking in general. He had no problem eating frozen dinners every night. Skye didn't know what to think about that.

As for Matt, he wasn't her type at all. They had nothing in common. He could talk about antiques all day, like he was perhaps stuck in another century. Skye had more in common with Diehl than with Matt...

Diehl.

"What do we have in common?" Skye asked herself.

They both liked Brinley's beach house, including the side yard and the ocean view.

He seemed to enjoy cooking when he helped her cook breakfast on the day Marlo called in sick. If there was one thing that tugged at Skye's heart, it was a man who loved to cook.

Did Diehl love to cook?

Skye knew a lot about him because Brinley had told her a lot in the last few years that they had been friends and praying partners. Skye wouldn't call it gossip since nothing left the room. However, the way Brinley put it, Diehl had a lot of problems.

And he had strayed from God so far away that no one knew if Diehl was saved or not.

While that might not be a big deal to others, it mattered much to Skye. He had kissed her twice.

The only way the relationship could continue was for them to be on the same page with each other.

"That's my prayer, Lord," Skye said aloud. "If Diehl is the one for me—if we are to date, say—then I need confirmation that we're on the same page with each other in our faith and belief in God."

She knew that she could not date someone who was not a Christian, who might not want to go to church with her. Half her life was spent in church. Someone who did not appreciate church would not appreciate what mattered to her.

They could still be friends, but that was all.

Kissing friends?

Perhaps those kisses had been premature.

"Forgive me, Lord," Skye prayed. "It just happened."

There was no doubt she and Diehl were attracted to each other.

But the Bible said she had to walk by faith and not by sight.

"That's my other prayer, Lord. That I would walk by faith in You and not by sight in my circumstances or the world around me."

She wondered what Diehl did all week when her crew wasn't in his kitchen. According to Brinley, he was supposed to be on a no-work sabbatical. How did he spend the rest of the day? Read a book? Watch TV? Walk on the beach?

What was he doing at this moment?

Skye tapped her phone on the side table to see what time it was. Nearly midnight.

"Lord Jesus, whatever Diehl is doing right now, I pray that Your perfect will would sweep through his life and prevail over the difficulties and hardships that he had—or has. I don't know what he's going through right now. It's hard to know what's on his mind when he doesn't show it. As it says in the Bible, we humans look at the outer appearance, but You look at the heart, Lord. I pray that You will deal with Diehl, whatever he is going through."

She chuckled at her own words.

Deal with Diehl.

Sometimes Skye wondered how different Diehl's life was from hers. Their jobs, incomes, and lifestyles differed. Was Diehl more like Jared? That flamboyant billionaire liked to throw money around as though paper money trumped all. Someone should tell Jared that money wasn't everything—but then he might take that as a challenge to prove them wrong.

Then again, even though Diehl and Jared had run in the same circles back when they were younger, Skye found Diehl different than Jared. While Jared was loud, Diehl was quieter and more thoughtful.

I prefer thoughtful.

While Jared looked at Skye as another woman to conquer, Diehl had talked to her with respect—although she wondered if Diehl had taken advantage of her by kissing her before she fully sorted out her feelings for him.

Their relationship was still in the early stages of a work in progress.

In any case, since Diehl knew Jared and how the latter ticked, perhaps Skye should ask Diehl for some business advice on how to handle Jared.

She had broached the potential sale of her shares

to Chef Onada, but he wasn't interested. He said he did not want to own a restaurant.

Well, neither did Skye. Not anymore.

Skye's mind wandered to the future. When she got up the next day, the first thing she had to do after reading her Bible and eating breakfast was to pack for her weeklong trip to Atlanta. She looked forward to seeing her brother again after all these busy months.

Accompanying Sebastian to food festivals had been their thing for many years. She missed those times away, even when they did not participate in competitions. They would attend just for the sheer fun of it.

Okay, so she would pack on Saturday, and then fly out to Atlanta after evening church on Sunday to catch a connecting flight to Miami Beach. She wished there was a direct flight, but not now.

Chef Joseph would not only manage things for her while she was gone, but he would also cook in her place at Diehl's house next week.

Would she miss Diehl?

Would they call each other?

She left the questions unanswered as she fell into a deep sleep.

CHAPTER TWENTY-EIGHT

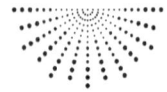

*B*right and early on Saturday morning, when she was supposed to sleep in, Skye found herself driving on an empty street. She turned into the driveway of Brinley's beach house, and parked behind Chef Joseph's van. His door opened and he stepped out of the passenger side, dressed in a blue chef's coat. Above them, the clouds moved. Rain clouds were coming in.

"We rang the bell, knocked, rang, called, texted, the gamut," he said.

"No note today?" Skye walked toward the front door.

"None."

Marlo exited the vehicle on the driver's side.

"Let me check the back before we try to get inside." Skye hadn't done that in weeks past, but today was the day that they could cook for Diehl again, so she wanted to make sure he hadn't extended that request for the entire weekend or something.

Marlo followed her around the house, and they stepped up on the deck. The curtains were drawn, but Skye did not attempt to open the French door. If the alarm was set, it would take a sprint to the front door to unset the alarm. Brinley had given her the code, but she had no idea how many seconds she had.

She walked back to the front of the house and texted Diehl.

No reply.

"Maybe he's still at his mother's house," Skye said.

Why would she hesitate now? For the last two weeks, she had been given permission—first by Brinley and then by Diehl—to walk into the house to cook for him so that he didn't have to get up to open the door for them.

Maybe I'm afraid of what I might find inside.

Skye prayed, mustered up her courage, and unlocked the front door. The alarm didn't go off. It wasn't even set.

Strong whiskey smell assaulted her nose.

Uh-oh.

Chef Joseph and Marlo were right behind her, carrying groceries.

She opened the door wide to let them in.

Marlo made a face as he took a whiff. The house reeked of a combination of booze and sweat, like someone had forgotten to turn on the air-conditioner.

As Skye walked into the foyer, she spotted Diehl passed out on a couch in the living room. He was not moving. All over the coffee table were bottles, some upright, some on their sides.

Skye's heart skipped a beat and she nearly dropped her keys. She put them back into her crossover bag and made her way to the living room, holding her breath.

Help me be strong, Lord.

She pushed away the memories of her drunken parents stinking up their childhood home with untold brands of liquor. After they died in the car wreck, Skye and Sebastian cleaned out every single bottle they had left behind in their house.

They vowed that day never to marry anyone who was a drunk.

As she neared Diehl, she could see his chest rise and fall under the white undershirt and gym shorts.

Well, at least he was clothed. And alive.

Somewhere in the living room, a phone pinged several times. Skye heard it, but she could not see a phone anywhere.

Skye could hear Chef Joseph and Marlo talking in the kitchen. Neither of them had been surprised by the scene. Being a personal chef meant that they had to go to people's homes. Those homes were not always perfect. Their job was to cook the meals and leave, and not to judge whether the rich and famous lived up to community expectations.

In fact, whether their clients were rich or poor, they all still had the same problem: sin.

Skye herself had seen couples fighting and throwing projectiles at each other while she and Marlo were trying to prepare a romantic candlelight dinner for them.

She had seen kids being dragged upstairs for talking back to the parent—and it didn't matter which one.

She had also seen kids and adults alike telling her that a dish she just made them was the worst in the world and other subjective evaluations.

However, this time it was different.

Skye walked past the sleeping Diehl and heard her name.

What?

"Skye, I'm sorry." Diehl's eyes were still closed.

He was not awake.

Skye pulled back the sheer drapes, unlocked the French door, and opened it. The gentle roar of the ocean filled the room, together with the morning breeze that swirled around Skye's hair. There wasn't enough sunshine this morning to kill the germs in the house, but the wind picked up, playing with the drapes. She tied up the drapes.

She turned on the fan to get more circulation going.

Lord Jesus, help this man. Something is going on.

As she entered the kitchen, Marlo was leaving with an empty basket. Chef Joseph was clearing the island. There were boxes of takeout Chinese food. The trash can was overfilled.

On the floor in front of the refrigerator were milk spills.

"Have you started the coffee?" Skye asked.

"Yep. Kona."

Skye nodded. The Brooks family liked Kona coffee. They sourced it themselves from Hawaii.

Skye opened the windows by the breakfast nook to air out the kitchen.

She donned some disposable gloves that Chef Joseph had brought with him, found a rag, and cleaned up the spill on the tile floor.

Marlo came in with more groceries. "That coffee smells good."

"Compared to the rest of the house." Chef Joseph got busy chopping up bell pepper and mushrooms.

Since Skye still had on her gloves, she tied up the trash bag.

"I'll take it out," Marlo said.

"Thank you."

Skye found new trash bags in the pantry and lined the tall trash can. She felt an urge to take another trash bag and clear out all the bottles in the living room, but they were not her bottles, this was not her house, and she did not want to overstep her boundaries.

While Chef Joseph prepared the food, Skye unloaded the dishwasher and put away the dishes.

Marlo returned, washed his hands, and started loading the dishwasher with Skye.

None of them mentioned Diehl, who was still in the living room.

When the coffee was ready, Skye poured a cup. It was hot. She placed it on a small tray and took it to the living room.

As she approached Diehl, his eyes opened. They were bloodshot red. "Skye?"

"Would you like some coffee?" she asked, trying to keep her emotions in check.

She had no idea what this man was going through.

"Do you have food?" Diehl sat up slowly, held his head with one hand as he took the cup from Skye with his other hand.

"Be careful. It's hot." She stepped closer to prevent a spill.

He smelled pretty ripe. Skye wondered when he had showered last, and whether he had remained in this state since Thursday when he left the note on the door, telling them not to cook for two days.

"Chef Joseph is making a frittata," Skye said.

"Good." He sipped the hot coffee.

"How about you go shower and clean up?" Skye asked. "Then breakfast will be ready."

He nodded slightly.

Then his eyes were on her.

Skye wanted to leave.

Outside, it started to rain a little. She had left her umbrella in her car, but it was a short dash.

She stood there listening to the rain, and prayed for Diehl.

Sometimes personal chefs were privy to private lives, but this time it was a man who had kissed her. It was getting too personal.

Thank God he hadn't been out there driving around while intoxicated—although he might have, because at some point he had to bring his stash home.

The smell of hot coffee and fresh rain began to push away the smell of liquor and human sweat.

"I have to go," Skye said.

Don't judge him.

"I'm sorry," Diehl said quietly.

To Skye, there was no problem in the world that God could not solve. To find a solution elsewhere—to attempt to drink away a problem—was a fool's errand.

Her parents had found out the hard way. No matter how much they drank, their money woes remained week after week. At thirteen years old, Skye couldn't understand why Dad would say they "deserved a drink" when the very next day, they ended up where they had started—or worse. Drinking had put them deeper into debt as they lost work and time with their kids.

Skye blinked. "You said sorry earlier." *How many times have you said it, Diehl?*

"I don't remember."

"In your sleep."

"Will you let me explain?" Diehl asked.

"To me? I have nothing to do with your problems."

His phone pinged again.

"It did that earlier too," Skye said. She still could not see the phone.

Diehl winced. "Can you get me some aspirin? Drawer in the kitchen."

"Which one?" Skye asked. She hadn't gone through all the drawers in the kitchen.

"Or maybe I put it in the pantry."

Before Skye could go to the kitchen, Marlo appeared with the bottle.

"Thank you," Skye said. "Did you want some water, Diehl?"

"No. I'll drink it with my coffee." Diehl held his head.

His phone rang.

"Where's my phone? Help me find it? I think I dropped it last night."

Skye was on her hands and knees looking under the couch and coffee table. She found it under an armchair on the other side of the table. By then, the phone had stopped ringing.

"Please check for me." Diehl swallowed the tablets with his coffee.

Skye read the notifications on the screen. "A bazillion missed calls from your son."

"Not my son." Diehl's chest shuddered and he began to weep.

"What are you talking about?" Skye swiped up. More notifications. Text messages from Ethan. No content. "Looks like he's been texting for a couple of hours."

"Ethan...Elisa... They're both not mine." Diehl lay down on the couch and covered his face with his arm. "What's the probability of that?"

"What on earth?" Skye sat down on an armchair near Diehl's head.

"The DNA test was negative."

"What? Seriously? But they sort of look like you —maybe."

"Not mine. They look like my dead wife, to be honest with you. However, their daddy is her Italian boyfriend—whom she'd been carrying on with for at least thirteen years."

"Thirteen years?"

"I know, right. Can you imagine?"

She could not.

"I'm responsible for them, but they're not my flesh and blood. How could it be?"

"That's tough."

Tears streamed down the sides of Diehl's face.

"Elisa...Ethan..." he moaned.

"They're in God's hands." Slowly, Skye began to sing Charles Wesley's hymn, "And Can It Be."

> Long my imprisoned spirit lay
> fast bound in sin and nature's night;
> thine eye diffused a quickening ray;
> I woke; the dungeon flamed with light;
> my chains fell off, my heart was free,
> I rose, went forth, and followed Thee.
>
> No condemnation now I dread;
> Jesus, and all in Him, is mine!
> Alive in Him, my living Head,
> and clothed in righteousness divine,
> bold I approach the eternal throne,
> and claim the crown through Christ
>   my own.

Skye thanked God she made it through the last verse without her voice cracking, even though she hadn't warmed up her vocal cords this morning. She had sung this hymn a countless number of times.

"I've lost everything," Diehl muttered.

"No, you haven't lost God."

Diehl seemed to ignore her. "You? Have I lost you too?"

Skye moved. She sat down at the edge of the couch where Diehl was, and put a palm on his chest. "I'm here."

He placed his palm over her hand. "Stay with me."

"Better yet, God stays with us," Skye said. "Once you belong to God, He does not leave you nor forsake you. '

"I need God."

"We all need God. He can solve all our problems."

"Isn't that simplistic?"

"Our problems are nothing to God. He has already solved the biggest problem of all: sin."

"I suppose."

"You think he didn't know about your DNA? He made your DNA."

"You're right."

"God is right," Skye corrected him. "Line up with God and He'll solve your most difficult problems. Nothing is impossible for God."

"I've heard that before. Grandpa Brooks..."

The phone rang.

Skye handed it to him. "Your son needs you."

He shook his head. "I can't. You talk to him."

So Skye answered the phone. "Hello?"

"Skye?" Ethan's voice was peppered with breathing. "Are you cooking for Dad today?"

"My chef is helping me. You're up early on a Saturday."

"Where's Dad?"

"He's... How are you?"

"We can't find Elisa."

"What?" Skye nearly fell off the couch. "Since when?"

"This morning... She wasn't in her room."

Skye stood up. "Did you call 911?"

"Grandma Rose did. We all tried to call Dad forever."

Diehl sat up and stared at her. He mouthed, "What?"

"What time is it?" Skye asked.

"I don't know," Ethan said. "The police are here. They want to talk to Dad."

"Okay. We'll be over there as soon as we can. Stay with your grandma. Don't leave her side."

Skye's hand shook when she hung up. "Elisa's missing."

Diehl jumped up, and immediately his hands reached for the armrest on the couch. "Owww."

"Drink the rest of your coffee. Go take a hot shower," Skye said. "Come downstairs and eat some breakfast. I'll drive you to your mom's house."

Diehl nodded. He could barely walk.

Skye could help him as far as the top of the stairs,

but she did not want to enter his bedroom. She caught Marlo's eyes and pleaded for help without a word. He instinctively understood and nodded.

He left the open kitchen and came over. "Sir, may I help you up the stairs?"

"Yes, please."

CHAPTER TWENTY-NINE

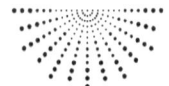

*R*eally, he should sleep it off.

Diehl leaned back in the reclined passenger seat as Skye took him on the short drive to Seaside Island across the bridge from St. Simon's Island.

"See if you can take a five-minute nap. I'll wake you up when we get there," Skye said.

"Do you know where the house is?"

"Yeah. Seb and I catered for your family when he was still in town."

Before Diehl realized it, Skye parked her car on the other side of the circular driveway to get out of the way of the police vehicles at the front door of Brooks Cottage.

There were several police officers in the yard and driveway. One came up to them on the driver's side. Skye rolled down the window, but Diehl spoke first.

"I'm Diehl Brooks, Officer. Elisa's father. I just got the message that my daughter's missing."

"Yes, Mr. Brooks," the officer said. "Detective Jeong wants to talk to you. He's at the guest cottage."

"Are my son, Ethan, and mother, Rose Brooks, over there too?"

The officer nodded. "That's where we're talking to the family. You cannot go in this house, sir. We're still going through it."

"Going through it?"

"It might be a crime scene or we might find something helpful."

"Please find my daughter." As Diehl heard his own words, he realized that, biological or not, Elisa was officially his. And so was Ethan. Diehl's name was on the birth certificates as the father of these children. They were his responsibility now.

God, if You hear my prayer, please bring Elisa home to us safely.

"We're working on it, sir." To Skye, he said, "Ma'am, if I may ask you to park outside this driveway —maybe on the curb in front of the neighbor's house, it will make it easier for our vehicles to get in and out."

"Okay. I'll do that."

After the officer went back to work, Skye put her car in reverse.

"It might be easier if we park next door at the guest cottage, rather than have to walk there." Diehl pointed down the road.

"I've gone there before, but whenever I did, it was with Seb's catering van—and someone else was doing the driving. Am I remembering it correctly that there's a winding driveway through some trees by a pond?"

Diehl nodded. "It's narrow and just one lane, so Mom got the house for a steal."

"And then they don't use it unless there's a party or for housing guests."

"That's what happens when there's money to spare and parties to throw—although I must say that my parents are getting a bit too old to host seasonal luncheons for power-grabbing politicians. So I wouldn't be surprised if they sell the guest cottage in the next five years."

Skye navigated the winding road slowly. "Wow. Don't let me drive into the pond, Lord."

Diehl grinned. "So far no one has done that."

"There's always a first for everything."

They were quiet for a while in the car as Skye tried not to hit a tree on the way to the guest cottage. "Glad I brought my little car instead of my usual van."

"This is a nice car." Diehl patted the seat's edge.

"My trusty Honda Accord." Skye parked the car and thanked the Lord.

She did it so casually that Diehl wondered what it must be like to be able to talk to God that way. Perhaps it was something she had trained herself to do over time.

"So much for my power nap." Diehl tried to get out of the car, but he still had a headache. The aspirin was kicking in, and so was the coffee, but he still felt dizzy.

He did not want Skye to help him out of the car. It would be caught on the security camera and perhaps used against him later by the Bishops to gain custody of the kids. That would be a fight he did not want to lose.

Then again, Isobel had done him much harm—led him down to the valley of the shadow of death with her deceits over the years. How could he not see through them all? How?

Perhaps he wanted to be blind to her faults. Was it love to dismiss sins? How was the way he had handled Isobel different from how Skye dealt with him this morning?

"Skye?" Diehl asked softly as he closed the car door.

Skye stood outside the driver's side. She was adjusting her crossbody bag over her shoulder. "Yes?"

"About this morning..."

"Let's talk later." Skye locked the car.

Nearby, the front door of the guest cottage opened. Cara walked briskly down the stone driveway toward them. "We've been trying to get a hold of you all morning. Your mother almost sent the police to your house."

"We're here now," Diehl said.

"Detective Jeong was in the family room talking to your mom. They dispersed a few minutes ago, and the detective went with Malik to the security office."

"Thanks, Cara. I'll go there."

"Hello, Skye." Cara nodded to Skye. She didn't say anything else to Skye.

"Nice to see you again," Skye said.

Ethan came running to the foyer as soon as Diehl stepped into the house. "Dad! Dad!"

Before Diehl could stop him in his tracks, Ethan wrapped his arms around Diehl and wept into his polo shirt. He could feel the boy's warm tears on his stomach.

"Have you eaten breakfast?" Cara asked.

"Yes," Skye said. "But if you have some toast and jam, Diehl might want some."

Diehl's eyes met Skye's. He knew she tried to help him with his hangover without making a fuss about it in front of his family.

"I'm not feeling well," Diehl said. "Might be something I ate."

Or drank.

"I have Pepto," Cara said. "Or Tums."

"I might ask you for them later."

"Everyone has been in and out of the family room getting interviewed," Cara said. "I've already talked to the police. Detective Jeong was going to interview the Bishops after he and Malik check all the security videos."

Didn't Ethan say that Elisa had been gone awhile? "When did they arrive?"

"About an hour ago. They came as soon as your mother called."

"An hour ago?" Diehl gently unraveled Ethan off his waist. "Didn't you try to call me and text me for the last few hours?"

Ethan's lips quivered.

"When did you know that your sister was missing?" Diehl asked.

Ethan didn't say anything.

"An hour ago? Two hours ago?" Diehl pressed.

"I don't know, Dad. This morning. The sun was up when she was gone."

Diehl felt warm fingers on his arm. Skye.

"Let's pray that she will come home safely. Right now you need to go to your mom," Skye said. "Ethan, have you eaten your breakfast?"

"I had cereal," Ethan said. "But if you cook me pancakes, I will eat them."

"We have pancake mix," Cara said.

"With chocolate chips in it?" Ethan's eyes grew wide.

Diehl chuckled. To Cara, he asked, "Have the police talked to him?"

"Ethan wouldn't talk to them until you got here. He's Dad's boy."

Diehl barely smiled. "Either that or he has a lawyer sense about him."

"Now that's scary." Cara laughed.

He watched Ethan hold Skye's hand and drag her down the hallway. "The kitchen is this way!"

Diehl walked upstairs where the family room took up the entire third floor. Before he reached it, he could hear Zeta's voice.

"If he can't even keep Elisa safe, then he's unfit to be her dad." Her voice was sharp. "We want custody of both kids."

Diehl hesitated at the door.

Should he go in?

Someone tapped him on his shoulder. He turned to look. A badge met him.

"Detective Terence Jeong," the man said, briefly shaking Diehl's hand. "Is there a place we can talk?"

"Not in there." Diehl shook his head.

"In-laws, huh?"

Diehl sighed. "We can go to the conference room downstairs in the security department."

"I just came from there. Ran up and down the stairs. Got my exercise quota for the day." Jeong panted. "And they call this a cottage?"

"Yeah, one of those things. The primary designer of most of the houses on the island called his creations cottages," Diehl said as he led the way to the stairs. "If you'd like to take the elevator, we could."

"No. It's fine."

As they went down the stairs, Diehl asked how the investigation was going. "I would ask if you made any progress, but you're still here and not out there looking for my daughter."

"Your daughter?" Jeong noted. "Zeta Bishop insisted you're not the father."

"My name is on the birth certificate. I was married to Elisa's mother when she was born. By law, I am the father. Also, I've raised Elisa and Ethan as my own. I've been there more times than Isobel when she was alive. I've also put aside college funds for them."

"Wish everyone had a father like that."

"Elisa's mother never said a word to me about the children's paternity." Diehl drew a deep breath. What if Isobel hadn't cared who her children's father was? Perhaps her main concern had been to stay with the man who could provide for her and the children.

That would be me.

"We arrived an hour and a half ago," Jeong said, jarring Diehl out of his thoughts.

"I found out Elisa was missing only half an hour ago." Diehl determined he had to be strong for Elisa. No matter what had happened to her since her disappearance, she needed her dad more than ever now. He had to do his best to protect her. And that included keeping full rein over his emotions and faculties.

That meant he couldn't be intoxicated. Not like Thursday and Friday.

It's my fault. I dropped the ball.

If he hadn't been having his own pity party at the beach house, he could have been at Brooks Cottage instead, spending time with his two children, keeping them safe.

Had Elisa overheard the adults talking about her biological father? Had Ethan?

Diehl wouldn't put it past the Bishops to be loud about it.

After the first revelation on Wednesday, the Bishops had adjourned to the guest cottage. Diehl decided to stay overnight in his old bedroom in his mother's house so that he could be with Elisa and Ethan. More than feeling sorry for them, he felt that he was the only person they had. He felt that the Bishops were after their own interests.

Late into the night, when he should have been sleeping, Diehl had doubts about his ability to be a father. Never mind that he had been one for the last twelve years.

He kept telling himself that he was a bad father, until he couldn't sleep. Shortly after midnight, he wandered around the house, berating himself for not finding out about Isobel's infidelities or believing they had been true. Before he knew it, he was sitting in Dad's cellar, inspecting vintages.

A few hours later, he drove home in the middle of the night and crashed in the beach house after scrawling a note for Skye and taping it to his front door. He couldn't remember the rest of it.

He hadn't emerged from his beach house until this morning when Skye drove him to Brooks Cottage.

"Lead the way," Jeong said at the bottom of the stairs.

Diehl nodded to Malik, who came to greet him. "Is the conference room available?"

"It is now," the chief of security said. He led them down the hallway to the room about a third of the size of the meeting rooms that Diehl was used to back home in Atlanta.

"Malik, Jeong is asking me some questions. Why don't you stay?" Diehl asked.

Basically, he needed a witness.

Malik nodded.

The door shut behind him, Diehl was alone with Jeong and Malik.

"Do you mind if I record this?" Jeong asked.

"Not if you don't mind that we record it as well." Malik swiped his phone and placed it on the table.

"Just asking some questions."

"Of course," Diehl said.

"When did you find out that your daughter was missing?" Jeong asked.

"Around eight thirty this morning when my personal chef was at my house. They woke me up, made me breakfast."

"They? One personal chef and at least one assistant?"

"Well, two personal chefs and one assistant."

"Big breakfast?"

"Not really. One chef was supposed to show up, but he didn't have the house key. I was fast asleep and didn't hear the doorbell. He called Skye, who does have the key."

Jeong nodded. "Details matter."

Diehl glanced at the clock. It was 9:15 a.m. "As soon as I found out, I showered, ate breakfast, and rushed here."

"Your girlfriend drove you here."

Diehl didn't correct him. "I have a headache."

"Where were you between the hours of seven and eight this morning?"

"I mentioned I was asleep."

"Your mom said between her and your son, they made many calls."

"Like I said, I was *very* asleep."

Detective Jeong waited.

Diehl glanced at Malik, who was stoic and silent sitting there.

"I was passed out," Diehl confessed. "I have no idea how long I slept. I only remembered eating some leftovers last night. Then I went to my living room and downed a few bottles of..." He waved his arms about.

They all waited.

"I can't even remember what I drank."

"You were passed out," Jeong said. "For how long?"

"Until Skye woke me up. My phone was making horrible noises. We had to find it. It was under an armchair."

Jeong scribbled on his notes. "Was she the only person with you in the house?"

"No. Chef Joseph and their assistant, Marlo, were there. They made me a delicious breakfast, made sure I had a steady stream of coffee."

"They? Does Skye cook?"

"She's my personal chef. Joseph fills in on the weekends when Skye doesn't work."

"What's her last name?"

"Langston."

"Was she a cook first or your girlfriend first?"

"Chef, sir. She's a chef."

"Sorry."

"She's my chef first." Diehl wondered what Skye would tell the detective if asked. "We just started hanging out these couple of weeks."

"Do you get drunk a lot?"

"No." Diehl was sure of it. "The last time I was drunk was right after Isobel's funeral one year ago, when I was upset she had died and angry that she left me with two motherless kids. I felt so bad for them. They were so young. However, I hired a nanny who did a great job before we had to let her go. The kids went to stay with their maternal grandparents for the school year. And here they are having their summer break with my parents."

"Has Elisa ever run away before?" Jeong jotted down some things on his notepad.

"I don't remember. We might ask the nanny. She doesn't want to talk to me since I let her go six months ago, not because she didn't do a great job, but because we didn't need her anymore."

"What's the nanny's name?"

"Romina Myers... She got married recently," Diehl said.

"Harrison is her new last name. She divorced a few months later, but kept her married name," Malik said. "I'll give you the contact information."

Jeong looked up. "So it's been a year since you were last drunk. And it just happens that the one morning you were passed out, your daughter disappeared."

Diehl moaned. "It's my fault. I should never have gone into Dad's cellar. I should have stayed above ground. Then maybe Elisa wouldn't have run away."

"She might not have run away. We're looking at all possible angles."

"Is that why your officers are combing my mother's house?" Diehl asked. "Taking fingerprints or something?"

"Let's hope we find her but I wish someone had called us sooner." Jeong closed his notepad. "I need to talk to your son, but he said he won't talk to us until you're here."

"I'm here."

"The sooner we find out where your daughter might have gone, the sooner we can get her back. Where is your son?"

Diehl took out his phone from his pocket and texted Skye. She told him where he was.

"Skye says Ethan's eating pancakes in the kitchen," Diehl said. "Do you want to talk to him in the family room upstairs?"

"That's fine. Somewhere he can be comfortable."

Diehl texted Cara to tell her to get the Bishops and Mom out of the family room. Detective Jeong would be interviewing Ethan there. He also asked her to take his toast and coffee upstairs.

Diehl didn't want to see the Bishops.

"You asked me earlier why it might be a coincidence for me to be passed out drunk at home while my daughter went missing," Diehl said. "I admit that it was a bad coping mechanism after finding out that both my children are not mine."

"That must have hurt."

Diehl glanced over at Malik to see his reaction. Malik just sat there.

"However, I am stronger than that, and I pray to God that never happens again. I am determined now, more than ever, to stay sober for my two kids—whether they are mine biologically or not. When they turn eighteen, they can decide for themselves where they want to go."

Jeong's face registered appreciation.

Diehl felt that he had gained the detective's trust.

"Did you ask the Bishops why they appeared at our home without any prior notification, and are still here the day Elisa vanished?" Diehl asked. "Everyone in the house knows they want non-parental custody of my children. They want to take me to court. My family attorney, Mark Gill, can fill you in on the details. Malik, could you give Detective Jeong his number too?"

Malik nodded.

"Do the two kids know what you all were discussing?" Jeong asked.

"To be honest, I don't know. All I know is that the adults agreed to keep it among ourselves until our lawyers get together."

"Walls have ears, Mr. Brooks. Walls have ears."

CHAPTER THIRTY

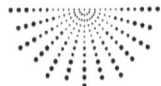

hile Diehl and Ethan were upstairs at the interview, Skye remained in the gourmet kitchen downstairs. She had been here at the guest cottage kitchen before. This had been where she and her brother would prepare dishes for Rose Brooks's many dinners, usually held in the ballroom on the same floor.

Since Sebastian married and moved to Athens, he ended his catering business. Skye still catered some via STL, but not for the Brookses. Chef Pierre had started his own catering business and had taken over all the work.

Skye missed this kitchen. It was charming, bright, and airy. In fact, she could see a hint of it in Brinley's beach house, which would henceforth remind her of Diehl.

Skye called Ivan and asked to be in the loop. Matt

had been keeping everyone updated, so Skye ended up in the group chat. She asked if she could participate and they said they had enough volunteers. Everyone at church was combing their own neighborhoods.

"Your job is to pray," Ivan told her over the phone. "And keep Diehl away from his dad's cellar."

Skye should have expected Ivan to know about his brother-in-law's problems.

"Something I should know?" Skye asked.

"I'll let him tell you himself. Pray for him. I'm assuming you're already on Mrs. Gonzalez's prayer loop."

"Yes. All of us in the women's group are."

"Good. We'll update Brin, and she'll post."

"Thank you, Ivan. How is Brin doing? I was going to call her instead of you, but I didn't want to bother her."

"Good. She's asleep right now, and her phone is on airplane mode."

After ending the call, Skye busied herself cobbling together cheesecake ingredients. It was a good thing that Cara and Chef Pierre kept the pantry and refrigerator in the guest house stocked. Otherwise, she'd have to bake something else.

When Ethan came back to the kitchen in tears, hugging his dad's waist like he couldn't possibly let go lest the cruel world also took him away, Skye's heart broke into a million pieces.

Lord Jesus, I pray for this poor boy. Comfort him, make him strong. Bring his sister home to us alive.

She would have gone to Ethan, except her fingers were covered with butter. She had been pressing her graham cracker mix to the bottom of a pan while waiting for Ethan to finish his interview so that they could make the rest of the cheesecake together.

Skye washed her hands quickly in the sink, dried them on a clean dish towel. "What happened?"

She couldn't ask if everything was okay, since it clearly wasn't.

Her eyes met Diehl's. His were pained, as though whatever hurt his son also hurt him. This was clearly Ethan's father, no matter what the DNA results said.

"We had a difficult interview upstairs." Diehl grabbed a clean paper napkin off a countertop and dabbed his son's face. "Ethan didn't remember much because he was sleeping in his own room this morning."

Of course. "Would you like a glass of water, Ethan?"

Ethan nodded.

Skye gave Ethan his water in a cup so he could hold the handle. She patted his head gently. When he handed her the cup back, she wiped the tears off his face with her apron and brushed back the hair matted to his forehead.

Diehl poured himself a cup of coffee. "Do you know where the sugar cubes are?"

"I have no idea. Cara's gone to the grocery store with Chef Pierre." His sous chef, Hans, was taking a cigarette break outside. Skye would've preferred a non-smoker assistant, but this was not her house.

"I'll survive." He drank the coffee black.

"Cream might help."

Diehl shrugged.

"Do you still have a headache?"

Diehl nodded. "I should lie down."

"You never did get your toast." Skye opened the refrigerator, where Cara stored some sprouted spelt bread. "I see jam here. Mixed berries. I can make you a piece of toast."

"Okay." Diehl took the bread and jam from her. "I can make my own toast. I'm not helpless."

"Did I say you were?"

Ethan raised his hand. "I'm helpless."

Skye smiled at the boy, but his eyes were elsewhere now. They grew wider as he stared at the springform pan on the island countertop where Skye had poured the graham cracker base.

"Did you get started without me?" Ethan asked.

"Just the base. We'll do that soon, but you know that we have to keep it refrigerated until tomorrow before we can eat it."

"Tomorrow?" Ethan frowned.

"It will set overnight."

"What do we eat now?"

"Well, we have fruits and such for snacks, and then Chef Pierre is grilling some fresh fish for lunch."

"I don't want fish. I want cheesecake."

"I can text Cara and ask her to get a small cheese-cake at the grocery store if you like."

"No!" Ethan snapped. "I want *your* cheesecake!"

Skye couldn't be flattered at the tone of the nine-year-old. Without glancing at his dad, who was still nursing a hangover, Skye prayed for words to calm the boy down.

"I'm glad you like my cheesecake, Ethan." Skye bent down so that she was eye to eye with him. "Did you know that I can make more than cheesecake?"

"Like what?"

"I can make all sorts of cakes and pies and *fruit* dishes." Her emphasis on fruit made Diehl chuckle. "Those might be ready faster than cheesecake. Take a blueberry pie, for example. As soon as it comes out of the oven, we can eat it. We don't have to wait overnight like for cheesecakes. However, I heard that your grandma's Chef Pierre is making a special dessert just for you."

"What is it?"

"It's a big secret that even I couldn't guess. He wouldn't say. It's a special top secret."

"Wow. A secret. I like secrets."

"You do?" Diehl's eyebrows rose. He finished his coffee and was going for another cup. But there was no more coffee left.

"I can make more coffee," Skye said.

"It's your day off. You don't work here." Diehl put the coffee mug into the sink.

"She works hard, Dad." Ethan placed his hands on Skye's arm.

"I know she works very hard. Today, she shouldn't be working."

"Then who's going to make my cheesecake?"

"Except for that."

Skye's phone pinged. She checked it. The search for Elisa had started. She closed her eyes and prayed. She couldn't say too much in front of Ethan, but she wanted to encourage Diehl.

"Our entire Sunday school class—and half the church—is spreading out all over the island in their own neighborhoods to see if anyone saw Elisa," Skye said.

Diehl was visibly moved. "Ivan meant it when he said the church would help."

"That's what we do."

"I should go with them."

"This is your neighborhood though. Stay in this area?"

"Malik has already made the rounds—all the security guards for the different cottages are on high alert."

Skye nodded. "And?"

"And nothing. No one saw anything."

"She just vanished," Skye said.

Ethan tugged at Diehl's shirt. "Is Elisa dead?"

Diehl knelt down in front of his son. "I don't think so."

"It's my fault." Ethan cried.

"No, no." Diehl hugged him.

Skye placed her hand on Diehl's shoulder. "Guys, we've been indoors for a while. It's nice outside, so how about we go for a walk and get some sunshine? Then we can come back in and make the cheesecake?"

"Good idea. I need some fresh air," Diehl said.

Skye put away the pan and the rest of the cheese-cake ingredients into the refrigerator.

Ethan grabbed Skye's hand. "I know how to get outside."

It must be the sheer size of this cottage that caused a little boy to declare such a thing. And this was only the guest cottage. Skye shook her head.

Ethan led them down the hallway to a large ball-room, where Skye and her brother had catered many Christmas dinners and fundraisers over the years. They crossed the floor to the French doors.

They were locked.

"Good thing I came along." Diehl pressed a button on a panel by the door. "Malik, could you unlock this door for us, please?"

"Yes, sir." The reply came just before a click.

They were outside on the terrace, the midmorning sunshine basking down on their heads as they made their way down a stone path.

Ethan dragged Skye toward a garden gate. "We're going to Grandma's garden."

He declared it like everyone was just going to go along with the kid, and sure enough, both Skye and Diehl didn't say anything.

Skye had no plans beyond being outdoors. She knew about the backyard of both the guest house and the main house, but she hadn't had the opportunity to wander around the Brooks properties. Every time she had been here prior to today, she wore a chef's hat and worked with her brother's catering crew in the kitchen.

Today, she wasn't sure what hat she was wearing. A family friend?

No one had questioned her presence here so far.

Oddly enough, Diehl's mother, Rose, didn't care whom he brought home today. Skye recalled Brinley telling her and Avery that Rose had been trying to find a girlfriend for Diehl since his wife died, but she had not succeeded. Today, Rose was distraught, in her own little bubble, and had gone upstairs to rest. She had been complaining about wanting to go back to her own house next door, but the police were still combing the grounds. That was what they got for having such a big house.

Cara had seen Diehl kiss her outside the grocery store last Sunday afternoon, and probably assumed they were an item.

"Dad, hold Skye's hand," Ethan ordered.

Diehl hesitated.

"Now."

He did.

It bothered Skye a little bit that he had hesitated. They had kissed twice, and now he was coy? What was that about?

His warm fingers intertwined with Skye's. He said nothing as they followed Ethan through the garden gate to a pretty garden courtyard—like those she had seen in Savannah—with wrought iron benches here and there surrounded by hydrangeas and tall Japanese crepe myrtles.

"Wow," Skye said.

"This used to be just grass," Diehl said. "Mom

decided to put a garden between the two cottages. She had the trees planted fifteen or twenty years ago, and no matter how much they grow, they won't block our view of the ocean since it's to the side."

Skye nodded, noticing that Diehl hadn't let go of her hand.

Ethan tore away and ran around the garden, his arms wide, the wind in his hair, and he made a roaring sound.

Skye wanted to take a photo of the moment, but she was afraid to overstep her boundaries. When she realized that Diehl had let go of her hand, he was already five or ten feet away, recording Ethan running laps around Skye.

She laughed as she watched Ethan.

Was this how it felt to have a child? Skye wouldn't know. She used to feel that she was too busy for relationships, but now...

Ethan collapsed in a heap on the grass. "That was some exercise."

Diehl stopped recording. He pointed to a bench nearest to them. "Would you like to sit down?"

Ethan sat up. "Would you like to hear a story?"

"I love stories." Skye sat down on the bench first, and Diehl put his arm around her shoulders.

"Mommy told us this one."

Mommy? As in Isobel Brooks? This, Skye had to hear.

Diehl stiffened next to Skye.

"Once upon a time, there was a boy and girl who loved each other very much." Ethan jumped to his feet.

"Their moms and dads didn't like them to be together, so they had to meet in secret."

Uh-oh.

Diehl retracted his arm.

Skye could hear him expel a breath.

"For many, many, many years, they had to find ways to see each other." Ethan clasped his hands together. "Many, many years."

Even after they had married other people. Skye saw the picture now.

Elisa and Ethan were Isobel's love children.

Skye glanced over at Diehl. His face was literally frozen. He crossed his arms over his chest.

"The boy and the girl grew up, but they still loved each other." Ethan separated his hands and stretched them apart. "One day the boy said he didn't love her anymore. He was tired of waiting for her to get a divorce. So he married someone else."

Whoa.

"Out of the mouth of babes," Diehl muttered.

"But!" Ethan ran around the small courtyard, arms outstretched. "They still loved each other. So they flew back and forth, and back and forth, to keep their little secret."

The garden gate creaked.

"What little secret?" Rose Brooks stood there. Her hair was disheveled, and her makeup looked pasty in the morning sunshine.

"Grandma! Grandma!" Ethan ran to her and hugged her. "Did you enjoy your nap?"

"No. Malik said the police are done and I can go home now. What are y'all doing here?" Rose asked.

"I was telling a story, Grandma. You missed it. Want me to tell it again?"

Diehl cleared his throat. "What did Detective Jeong say? He hasn't texted me."

"I caught him just as he was about to leave minutes ago," Rose said. "He has interviewed everyone, and he's putting a team together. I should donate more to the police. Do you think they could use new vehicles or something?"

Skye didn't say anything.

"Thank you for being there for Diehl and Ethan," Rose said to her.

"No problem. Today is my day off, so I have time."

"Ivan called, saying that Pastor Gonzalez will be stopping by after lunch," Rose said. "I don't want this event to turn into a religious fest."

"Fest?" Skye asked. She wanted to know what Rose meant by that, but it might lead to an argument. Instead, she tried something else. "Our church prays for people all the time. We'll pray for Elisa's safe return."

"Does that even work?" Rose snapped.

"God is all knowing, all powerful."

"Y'all are so naive." Rose frowned.

"Mom," Diehl said.

"We tried prayer. Parker still died. Now I have only three kids left." Rose's voice cracked. "And Diehl's marriage was always broken. Now the kids are not even his, and they're in his will."

Ethan burst into tears.

Apparently, Rose had forgotten that Ethan was standing right there.

"Mom, stop." Diehl was on his feet, rushing toward Ethan. Skye followed him, leaving Rose standing at the gate.

"No!" Ethan backed away and started to run toward the ocean.

CHAPTER THIRTY-ONE

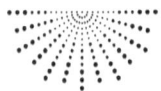

*E*than dashed past the swimming pool shaped like a violin, beyond the grass, over the board-walk, and out to the beach and ocean.

Skye couldn't keep up because of her sandals. She stopped at the edge of the dunes and took them off. Then she ran barefoot across the boardwalk, chasing after father and son. Before she could reach them, her phone pinged again.

It was a prayer update from Brinley. Even though she was on bedrest, she could still pray. Everyone was doing everything they could to help out.

Pray for God's wisdom for Detective Jeong and the police department.

Skye immediately stopped walking. She closed her eyes and prayed.

When she opened her eyes, Diehl had tackled Ethan, rolled him over on the sand, and tickled him. Sand flew everywhere as Ethan kicked and laughed.

For a snapshot moment, father and son seemed to have a break from missing Elisa. Skye prayed they would have many days like this.

Yet we're not promised tomorrow.

By the time Skye reached them, they were covered with sand. Sand stuck to Ethan's face, smeared over his tears.

"We better go wash in the ocean or Grandma won't let us in the house," Diehl said.

"Grandma." Ethan's voice lowered. "What did she mean in the garden? What is a will, Dad?"

"It means I *will* tickle you some more." And Diehl did.

"Stop! Stop!" Ethan laughed and laughed.

Diehl glanced over at Skye. "Want to join us?"

"Nope. I'm not getting sand in my hair." Skye stood where she was, about five safe feet away.

"Take a picture of us?" Diehl asked, reaching for his phone.

"I'll use mine." Skye retrieved her phone from her pocket, and then realized that she had left her purse in the kitchen back at Brooks Cottage. She hoped it was safe there.

She took several snapshots of Diehl and his son posing in the sand. She wondered how long they could distract Ethan from the reality of his life.

That story that Ethan had told them in the garden wasn't a fairytale, was it? It was Isobel's tragedy. How awful it must have been for her not to be with the person she loved.

Skye wasn't privy to all the details, but it seemed

like a strange tale of love found and love lost. Caught in the middle of it was Diehl. What kind of loveless marriage had he been in? Had Isobel married him for his fortune?

She could not see Diehl as a tortured hero, but the poor man had an unfulfilled marriage. He had told her last Monday, when they made breakfast together, that he had married Isobel when she was pregnant with their first child. That child died, but they stayed together.

If Ethan's story was to be believed, then Isobel had continued her affair with her boyfriend throughout their marriage in a twisted tale of deceit and deception, producing two children, whom she had passed off as belonging to Diehl.

How could she do that to him? How could he not know, though? Had his work taken so much of his time that he could not get away to be at home?

Skye remembered Brinley mentioning that her sister-in-law often stayed for months on end in Hawaii and Italy while Diehl worked in Atlanta, not taking any vacation in years.

If Skye were his wife, she would love him and only him for the rest of her life. She would love no one else, be with no other. She would always stay with him and raise their kids together.

Of course, it was all hypothetical.

Nothing could come out of their summer romance. Skye felt that there was still something holding Diehl back from showing her whether he really wanted to be with her or whether she was only a filler for his lonely summer days before he returned to his corporate world in Atlanta.

Perhaps his heart had been broken to the point that it had hardened toward things related to love.

And things of God.

Until Diehl was aligned with God again and experienced the full measure of God's love, he could never truly love another person. He wouldn't know what it meant for Christ to love the church, and for a Christian man to love his wife.

"Thank you." Diehl brushed off the sand from his shirt, pants, and knees.

Ethan was running again. This time, toward the ocean.

"Ethan!" Diehl kicked off his shoes, and went after him.

Skye stood where she was, looking at the private beach. There was no one else out here at this time. Diehl and Ethan played at the ocean's edge, the waves swirling around their ankles. Above them, the morning sun shone through puffy clouds against a sky-blue backdrop.

Mom had told her that they named her after the sky.

She had rarely mentioned her middle name to anyone. Who wouldn't laugh to hear that her full name was Skye Blue Langston. At least Sebastian had a normal name.

Skye made her way across the packed beach sand

toward Diehl and Ethan. They had plunged into the ocean in the clothes they were in.

Ethan splashed water with his palm. "I wish Elisa was here!"

And then it started all over again. Tears streamed down his face.

"Shhh." Diehl put an arm around his son's shoulders. "We'll get her back."

Skye motioned for them to get out of the water.

Diehl nodded. Father and son came onshore.

Ethan was still crying. "Why did they take her?"

"They? Who?" Diehl asked.

Ethan quietened. "Don't let them take me too."

"No, I won't." Diehl held his hand.

"I'm so afraid, Dad."

"Don't be afraid."

Skye tried to find something to say, but all she could think of was an old verse. "Psalm 56:3 says, 'Whenever I am afraid, I will trust in You.' *You* being God. That's how I'm not afraid, Ethan."

Diehl nodded to Skye. "That's a good verse."

"Whenever I'm afraid, God is with me," Skye said. "When I'm happy, God is with me. When I'm sad, God is also with me. Good days, bad days, He's still with me. There's no need to be afraid."

Diehl reached for Skye's hand. "When are you sad?"

"Not right now." She let him hold her hand as they walked back toward the boardwalk.

This was just like the beaches on St. Simon's Island across the bridge. All these beaches faced the

Atlantic Ocean. The only difference—other than the fact that Seaside Island beaches were all private, whereas St. Simon's Island beaches were a mix of both private and public—was the type of beach houses here.

The main Brooks Cottage over the dunes was typical of the houses here. Built in the twenties and thirties through the fifties, they had been designed for the then nouveau riche as well as those who had inherited wealth, like the Brooks and Urquhart families. Being more affluent, the Urquharts had bought an island of their own between St. Simon's Island and Tybee Island, an hour north.

Skye hadn't been here on Seaside Island for at least a year since Sebastian moved away, but the houses looked the same like they had been—

"What's that? A green roof. Most of the roofs are brown or red." Skye pointed to a coastal style roof peeking over some dunes several houses to the right of Brooks Cottage. "Ooh, look at all those windows. I've always wanted..."

She didn't finish her sentence.

"Not just a new roof," Diehl said. "They razed a house built in the fifties down to the foundation, and rebuilt a brand-new cottage sometime last year."

"When was the last time they allowed such a thing on Seaside Island? Was that a historic home?"

"Yeah, but somehow they got permission to destroy it. It's the same floor plan as a few others on the island, so I guess they won't miss it. They wanted an open floor plan."

"I love open floor plans." She wanted to ask them

to go on ahead, while she walked down the beach to take a look.

"Let's go see it," Diehl said.

"No," Skye said. "We need to get back to the house and put the cheesecake in the oven."

"Just the outside. A quick peek?"

"No. Let's get back to the kitchen." Skye started walking toward the boardwalk leading to Brooks Cottage.

"Don't you ever leave the kitchen?" Diehl followed her, Ethan in tow.

"It's my comfort zone."

"Where the comfort food is," Ethan said.

"I know who owns that house," Diehl said. "I'll take you there someday when all this is over."

"Sure." Skye nodded. "I was only curious, is all. Sorry I was distracted. It's a lovely beach house. Someday..."

"Do you want it?"

Diehl's question caught Skye by surprise and she had no answer for him.

"I'm serious," he added. "He might sell. He doesn't live there anymore. He prefers Palm Beach."

Skye felt uncomfortable. She couldn't afford such a house, and Diehl's offer seemed to imply something. She didn't want to go there. "Right now, I'm thinking of cheesecake."

"Cheesecake!" Ethan jumped up and down. "And a surprise dessert from Chef Pierre!"

"You don't miss anything, do you?" Skye asked.

"Nope." The boy shook his head vigorously. "I miss Elisa though. I hope they bring her back."

"They who?" Diehl asked.

Ethan clammed up.

"Ethan." Diehl squatted down in front of his son. "Whatever you can tell me could help bring Elisa home safely."

"I don't know anything, Dad."

Skye wondered if Diehl had the same thoughts as she did. They should get a child counselor or a psychologist to talk to Ethan. He seemed to know more about his sister's disappearance than he let on.

"If you remember something important, please tell me, okay?" Diehl held Ethan's arms gently.

"I will, Dad."

Skye touched Diehl's arm, as if to say something. He looked her way and nodded, as if to say he got it. Then he reached for her.

All three of them walked together back to Brooks Cottage, hand in hand.

Cara greeted them before they stepped off the boardwalk. "Your grandma was looking for you, Ethan!"

"Which one?" Ethan broke free from Diehl and Skye and sprinted toward Cara.

"The one from Hawaii. I'll walk with you to the guest cottage, if that's okay with your dad." Cara glanced at Diehl.

"Stay with him and bring him back," Diehl said.

"Will do." Cara followed Ethan as the boy hopped

and skipped along the stone path on the grass toward the guest cottage, where his other grandparents were.

Diehl was still standing on the boardwalk. His eyes were on his son.

Skye looked around. There was no shade. And no benches on the boardwalk. A railing separated them from the tall sea oats swaying in the afternoon sun. It was hot, but they were both wearing sunglasses.

"Let's go inside," Diehl said.

Skye nodded. "How are your in-laws doing?"

"Their own thing. Not talking to me much. You see that they keep to themselves and eat their own meals."

"Makes no sense to me, but I don't know them."

"Makes no sense?"

"Well, they're your mom's guests, right? Free room and board. So why wouldn't they eat with your family?"

"I don't know. That's how they've always been. In fact, Isobel…"

"Yes?" Skye wanted him to finish his sentence. A long time ago when she had been grieving for her parents, it took her a while to be able to talk about them. Once she could, the healing began. "Was she like her parents too?"

"She swung back and forth. Sometimes she liked to be with people. Other times, she liked to be alone—not even with me. Just alone all by herself, doing her own thing, in her own room."

"Her own room?"

"We each had our own home office."

"Oh, I see."

Diehl led Skye across a yard of freshly cut grass. Beyond some butterfly bushes, a stone pathway led to the Brooks Cottage backyard terrace.

It was a little bit cooler in the shade, but Skye would prefer to go indoors for the air-conditioning.

"I think the Bishops felt bad for bringing the DNA news, and then while they were here, Elisa disappeared. In a sense, they can't blame my mom or me. They were here too on Friday night and Saturday morning," Diehl said.

He was back to talking about the in-laws. Isobel was a memory.

"How much do the kids know about their biological father?" Skye asked. "I wonder if that could have made Elisa run away—if that's what she was doing."

"That was one of my first thoughts too." Diehl unlocked the back door by texting Malik to open it. "Zeta has a sharp tongue, but also loose lips. I wouldn't put it past them to talk about it in front of the kids or within earshot. Do you think Elisa ran away?"

"You mean to Italy to see her biological dad?" Skye hadn't thought about that option, but she did now. She followed Diehl up the stairs. "She's twelve, so they would probably let her fly alone, but she would need a ticket and a valid passport."

"None of our credit cards were used. Someone might pay for the tickets for her, but her passport expired last month. I haven't had time to renew it."

"So we hope she's still in the country."

"Hopefully."

"Best thing we can do is pray," Skye said.

"Is it?" Diehl asked.

"Well, what else can you do but wait for Detective Jeong to find your daughter? Of course, Ivan's search party will help. Ultimately, you need divine intervention to keep Elisa safe."

"I believe you."

"Believe God." Skye entered the empty kitchen. There was a note on the table.

Gone to get groceries.

The scrawling signature had a chef's hat illustration on top of it.

Diehl ran a finger on Skye's arm. "Warm."

"Sticky and sweaty," Skye said. "I need a shower."

"You can freshen up in any of the guest bedrooms upstairs."

"Thank you, but after I show Ethan how to make the cheesecake, I need to go home. I have a lot of things to do before my trip to Miami Beach."

Diehl nodded. His eyes were on her lips.

Skye slipped away to wash her hands in the sink. She did not want him near her because she was sweating all the way through her blouse, back and front. If she had thought about it before they went outside, she would have stayed indoors. It was a warm day in June. How could she forget?

"Are we okay?" Diehl asked.

"I'm sweaty," she admitted.

"I am too."

"Could you get me the cream cheese and eggs and

the rest of my ingredients? It's in the fridge in a folded shopping bag."

Diehl chuckled. "You're putting me to work."

"Wash your hands first."

"Ordering me around." He did as he was told. He put the bag on the island. "When did you go to the grocery store?"

"I didn't. Cara said I could use whatever she has and she has everything."

"I feel like this is all wrong." Diehl stood close enough to Skye so that he didn't have to raise his voice to be heard.

"Wrong how?"

"I can't be in the kitchen while my daughter's out there."

"As soon as Ivan gets organized, join the search team."

"Malik said I might be in the way."

Whatever his net worth was, surely there was a way for him to canvass the neighborhood—if it would be helpful.

"Are you in the way? Or are you afraid to show yourself in town because you feel that you don't know anyone and have not socialized? Now you need help, and you're concerned that no one out there would care about your daughter going missing. Am I right?"

Diehl's eyes flared up, like he was about to get angry.

Skye wondered if she had overstepped the line in the sand. She placed a hand on his chest. "I'm sorry. Let me rephrase that."

He placed his palm over her hand. It was warm to the touch. "You are right. I don't feel worthy of getting help from the community because I don't actually live here. I come once a year at Christmas or not even that."

"You work too much."

"Now I don't work at all."

"Pray about—I mean, let's pray about how you can be most useful," Skye said. "For example, Tristan Rao from church is too busy to walk from house to house on your behalf, but he has many patients all over the island and he's got a following on social media. Since you gave Ivan and his team permission, Tristan has posted your daughter's photo all over social media. Someone should see something."

"How did you know what Tristan did?"

"We're friends on Facebook."

"I'm not on Facebook."

"So find something you can do. For example, you can go to Malik's office in the guest house. Isn't that his operational center? Whatever he and Detective Jeong do, you'd be in the know."

"Good idea. Why didn't I think about that? It seems to be common sense now that you mentioned them."

"Because you're in the fog. You're used to being the CEO of a corporation, but this is...uh..."

"Real life?"

"Well, you also have a son. He needs something to do. Keep him occupied." Skye didn't have to say that if they spent enough time with Ethan, they might hear him say something noteworthy about his sister.

"I'll call Ivan and ask to be in the loop."

"He doesn't want you to worry."

Diehl raised his eyebrows. "I don't need to be coddled."

Skye smiled. Ran a finger down his arm. "No?"

He chuckled. "No."

"If you want to go with Ivan, then ask Malik to send along some bodyguards. Matt and Ben are with him, but they're taking separate trucks."

"How do you know all these things?"

"I know you've got a lot on your mind."

"So you kept up with Ivan for me." Diehl sounded...jealous?

"Not Ivan. Matt. He texts me with updates, but I haven't heard from him in a few hours."

"Matt. Should I be worried?"

And her phone pinged. She checked it. "Okay. Tristan says one of his patients saw a girl about that age going into a Walmart in Brunswick. They called Detective Jeong, but Hayden lives in Brunswick near the Walmart, so he's checking it out."

"Add me to that loop." Diehl retrieved his phone. "I'm out of battery again."

"Right now, I need to finish making this cheese-cake to keep Ethan occupied."

"I need to keep busy too." Diehl pecked Skye's cheek before she realized what happened. "Sweaty."

"I told you." She stepped away. "I don't want to get too far ahead before Ethan shows up. He'll be upset or something. I don't have time to start over with a second cheesecake."

"Text Cara to bring him back." He gave Skye Cara's number. "I'll have to charge up my phone."

"Well... He needs to spend time with his other grandparents." Skye retrieved the pan of graham crackers from the fridge. "This is the longest time I've taken to make a cheesecake. And it needs to set overnight, besides."

"Do you keep all these recipes in your head?" Diehl asked.

"Well, only those I make often." Skye looked around. "Could you help me find an electric mixer?"

"I can't believe you're cooking again. Don't you get tired of it?"

"Not most of the time. Occasionally, I do get tired and need a break. That's why I take weekends off. If I don't do that, I'll burn out."

"Like me," Diehl said. "I worked every day of the week non-stop."

"That's bad for your health."

"I burned out, as you know. And got banished to this island..." Diehl stood near her at the kitchen island, but he did not touch her. "Where I met the most beautiful woman in the world, who doesn't judge my past or my present—but treats me fairly."

Skye didn't know what to say.

"I believe God brought you into my life." His eyes looked pained. "I hope you'll stay. Don't go."

"You mean right now literally or do you mean figuratively?" Skye asked.

When Diehl didn't reply, Skye said, "Are you projecting someone else's behavior onto me?"

Diehl bristled. "What do you mean?"

"I'm still here, Diehl. I haven't left. In fact, I'll probably always be living here on this island until I grow old and die. The question is where *you* will be."

Diehl couldn't answer her, and it told her all she needed to know.

CHAPTER THIRTY-TWO

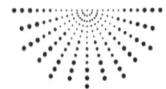

"*H*ow could there be nothing?" Diehl was upset, and he couldn't hide it. The security videos on the giant screen in front of him in Malik's office clearly showed no strange activity for the past twenty-four hours.

Mom grunted. She was sitting in the office chair next to Diehl. They had been watching a series of sped-up videos, a presentation from Malik Metcalfe, only one of the best chiefs of security whom Dad could hire.

It was only four o'clock, but it felt like the longest day of Diehl's life—longer than the day Isobel died. After this meeting with Malik, he wanted to catch Skye before she went home to shower and pack for her trip. Diehl didn't want her to go to Miami Beach for the week, but this wasn't her problem. Besides, he wanted to show her that he was a leader, not a follower.

Somewhere at the back of his mind, he knew she was concerned about him personally. He made a decision not to be intoxicated anymore—for the sake of his children.

So help me, God.

Diehl took Skye's advice to keep busy at Malik's operational center. He was in a familiar setting—an office—and he felt like a CEO again, meting out orders and getting status reports. He was in his zone. How did Skye know exactly what to advise him?

And earlier, she knew what he needed to cure his hangover so he could be functional today. Where he had fallen short, she'd picked up the slack—keeping in touch with Ivan's search team to filter information for him so that he didn't get overwhelmed while having a headache.

Now he felt better physically, though his body was still tired. He hadn't gone back to the gym since he arrived on St. Simon's, so perhaps it was time for him to get in shape again. Exercising was also a good stress relief.

If something fatal happened to his daughter, he knew he was going to break.

"Remember a few years ago when Aunt Ella was here?" Mom asked. "She walked right out of Brooks Cottage and nobody saw her. Something is wrong with this multi-million-dollar security system, is all I can say."

Diehl shrugged. "What kind of planned operation was it that could abduct a twelve-year-old right under our noses?"

"That's the same question Detective Jeong is asking," Malik said. He worked the mouse on his laptop that mirrored the bigger screen hung on the wall. "So we went back through the tapes for the entire evening, from the time Elisa had her dinner—the last time we saw her—through this morning when Ethan ran to Mrs. Brooks's bedroom to tell her that she was gone."

"And that was shortly after eight o'clock this morning." Diehl recalled that had been around the time Skye found him asleep in his living room.

However, Skye also said that the notification history on his phone said Ethan had been trying to call Diehl for a couple of hours.

Diehl retrieved his phone. He checked the notification history, which he thankfully hadn't cleared. The first time Ethan texted him was at 6:07 a.m.

Ethan had known that Elisa was gone at least two hours before he let his grandma know.

Diehl's first thought, as nefarious as it might be, was whether the Bishops had anything to do with it. Diehl had disclosed his concerns about his in-laws to Detective Jeong.

"Have you given all of this information to Detective Jeong?" Diehl asked.

"Yes, sir." Malik looked up from his laptop. "As soon as we put it together, they had it."

"Put what together?" Mom asked.

"Data from all fifty-seven cameras around the Brooks Cottage, ma'am."

"And the guest house?" Diehl asked.

"That too. Also no activity there. The Bishops stayed in." Malik drew a deep breath. "Frankly, we're stumped."

Mom made a face. "Interesting timing they have, to come here just in time for Elisa to disappear."

"Mom." Even as Diehl said it, he felt the same.

"We'll keep an eye on them if you want us to," Malik said.

"Go back through the tapes again," Mom said. "Maybe you missed something."

There they went, talking about *tapes* again in the twenty-first century. Mom and Malik were not the same age, but they seemed to speak the same language. Dad too.

Mom and Malik chattered away about tightening security around the perimeter. She was afraid she might get abducted.

"Don't worry too much about that," Diehl said. "Not only does the cottage have security, the entire island does too."

"But we don't have a fence around the house."

"Dad doesn't want a fence," Diehl reminded her. "It ruins the view of the beach and ocean, he says."

"Oh, the irony." Mom laughed. "Now he's in Atlanta, landlocked and no ocean."

Landlocked.

Oddly enough, Diehl missed his job in Atlanta. Was this sabbatical long enough for him? It had only been two weeks. At some point—after they found Elisa

—he'd have to go home to Atlanta before the new school year started. Already the private school the kids would return to had sent him copious emails about this and that.

He hadn't had time to read them all.

But the eventuality was clear: he had to go home to Atlanta by August.

Landlocked.

Would Skye appreciate the big city? She had been to Atlanta before, but would she want to stay there?

It didn't look like anything could come of their relationship, could it? Once summer blew over, they'd each return to their regular lives.

He shouldn't have kissed her.

But he'd wanted to.

He wanted to be with her more and more.

Focus, Diehl.

He told himself twice to not think about Skye right now.

He stared at the frozen collage of videos on the big screen. They showed various camera angles all around Brooks Cottage where Elisa had spent her last night on the island. There was nothing more to see.

"When did Cara leave last night?" Diehl asked.

"Eleven, as usual. She never leaves until Chef Pierre does."

"When did he leave?"

"Chef Pierre and Hans left at nine o'clock," Malik said. He cleared the screen and displayed the chef's van, parked outside the kitchen, where catering vans parked whenever the Brooks family hosted dinner parties in the ballroom on the other side of the kitchen.

"That's a big utility van," Diehl said. "His usual?"

"He usually drives a smaller van, but it was in the shop. This was his catering van."

"With lots of room inside." Diehl wondered if Elisa had stowed away. "Who drove it?"

"Hans," Malik said. "The police questioned Chef Pierre and Hans extensively twice before they left this afternoon."

"After they see this video, they might have more questions for him." Diehl turned to Mom. "Do you have Dr. Endecott's number?"

"Why?" Mom asked.

"Just in case we need him for any reason."

Mom blinked. "You mean if the kidnappers hurt Elisa in any way?"

Well, Diehl hadn't thought that far, to be honest. He only wanted to ask Dr. Endecott for local referrals to a child psychologist who might be able to coax more information out of Ethan. Someone who worked on weekends. Monday might be too late.

Diehl was convinced that Ethan knew something more that he hadn't told Detective Jeong in the interview this morning. The child had been distraught, like his grandma was all morning.

As for Diehl, he felt better this afternoon. His headache had gone away. He could use a nap, but he'd just go to bed earlier tonight.

"Did you check my house in Atlanta?" Diehl asked Malik.

"Yes, sir. Nobody's there. It's all locked up. Alarm is working."

"Okay. So Elisa didn't find her way back home to our house."

"Not that we know of," Malik said. "If I may, there's one more thing."

"What?" Diehl and Mom said together.

"May I suggest that we offer reward money for the safe return of your daughter?" Malik asked.

"How much do you recommend?" Diehl asked.

"Ten thousand is a good start."

"Double it," Diehl said. "It's my daughter we're talking about."

And he meant it.

Mom looked tired, worn out. She started to cry softly. She chuckled as she cried. Very odd. "Look at me. I'm crying over my granddaughter—and yet she is not mine, not biologically."

"My name is on the birth certificate. I'm her father." It was all Diehl said. He realized that he had been aggrieved for two days over Isobel's deception, but Elisa's disappearance changed everything. He wanted her back alive and well. They could fix or sort out the rest.

Malik nodded slightly. "Spoken like a father, sir."

Diehl didn't reply. He wasn't sure if he was much of a father—being drunk on the job. If he had stayed at Mom's house instead of passing out at Brinley's beach cottage, would Elisa still be with them today?

Well, that won't happen again.

He made the promise to himself and to God—if

God heard him. He wanted God to hear his prayers. But the barrier was there. Skye had pointed it out the night they FaceTimed.

You know you can't be partially saved. Either you're all saved or you're not. You can't be half-saved.

Was that why there seemed to be something preventing Diehl and Skye from being transparent with each other? They didn't seem to be on the same page spiritually.

"Mom, do you want to rest for a little bit before dinner?" Diehl asked. "I'll walk you back to the big house."

Diehl didn't disclose his real reason for wanting to take Mom back to her own house next door. After Detective Jeong and his people had cleared the premises, Diehl had sent Skye and Ethan—together with their refrigerated cheesecake—to Brooks Cottage, accompanied by one of the security personnel. He did not want his family to stay any longer than necessary in the guest cottage with the Bishops.

Truth be told, he did not trust the Bishops at all.

"A short nap will do me good. I'm worn out." Mom nodded. "Oh, I need to call Brin. See how she's doing on bedrest."

"I'll come back," Diehl said to Malik.

"Very well, sir," Malik said. "I've called Helen Hu per your request. She's sending one of her PIs and he's arriving after dinner at eight."

"I want to be here when you brief him. Who is Helen sending?"

"Earl Young. I was his commanding officer in the Army. He's solid."

"I don't know him though. Is he one of Helen's best?"

"Yes. She said to trust him like you'd trust her. If you like, I can text you when Earl gets here," Malik said.

"Do that."

"We go to night shift at eleven, but I'll stay through the night."

Diehl nodded. "Feel free to use any guest bedrooms if you need a rest."

"Thank you, sir."

"Do you have food?" Mom asked.

"Yes, ma'am." Malik helped her get out of her chair. "Chef Pierre cooked a whole refrigerator of food we can heat up. We probably have enough to last us through Sunday night."

Before they adjourned the meeting, Diehl asked Malik to do something for his kids.

"Is that necessary?" Mom asked when she heard what Diehl wanted.

"They're my kids," Diehl said.

"Not biologically."

Mom's words hurt badly. Diehl tried not to react, tried not to recall the lies that Isobel had told him in their years together. He tried to compartmentalize it, file it away for later.

"Officially, they are," Diehl said. "If I'm not responsible for them, who would be?"

"My cold son has a heart, after all." Mom squeezed Diehl's arm.

"I will let you know, sir," Malik said.

"You do that." Diehl didn't have to add that he didn't care how much it cost.

Diehl accompanied his mom across the lawn to Brooks Cottage. He wondered why they didn't build a covered walkway, but Dad might say it'd ruin the view.

"I wish your dad were here," Mom said. "Even though he doesn't know what to do every time, I like him around. He's the stable type, you know?"

"Yes, he is. I feel guilty that he has to go back to work because I couldn't handle it." Diehl followed Mom to the terrace. That was the closest entrance from the guest cottage.

Mom smacked her lips. "You can handle it. You just need to manage your emotions."

"My emotions?"

"Yes. You lost Isobel, but you didn't give yourself time to grieve. You sent the kids away to live with their other grandparents—not us, but that's another matter—so you didn't have to see the kids, who remind you of your dead wife."

"Was that it?" Diehl wondered if there was some truth in what Mom just told him.

Mom nodded. "I'm always right. So listen. Isobel has been gone for just one year. Some people grieve longer. My friend Marguerite is still grieving, and her husband's been dead four years."

"Really?" Diehl hadn't seen Marguerite Urquhart

since Sherman's funeral. "I thought she was keeping busy."

"Yeah, trying to marry off her nieces." Mom chuckled. "I don't think you like Siobhan as much as you like Skye, do you?"

"Siobhan and I are friends on account of her cousin, Jared, but no, there is nothing between us." Diehl didn't say that he would like to date someone older than Siobhan.

Someone like Skye.

They took the elevator upstairs.

"Do I need to look up my Rolodex of eligible girls for you?" Mom asked.

"That won't be necessary." Diehl tried to be nonchalant about it so that Mom didn't read too much into it.

Yes, he was trying to keep his emotions in check.

"Because you have found the one?"

Diehl held the elevator door while Mom exited. "Maybe I have. But right now, the only thing that matters to me is to get Elisa home safely."

The carpet on the second floor was plush and new. Every few years, Mom would replace the carpet and some furniture and repaint the entire house—including the library on the third floor that hardly anyone used. It was a waste of money, but it gave Mom something to do between her trips to Paris to see her youngest daughter, Zoe, and her family.

Diehl himself hadn't seen Zoe in several years, but it made no difference to him. He was closer to his other sister, Brinley, primarily because he had nothing in common with Zoe.

"Right. So you are keeping your emotions in check." Mom walked toward her bedroom door.

"Not when we find out who took Elisa. I'm going to beat the tar out of her abductors."

"Emotions." Mom wagged a finger. "Let the law work its course."

"You're so wise, Mom." Diehl hugged her. "Do you want me to come get you at six?"

"Don't forget I'm eating dinner with the Bishops tonight."

"Ah, that's right." Diehl had already forgotten. Truly, he did not want to see Zeta. Isobel had looked like her, with dark wavy hair. Every time Diehl saw Zeta, all the memories of his sorry life with Isobel kept flooding back. That had been one of the reasons he went home to Brinley's beach house on Wednesday night instead of staying here with his kids.

"If you don't mind, I'll have Malik come get you," Diehl said.

"You're not eating with us?" Mom asked.

"I'm not hungry."

"You will be in two hours."

"I'll be working at Malik's office. You heard him. Helen's PI is coming to town. I'll have a working dinner with Malik. We need to go over some stuff." Whatever stuff it was, it was going to be more important than eating dinner with the Bishops.

After Mom shut her bedroom door, Diehl bounded down the stairs to the kitchen, and heard laughter even before he reached there. Skye and Ethan having fun.

"Dad!" Ethan said when Diehl entered the kitchen. He was stirring something in a mixing bowl. Flour was on his forehead. "We're making Elisa's favorite food. She might be hungry when she gets home."

If she comes home.

"We just made pigs in a blanket." Ethan pointed to the oven. "When do they come out of the oven?"

"In a few more minutes," Skye said. She had on an apron, and looked very domestic.

"If you eat all that, you won't be able to eat dinner," Diehl said.

"Grandma said it's okay if we eat our own dinner at five instead of at six."

"Did she?"

Ethan nodded. "She said she'll eat with my other grandparents, but she really wants Grandpa Ned here. Can you call him and tell him to fly home for dinner?"

Diehl felt bad. It was his fault that his parents were living apart for the summer. He made a mental list to call Dad and talk to him about the family business. There was something he had been wanting to talk to him about—long before he burned out.

The signs had been there.

The oven buzzed and Skye opened it. The pastry-wrapped hot dogs looked delicious.

Ethan jumped up and down.

"Don't get too close to the oven door." Diehl put out his arm between Ethan and the oven.

"We have to taste-test them," Ethan declared. "If they're good, we'll make another batch when Elisa gets here."

Elisa?

Diehl approached them. "Ethan, do you know something we don't? When is Elisa getting here?"

Ethan shrugged.

What if Elisa didn't come home? What if she was dead?

Diehl drew a deep breath. "Where's Cara?"

"She just left before you walked in. Said she was going next door to the guest cottage." Skye sifted more flour into the bowl that Ethan had been stirring in. "Something about keeping an eye on things."

With the Bishops, no doubt. "Chef Pierre with her?"

Skye nodded. "She said the Bishops are eating dinner with Rose and Ethan tonight. Are you going?"

"No, I'm not invited." Diehl wondered if he should ask Skye to dinner, just the two of them. He could use a break. They could drive to The Priory.

"Do you want me to make you dinner before I leave?" Skye asked.

"You're not staying?" Diehl held his breath.

Skye shook her head. "I need to get home. I have a lot to do before I fly out tomorrow evening."

In the chaos, Diehl had forgotten that Skye would be going out of town the following week. "When are you coming home again?"

"The food festival is over on Thursday, but I'm

going to spend the long weekend with Sebastian and his wife."

"Oh." Diehl hoped no one saw his heart drop to the kitchen floor. "I'm...we're going to miss you."

"I'll be praying for Elisa to come home safely," Skye said. "Pastor Gonzalez called. The whole church is praying."

"Tell them thank you. Wasn't he supposed to come over?" Diehl hoped he hadn't dropped the ball on being a good host to the pastor's visit.

"Grandma told him not to come," Ethan said. "I heard her say it on the phone."

"Oh." What else had his son heard on the phone or elsewhere?

Diehl felt unhelpful simply standing there watching Skye and Ethan work. "Is there another apron for me?"

"A few are hanging in the pantry behind the door." Skye pointed. "Does that mean you're helping us make cookies?"

"What happened to the cheesecake?" Diehl found a white apron. He was trying to put it on when Skye came over to help him tie it around his waist in the back.

"Still in the refrigerator. Don't touch it until tomorrow after church," Ethan said. "Are we going to church, Dad?"

"Yes, tomorrow morning." It dawned on Diehl that it was still Saturday. "Today is such a long day."

"Seems like it," Skye said softly.

Diehl reached for her hand as she started to walk back to where Ethan was, still stirring the mixing bowl.

Skye stopped in her tracks.

"I'm glad you're here," Diehl said.

"I'm glad she's here too!" Ethan shouted. "Now come over here and help me."

"Yes, Chef Ethan. Coming." Diehl chuckled. "But first..."

He nuzzled Skye's ear.

"We need to talk," he whispered.

Before Skye could say anything, the oven timer went off. And she walked away.

CHAPTER THIRTY-THREE

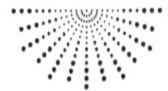

*A*fter Skye left to let the Brooks family have dinner by themselves, Diehl missed her so much he texted her before and after dinner, and before he went to bed. He made sure to tell her he hadn't had a sip of anything stronger than Cara's sweet tea—which was probably potent in itself.

After eleven, Skye stopped replying to his text messages. Diehl figured she must have fallen asleep. He wondered how she looked with her eyes closed.

Well, at least she could sleep.

Diehl could not.

Maybe it was all that sugar in the sweet tea that kept him awake. Maybe he was worried about Elisa's well-being. Maybe he was even more worried that Ethan had kept secrets from the family—secrets that could very well determine whether Elisa was dead or alive.

He had called Dr. Endecott on his private line

after dinner, and the family doctor promised to send a child psychologist after church on Sunday to have a talk with Ethan.

Past midnight, Diehl still couldn't sleep. He was in his old childhood bedroom again, facing the ocean. This was his sister's favorite room in the entire cottage. It might be why she had constructed a similar top-floor main bedroom in her beach house to echo this design, where French doors opened to a balcony that overlooked the beach and ocean.

He sat outside on the open deck, listening to the waves of the ocean. The moonlight cast a pale, charcoal-like hue across the entire beach and ocean.

Diehl felt nothing.

He didn't feel any sorrow about Isobel anymore, not after what she had done to him for the last fourteen years. The secrets she had hidden from him. The lies. The deceit.

He could shed no tears for her.

Also gone was his desire to run to the bottle tonight. Two floors down from here was the pit of despair. Right now, all he wanted to do was run to God —like Skye would do.

Indeed, Skye had been a good spiritual influence on him.

Diehl also had good feelings toward Elisa and Ethan, in spite of their circumstances. They had come to the world through no fault of their own. At least Isobel hadn't aborted them. Once they found Elisa, he would take them both home to Atlanta, and they could start over.

God, let us find Elisa safe. If You would do that for me, I'll go to church the rest of my life.

As he said it aloud in the wind, he wondered if God heard his offer to bargain.

Would Skye have approved such a prayer?

He wondered what she would say. The strong Christian that she was, Skye might tell him not to test God. Something Grandpa Brooks had said so long ago.

Never test God, kids.

Diehl knew he could not begin to approach the spiritual maturity that Skye had. How long had she studied the Bible to get there?

He recalled the conversation they had on Face-Time on a Friday night, when she questioned his salvation. Well, she hadn't put it that bluntly, but what was he to think when she told him at least twice how to accept Jesus. He was sure he had done so back in his college years.

Pre-Isobel.

Diehl remembered thinking that he had been too good for Isobel. Now he thought that Skye was too good for him.

Had he fallen in love with a woman he could not have?

Skye seemed to be set on living on St. Simon's Island. He had a job in Atlanta he could not leave. Although the two places were only five hours of driving each way, Diehl had made up his mind not to be separated from his significant other ever again.

Was Skye his significant other?

He wanted her to be.

"God, I think she's the one." Diehl could tell right away. In his mind, she was perfect.

Her Christian faith was stronger than his—wait. He wasn't sure if he had faith in God at all. For the last fourteen years, he had only reserved faith for himself. He hadn't been to church in years—except for funerals and weddings—until two weeks ago when he suddenly attended all services at Seaside Chapel.

Thanks to Skye.

The songs she sang, the trio she organized, had both drawn Diehl back to church. Who'd think that at nearly forty years old, he'd start playing accompaniment for a couple of Christians at a church he had rarely frequented since Grandpa Brooks died.

"Welcome home," Pastor Gonzalez had said to him the first Sunday they ran into each other two weeks ago.

Home?

How could he be home when he did not feel close to God?

He felt a light spray of rain on his face. He padded back into his bedroom and shut the door. He felt a bit thirsty from the salty teriyaki chicken that Chef Pierre had cooked at dinner.

However, thank God he did not feel any desire to run to the bottle. Maybe he didn't want to apologize to Skye again. Maybe God was in the process of removing that desire from him.

All he wanted to do right now was run to God.

Diehl left his bedroom. The hallway had night-lights here and there. Ethan's room was dark, but the door was cracked.

Diehl walked quietly down the stairs to get some water from the kitchen. At the foot of the stairs, he saw that the kitchen light was on even before he reached it. He heard the refrigerator door opening and closing.

There was Mom at the island, eating a dollop of cheesecake.

"Mom." Diehl sighed.

"Busted." She grinned. "Want some?"

"Is that Skye's cheesecake?"

Mom shrugged. "There's only one in the fridge."

"Is it done yet? I heard her say it has to stay overnight."

"It's a bit jiggly, but it's good enough. Want some?" Mom opened and closed several drawers until she found a cake cutter.

"Well, okay. A small slice." Diehl found a dessert plate in one of the cabinets.

This kitchen was entirely too big for him. He liked that smaller kitchen in Brinley's beach house, the one that Skye cooked in.

Mom cut a piece of cheesecake for him. They sat at the island and ate in silence.

Then Mom spoke. "I want you to know that you, Brin, Zoe, and Parker all belong to your dad and me."

"Good to know." Diehl kept eating.

"You were never adopted. I never had an affair."

Diehl noted that she did not say whether Dad ever did.

"It never crossed my mind that Isobel would..."

Mom stopped herself. She ate another bite of cheesecake.

"She was lost, Mom," Diehl said.

"Lost?"

"Lost—when you don't know God, you're lost."

Mom pointed a fork at him. "Are you lost?"

"I might be. I'm closer to God now than I ever was, but I think I am not yet in His family. I feel like I am still outside the fence, looking in." And holding hands with Skye on the other side of the fence.

He wanted to be on the same side of the fence with her. Very much.

"Did Brin get to you?" Mom rolled her eyes. "She's been inviting me to church. Usually she tried non-Sunday events, you know, as if I'd overlook the fact that it's still at church."

"Grandpa used to take us to the same church."

"He's dead now."

"And in heaven. Christians believe that they will go to heaven when they die."

"This is heaven for me." Mom said it like she truly believed it.

"Is it, Mom? Our bodies grow old, and we have health problems. Aging notwithstanding, we have problems. Work problems, family problems. We still don't know where Elisa is, for example. For all we know, she might be..." Diehl dared not say it.

Mom shook her head. "So young. So young."

Diehl reached over to pat her shoulder.

"When I was twelve, I never thought of running away," Mom said. "Who would run away from free food and free lodging? We might not have been wealthy like your dad's side of the family, but we had enough to get by. Elisa stands to inherit billions—unless we choose not to give any to her. Why would she run away?"

Diehl decided not to parse what Mom just said. Yes, there were people who lived better lives while earning less than the Brooks family.

Like Skye.

"That's the thing, Mom. Brin, Ivan, and Skye have something we don't." Diehl was sure now, more than ever, that whatever he had tried to believe in college had been incomplete. If he had truly believed in Jesus, then whatever Pastor Gonzalez preached at church wouldn't have sounded half-foreign and half-familiar. It would all be familiar, wouldn't it?

"Don't go there. Jesus is just an idea, you know?" Mom slid off the barstool to put away the rest of the cheesecake.

"I used to think that too," Diehl said. "To some, He might be a concept, a character. To Brin and Ivan and Skye, Jesus is the Son of God, who can save my soul—and yours too, Mom—from the pit of despair and rescue me from the fires of hell. That's what they've been telling me. It's a bit different from what I heard in college. To be honest, I don't know what I believed in college. It's like I need a spiritual reboot or do-over or something."

"Don't be dramatic, Diehl. Don't make me disown you." She closed the refrigerator door.

"What is disown?" A little voice asked.

Ethan.

Diehl spun around on the barstool. "Aren't you supposed to be sleeping, young man?"

"You too, Dad." Ethan frowned. "Why are you eating Skye's cheesecake?"

"I thought this is a community cheesecake." Diehl put his fork down slowly.

"Uh-uh. We worked very hard on that." Ethan approached the remaining cheesecake on Diehl's dessert plate. "I don't think it's set."

"Do you want to check and see?" Grandma asked, opening the refrigerator door again.

"Do I have to brush my teeth a second time tonight?" Ethan looked at Diehl for an answer.

"Yes, son."

"Then no. I'll just have water, thank you." Ethan waited by the island, next to Diehl's cheesecake.

"Sounds good to me. Get it yourself, Ethan." Diehl continued eating.

Mom shook her head at Diehl's response. Whatever. "The child is nine. He knows how to push the tab to get cold water from the fridge."

"He can't reach the shelf to get a cup," Mom said.

"Let's not spoil our little prince."

"Is my father a real king?" Ethan's eyes widened.

"Figure of speech," Diehl said.

"I figured you were fibbing." Ethan took the cup of water from Mom. "Thank you, Grandma. You're so good to me."

Mom patted his head.

"When is Skye coming back?" Ethan asked in between sips. "She didn't have dinner with us."

Diehl shrugged. "After church tomorrow—today—she's going to visit her brother in Atlanta."

"Atlanta? We live there too. Can we go?" Ethan put the cup of water carefully on the island.

"No. We're going to stay right here until Elisa comes back." Diehl polished off the last bite of cheesecake. It was delicious, but he knew he'd have to walk off about two pounds in two months. Or more.

"Are you joining Ivan's search party?" Mom asked.

Diehl nodded. "They're having a search committee meeting Sunday after the evening service at Ivan's house. I'll go for us."

"What exactly are they going to do?"

"The committee wants to strategize. So far, Ivan has led the charge to distribute fliers all day Saturday. The whole church is involved, going door to door in their own neighborhoods to ask if anyone has seen Elisa. The techno-savvy high schoolers and college kids are going online to show her photo in every social media platform."

"Twenty thousand dollars might get us a lead or two," Mom said.

"At least." That was Diehl's hope. "Of course, Detective Jeong will take the calls and sift through the tips."

"Dad?" Ethan asked.

"Yes?" Diehl rinsed off the dessert plate and fork, and put them in the dishwasher. After church, Cara would come over and add more dirty dishes and start the dishwasher.

"Take me to church, Dad."

Diehl pointed to the clock on the wall. "We'd better go to bed if we want to make it to the church service on time."

"What about Sunday school? I want to see my new friends."

"Sunday school starts in eight hours." Diehl could survive on four or five hours of sleep, but Ethan needed more sleep than that. "If we stay up all night, we won't make it. Or we'd sleep in church."

"That's what happened to Elisa last week." Ethan laughed. "She stayed up all night Saturday night, and she fell asleep in church. Do you remember, Dad?"

Of course he remembered. Elisa fell asleep even before Pastor Gonzalez began his sermon.

"What was Elisa doing staying up all night?" Diehl asked.

Ethan's eyes widened. He pursed his lips.

"Ethan?"

"I'm not a tattletale."

"No," Diehl said. "We're beyond that. If you know something that can save Elisa's life, you need to speak up now."

"Or your sister might die," Mom added.

"Mom." Diehl glared at her.

"Die? I don't want Elisa to die." Ethan burst into tears.

"Shhh. Mom, you're scaring him." Diehl reached for his son. "Ethan?"

"I didn't mean to listen at the door, but she was talking loudly," Ethan said.

"What did you hear?"

Ethan refused to say.

"You better tell your daddy," Mom said.

"Shhh." Diehl turned to Mom. "Why don't you go to bed and let me talk to Ethan?"

Mom walked out of the kitchen. "Good night, y'all."

"Is Grandma mad at me?" Ethan's lips quivered.

"No. She's just tired and needs to get some sleep, you know?" Diehl hoped it was true.

Ethan nodded.

"Son, you remember when you were learning to wear big boy pants?" Diehl asked.

"I was growing up."

"Yes, you were. Now I'm asking you to grow up here." Diehl pointed to his head.

Ethan's jaw dropped. "You want me to wear big boy pants on my head?"

Diehl choked. "No, that's not what I meant. I want you to grow up overall. Like Dad is a grownup. So I'm speaking to you like you're a young man growing up."

"Oh. Okay. Whatever that means."

"It means that your sister is missing, and we're doing everything we can to find her. We need to put on our thinking caps and try to remember everything that can help find your sister before something bad happens to her."

Ethan nodded. "Skye said that God knows where Elisa is."

"Yes, He does."

"And that God will keep her safe."

"Yes, while we try our best to find her. Are you with me?" Diehl put out a fist.

"Okay." Ethan gave Diehl a fist bump.

"So. Let's talk. What did you hear one week ago last Saturday night?" Diehl asked again.

Ethan made a face, like he was in deep thought. "Elisa was talking to someone on her phone."

"Who was this person?" Diehl wanted to ask if it was a friend from her school in Hawaii, but he didn't want to lead the witness. "Did it sound like anyone we know?"

"I couldn't hear that part. I only heard Elisa's voice."

"Makes sense." Diehl wondered why Ethan was eavesdropping on his sister. However, he recalled that when he had been in middle school himself, his younger sister Brinley had often dropped in unannounced in his room to see what he and Parker were doing. Often they were talking about girls at school, but most of them might have been Brinley's friends or classmates. She hated it that they wouldn't let her in on their little conversations.

"What did Elisa talk about on the phone?" Diehl asked.

"I don't remember." His words were curt.

Hiding something? "It might help the police find her."

"Is she in danger?" Ethan asked.

"Yes." Diehl believed so.

"She talked to Romina."

Romina! "Your nanny?"

"You know she and Romina are closer. She cried a lot after you let Romina go."

Okay. We're getting somewhere.

Diehl tried not to freak out. He had no idea his daughter felt that strongly about her nanny. Perhaps Romina had become more of a surrogate mother than he had thought. "And?"

"Elisa wanted to know how to find a Greyhound. Is she getting a dog, Dad? I want a dog too."

Greyhound? As in Greyhound bus? That was news to Diehl.

"When Detective Jeong asked you this morning—I mean Saturday morning—whether you heard anything, why didn't you tell him this?" Diehl hoped he hadn't lost the tenuous connection he had with his son this moment by bringing up the interview on Saturday that hadn't gone as well as he'd hoped.

"Elisa will be mad at me for listening at her door," Ethan mumbled.

She wouldn't be mad if she were dead.

Diehl swallowed.

"I don't want to get Elisa in trouble, Dad."

"She's already in trouble." Big trouble.

CHAPTER THIRTY-FOUR

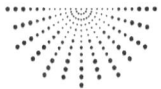

e need to talk.
　　　　While getting ready for church on Sunday morning, Skye wondered what Diehl had in mind when he whispered those words in her ear at Brooks Cottage the afternoon before.

She prayed that it wasn't bad news.

Without reading too much into it, Skye reminded herself that their more-than-friendship had been on the fast track. While they had known of each other for years, they wouldn't have interacted with each other had it not been for Diehl's sister.

As far as Brinley was concerned, Diehl hadn't shown Christian fruit.

No doubt he was an upright citizen and a moral man. In spite of his wife's infidelity, Diehl had not cheated on her, according to Brinley.

Skye could see why Diehl had driven himself drunk. The news must've been awful the first time he had heard it. She could not imagine how Isobel had hidden the secret from him for thirteen years, and died without personally explaining her side of the story— although she had left clues of it with her children, which Ethan had expressed in his skit in the garden on Saturday.

Bizarre.

Skye picked a simple pastel summer dress from her wardrobe and paired it with a pair of light teal sandals. She hadn't worn that dress since the year before, but she had pressed it before storing it away.

It wasn't her turn to bring breakfast to Sunday school, so she decided to eat oatmeal instead. Usually, she would cook steel cut oats on the stove-top, but today, she felt lazy. Instant oatmeal to the rescue!

She scolded herself for dressing up first before she ate because she spilled a blob of oatmeal—with cinnamon and apple bits—on the front of her dress. Because it was plain pastel, she could clearly see the stain.

Sigh.

As she ran upstairs to change, her phone rang. It was Diehl. He wanted to FaceTime.

"Not while I'm changing, buddy." Skye chuckled.

She almost hadn't taken the call. "Could I call you back in a couple of minutes?"

"Sure."

Skye took more than a couple of minutes to select another dress because she wanted to look halfway decent on FaceTime.

She found a modest dress with a buttoned-up front and puffy sleeves. Was this too old-fashioned?

She berated herself for being ridiculous because the clock on the wall warned her she was going to be late for Sunday school if she didn't hurry up.

At the end of the long five minutes, she ended up with a light pink silk blouse over a pair of white stretch trousers.

And out the front door she went. In her car, she put on her headset—which messed up her hair—and called Diehl back as she drove to church.

After all her hard work of choosing what to wear to FaceTime Diehl, she ended up on audio only so that her hands were free to drive.

"Sorry," Skye said. "I spilled oatmeal on my dress and had to change. I'm on my way to church. Sorry, can't FaceTime."

"You don't want me to see you driving?" Diehl sounded amused.

"I don't want to be distracted in the fifteen minutes it will take me to drive to church."

"Well, I have a progress report that you can share with our Sunday school class, although Ivan will probably do it if he's there today."

Our Sunday school class.

Did he say *our?*

"Any progress is good. Praise the Lord." At the red light now, Skye waited patiently for Diehl to explain.

"I've been up most of the night," Diehl said. "Detective Jeong just left us after talking to Ethan, Mom, and the Bishops."

"Ethan is talking?" That would be progress indeed.

"Yeah. He overheard Elisa talking to Romina last week, so the police are following up on that," Diehl said. "You know, his former nanny? She still lives in Atlanta. It could be a big clue."

"Hopefully it's not child trafficking." Skye wished she didn't have to mention it.

"I hope not." Diehl went silent for what seemed to be at least half a minute. "Please pray it's not that."

"Why don't we pray now?" Skye asked.

"Now?"

"Yes. Dear Heavenly Father, we turn over Elisa to You right now. You know who took her and where she is. You said that if we don't ask, we don't get, so I pray that You will bring Elisa home to us safely and unharmed. In Your Holy name, I pray. Amen."

"Amen," Diehl said. "Why didn't they take both Elisa and Ethan? Only Elisa vanished. The police said there's no sign of a break-in. Cara set the security alarms before she left the night before. And she unset it at six when she came back on Saturday morning."

Skye remembered something. "I've been meaning to ask you about the security cameras, but had no chance yesterday."

"You left before dinner."

"I had a lot to prepare before my trip out of town."

"Well, Malik found nothing. I wish I had been here the whole time. It never crossed my mind that Mom's house would be unsafe for my kids."

"Not unsafe, is it? If Elisa left the safe place, then she is outside the circle of safety."

"Good point." Diehl yawned. "I sent Ethan to bed at three in the morning, and he's still sleeping right now."

"How much sleep did you get?"

"I haven't gone to bed. After Detective Jeong talked to Ethan again, he wanted to talk to the Bishops. I hung around in case he needed me for some reason. After he left, I spent the last half an hour talking to Ivan. I had to wait until dawn to call him. Didn't want to wake my sister."

"That's considerate of you." Skye pulled into the Seaside Chapel parking lot in record time due to low traffic this early in the morning. She put her car in Park and continued listening.

"Mom is up now. I don't think she had enough sleep. She's all cranky and upset," Diehl said. "She's getting all sorts of crazy ideas about the Bishops. She thinks there's a conspiracy to make me look like a bad father so that the Bishops can take away my two kids—biologically theirs."

Skye unbuckled her seat belt. "What do you think?"

"I don't know, to be honest. Elisa is twelve. When I was that age, I got into all sorts of trouble without any help from my parents or grandparents."

"When I was twelve, I had no idea that one year later, I would lose both of my parents. My world changed." Skye didn't want to dwell on the past. "Anyway, sounds like you and Ethan won't be able to make it to church this morning."

"I doubt it. After I talk with you, I'm going to bed for a nap. We might make it to evening church."

"Or you can catch the live stream replay in your pajamas." Skye stepped out of her car with her purse and Bible. "If I see Ivan in Sunday school, I'll ask him about the search and rescue."

"Are you coming over after church?" Diehl asked.

Skye didn't directly answer him. "Are you still at your mom's house?"

"Yep. I'll be here all day so Detective Jeong can brief us all at the same place and time. Ethan would be glad to see you."

Skye wondered if Ethan was the only one. "Do *you* want me to?"

"Yes." He did not hesitate. "Please come for lunch. I'll save a seat for you."

Skye looked both ways before she crossed the small lane between the parking lot and the front door of Seaside Chapel. One couldn't be too careful—even if the parking lot was full of Christian drivers.

"I want to see you at lunch—if you don't have other plans." Diehl's voice sounded earnest.

"I was going to ask Avery to have lunch with me to discuss Brinley's baby shower that got canceled. Next week, she's delivering all the baby gifts without me since I'll be out of town."

"But you haven't asked her."

"Not yet. I will see her in Sunday school." Skye nodded to the greeters at the door. They had stopped handing out the Sunday morning bulletin because many people simply threw it away. To save paper and ink, the bulletin was posted on the church's app and on the website.

"I asked you first," Diehl said. "Please say yes."

When Skye didn't reply right away, Diehl kept talking. "I was hoping you'd have lunch with me, and then I need to talk with you about something before something else."

"So two things?"

"Yeah."

"And they can't wait until I get back next week?"

"One can, but the other can't."

"You could talk to me on the phone. Or email me. Or text me." Skye sat down on a bench outside her Sunday school class.

"It's not the same, is it?"

His answer seemed to be loaded with memories and angst. Skye figured that Diehl wouldn't do well with long-distance relationships.

"I haven't left town," Skye finally said, getting it.

"I know."

"All right. You can be quite persuasive. I'll see you at lunch at Brooks Cottage." Skye decided she'd have her meeting with Avery on FaceTime from Atlanta instead. "What time do you want me to be there?"

"I know church lets out at noon, so let's say twelve forty-five? We'll eat at one."

"Okay. I better go now. Good morning to you." She didn't mention his name in public. People were coming and going in the church hallway, and someone could pick up a name if she said it.

Not that it mattered.

Still.

"It'll be a good morning when I get my Elisa back," Diehl said.

"You know, it's still a good morning, no matter what. I've learned to be hopeful and yet be aware that this is a sorry world we live in, full of sin and despair. Job lost all his children, for example."

"That must've been tough."

"I know, right. More than his business and livestock, he lost his kids."

"That's one of the things I like about you, Skye," Diehl said.

"What?"

"You are honest with me. You don't sugarcoat your opinion. Thank you for the reality check." Diehl paused. "You're right. This situation could go either way, but God is still God."

"Yes, He is." Skye's heart soared. Diehl got it.

CHAPTER THIRTY-FIVE

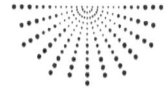

hen Skye drove up to Seaside Island after church, Diehl was sitting on the steps outside the front door of Brooks Cottage in an old T-shirt and faded shorts, waiting for her, apparently. He waved even before she pulled up. After she parked, he opened the driver's side door for her.

"Valet. Nice." Skye chuckled.

"At your service, ma'am."

"How long have you been waiting?" She stepped away from the car so that Diehl could shut the door for her.

"I don't know. I had to come out here to get some fresh air."

"A walk on the beach would be fresher." Skye walked with Diehl back to the house.

"Then I wouldn't see you coming up the drive-way." He hugged her and planted a quick kiss on her cheek.

"Prickly." Skye made a face.

"I'll shave soon." Diehl rubbed his own chin. "To my credit, I showered."

"Well, good."

"Thank you for coming to lunch."

"How is the investigation going?"

Diehl opened the front door for Skye. When she passed by him, he wrapped an arm around her waist. They hugged in the foyer. "I missed you."

"I saw you yesterday."

"I'm thinking about not seeing you all week."

"But you said *missed*, as in past tense."

"The more I thought about it, the more it felt like you were already gone." Diehl led her to the dining room.

"I'm still here, okay? My flight is not until after evening church, remember?" Skye let Diehl seat her next to Ethan. "Hello, Ethan."

Ethan pouted with his lips curled out. "They ate your cheesecake before it set."

Diehl cleared his throat. "Just a couple of slices."

"Grandma had two!" Ethan glared at Rose, who was coming into the room.

"Two what?" Rose asked as Diehl seated her.

"Your grandson is complaining about the cheesecake." Diehl returned to where Skye was and sat down on the other side of her.

"It was delicious, Skye," Rose said. "Glad you could join us. I would ask you how church was, but I really don't care."

Skye smiled. Good thing she and Diehl were only

just going out—barely. Imagine what she'd have to put up with if she and Diehl were...

Banish the thought.

Skye drank some water. "Good water."

"Spring water that Chef Pierre brought himself," Rose said.

"I'll have to ask him where it came from."

Ethan tapped her arm. "Why didn't you eat dinner with us last night?"

"I had to go home to pack and do some work," Skye said.

"What kind of work?"

"I have to make sure the chefs are going to be okay next week while I am gone. What kind of work do you do?" Skye asked.

"Well, I try not to get into trouble," Ethan said.

"That takes a lot of effort, doesn't it?"

"Sure does." Ethan's eyes widened when Chef Pierre and Hans entered the dining room with trays of Alaskan king crab legs and lobster tails.

Skye hadn't asked what they were serving for lunch, so these were a surprise to her. Her thought immediately went to her pink silk blouse and white pants. *Oh no.*

All that butter Chef Pierre had drizzled over the lobster tail...

Don't spill. Don't stain.

When she didn't say anything, Diehl touched her shoulder. "Are you okay?"

"Uh, yeah... No. I'm going to make a mess," Skye

confessed, pointing to her blouse. "This is the only silk blouse I have."

"At least she's honest—unlike some people," Rose said. "I don't think it's very messy. Chef Pierre made sure we can eat the crab legs and lobster without needing a mallet or cracker."

"I'm sorry, but I know I will make a mess." Skye smiled. "That's all right. Don't worry. I'll just have salad."

"It's my fault," Diehl said. "I should have warned you to wear something old."

"It's mine too. Once again, I forgot to put spare clothes in my car."

"I have an idea," Diehl said. "Just wear a shirt of mine. They're all washable."

"There you go," Rose said.

"Why don't we say a blessing and then you can go change?" Diehl asked.

"A blessing? When was the last time you prayed over your food, Diehl?" Rose asked.

"Starting now." Diehl turned to Ethan. "You learned how to pray in Sunday school. How about you thank God for our food?"

"Okay." Ethan closed his eyes. "Thank You, God, for the lobster and crab that we're going to eat. Don't let Skye spill food on her pretty blouse. Bring Elisa home to us. Don't let Grandma and Grandpa Bishop be mad at her."

Diehl said *amen* but Ethan wasn't done.

Skye felt a hand on hers. Diehl's warm hand enveloped hers as Ethan continued praying.

"God, please improve Grandpa Ned's golf swing. He needs a miracle. Show Grandma Rose where she put her lost bracelet. Help her not to be so forgetful."

Rose cleared her throat.

"Help Dad not to be lonely. Find him a wife who will love him the rest of his life—or her life if she dies sooner than he does. Amen."

Skye tagged on a silent prayer for the salvation of the Brooks family. That was what Brinley and Ivan had requested in Sunday school class for the last three years.

When everyone looked up, Rose drew a deep breath. "That's short and sweet."

"I could pray more if you want," Ethan said.

"No need, young man," Rose said. "You've blessed us enough. It would indeed be a miracle if Ned's golf swing improves."

"Do you want me to tell you where to go upstairs or show you?" Diehl asked Skye.

"I've never been upstairs."

"It's not that hard. Mom renovated the entire second floor, so there aren't many rooms. You won't get lost." Diehl got out of his chair.

"I'm not trying to be démodé, but Pastor Gonzalez spoke this morning about avoiding all appearances of evil—which might include being mistaken for things done or not done," Skye said. "If you would please grab a T-shirt that you think would fit me, that's best. I'll wait here."

Diehl nodded. He patted her shoulder before he left the dining room.

When Skye turned back to the lobster tail, she realized that Diehl's lunch would be cold if he didn't hurry back.

Rose's eyes were on here. "You're sure different from all the other girls Diehl has dated in his lifetime."

Dated?

"I'm not sure if we're dating yet," Skye said.

"No? He's positively in love. I can tell." Rose reached for a bowl of quinoa. "I haven't seen that look on his face since he was in college."

"Oh?" This she had to hear. "Tell me more."

"Amanda Hall is her name. She lives in England now, next door to Talia Cavanaugh-Perry."

"Really? And who is this person?"

"Do you know Siobhan Urquhart, Jared's cousin?"

"I know who Jared is, but not his family," Skye said.

"Well, Amanda is Siobhan's other cousin on her mother's side. She's Diehl's age. She used to party with Jared and Diehl, plus some of their best buddies. They'd take vacations together and all. College kids, you know."

No, I don't know.

Back when Skye was in college, she was either working or studying all the time. No time to play.

"Anyway, Diehl was madly in love with Amanda, but she spurned him." Rose drizzled drawn butter on her lobster tail.

Unrequited love. Poor Diehl.

"And to top it off, she married one of his friends," Rose added. "I think that was the trigger that got him so drunk on the day of Amanda's wedding that he bedded a random woman and made her pregnant. To do the right thing—being a traditionalist that Diehl was—he married her."

Isobel.

Skye wondered what Diehl would say when he heard his mother call his deceased wife a "random woman."

"Mom!" Diehl's voice was sharp and harsh.

Skye nearly dropped her goblet of pure spring water.

"May I remind you that there's a child in the room?" He pointed to the back of Ethan's head.

Ethan chuckled. "I've heard worse. Mom said someday I'll know what it all means."

Diehl's eyes were as wide as Georgia peaches.

"What did that woman teach your kids?" Rose laughed.

Skye got out of her chair to take the shirt from his hand so that he could sit down and eat. "I'll be right back."

Walking down the hallway, she wondered why the Bishops didn't join the Brooks for lunch. Didn't they want to be with Ethan, their biological grandson?

Strangely though, Diehl's in-laws kept to themselves in the guest cottage. They hadn't stepped foot in the Brooks Cottage on Saturday when Skye had been there.

In the half bath down the hallway from the kitchen, Skye pulled Diehl's cotton T-shirt over her blouse. It was big enough to cover her entire blouse.

The sleeves reached her elbows, and the bottom of the T-shirt was halfway down her thigh.

She guessed that Diehl had picked the biggest shirt he had so that it would also cover her white pants. How thoughtful.

His cotton shirt was baby soft and comfortable, something Skye would have napped in. Unfortunately, she had to stay awake until she reached Miami Beach tonight. Her flight from Brunswick Golden Isles Airport to Atlanta was only one hour long. From Atlanta to Miami, she'd be in the airplane for under two hours. However, extra time was needed for check-in and waiting at the gate. She figured that by the time she and her brother checked into their hotel, it would be past midnight.

She washed her hands and prayed for Elisa. Where had the middle schooler gone to? Had she run away? Had she been abducted?

Ironically, because of the girl, Skye found herself spending more time with Diehl, at his request. Even this afternoon, he wanted her to have lunch and talk with him afterward.

Skye was about to go out of the bathroom when she heard noises—voices—outside the bathroom window, which meant they were in the courtyard behind the kitchen. She could barely make out whose voices they were, but she guessed that they were male.

"...gone too far," one voice said.

"Told you so," another voice added.

Skye thought it could be a benign conversation. However, they continued.

"...get on the bus."

"...won't end well..."

She couldn't hear anymore.

Quietly, she unlocked the bathroom. The hallway was empty. She walked slowly, quietly past the kitchen. She heard the back door open. Feet shuffled into the hallway. Then the sound of pots and pans.

She had to see who they were.

Skye turned around and walked back to the kitchen.

Sous Chef Hans put away a box of cigarettes into his apron pocket. "I smoked outside."

Skye shrugged. "I'm looking for more melted butter for the crab legs. Do you have any left?"

Hans looked for it. "Chef Pierre left it somewhere... There. How much do you want?"

"Just a bit more." As Skye waited, she watched the other guy wash dishes. He didn't say a word to her nor did he turn his face to look at her. "You guys did such a great job with the crab legs and lobster tail. Thank you."

She felt like she had to say something even though she hadn't eaten any of what she mentioned.

"It was all Chef Pierre's work, but thank you." Hans smiled. Cute dimple. Hans heated up a small saucepan and melted some butter in it. He sprinkled some dried herbs in it.

"Ah, the secret ingredient?" Skye smiled.

"It's just a bit of basil." He poured it into a small dispenser and handed it to her.

353

"Thank you." Skye waved and returned to the dining room down the hall.

She held her breath.

Maybe it was nothing. Maybe she had imagined what she heard.

"Where have you been?" Diehl whispered in her ear when she took her seat.

"I'll text you right now," she whispered back.

CHAPTER THIRTY-SIX

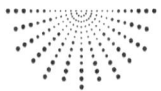

*A*s soon as Diehl received the text message from Skye explaining what she had heard and seen, he felt a shock through his system. It might be nothing, but it might also be the lead they needed.

Get on the bus?

Greyhound?

He texted Malik and Detective Jeong with rapid speed. Within seconds, Jeong texted back, advising him to remain in the dining room and eat lunch as per usual. If they abandoned the dining room, which was down the hallway from the kitchen, it would arouse suspicion.

Malik also texted Diehl, saying that he was coming over with his security team to guard the exits from the kitchen until the detective arrived.

When, though?

Diehl wanted them to hurry up for two reasons. It had been over twenty-four hours since Elisa disappeared. The longer it went on, the more danger she was in.

The other reason had to do with Skye. Diehl longed for some alone time with her. He couldn't wait to get her out of the dining room to speak to her privately before she might have to leave. Evening church was in three hours, and then Skye would fly out and away from him for a whole week.

When Chef Pierre didn't show up with the dessert, and Cara brought Skye's partially eaten cheesecake instead, Diehl knew that Malik and Detective Jeong were up to something.

"This is a good cheesecake," Ethan said. "Just the right consistency and taste. Five stars."

"Thank you, Mr. Ethan," Skye replied. "You made my day."

Before dessert was over, Malik and the detective entered the dining room. Malik smiled. Detective Jeong did not.

"Detective?" Mom looked startled. "What brings you here?"

"I had some questions to ask Malik, ma'am," Jeong said.

Malik nodded.

Diehl glanced at both of them, keeping a straight face. What about Hans and the dishwasher?

"I may need to re-interview a number of people," Jeong said.

"I told you all I know." Mom lifted her wine glass. She liked a glass of bubbly with her lunch.

Strangely enough, Diehl had no desire for another drink—especially not in front of Skye and her God.

"I just talked to some of your kitchen staff," Jeong added.

"Chef Pierre's staff?" Mom sounded genuinely surprised. "We vetted all of them, didn't we, Malik?"

"Yes, ma'am," Malik said. "They have clearance to be here, including Bailey, the dishwasher for today."

"If I don't do my due diligence, I wouldn't be doing my job," Jeong told her.

"She's been gone for more than a day." Mom frowned.

"We're doing our best," Jeong said. "In fact, the FBI is helping us."

"FBI?" Mom rubbed her temples.

Detective Jeong nodded. "GBI and the FBI."

Whoa.

Diehl almost couldn't breathe. If the Federal Bureau of Investigation was helping the Georgia Bureau of Investigation with the case, it must be deadly serious.

Diehl expelled a breath. "Are you saying...?"

"The FBI is interested because your daughter is only twelve years old," Jeong said.

"We can use all the help we can get, sir," Malik added.

Jeong excused himself, and Malik followed him out of the dining room.

Diehl glanced at Ethan, who was engorging on his second slice of cheesecake. Diehl hoped Ethan didn't catch what the adults were talking about.

Cara walked in and went to Mom directly. "Ma'am, Chef Pierre wants a word."

"Not right now." Mom lifted a hand. "I think I'll go upstairs for a nap."

Cara nodded. Without being prompted, the once-nanny asked if she could watch Ethan this afternoon.

Diehl was grateful for that. He figured she could tell that he wanted some time with Skye. As he was still sitting with Skye, Hans walked in, pushing a utility cart.

Diehl was surprised. He thought Detective Jeong would have asked Hans and Bailey to go with them to the station for further questioning. He figured they didn't want to go.

"Excuse me, sir," Hans said. "I thought y'all finished lunch."

"We have. We can go elsewhere, but I was talking to Skye about my daughter," Diehl said.

"I'm sorry about her." Hans shook his head. "Who-ever took her, I hope they catch them, you know? Can't believe it."

"I know. It makes no sense. Malik has so many cameras all over the place, and yet she sneaked out and vanished."

"Sneaked out?" Hans asked.

Diehl nodded. "I think she ran away."

"Yeah? I guess kids can do that." He seemed to relax a little bit.

"It's that age between a child and high school."

"I guess. I don't remember wanting to run away, though." Hans seemed to be in thought. "My dad made my brothers and me work, so we were too busy."

"Work is good. Speaking of work, you were working Friday night, right?"

"Yes, sir. I was here with Chef Pierre until nine o'clock. I told the detective."

"Did you see Elisa before then?"

"Only until dinnertime, sir. Cara was talking to her. I was busy next door at the guest house."

"Where was Chef Pierre, do you remember?" Diehl hoped that the sous chef would let down his guard further if he asked about someone else.

"The chef came and went. I wasn't paying attention," Hans said. "Bailey cleared the tables next door, loaded the dishes, and we pushed the cart back to our van."

A cart! How big was the cart?

"Cart? Of leftovers?" Diehl feigned ignorance.

Hans laughed. "No leftovers! We had prepared some food for Malik and his night shift crew. They eat a lot."

"Your food is good. That's why."

"Thank you, sir."

"Why didn't you drive the van over?" Diehl asked.

"It would take longer to drive around the lake to the driveway than to just roll the cart across the stone path. We filled it with covered dishes, plates, and whatever else the chef wanted, and off we went."

"Sorry I asked all those silly questions."

"Not silly, sir." Hans seemed genuine in his reply.

"Mom is the one throwing all the parties that I

rarely—if ever—attend. I hope she didn't work you too hard."

"Not too hard, sir. And she pays well. So I appreciate that."

Diehl lowered his voice. "Do you like working for Chef Pierre?"

Hans nodded. "I'm learning a lot from him. When I save up enough, I'm going to open a restaurant of my own."

That would be a very long way off from where Hans was, but it told Diehl something. Maybe Hans needed money. *Hmm.*

"Are you planning on going to chef school also?" Diehl wanted to keep the conversation going.

"I don't have to if I can hire a chef to work for me. I'll be giving out orders. It'll be a reverse of what I'm doing now." Hans clammed up.

All this time, Skye hadn't said a word.

"You work hard, Hans," Skye finally said. "The sauces you made. You'll do well in the future."

"Thank you, ma'am. Coming from a chef, I appreciate it."

Diehl wondered how Hans knew that Skye was a chef. Perhaps Chef Pierre or Cara had mentioned it.

"I'll be sure to tell Chef Pierre," Skye added. "By the way, you know what I do."

Hans nodded. "Chef Pierre talks about wrestling the catering from you."

Skye laughed. "Wrestling?"

"There are many dinners next door. You set the gold standard."

Skye brushed it off. "Chef Pierre's a really good chef himself. He sets the standard now."

Hans nodded. "Just let me know when you're ready for me to clear the table, ma'am."

"Where are Chef Pierre's other helpers?" Diehl asked.

"He let them go, sir. Downsizing."

"So he's making the sous chef clear the table?"

"We multitask," Hans said.

"Sous chefs do a tremendous amount of work," Skye said. "I should know, although I do it all."

"You do understand, ma'am."

"Of course, I do." Skye stood up and picked up her own plate.

"Ma'am, let me do that." Hans reached for the plate.

Skye did not give it to him. She put it on the trolley instead. And then she picked up silverware.

"Thank you, ma'am." Hans cleared the other plates.

Diehl stood by watching, wondering what Skye was up to.

"Do you have to cook a whole lot more when Diehl and his kids come here?" Skye asked.

"Depends. The last time they came here, it was only for one week," Hans said.

Seven months before.

"Thanksgiving week," Diehl said. "I had to work. I wasn't here. I sent the kids with their nanny."

"I forget her name," Skye said. She seemed to be

directing the question to Diehl but she wasn't looking at him.

"Romina," Hans mumbled under his breath.

Interesting.

Would that be of interest to Detective Jeong? Diehl wondered.

"Thanksgiving is such a busy week." Skye picked up the salt and pepper shakers. "Did you get to see your family, Hans?"

"I don't have family nearby." Hans cleared the flower arrangements on the table.

"I don't either—except for my church family." Skye helped him fold the tablecloth so that all the crumbs were inside the tablecloth.

Diehl wouldn't know what to do there because he hadn't paid attention all these years.

"I don't go to church," Hans said. "Not my thing."

"I need God because my parents died many years ago, and my only brother has moved out of town." Skye laughed. "Not that I'm needy and all."

"I'm sorry your parents died." Hans put the chairs back at the table. "Mine are still alive but we don't talk. They are dead to me, pretty much."

"Well, you work quickly. I'm impressed," Skye said.

"You helped."

"No problem. I wish you God's best in your endeavors," Skye said. "I'm going to Miami Beach for a food festival so maybe I can bring home some recipes for you. Any particular thing you want to try?"

Hans didn't seem to have to think about it. "I'm

looking for new she-crab bisque recipes. If you come across any..."

"I'll ask the chefs for you," Skye said. "There will be some Michelin chefs there, and my brother knows a few. If they won't share their secret, they could at least give us some tips, you know?"

"Wow. Thank you, ma'am."

Diehl was impressed that Skye used the word *us*. It seemed to make Hans open up and trust her.

At the same time, he worried that she was too friendly with everyone—especially the men. It seemed that all the men she knew at church liked her.

Or was he just protective of her?

Jealous?

CHAPTER THIRTY-SEVEN

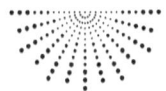

$\mathcal{J}$ust about the only place Diehl could get privacy for Skye and himself in the twenty-thousand-square-foot cottage was outside on the terrace level downstairs. It was warm outdoors, but not too bad under the ceiling fan. He made Skye wait for him on the terrace as he sent a long text message to Detective Jeong and Malik about the dining room conversation that had transpired.

Skye sat on a porch chair, checking her phone. It had been pinging since she unmuted it.

When Diehl got off the phone, so did she.

Here on the terrace, they could look out to the garden, the green grass, the dunes, and the sky. Diehl could not see the ocean from this secluded backyard, but he could hear the roar of the waves. Above them, the sun was up in the sky, but it was cloudy enough for them to stay out here to talk privately.

"I can't believe it," Diehl whispered. "Under our noses."

"We don't know yet," Skye whispered back. "I might have misheard."

"He knows Romina..."

"Shhh. Let Jeong and Malik handle it."

"If you watch the news, a lot of times the bad guys are closer than we think."

Skye gave him a funny look. "I thought you were a busy man. When was the last time you watched the news?"

"It's common knowledge."

"If this is a false lead..."

"Then we're back to square one." Diehl crossed over the terrace to sit on the low brick wall so that he could be close enough to hold Skye's hand if he wanted to. "However, if it's a good lead and brings Elisa home, you get the reward money."

"That never crossed my mind, so if it works out that way, please write the check to Seaside Chapel. They can use it for their ministries in the community."

That was generous of her, and Diehl respected her even more.

"So what would you like to discuss?" Skye asked. "I need to leave by four to go home, pick up my luggage, and be back at church for the evening service."

"And then you're gone for one whole week." Diehl didn't know how to say it so he just went for it exactly as he thought. "About yesterday morning, I'm truly sorry you had to see me in a state like that."

Had it only been yesterday?

"Is that what you wanted to talk with me about?" Skye asked.

"Part of it." He truly didn't have any idea when he might expose his heart to Skye. What he would say next would be a test for her. "As embarrassed as I was, you saw both sides of me."

"We personal chefs see a lot."

"Are you distancing yourself from me now?"

"What do you mean?" Skye asked.

"You said, 'we personal chefs see a lot.' You're compartmentalizing what you saw into a work situation."

"I can't take it personally."

"No? Saturday was your day off. You came to the house because I wasn't awake to let Chef Joseph in. Since Brin gave you the key to the house, you're the only one who can open the door for them."

"Well, he had to cook."

"If I had been passed out upstairs in my bedroom, you would never have known that I sometimes drink—or drank, though not as much as I used to when Parker was alive, probably because I need to be a sober single dad for my kids' sake."

"The terrible news pushed you back to an old habit that you had done away with. Is that what you're saying?" Skye tried to keep her voice calm, but it was cracking.

Diehl reached for her hand. "Again, I'm sorry. I should have run to God instead of to the bottle."

"I will pray for you that you will not be where my

parents were." Skye drew a deep breath. "They tried to solve all their woes with wine. When that didn't work, they tried something stronger and stronger. Next thing they knew, bam. Train wreck. Literally."

She wasn't smiling. Tears pooled in her eyes. "I don't want you to be like that."

Diehl remembered that day when she sang "His Eye Is on the Sparrow" at the beach house while he accompanied her on the piano. Afterward, she was in such sorrow that he felt compelled to wipe the tear from her cheek.

There it was again.

For the first time in his life, he wanted to be her champion and protector, to be her alert watchman on a tower to keep her safe from the cruel world out there. To do that, he had to be aware of her every concern. He had to be alert.

And sober.

"If all the solution you can see is through the cylindrical glass on the bottle, your perspective will always be distorted," Skye said quietly as Diehl kissed her softly on her forehead. "See your problems through the eyes of God, and you will not have a vision problem. Or a hangover."

She said it matter-of-factly, like she had no dog in the fight. Her objectivism frightened Diehl because he wondered if she could compartmentalize him out of her life.

He didn't want that.

At the same time, what she said was true.

This paternity problem was here to stay. He had to

deal with it. If he hadn't been drunk out of his mind on Friday night, he wouldn't have been passed out on Saturday morning when his family tried to contact him.

If Skye hadn't shown up, his mom would have. And then she'd be totally disappointed in his lack of control. Then again, was Skye disappointed too?

"Are you...uh..." Diehl couldn't get the words out.

"What, Diehl?"

Diehl cleared his throat. "Are you disappointed in me?"

To be fair, he only drank when he wasn't working. That was why he had to work all the time so that he didn't have time to waste on things like getting drunk. There was so much work to do, but he had lost control of himself on Friday night.

And Thursday night.

Dad's cellar was potent. He should never have gone down there. The temptation had been too great.

Once upon a time, he and Jared had been drinking buddies. He replaced Jared with Isobel, who could knock down way more than Diehl. Since they had a chauffeur, Diehl didn't have to worry about being the designated driver.

He couldn't remember drinking the nights away with Isobel, but the last sermon he had heard in a church while he was in college was about a "strange woman" in Proverbs 2. Two verses jumped out at him then, and had stayed with him to this day.

For her house leads down to death,

And her paths to the dead;
None who go to her return,
Nor do they regain the paths of life...

Proverbs 2:18-19 had convicted him much, but the nail in the coffin had come in Proverbs 7. Somehow at this minute, he recalled the elderly pastor Reverend Cole—still standing at that time but with a cane in one hand and a Bible in another—preaching God's Word to him.

With her enticing speech she caused him to yield,
   With her flattering lips she seduced him.
   Immediately he went after her, as an ox goes to
the slaughter,
   Or as a fool to the correction of the stocks,
   Till an arrow struck his liver.
   As a bird hastens to the snare,
   He did not know it would cost his life.

How could Proverbs 7:21-23 not be about Isobel? The description fit her perfectly.

Since then, Diehl had stopped attending church because he did not want to lose the company of his then girlfriend. In fact, he had married Isobel and invited no one from his old church to attend. From then on, it was all about the pursuit of Isobel's happiness over his own and everyone else's. If anyone had asked him back then, he would say that yes, he worshipped her.

Was it possible for a Christian to sin this much?

Maybe he wasn't a real Christian, after all?

Could a Christian keep on sinning without remorse?

Many years later, after one heated night of quarreling after another, Diehl had moved downstairs to sleep in their basement while Isobel stayed alone in their master bedroom upstairs.

One night, with his brain tired from overwork, and nothing else to do, and somewhat regretting his relationship with Isobel, he googled Reverend Cole, only to find that he had passed away, leaving behind his sermons online and a warning for him in Proverbs 7:25-27 inside that one sermon that had bothered him for years.

> *Do not let your heart turn aside to her ways,*
>> *Do not stray into her paths;*
>> *For she has cast down many wounded,*
>> *And all who were slain by her were strong men.*
>> *Her house is the way to hell,*
>> *Descending to the chambers of death.*

That had been Isobel's legacy with him. Wrapped up in his life with her was everything he needed to know about how to mix strong drinks, how to get intoxicated, how to forget the world and all their woes.

Then again, no. He had chosen to be with her. He had chosen that legacy.

Besides, Isobel was gone now. Who made him get drunk at his own pity party? No one but himself. He knew he had to own the decisions he made.

And the consequences thereof.

He waited for Skye to reply. When she didn't, he repeated his question. "Are you disappointed?"

"In how you handled the paternity news, specifically. How you drank your sorrow away for two days was totally unnecessary."

"I could have done better."

"How?"

"I don't know."

"Well, to be sure, if you and God were close, you'd pray for those two poor kids. God would give you wisdom. People adopt kids all the time, right? If God wanted you to have those two children, does it matter how He brought them to you?"

"I want to have my own kids too, from my own seed..." There, he said it. "Sorry. Too much information."

"If the Lord wills it, you may someday have kids of your own. However, if God chooses to give you kids another way, would you not thank Him for it, regardless?"

"My kids made me feel better about my marriage to Isobel, but when I found out she had cheated on me for my entire marriage to her, for both children..." Diehl resisted running back to the house. The cellar was on the other side of the terrace.

No.

Skye placed a finger on his lips. "Shhh. Listen."

"What?"

"Hear the waves of the ocean?"

"Yes."

"Back and forth, perpetually. Isn't that a reminder from God that time continues? Life goes on? What was in the past remains in the past."

"I don't know. I'm still thinking of them. My kids, Isobel, her extramarital affair."

"Turn them over to God. He sees the past, present, and future. He has things under control. He's got this."

Diehl nodded. Barely. Like he wanted so hard to believe what Skye said.

"Forgive Isobel," Skye added. "Let her go."

Diehl was shocked at what he just heard. "It's easy for you to say. You're outside, looking in."

Skye stepped away from him. "I guess I expected more of you, even though I've heard many things about you—never mind."

"What did Brin say about me?" There could be a million things. His life hadn't always been exemplary. His business decisions had often been brutal. His choice of investments could be over the top. His private purchases —and his art collection in Atlanta—were extravagant.

He had brought none of that with him to St. Simon's Island. His sister's beach house was austere. Whitewashed walls and blue accents. Nothing more. There were very few art pieces in the house. The only thing more expensive than the kitchen makeover was the Steinway grand piano in the living room.

However, he had brought himself to the island.

And now his old life was affecting his new relationship with Skye.

He touched her arm. Her skin was soft. Her fingers

might be rough from working in the kitchen a lot, but the rest of her arms felt delicate. She was so beautiful and pure that Diehl didn't believe that he should inflict the sins of his past life on her.

Perhaps Skye wasn't for him. She deserved a better man. Maybe a Bible-teaching man like Hayden What's-his-name.

Diehl could see it now.

Why would God bless him with love a second time around when he failed the first time?

He was trying to figure out how to say it nicely when out of the corner of his eye he saw Malik walk toward them, coming down the stone patch by the violin-shaped pool that Grandpa Brooks had installed in the backyard of Brooks Cottage.

Malik waved.

Diehl waved back. "Got something for me?"

"We have a lead!"

"Thank God." Skye grabbed Diehl's arm. "Good news there."

There was a smile on her face. No malice, no anger there. She had said she was disappointed, yes, but only in his response to a problem and not him as a person. Diehl had noticed that bit of detail.

When was the last time Isobel hadn't attacked him personally for a behavior he could have corrected and then held a grudge for days?

On the other hand, Skye had been calm since Saturday morning's episode and didn't raise her voice at him. Instead, she spent most of the day with him and Ethan. She was like cool spring water on a hot summer's day. Refreshing.

Diehl wanted to stay with her forever.

And yet...

"Detective Jeong is keeping tabs on Hans and Bailey—as are we," Malik said.

"I figured."

"Well, Hans knows our security personnel, but he might not know Helen's people."

Diehl nodded. "Good move to call her."

"Have to protect the family."

"You called Helen Hu?" Skye asked.

"Yes," Diehl and Malik said in unison.

"She helped my sister-in-law find her brother," Skye said.

"I remember that." Malik nodded. "On top of that, an anonymous tip has led the police to a couple of persons of interest. One is a parolee living in the foothills of Tennessee. The man stalks teenagers online."

"A man?" Diehl recoiled.

"Thirty-five years old going on eighteen—offering free car rides."

"For a price," Diehl said. He prayed to God that the price wouldn't be Elisa's life. Everything else, he could handle—with God's help.

He saw now how much he needed God.

In times like this, none of his billions of dollars in the bank could lift his spirits more than God and His godly people could.

He glanced at Skye.

"The other persons of interest?" Skye asked.

"All men."

"That doesn't sound good at all." Diehl hadn't felt this angry in years.

"We'll keep praying for God to protect Elisa," Skye said. "God is bigger than this problem."

Diehl very much wanted to believe that too.

CHAPTER THIRTY-EIGHT

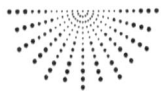

*D*iehl wasn't happy that Mom organized a last-minute playdate at Marguerite Urquhart's house on the other side of Seaside Island. He knew how it would go. Several kids Ethan's age would play and picnic in Marguerite's big yard, with overpriced nannies watching them, while their ultra-wealthy grandmothers ate dinner indoors and talked about their next shopping trip at Sotheby's or Christie's.

If it had been at another time, he wouldn't have been too upset about it, but Mom had picked five o'clock on Sunday afternoon—the same time as evening church at Seaside Chapel. Plus, a sleepover if the kids were so inclined. Who'd turn down a sleep-over in a palatial mansion with free food?

On the other hand, since he had planned to attend the search committee meeting after church, it was probably best for him not to have Ethan with him. He might run off and disappear like his sister.

Since Diehl had missed church that morning and had promised Skye that he'd make up for it this evening, he had to be there, with or without his son. It would be the last time he would see Skye before she left town for the week.

And he wanted to see her badly.

The two hours between the time she had left Brooks Cottage and evening church had been long without her.

Diehl filled the time by talking to his brother-in-law about the latest developments this afternoon, and Ivan agreed that their best grassroots effort would be online. After all, if Elisa had somehow hopped on a bus, she could be anywhere in the country by now and certainly not still on St. Simon's Island, Seaside Island, or any of the barrier islands nearby.

Where are you, Elisa?

Diehl entered the Seaside Chapel sanctuary and looked for Skye. When he couldn't see her, he looked for Avery or anyone in his Sunday school class. They would know where Skye was. Probably.

He didn't see anyone he recognized.

Oh, well.

He sat down at the last row, and checked his phone. Malik had texted him a few times. He'd been in touch with Detective Jeong and had taken to summarizing the situation for Mom and Diehl. While Diehl would like to know every single detail of the big search for his daughter, he was more the CEO type. He was most concerned with the results.

Did you or did you not find my daughter?

Skye had told him that God knew where Elisa was.

Tell me where she is, God.

He closed his eyes, trying to feel God's answer. He sensed nothing at all. It was like he was staring at a blank wall.

He wasn't sure why his belief back in college hadn't carried through to today. What on earth had he believed then?

He recalled his conversation with Mom, how he had told her about his own spiritual condition.

I'm closer to God now than I ever was, but I think I am not yet in His family. I feel like I am still outside the fence, looking in.

Truly, his thoughts had been about Skye. He wanted to be with Skye, but would she go out with someone who was not sure about God or where he stood with God?

Diehl felt that perhaps he should spare her from himself. He was no good for her. He would never be good enough for her.

Even though he had given up those bad-boy days when he married Isobel, she had damaged his heart and emotions so much that he was not sure if he could ever love another woman—especially Skye—with the care she deserved.

The piano began to play.

Still no sign of Skye.

Just as well.

Throughout the congregational singing, Diehl found himself unable to participate with his whole heart. He did not feel like the hymns were his—that he could own the words to the songs or that the lyrics were his own praise to God. He mouthed the words and waited for the songs to be over so he could put away the hymnal.

He felt like a fraud standing here singing to a distant God.

A casually dressed Pastor Gonzalez took the microphone to pray. "Father God, if there is anyone here with unconfessed sins, let them confess to You now so that they can worship You with a free heart for the rest of the service. This evening we're going to study 1 John 1. Let Your Word shine in our hearts so we might know the truth of God. Your truth sets us free. In Jesus' name, I pray. Amen."

Your truth sets us free.

Quietly, Diehl prayed to God. He wanted God's truth. He wanted to be free from the bondage that had tied up his heart for so many years.

He wanted to be free to love Skye with God's love. If he could not love her with His love, then he would not love her at all. But how? What was God's love?

After several teenagers sang a song that Diehl had never heard of, Pastor Gonzalez returned to the podium. "Turn with me to 1 John 1. My focus tonight is on verses five to ten, but I want us to read the last part of verse four as well. 'And these things we write to you that your joy may be full.' Christian, is your joy full?"

I have no joy.

"Has the enemy stolen your joy?" Pastor Gonzalez asked. "Let us examine our hearts and get back on the right track with God. Broad is the road that leads to destruction, as the Bible tells us. The narrow road is where we want to be because it's the only path to joy in the Lord—which Nehemiah tells us is our strength through tough and hard times in life."

Diehl sat there, trying to absorb all that Pastor Gonzalez had said. It seemed like a lot to take in.

Perhaps tonight's sermon might be why Skye was not sitting next to him. If he was right about the trajectory the pastor was going with his sermon, it was about to get painful in a minute. Diehl would rather Skye not see his reaction.

"What is this narrow path I just mentioned?" Pastor Gonzalez put his Bible down on the lectern. "One word: Jesus. Listen to what our Lord told Thomas in John 14:6. 'I am the way, the truth, and the life. No one comes to the Father except through Me.' He is the only path to God. Do you doubt that?"

Diehl wondered if he was a doubting Thomas.

"Jesus is the path of light to God. 'This is the message which we have heard from Him and declare to you, that God is light and in Him is no darkness at all.' Do you believe 1 John 1:5 when it says that there is no darkness in God? God is all light."

Diehl looked down at his phone only to realize that

the battery was out. He had forgotten to charge it all day long. So now he couldn't look up the Bible verse that Pastor Gonzalez referred to.

At the back of the pew in front of him, there was a Bible. Or at least it said "Bible" on the cover. He was afraid to reach for it because he had no idea where 1 John was.

So he looked back at the pastor on the podium. Behind the pastor, two big screens displayed the Scripture passage in question. Good. He would have to read the screen to follow along.

"Light and darkness," Pastor Gonzalez said. "I don't know about you, but when I wake up at night and walk around in the dark, I am liable to stub my toes—or for you younger people with kids, you might step on LEGO bricks."

The congregation laughed.

Diehl did not recall stepping on LEGO blocks in his house. Elisa and Ethan had a nanny who cleaned up after them, but they also had playrooms where toys never left.

He could not imagine a house with toys all over the floor.

"When you turn on the light at night, you can see just as well as in the day, but that light is artificial," the pastor said. "I want you to think of the brightest sunlight you've ever been under. We get plenty of sunshine here in this beach town, but some days are hotter than others. The sunlight can be so bright we need to wear sunglasses and slather in sunblock, yes?"

Diehl felt movement next to his seat. He glanced over to see Ivan sitting down next to him. They nodded to each other. Ivan opened his Bible.

"We know that depending on the time of year, the sunlight might be weak or strong. Contrast that with God, who is always strong and never weak. God is the perfect light and 'in Him is no darkness at all.' Do you see that now? In God, there is one hundred percent light and zero percent darkness."

Perfect God.

Diehl felt sorry that he never knew this God. To him, God hadn't answered his prayers all these years when he pleaded for help with his marriage and with the kids. Even if God hadn't gotten him into the mess in the first place, wouldn't God help him out of it—because of His compassion?

Ivan was taking notes in the margins of a handout, seemingly unaware of the thoughts that roiled through Diehl's mind.

"Friends, my question for you is this: are you with light or with darkness?" Pastor Gonzalez asked. "You might say, 'Christians sin too. Does that mean we walk in darkness?' Let's read the next verse, 1 John 1:6. 'If we say that we have fellowship with Him, and walk in darkness, we lie and do not practice the truth.' If you are a true believer, you consistently walk in the light of Christ. You're not perpetually wandering around in darkness. Maybe you fall every now and then—so you ask God to forgive you and you get back on track—but it's not a habit for you to walk in darkness. It's not your lifestyle. Your lifestyle is one of light."

Diehl had told anyone who asked that he was a Christian, but he would admit that it certainly hadn't been his lifestyle to live as one. Wasn't it enough to just believe once? He didn't realize that he had to live the life too.

I still don't know whether I believed in Him in part or wholly back in college.

"Are you walking in the light of Christ?" Pastor Gonzalez asked again. "Here's the test, Christian. 1 John 1:7 says, 'But if we walk in the light as He is in the light, we have fellowship with one another, and the blood of Jesus Christ His Son cleanses us from all sin.' You know in your heart that Jesus Christ has forgiven you of all your sins. You also have sweet fellowship with other Christians. Not that it's always smooth-sailing, but your friction is small and you're on the same page."

Same page.

Diehl had been sure there was a barrier between him and Skye. No, they were not on the same page.

The problem is me.

"Which side of the fence are you on?" Pastor Gonzalez picked up his Bible. "Are you standing in darkness, looking in at the light? Are you in the light, and know it in your heart? Or are you on the fence about Jesus? Don't you want to be sure about the condition of your soul? Sitting on the fence can be painful."

The congregation laughed.

Diehl did not.

"A real believer walks in the light. A non-believer

walks in the dark. How do you know whether you're a real believer or not?" Pastor Gonzalez turned a page in his Bible. "We get our answer in the next chapter. 'He who says, "I know Him," and does not keep His commandments, is a liar, and the truth is not in him. But whoever keeps His word, truly the love of God is perfected in him. By this we know that we are in Him.' I John 2:3-5 says that your life is the test. If you know Jesus, you're with Him in what you do. You do the things that glorify God and edify those around you. If you don't know Him, you don't care what the Bible says. And you live your life as you please."

Diehl knew where he was and where he had been. He was in darkness, and Skye was in the light. It was finally as clear as day to him.

"If you don't know Jesus Christ as your Lord and Savior, then you are walking in darkness. How do you transfer from the domain of darkness into God's kingdom of light?" Pastor Gonzalez opened another page in his Bible. "Acts 16:31 says, 'Believe on the Lord Jesus Christ, and you will be saved, you and your household.' That doesn't mean everyone else will be saved just because you are. It means that when you are saved, your family will see your salvation, and perhaps for such a time as this, they too shall believe, and thus will be saved as well."

Diehl thought of his kids. Would God keep Elisa safer if she believed in Jesus? Was Ethan old enough to believe in Jesus for the salvation of his soul?

What about me? Am I too old to be saved?

"Maybe you say, 'Pastor, once upon a time I was

saved and walked in the light. Now I am walking in darkness. What am I?' To that, I would ask you a couple of questions. Were you truly saved in the first place? Have you accepted Jesus for real? If you're not sure if you're saved, then get saved now. It's not too late. Admit to God that you're a sinner. Ask Him to forgive you of your sins. Believe in Jesus Christ as your only Savior."

Pastor Gonzalez looked around the sanctuary, as though he was searching for a lost sheep. "If you're saved and still sinning, then get right with God. Repent. Confess. Ask God to forgive you, and He will take you back. 1 John 1:9 says, 'If we confess our sins, He is faithful and just to forgive us our sins and to cleanse us from all unrighteousness.' Christians can sin too, but we get right back to God. We're not sinning and sinning over and over again. Dear friends, which are you?"

When the pastor prayed the closing prayer, Diehl felt that perhaps it was time to resolve his confusion once and for all. Which one was he? Was he a Christian who had strayed from God? Or had he been a non-Christian all this time?

As the piano played again, Ivan turned to him. "Glad you're here, brother. How's Ethan doing?"

"Partying with his friends and their grandmas."

"Ha. Is that something my child has to look forward to?" Ivan asked.

"Protect my nephew at all cost," Diehl said. "How's Brin, by the way?"

"Bedrest, bedrest. She's sick and tired of my cooking. We might have to hire Skye soon before Brin kicks me out of the house for failing to deliver anything beyond soups and sandwiches."

Diehl laughed. "Skye can cook."

"She sure can. I was trying to save some money, you know. I figured I could learn to cook."

"Yeah. I don't know if Brin is up to you learning on the job, though."

"That's what I'm finding out." Ivan got out of his seat. He seemed to be waiting for the crowd to clear from the aisle. "So what do you think about the sermon?"

"Good," Diehl said. "Showed me a few things."

"Like?"

"I've tried to live the life but I don't measure up." It was the truth, and Diehl knew he could tell his brother-in-law.

"We've all failed. If we could reach God on our own, we'd be at His level," Ivan said. "God is sinless and holy. Only God can reach His own level. That's why He had to send God the Son to bridge the gap between us and God the Father, whose forgiveness we seek."

"Good point." Diehl debated whether to broach the subject. "I'm not sure if I was ever saved in Jesus."

"You can be sure now, once and for all."

"What about what I believed—or thought I believed back then?"

"Are you living it like the pastor said? Are you walking in the light as God is in the light?"

"Not really. But I've started to attend church..." Thanks to Skye.

"Anyone can attend church, but do you have Jesus in your heart?"

"I'm not sure. How can He get in my heart?"

"When you accept Jesus, the Holy Spirit of God enters your heart and seals you with a promise that you belong to God. You will know without a shadow of doubt that Jesus is your Lord."

"In that case, I never knew Him."

"It's not where you've been or what you have or haven't done, but what matters is whether Jesus is in your heart right now and henceforth and forevermore. Where you're going is more critical than where you came from. Today can be a new start for you, brother."

"I'd like that."

"Do you want to ask Jesus into your heart to cleanse you of your sins and give you eternal life?" Ivan asked.

"Yes." Diehl meant it.

"Then let's pray. You can pray after me or use your own words." They bowed their heads as Ivan led Diehl in a prayer.

"Dear Lord Jesus, I recognize that I'm a sinful man and You are the only holy God. I cannot reach You by my own effort. I need a Savior," Diehl repeated after Ivan. "I believe that Jesus Christ died on the cross to pay for the penalty of my sins. I ask You to forgive me of all my sins because of what Jesus has done for me. I accept Jesus as the final payment for all my sins. I believe in Jesus Christ as my Lord and Savior. In Your Holy name, I pray. Amen."

"Now your sins are paid in full," Ivan said.

"All my sins?" Amazing.

"Yes, all of them. Even sins you haven't committed yet."

"Wow."

"Of course, it's not a license to sin," Ivan reminded him. "Jesus told the woman in the New Testament to 'go and sin no more.' That is to say, we're to study the Bible, learn more about God, and sin less and less as we mature more and more in Christ."

"I guess I'll need to find Grandpa Brooks's Bible," Diehl said.

Ivan handed him his Bible. "Here. You can read mine in the meantime."

"You don't need it?"

"I do, but I have dozens of Bibles at home."

"One is not enough?" Diehl laughed.

"Aren't we blessed to have as many Bibles as we want?" Ivan patted Diehl's shoulder. "Now we need to go to our search committee meeting. You have a lot of updates to report. Everyone's been handing out fliers and posting on social media, but if the bus clue pans out, we're talking multi-state or maybe international."

"God knows where Elisa is," Diehl echoed what Skye had told him.

Now it was real. He could feel it in his heart.

He had taken a step of faith to trust God with his salvation, and now he felt the reality of salvation in his heart and soul.

The burden that had once weighed heavily on his shoulders lifted. The memories of Isobel were still there, but the anguish that had come with them was dissipating. It was as though the door had closed on that chapter of his life, and he stood at the cusp of a new beginning.

Did that mean he was now free to love Skye?

CHAPTER THIRTY-NINE

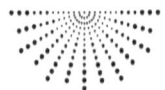

*S*kye was late to evening church and caught the tail end of the offertory prayer before sitting down in the balcony upstairs with Avery and her cousin Gillian.

She wasn't sure if Diehl made it tonight, but there was no time to check. She was leaving right after the closing prayer to catch a flight out of Brunswick on the mainland. There wasn't a lot of time in between arriving in Atlanta and taking off again for Miami Beach, and she wished she had found a later flight.

Or flown this afternoon instead.

On the other hand, she was glad she hadn't flown out after morning church because she had a good lunch with the Brooks family and even heard something useful that the police might be able to use in their search for Elisa.

When she got off the plane in Atlanta, her phone

made so much noise she wondered if STL had exploded while she had been gone for only one hour.

Chef Joseph had questions about the menu for Mrs. Morton. Chef Pamela had problems with her sous chef. Two other chefs had vacation questions. Already? And Marlo decided to apply for a scholarship to chef school.

And what is this text from Brinley?

She nearly fell out of her seat at the gate.

Diehl got saved. Ivan led him to Christ after church.

After fumbling around for words, Skye texted Diehl with just one word.

Wow.

He did not reply. He was probably still at the search party meeting with Ivan.

Someone waved to Skye in the distance. Her brother, Sebastian. She waved back excitedly.

"You seem glad to see me." Sebastian put down his backpack in the seat next to Skye.

"Diehl got saved!"

"Oh, and here I thought you missed your own brother." He made a face. "No, seriously. That's amazing news. I'm happy for him. Finally. How long have we prayed?"

"I know, right. Ivan prayed with him after church."

"Why now?"

"Brinley said Pastor Gonzalez preached a convicting sermon."

"He always does." Sebastian sat down and stretched his legs. He was wearing sweatpants and a T-shirt, like he was going to bed.

"You look casual."

"Well, you look like you just came out of church." Sebastian pointed to her stretch pants and cotton blouse.

"Yes, actually. About two hours ago. No time to change." Skye glanced at her phone. Still no reply from Diehl.

The flight from Atlanta to Miami Beach was smooth and uneventful. By the time they checked into their hotel near the outdoor food festival, Skye was bushed.

She brushed her teeth and washed her face. She didn't bother to unpack her suitcase.

She was in bed when the text came from Diehl. She asked him if he was still awake, and next thing she knew, he called her. Audio only because she did not want him to see her in her pajamas.

"How was your flight?" Diehl asked.

"Which one?"

"Both legs."

"Not bad. Short and sweet." Skye tapped on the speakerphone icon and placed the phone on the side table. Her head was on the pillow, her eyes closed. "I heard the good news."

"My sister told you?" Diehl asked.

"Praise the Lord," Skye said. "Tell me how it happened."

Diehl did. His voice was calm, and he sounded at peace. Skye couldn't wait to get home to St. Simon's next week. She wanted to look at his face to see if there was any visible change.

"Best decision I ever made was to accept Jesus as my Lord and Savior," Skye said. "The rest of my life fell in place."

"I don't know what I believed in college. This is a do-over for me. A reboot."

"Better saved than sorry."

"Yep. When it comes to life and death, it's no joke."

Skye couldn't see Diehl's face when he said that. "Being a Christian doesn't mean that life is going to be perfect from here on out."

"God is with me no matter what happens." He seemed genuine about the statement.

"Even if things don't turn out the way you want," Skye said softly.

"I know what you mean."

"Good."

"Thank you for the reality check." Diehl cleared his throat. "I think we're on the same page now."

"Oh?" Skye prayed that Diehl hadn't accepted Jesus on account of her at all. Diehl's salvation was between him and God.

"Our yoke is equal now," Diehl added.

Skye recalled 2 Corinthians 6:14 that Avery had reminded her about the other day.

> Do not be unequally yoked together with unbelievers. For what fellowship has righteousness with lawlessness? And what communion has light with darkness?

Now that Diehl was on equal footing with Skye, where would they go from here?

"Sometimes it takes difficult times in life to get people to run to God," Diehl said. "Today, I know I believe in the real Jesus, not my own idea of who God is."

"That's good to hear." Quietly, Skye prayed that Diehl would grow in his faith in Jesus Christ.

"Well, it's almost midnight, and you've had a long day. I have to get up early to go to the men's Bible study."

"That's why the women's Bible study is in the evenings." Skye yawned. "I need to read my Bible and then go to bed."

"What verse are you reading?"

"Our women's group is starting the book of Galatians next week, so we were told to read through chapter one this week. I figured I'd do that since I will miss Bible study on Tuesday night."

"We're on a summer schedule, apparently, in the men's study," Diehl said. "I don't know who's speaking tomorrow morning, but it's topical. Last week, we studied Galatians 6."

"That's a good chapter."

"We went over a couple of verses, but I can't remember which ones."

"Who's teaching tomorrow?" Skye asked.

"I have no idea."

Skye nodded, though Diehl couldn't see her. "Have fun. You can tell me what you learn tomorrow and I'll do likewise."

"Will do. Good night, sweetheart."

Sweetheart? Did he mean it?

Skye didn't reply.

"Skye?" Diehl asked.

"Yes?"

"Is something wrong?"

Skye wasn't sure how to say it.

"Tell me," Diehl said quietly.

He seemed to want to know what was on her mind. Should she tell him?

"There are verses in the Bible that talk about the old man versus the new man," Skye said. "When we get saved, we do away with the old things. The old things pass away, the Bible says. We're no longer who we were before."

Specifically, Skye thought of Romans 6:6, but she wasn't sure whether Diehl was ready for it. She knew that God would work in his heart in due time.

...knowing this, that our old man was crucified with Him, that the body of sin might be done away with, that we should no longer be slaves of sin.

"I know. God opened my eyes and I can see clearly," Diehl said. "Is that what you meant?"

"There's more, but God will show you in His time." It was all she could say.

In her mind, she asked a question that she dared not voice: *What about your drinking issues?*

Perhaps that was something that Pastor Gonzalez or Ivan would have to address or confront. Skye remembered Brinley saying that her brother was a casual drinker. However, what Skye saw on Saturday morning questioned that premise. Clearly, Diehl had used alcohol as a coping mechanism when he found out that the two children he had been raising since their births were not his. His wife, whom he had remarried twice, had cheated on him throughout both marriages.

It must have made him look terribly foolish, especially for a businessman who had been successfully managing a multi-billion-dollar corporation.

How many times had Diehl used alcohol to manage his personal problems?

Skye had avoided thinking about that matter since Saturday's chaos. It wasn't her problem unless she made it so. After all, even though they had kissed and spent time together, Skye could not imagine Diehl lasting more than the season. After summer, he'd go home to Atlanta, and that would be the end of their relationship. Whether he drank or not, it would not be Skye's problem anymore.

"Are you thinking of what I am thinking?" Diehl asked.

"What is that?"

"You're trying to tell me that as a Christian, I shouldn't be drinking."

"Well, the Bible does say that kings shouldn't drink. 'It is not for kings, O Lemuel, it is not for kings to drink wine, nor for princes intoxicating drink; Lest they drink and forget the law, and pervert the justice of all the afflicted.' That's from Proverbs 31:4-5."

"Interesting that there's such a verse."

"I know that some Christians drink alcohol. I don't because I have a testimony to protect and I need to be in full control of my faculties—I cannot afford to be intoxicated even for a moment—but this is my choice. You make your own choices. We all have to answer to God individually, so you can't answer for me and I can't answer for you."

"But you would prefer that I don't drink."

"I would ask that you pray about it as a matter of being a leader—a king, as Proverbs 31 says—setting an example for your children."

"I've thought of that long before I was saved, especially since their mother was a heavy drinker." Diehl went quiet.

"My parents were alcoholics and they died because of their disease. My brother and I have to live with that the rest of our lives. Neither of us drink because we cannot go down that path. In my house, there is no alcohol—and there will never be. My chefs might cook with it, but I don't."

Now Diehl was silent.

Perhaps it was what she just said.

In my house, there is no alcohol—and there will never be.

That was to say, due to a family history, she could never marry someone who drank. She would not inflict such pain on her future children.

Where could she find a husband who could kiss her as passionately as Diehl and yet was a teetotaler?

Brinley found Ivan. Sebastian found Emmeline.

What about me?

"It's late, so let's get some sleep," Diehl said. "Good night again."

This time he did not say *sweetheart*.

"Good night. I'll be praying for Elisa's safe return. Keep me posted, okay?"

"Will do."

When he hung up, Skye prayed. She did not want to judge Diehl, and God knew she hadn't. However, when it came to her own personal life and future, she could not compromise her own convictions.

If Diehl believed that he could still get drunk with impunity after salvation, that would be something between him and God.

As for me and my house, we will be alcohol-free.

At some point in time, Diehl would have to go home to Atlanta, back to his job in the corporate world. His father could not possibly hold the fort for long, while Diehl stayed on St. Simon's Island with nothing much to do.

Diehl had burned out at work in Atlanta. However, on the island, he seemed rejuvenated. That was, until the DNA test results came. That would have been devastating for anyone, especially someone who didn't know the Lord and did not have undergirding divine strength to endure the news.

What a difference one day had made.

Skye read her Bible starting in Galatians 1. When she reached the fourth verse, she prayed for Diehl. Then she screen-captured Galatians 1:3-5 from her Bible app and sent that to Diehl.

Grace to you and peace from God the Father and our Lord Jesus Christ, who gave Himself for our sins, that He might deliver us from this present evil age, according to the will of our God and Father, to whom be glory forever and ever. Amen.

Diehl did not reply. On her phone, Skye noticed that Diehl hadn't even read it. Of course, he might have read it in the notifications, and as such she wouldn't be able to tell from over here.

"Lord, please forgive me. I wasn't trying to tell him what to do. I want him to do what is right in Your eyes," Skye prayed. "Forgive me for my own sins. Help both of us to be the man and woman You want us to be for Your glory."

Skye wondered if she might ever be able to breach the topic with Diehl again. They could be on different pages on that one matter.

It was important to her.

But it might not be of any significance to Diehl at all.

Equal yoke? The jury was out.

CHAPTER FORTY

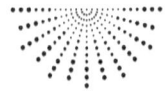

$\mathcal{D}$iehl parked Dad's Bugatti Veyron outside Matt's antique store, and watched Ivan arrive on his shiny new bicycle, riding in the morning wind, his messenger bag across his back. He got off the bike, pushed it to a bike rack, and locked it.

"I envy you," Diehl said as he locked Dad's sports car. "Maybe I should get a bike."

"Envy is a sin." Ivan must have seen Diehl empty-handed, so he said, "Did you bring a Bible?"

"App on my phone."

"Lots of distractions on your phone. Brinley wants me to give you a new Bible." Ivan unlocked the door for Diehl.

So Ivan had a key to Matt's shop. Maybe it was because he taught the Bible study from time to time.

Ivan locked the door behind Diehl.

At the back of the store, Matt was making coffee. "Good morning, y'all."

Benicio was stretched out on a blanket covering an old couch that looked like it came from the nineteenth century. "Is there any way we can move the Bible study to the evening? The ladies have theirs at seven, usually with dinner."

"That's nice. Who gets up this early, huh?" Ivan opened his messenger bag and handed a wrapped gift to Diehl.

"A present for me?" Diehl opened the card taped to the gift.

"If it were up to me, it'd be unwrapped—as is. But your sister insisted it has to be not only wrapped, but accompanied by a handwritten note in cursive, no less."

Diehl finished reading the card. "That's nice. Tell her I'm glad to be saved too," Diehl said. "How's she doing?"

"Still on bedrest. From the size of her, we might as well be having twins."

"Well, Brooks babies are large."

"McMillan babies are normal." Ivan laughed. "Well, Brin was so tired of my gourmet cuisine that I finally caved in and asked Skye to return."

"Not that you can't afford her." Diehl unwrapped the gift, knowing what was in it.

"Unfortunately, she's sending another chef. Brin would prefer Skye herself, and now she's probably doubly mad at me."

"Skye is busy because she's cooking for me, except this week. Chef Joseph is filling in for her while she's in Miami Beach." Diehl recalled the rather strange ending to their conversation the night before. However, he had fallen asleep before he thought too much about it.

Right now, he was holding the greatest gift ever: the Word of God. The leather-bound Bible had tabs so he could find the books of the Bible, since he hadn't gotten their order memorized.

"This is beautiful," Diehl said. "You just have Bibles like this lying around the house?"

"Pretty much. Never know who you might need to give it to—although Brinley has saved that one for you for a few years."

"She has?" Diehl was moved.

Ivan slapped his shoulder. "Your sister loves you and has been praying for your salvation since she herself was saved."

Diehl wondered if Skye had prayed for his salvation too—since Brinley and Skye were close friends.

"We have all prayed for your salvation." Matt came over with hot coffee in stoneware mugs designed to look like enamel-coated steel camping mugs. He didn't ask what Ivan or Diehl wanted in their coffee. It was like they were out camping in the wilderness, and there was only one type of coffee.

Take it or leave it.

The coffee was good. "Wow. What is this?"

"Costa Rica. Organic." Matt handed a mug to Benicio, who sat up with his eyes half shut.

Even coffee tastes better with Jesus in my heart.

Diehl found his seat between Benicio and Ivan. He did not have to sit next to Ivan, but the edge of the old sofa seemed to be most comfortable. He didn't want to sit in a folding chair today, and was glad there were options.

Boy, I am getting fussy in my old age.

Was that it? Had Skye said what she said last night because she thought he might be set in his ways and was unable to change? She didn't know that since he accepted Jesus after evening church, his entire way of thinking had changed.

Life might begin anew for him at almost forty.

His heart no longer felt heavy. His anger about Isobel's betrayal was gone. He felt even more compassion toward his children. He had sympathy toward his mother. He started to pray for her salvation.

As for Dad, his friend Argo Perry had gotten him into Christian things, but Diehl wasn't sure if Dad was exploring Christianity or whether he was one. Diehl was scheduled to call Dad this afternoon, so he'd try to remember to ask.

All in all, he felt that his heart had changed dramatically. It was like night and day.

Never once in the last however many hours had he thought of drinking the night away. Usually, after two nights of drinking, he'd keep doing it, particularly if Isobel goaded him on. Not this time.

Sure, his descent into a pit of despair had been interrupted by his daughter going missing. And for the sake of his other child, he could not afford to be inebriated—not when the detective might need to talk to him.

However, now it was different. He knew there was

a big change inside his heart. His perspective had changed.

"In the interest of time, we're going to start taking prayer requests by email," Matt announced. "I'll email you a Google document, and you update it with your name, prayer requests and praises. Be succinct. Every Monday, we'll go over them."

"Paperless?" Benicio asked.

"Why not?" Matt said. "Some people are not here today, but they want to get updates too. Tristan Rao is traveling in Canada with his family. Adam is also out of town—I sent him on an errand in South Georgia. Hayden Hartley might join us."

Hayden. That dude who put his arm over Skye's shoulder one Wednesday night at the Fire Pit Service at church.

Diehl tried not to react to the idea that Hayden might be sitting in this circle listening to his personal problems.

A runaway or abducted daughter.

Two motherless children.

A new believer navigating the Christian life.

A family business on the brink of restructuring.

Diehl thought about his own parents, how he had split their living arrangements into two cities. Maybe downsizing the family business could give more life to the family. Did they really need to invest in manufacturing and transportation? Would they be fine dealing with only properties? Or maybe they should drop real estate and focus only on transportation? Which income stream should they drop to save their sanity?

Perhaps Dad didn't have to work so hard if Mom could cut expenses. She had been taking entirely too many trips to Paris on the mostly empty Gulfstream. Maybe she should consider taking commercial flights instead.

And yeah, she could stop going to auction houses to buy antique jewelry and whatever else she bought. How many pieces of jewelry could a person wear, anyway?

Then again, Mom was not Diehl's problem—unless Dad dropped dead. Then Diehl and his sister would have to take care of a high-maintenance mother.

Diehl's only happy thought—apart from Christ—was Skye.

He could not think of anything wrong with Skye. She was quiet, thoughtful, kind, generous—all the attributes he wanted to have.

Sometimes Skye was sad, and he wanted to hug her and wipe away her tears—although God would always get to her first, as He should.

Matt gave a stack of paper to Ivan to pass around. "As you can tell, I'm teaching again. I'm going out of town next week when Adam gets back. Ben will be teaching next week."

Ben nodded. Suddenly serious, he had probably been joking earlier about moving the Bible study to an evening slot.

"Well, guys, we let the time run away from us, so let's do this. I'll open with prayer, and we can study God's Word. When we're done, Ivan and Ben can split up the prayer list and pray for all the requests. If you have to leave, sneak out quietly and make sure the door is shut before you run off." Matt looked at the front door as he spoke. "I guess Hayden is not coming."

Matt prayed for them, and he thanked God for Diehl's salvation.

"Let's begin. Last week, we talked about doing good to others, especially those in the house of the Lord—that is, the church. That's an external activity. I was going to do another study on good works, but we want to rejoice in the Lord for our new brother in Christ, Diehl. So today we're going to talk about an internal transformation. Turn with me to Ephesians 4."

Fumbling around, Diehl found the table of contents of his new Bible to show him where Ephesians 4 was.

"Ben, would you read Ephesians 4:17-19, please?" Matt asked.

"Sure. 'This I say, therefore, and testify in the Lord, that you should no longer walk as the rest of the Gentiles walk, in the futility of their mind, having their understanding darkened, being alienated from the life of God, because of the ignorance that is in them, because of the blindness of their heart; who, being past feeling, have given themselves over to lewdness, to work all uncleanness with greediness.' That reminds me of Pastor Gonzalez's sermon on light versus darkness."

Matt nodded. "Yep, Scripture supports Scripture. So that's a laundry list of what we were before we were believers. What are some of the things we were?"

"Ignorant. Futile. Alienated from God," Ivan said in random order. "Lewd. Unclean. Greedy."

"Pastor Gonzalez spoke of light versus darkness," Benicio said. "Here we see the phrase 'having their understanding darkened.' That is, we walked in darkness before we were saved."

Matt waited.

"Do I need to say something?" Diehl asked.

"You don't have to, but if a word or phrase pops up, feel free to say it," Matt said.

"Well, an unsaved person's heart is blind," Diehl said.

"Good. That goes with some line from 'Amazing Grace,' doesn't it? 'I once was lost, but now I see.' Once we're saved, God removes the scales of sin from our eyes, and we can see everything clearly."

"I can attest to that," Diehl said. "I peeked into my son's room this morning while he was still sleeping. He looks different. I see a soul who is loved by God. I was astounded."

"Same here. When I got saved, I suddenly saw each person as an individual," Matt said.

"When did you become a Christian?" Diehl asked.

"Nine years ago—six months after my wife left me." Matt's voice seemed tinged with some unresolved pain.

"Really? You sound like you know a lot about the Bible."

"You don't have to be *old* to know the Bible. A person who is saved for twenty years might not know as much as a person who is saved for two years if the former doesn't spend time in God's Word at all. The closer you stay to God, the more you will learn and have tools to apply to your life."

Diehl nodded.

"Any one of us would be more than happy to meet with you one-to-one to study the Bible verse by verse," Matt added. "Additionally, we have our Bible study here, plus church services. You're going to get fed well."

"I should join the church too," Diehl said.

"And get baptized. We do believer's baptism at church."

Diehl wondered why Ivan had not offered to meet with him one-to-one. He'd ask Ivan later. Was it because they were brothers-in-law?

"I'd be happy to meet with you if you don't mind the fact that I go out of town once or twice a month to buy new stuff for my stores," Matt said. "My schedule is sort of touch-and-go."

"I don't know if you want to see me too much." Ivan laughed. "You'll get so tired of me and then I'll be in trouble with your sister."

Benicio lifted his hand. "We'll be your big brothers here in this men's group. I need someone to hold me accountable too. I sometimes fall off the bandwagon and get lazy about studying the Bible."

"The chaplain has confessed," Ivan said.

"Former chaplain. I retired, remember?" Benicio grinned. "Seriously, I'm helping in the youth group at church, so I've already met your daughter and son, and

Riley's daughter and son. I don't know if the kids will think I'm tattling on them whenever we meet."

"Thanks, guys, you're all very kind," Diehl said. "Looks like the only person who has no connection to me personally is Matt."

"Let's set a date," Matt said. "I think we should start as soon as possible, even while the police and the community are searching for your daughter. You need to know the power of His Word and His presence in your life. When going through difficult times, we need to pray powerfully in the Name of Jesus. How do we pray? We need to know Scripture so we know what prayers God listens to."

Wow.

Diehl was happy he picked Matt to help him study God's Word.

"What I just mentioned is where we are—or ought to be—as Christians," Matt continued. "We went over a list of things that unbelievers are before they get saved. And now we'll see who we are as Christians. Diehl, would you please read the next sentence? It's one long sentence split up into five verses in Ephesians 4:20-24."

"Okay." Diehl felt a little bit nervous. For the first time in his adult life, he was going to read the Bible aloud to three mature Christian men. He had to do well—not for them, but because this is the Holy Word of God.

He cleared his throat. "Here's the passage. 'But you have not so learned Christ, if indeed you have heard Him and have been taught by Him, as the truth is in Jesus: that you put off, concerning your former conduct, the old man which grows corrupt according to the deceitful lusts, and be renewed in the spirit of your mind, and that you put on the new man which was created according to God, in true righteousness and holiness.' Whew. It is one long sentence."

"With many loaded parts," Ivan said. "Bonus list of 'former conduct' we're to do away with. We were corrupt, deceitful, lustful."

Lustful.

That described Diehl's relationship with Isobel.

"The phrase 'the truth is in Jesus' reminds me of John 14:6," Benicio said. "Pastor Gonzalez mentioned it last night. 'I am the way, the truth, and the life. No one comes to the Father except through Me.' Once we are reconciled to God through Jesus Christ, the rest of the list applies."

"It's a call to action," Matt said. "Put off your old self. Put on the new self. What's the same and what's the difference?"

Diehl didn't understand the question. He waited for someone else to say something.

Benicio was at the coffee maker. He poured a half cup. "What's the same? Only Jesus can cleanse us from our past. And only Jesus can help us walk in the newness of life."

"And the difference is that our new life in Christ is internal," Matt said. "You are called to be 'renewed in the spirit of your mind.' The new man that God transformed you into is 'in true righteousness and holiness.' The next time I teach, we'll break down those two words in two studies. What is righteousness in Christ? What is holiness in Christ? For now, just remember that we can't have either unless we are in Christ."

"In Christ, we have everything," Diehl said. "Outside of Christ, we have nothing."

"That about sums it up." Matt nodded in approval. "Now let's turn to our list of prayers and praises. Are you having a fun summer? Rejoice in the Lord! Are you having a difficult and trying time in life? Pray to the Lord. He's sovereign over all the events in this world and everything that concerns us. He undergirds us with His strength."

Diehl felt good about the Bible study this morning until they started to pray about his lost daughter. Then he lost it and found himself on his knees weeping, pleading to God to bring his daughter back alive and in one piece.

He wasn't the only man on his knees. The other three men were with him, praying in turn and in earnest for Elisa, a girl none of them—except for Ivan and Diehl—knew.

When they were done praying, there was not a dry eye in the room.

"Even though I'm not married and don't have a daughter, I do have a niece," Benicio said. "I can't imagine what my sister's family would go through if my niece were missing."

"As someone who is the father of a soon-to-be-born child, I already know it's tough," Ivan said. "The search party has gone online, so we're not out there pounding pavement. It might not seem that we're doing much, but the college kids are on the frontline for this. The rest of us—mostly the older generations—have a lot to catch up on, connectivity-wise."

"Let's hope the leads lead somewhere," Diehl said. "I know it's only been two days, but a lot can happen in two days."

"Nothing is impossible with God," Ivan said. "Absolutely nothing."

CHAPTER FORTY-ONE

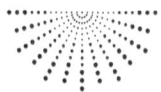

*D*iehl had texted or left voice messages for Skye all day Monday, and so had Matt, Ivan, and Brinley. Skye felt overwhelmed with the avalanche of information, prayer requests, updates from Malik, Helen's PI, and the good detective. However, she was happy to be part of the prayer support team at Seaside Chapel.

Praying was the best thing she could do, being so far away in Miami Beach, where she had a full schedule from morning until past dinnertime. Not only had she been busy helping Sebastian at his booth, Skye somehow ended up filling in for one of the competition judges who had come down with food poisoning at lunchtime on Monday.

Should she have volunteered?

"I don't know what overcame me," Skye told Diehl on FaceTime when he called her after dinner on Monday night.

She slumped back in the armchair in her hotel room overlooking the marina. It was dark now at ten o'clock, and she could not enjoy the much-touted view. Truth be told, she could have gotten a room facing the parking lot for a hundred dollars less per night, considering that she had been gone all day the last two days, mingling at the food festival.

And now judging.

"You have a kind heart," Diehl said.

Onscreen, he was dressed in an old T-shirt and a pair of faded plaid pajama pants. He was sitting in bed. He seemed to be looking into his iPad camera as he held his phone in hand.

"Do I? Or was I taken advantage of?" Skye asked.

"When is the judging over?"

"Wednesday night. The winners will be announced at the evening gala, where we get to taste the winning dishes."

"And then the next day, you'll be in Athens to see your sister-in-law."

Skye nodded. "Very late at night."

"And you'll be back here Sunday night." Diehl drank some mineral water straight out of the green bottle.

Skye was glad it wasn't anything stronger, but she did not ask him what else he had been ingesting. She was not his Holy Spirit. His convictions should come from God alone.

"No, I haven't had a drop since Friday night." Diehl seemed to have read her mind.

Three days.

"In fact, Mom asked me to go down to the terrace bar tonight. Pierre made her cocktails as she regaled me with oft-repeated tales of old about the Brooks family, how it came to be and all that. Even with the smell of booze around me, I had no desire for any of it. I am serious. The desire has evaporated from me."

"It's a God thing."

Diehl agreed. "God removed the desire for alcohol from me. Mom was stone drunk when Pierre and I helped her get to her bedroom. And Pierre remarked that I only drank mineral water all evening."

"God watches over His own."

"I found Jesus and He protected me from that which can destroy me. Maybe to other people, alcohol isn't a big deal. To each his own. For me, I can't go there. I have no desire to numb myself anymore. I think God plucked me out of a spiral I couldn't recover from. The more I drank, the more I drank."

Quietly, Skye praised God.

"The Spirit of God is greater than the spirit in the world." Diehl swiped his phone. "I learned this from Matt. 'You are of God, little children, and have overcome them, because He who is in you is greater than he who is in the world.' I John 4:4."

"I like that verse. Good reminder."

"I don't need alcohol anymore because Jesus is my Lord and Savior." Diehl's voice cracked. "God has done so much for me, Skye."

"Just be aware that sometimes the enemy will try to find a way to knock you over in the midst of your celebration."

Diehl nodded. "Whatever happens, I will still worship God."

"You're learning a lot."

"Matt's teaching me how to study the Bible."

"He's a good Bible study teacher." Skye didn't go into the other things, like her having gone out with Matt once. He had been single for a very long time and hadn't dated anyone for at least eight years, so Avery set them up on a blind date.

When Skye showed up and saw who it was, both she and Matt had a good laugh through dinner. Might as well, since the reservation took a few days to set up.

"Not just a Bible study teacher," Diehl said. "He's my accountability partner."

"That's great, Diehl. He's so busy, so for him to do this for you... It's amazing. Matt's a mature Christian. I know he wants God's perfect will to be done in your life."

Diehl put down his bottle of mineral water on the side table. "I told him about you."

"Me?" Skye wondered what they could be talking about.

"Us."

"What about us?"

Diehl grinned. "I wanted to know if it's okay for me to pursue a relationship with you while I'm having all those problems in my family."

"What did he say?" Skye asked.

"He said the most important thing right now is to get Elisa back."

"But you could have told yourself that. It's obvious."

"However, talking with you helped take the sting off my stress." Diehl drew a deep breath. "You know that you're my silver lining and the sun rays above heavy rain clouds."

"Be careful, Diehl." Skye wanted to prevent a misplaced focal point. "God is the one who brings you sunshine and rain."

"Yes, I know that God is the source of all things good—including sending an encourager to be with me through my tough times. If you hadn't shown up at the beach house on Saturday morning, I would have failed as a father. You covered for me, helped me through the day so I could at least muddle my way through. You didn't say a word to anyone so that I wasn't embarrassed in front of my family. Most of all, you were there for Ethan when I wasn't all there."

He had noticed.

In her heart, Skye thanked God. "To God be the glory."

"I know I'm not out of the woods yet, but we've all prayed with great expectations that God will bring Elisa home safely," Diehl said.

"Any word from Detective Jeong?"

"He's working around the clock with the GBI and FBI, and now the DHS is involved."

The Department of Homeland Security could only mean one thing to Skye. "So they think it might be child trafficking?"

"They're trying to rule it out." Diehl's voice was even.

He looked calm on the screen. Skye believed that God had given him internal fortitude to endure this. At this time, it could go either way.

"Of course, we will pray that all is well," Skye said.

"Fortunately, Dad's holding up the company so I can focus on Elisa," Diehl said. "I don't need to worry about what goes on at the office in Atlanta until all this is over."

Atlanta.

Five hours of driving away.

Skye tried to be strong, but inside her heart, she knew she could not carry on a long-distance relationship. FaceTime every day wouldn't cut it for her.

Maybe the only reason Diehl was on St. Simon's Island all summer was to get saved. Maybe it wasn't to find a new girlfriend.

Skye wondered how life would go on.

"It's amazing how my priorities have changed overnight," Diehl said. "Before this summer, I wanted wealth—lots of it. I wanted to earn more than Dad and Grandpa combined. I know that's a simple goal but if you knew their net worth, you might laugh at my impossible dream. Now, I want health—spiritual and emotional health."

"You still have to go back to work."

"I know, but..." Diehl leaned toward his iPad. "I want to be with you."

"Your office is in Atlanta. Mine is on St. Simon's

Island." Skye didn't have to remind him, but it was worth repeating.

"We can't meet in the middle because that's the Okefenokee Swamp." Diehl laughed.

It wasn't exactly, but Skye knew what he was saying.

Diehl turned solemn. "I don't want to leave you."

Skye wondered if they had plunged into a relationship too quickly. Now was not the time to bring it up. After Elisa returned, they would need to address it.

"I want God's perfect will to be done for both of us." That was all she could say for now.

"I agree, Skye. We can pray about this and see where He leads us." Diehl stared at the screen.

Skye smiled. "I'm just tired. I had a ridiculously long first day. I hope someone else will fill in the judging tomorrow so I don't have to do it. Frankly, I just want to help my brother at his booth and that's all I want to do."

"Then don't volunteer." Diehl folded his arms. "Tomorrow, go to the organizers and talk to them. Surely they have backups—or they should have made a list."

"Do you boss people around at your workplace?" Skye smiled.

"All the time."

"This is the first time you told me what to do."

"Is it?" Diehl raised his eyebrows. "Let me remind you that I skillfully wiggled my way into playing piano for the Treble Trio. Didn't I tell you what to do then too? Aren't you glad you agreed to let me do it?"

"You're just as good as your sister at the piano—after you scrape off the rust." Skye laughed.

"I do love the way you sing. Your voice is clean, crisp, and clear. Made me want to do my best at the piano."

"Thank you for your help. You took a load off your sister in her last trimester of pregnancy."

"And I haven't even been accepted as an official member of Treble Trio."

"You're filling in for your sister," Skye said. "If we make you an official member, then it's not a trio anymore."

"Well, you figure that out. It's your group."

"That's a problem for another day." Skye massaged her shoulders and stretched. "Right now, I'm tired, and I have to get up early to eat more strange dishes."

"I'll pray you don't get food poisoning," Diehl said.

"Thank you, Mr. Brooks."

"I'll let you go. Sweet dreams."

It was anything but sweet dreams.

Skye cried herself to sleep for the first time in many years, thinking about the *something* she had with Diehl, and the parting that loomed ahead at summer's end and his kids' school year beginning.

CHAPTER FORTY-TWO

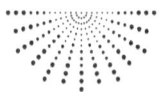

*B*eing woken up in the middle of the night by Malik rapping hard on his bedroom door created all sorts of anxiety in Diehl that he wasn't able to deal with at three in the morning. Or was it only two o'clock?

"Sir, they found Elisa." Malik's voice showed the strain of a father.

Diehl could tell that if it had been one of his three kids, he would have been distraught. The former Army colonel had a lot of tough training behind him, but when it came to kids, whether his own or the Brookses' children, Malik had a soft spot that he could not hide.

"Where?" Diehl asked, feeling like he needed to sit down. He had jumped out of bed when Malik showed up, freaking him out like the house was on fire.

"Decatur."

Metro Atlanta. He should have... No. Nobody would have guessed. Still, it was in the Atlanta area.

Diehl's house was across the interstate on another side of Atlanta. "We checked my house, didn't we?"

"Yes. None of the security cameras showed she had ever been there," Malik said. "Detective Jeong called a moment ago, saying that the GBI found her. She was with Romina Harrison."

Diehl's eyes widened. "Seriously?"

The nanny he had let go six months before. It wasn't because she failed to do her work, but the kids were going to school in Hawaii and living with their maternal grandmother. She wasn't needed anymore.

"Is my daughter okay?" Diehl felt both a sense of relief and foreboding. "Is she hurt?"

"Jeong didn't say."

"How did they find Elisa?"

"Based on what Ethan said he overheard on the phone, and the name you said Hans mumbled, Jeong asked Hans to go to the station. He refused, so Earl Young paid him a visit."

"Oh?" Diehl was surprised. "Are we liable for that?"

"Nope. Hans cooperated willingly." Malik paused. "There's more, sir, but I'll let Earl fill you in with what he knows. He's waiting for us at Peachtree DeKalb Airport."

"Give me a few minutes to brush my teeth and change," Diehl said.

"I've already asked Chris to fuel the jet."

"Thank you, Malik. Please wake my mother. Tell her to pack for a few days."

"Yes, sir."

"Get the Bishops."

"Ah, about them..."

"What?"

"They left," Malik said.

"Left to go home?"

"Apparently. They flew out on a private plane."

"When?"

"An hour ago."

"That doesn't make any sense."

"Detective Jeong is already in Atlanta, but he's going to follow up on it." Malik was about to walk away when he turned back. "Speaking of the detective, he wants you to bring a change of clothes for Elisa."

"Okay."

Diehl brushed his teeth and packed his toothpaste and toothbrush. The suitcase of clothes he had brought over from Brinley's beach house was still conveniently packed. When Cara washed his clothes for him, he put the folded clothes back into the suitcase. As such he didn't have to do anything but find his toothbrush and toothpaste.

He hadn't planned on staying at Mom's house long. He wanted to get back to Brinley's house for his own space. Now he wasn't sure if that house—so close to a public beach—was safe for his two kids.

Perhaps he was only paranoid.

Thousands of children had been brought up on St. Simon's Island for decades without abduction problems.

Diehl left his bedroom to wake up Ethan.

He reminded himself to text Dad when it was

closer to daybreak. And Skye, too, although he did not want to wake her before her upcoming long day at the food festival.

Before he reached Ethan's bedroom, he stopped at Elisa's room to get some clean clothes for her. He packed several sets of clothes, a couple of pairs of shoes —she had worn her favorite on Friday—and her favorite stuffed animals, which he picked up from her unmade bed. He put all that into Elisa's pink rolling carry-on.

Then he found a small tote bag in the closet, into which he tossed her toothbrush and toothpaste, together with a change of clothes for the hospital— because he didn't think it made sense to take the carry-on to the hospital. He rolled up the tote bag and stuffed it into his own backpack with his laptop and power cable inside. It fit in the larger compartment.

It dawned on Diehl that he hadn't thanked God for answering his prayer.

He dropped to his knees and closed his eyes. "Lord Jesus, forgive me for forgetting. Thank You for answering my prayer. They found Elisa. I don't know what condition she is in, but as long as she is alive, we can sort out the rest. I pray that You will catch the people responsible. Don't let them get away with it. In Your Holy name, I pray. Amen."

"Amen!" Malik's voice was sure and clear.

Diehl's eyes popped open. "You're a believer?"

"Yes, sir."

"I had no idea."

"We only talk about work."

"And you worked on Sunday morning."

"Not all the time. When required, I either attend the early service or watch it on live stream—as I did last Sunday."

"How long was the service?"

"An hour."

"You could have gone to church and come back," Diehl said.

"You could've too, sir." Malik smiled.

"Well...I stayed up all night, remember?"

"So did I, sir."

"I went to the evening service, though," Diehl said.

"My church doesn't have an evening service."

"Then come to mine. It starts at five and ends just in time for dinner." Diehl wondered if he should have referred to Seaside Chapel as his church when he hadn't joined it.

"Miss Brinley has invited me before." Malik turned toward a noise.

In her silk pajamas, Mom rolled her giant suitcase toward them. "Let's go, boys."

"Let me get Ethan," Diehl said. "I'll meet you downstairs."

"May I take your bag?" Malik asked.

"Yes. Thank you." Diehl quietly opened Ethan's door as Malik and Mom headed for the elevator. Even though they were only one floor down, Mom preferred not to climb the stairs.

Diehl opened Ethan's bedroom door slowly. His son was still sleeping—like a comfortable baby—under a blanket in the bed. Diehl hated to wake him up, but he wasn't going to leave Ethan behind.

"Elisa?" Ethan rubbed his eyes. "About time."

Diehl tried not read too much into it. If this was a hoax, he'd get to the bottom of it and everyone would pay—

No. I'll be glad to have my daughter back.

That thought remained in his mind all the way to the Brunswick Golden Isles Airport and through breakfast on board the family Gulfstream, when Malik told them that Private Investigator Earl Young would be meeting them at the airport.

Malik suggested that he and Diehl would go with Earl to the station to meet Detective Jeong, while Mom and Ethan would wait at Diehl's house with Dad.

Diehl was impressed that while he had been sleeping, the GBI and local area police department were hard at work hunting down the tracks that led to his daughter.

Speaking of sleeping, he turned to the seat where Ethan was buckled in, and the kid had fallen asleep again. Across from Ethan in a similar reclining seat, Malik was talking on the phone with Earl.

One row in front of them, Diehl and Mom sat across from each other.

Instead of texting Dad, Mom called him, not caring that it was four in the morning Atlanta time, and Dad was probably still sleeping.

"Checking on him," Mom whispered loud enough for Diehl to hear. "Trying to see who picks up the phone."

Diehl's jaw dropped. "We have PIs for that sort of thing."

"He's not going to cheat on me." Mom waved her hands. "He's not an Urquhart."

Diehl didn't reply. It wasn't polite for Mom to gossip about her own friends, although everyone felt sorry for Marguerite Urquhart when her husband of fifty years had an expensive facelift and ran off with his chief financial officer's daughter—only to die of a heart attack on an expedition trip in the Amazon rainforest.

While Mom talked with Dad, Diehl texted Skye.

She wasn't awake yet, he supposed.

She surprised him by calling him. "Good morning and good news there."

"You're up early." Diehl was happy to hear her voice. He put on earbuds so that only he could hear what Skye had to say.

He kept his voice low so that Ethan didn't wake up, but the boy had slept through the other conversations in the cabin.

She was wearing a T-shirt, and her hair was all tied up in a bun. Her face looked fresh. She wore no makeup.

Diehl wondered what it would be like to see that face every morning. When she smiled, he could hear a sparrow sing.

"For some reason, I woke up and couldn't get back to sleep," Skye said. "I've been praying for the last fifteen minutes before you texted me."

"Well, maybe God woke you up." One week before, Diehl wouldn't have believed that.

"I prayed for Elisa, Ethan, and you."

"Thank you. As I mentioned in my text, we're on our way to Atlanta."

"Thank God they found her alive," Skye said. "Anything could have happened in the last three days."

"Right. God answered our prayers." Diehl went on to say that Detective Jeong hadn't told them everything. "So we don't know what to expect."

"No matter what happens, God will work it out."

"I have to believe that." Diehl waited for the flight attendant to clear the breakfast off the table in front of him. He pointed to his coffee mug. She nodded.

"How's Ethan?" Skye asked.

"Asleep."

"Speaking of sleep, maybe I need to go back to sleep. I might be able to get three or four hours in before I have to get ready for more judging."

"Okay. Thanks for calling." He drank the hot coffee that the flight attendant brought him. "I appreciate it."

Skye smiled into the camera. "Before I go, let me ask you something."

"Anything."

"How are *you* doing?"

Maybe it was his voice or something. She seemed to sense his feeling.

"I'm taking it one day at a time," he finally said. "The days go better when you're here with me."

"Oh." That was all Skye said.

"But don't let me take you away from being with your brother."

"Speaking of my brother, he told me that you're undergoing a test from God, and that I should let you be so that you don't rely on people when you need to be relying on God."

Diehl thought about what Skye just told him. "He thinks this is a test?"

"To grow your faith in Christ."

"That's a good test," Diehl said. "Stay there. Let me pass this test."

"Does that mean you don't think you'll pass the test if I'm there with you?" Skye asked.

Could Skye distract him? "I don't know."

"You might turn to me for support instead of to God."

"While Sebastian might have a point, I want to see you because I enjoy your company. In fact..." How could he say it? He glanced over at Mom. She was off her phone and probably listening in to what he said, but she could not hear what Skye said because he was wearing earbuds.

Well, did it matter? He wanted to say it anyway.

"I want to be with you the rest of my life, Skye."

Onscreen, Skye looked visibly moved. "I don't know what to say."

"Do you feel the same?"

Slowly, she nodded. "It's an odd feeling, isn't it?"

"For the first time in my life, I know who I want to be with. I'm actually feeling pretty good."

"Same here."

Hearing her say that warmed Diehl's heart to no end, and lifted him above the clouds outside.

He considered it her vote of confidence that he was worthy of her time, space, and love. That, in spite of his failures, she still wanted to be with him.

The encouraging message conveyed made him feel like he could conquer anything.

Even this episode with Elisa—no matter her condition when they returned her to him.

"I would like to spend more time with you," Diehl said, even though he wasn't sure how yet.

His work would take him back to Atlanta soon. Either he had to relocate his office from Atlanta to St. Simon's Island, or Skye would have to move to Atlanta to be with him.

"God owns time," Skye said. "He will work it out."

She read my mind. Either that or she had been thinking about their situation.

"Keep me posted about Elisa," Skye said.

"I will."

The phone call ended without a commitment.

"Go after her or you will lose her." Mom's voice was loud and clear.

Yep, she had been listening—albeit only to Diehl's side of the phone conversation.

"Girls like that won't stay single long." Mom pulled up her blanket over her shoulders. "She's sweet, kind, always helpful. Doesn't smoke, never cusses. One in a million."

Kind.

That word again.

Diehl remembered telling Skye on Monday night that she had a kind heart. A kind heart like hers could be fragile. He didn't want to do anything that could hurt her in any way.

Lord, let me be the best man for her.

And he meant it.

"No criminal record—except for a couple of speeding tickets out of Jekyll—"

"Mom!" Diehl was appalled. "You didn't do a background check, did you?"

Mom shook her head, all innocent-like. "Not me. Uh, not directly."

"Malik?" Diehl said it loudly enough for Malik to hear.

"I just do what I'm told." Malik grinned.

Mom wasn't done. "She's single, never been married, of childbearing age—"

"We're not in the fifties anymore, Mom."

"Between Skye's the Limit and Saffron on Jekyll, she has a personal worth of nine million."

"What?" Diehl perked up and then scolded himself for doing so. They had invaded Skye's privacy.

"I know, right. So I asked myself how she could be worth that much running a personal chef business and being only a part-owner of a restaurant?" Mom inspected her manicured nails. They were a bright red.

"Mom. That's prying."

"Don't you want to know?"

"No." *Yes.*

"You're a curious one, aren't you?"

Diehl didn't reply.

"She started out with an inheritance from her aunt and uncle. Then she invested wisely, including in cryptocurrency."

"Good for her." Diehl felt proud of Skye that she had multiplied her income.

"She used to own a million-dollar oceanfront beach house, but she sold it to buy out her brother's shares. For whatever reason, she rents a condo now, but get this." Mom waited. "She has a piece of land on Seaside Island that has doubled in value in five years, but she hasn't built anything on it. Empty except for grass and trees. Why hasn't she done anything with it?"

"Seaside Island?"

"Half an acre of prime oceanfront, can you believe it?"

No, he could not.

"She doesn't look rich. She looks rather ordinary," Mom said. "Her brother is worth four million more than she is, and he looks like a regular guy."

"Not everyone flaunts their wealth like you do." Diehl frowned. "Did Malik dig all that up for you?"

Mom seemed pleased with herself. "The last part, I got out of Marguerite. She thinks if a cottage is built on the land, the value could be at least fifteen million and up."

Marguerite Urquhart, the matriarch of Urquhart Enterprises.

Jared's mom.

Which meant that Loose Lips Marguerite would eventually tell Jared that Mom had asked about Skye...

It could start a bidding war between Jared and Diehl for Skye's attention.

No, he could not lose Skye to Jared—not because Diehl had always been competitive against his childhood friend, but because he knew now that he loved her.

Then again, how could it possibly work out?

Your office is in Atlanta. And mine is on St. Simon's Island.

Skye's words from Monday night rang in Diehl's ears.

Both of Skye's businesses were ensconced on the Georgia coast. On the other hand, all three branches of Brooks Investments were headquartered in midtown Atlanta.

It would be too much to ask Skye to move to Atlanta. If he asked, Skye might think he didn't consider her businesses as important as his.

It was impossible for him to move Brooks Investments to St. Simon's Island unless...

Nah. It won't work.

Somehow there must be a way.

Is there a way, God?

CHAPTER FORTY-THREE

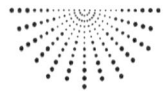

*P*rivate Investigator Earl Young greeted Diehl and his family at the disembarkation hall of the Peachtree DeKalb Airport after the Gulfstream jet landed, at the same time as Dad's chauffeur, Murray, who had brought a vehicle to transport Mom and Ethan to Diehl's house.

Murray wasn't alone. Two of Malik's security personnel accompanied him. Trevor and Miranda had been with Brooks Security for several years. They were both young and single.

"Trevor is going to be with Ethan at all times," Malik said quietly. "Miranda is coming with us to get Elisa."

In times like this, Diehl appreciated Malik more than ever. The chief of security had done what Diehl asked him to do on Sunday. He hoped these two people worked out to keep Elisa and Ethan trouble-free henceforth.

"Dad, I want to go with you." Ethan stepped toward Diehl, who was telling Murray to take their luggage to the house.

Diehl placed his hands on Ethan's shoulders. "We're going to the hospital—"

"Hospital?" Ethan's voice rose. "Is Elisa okay?"

"Don't worry. They're just checking her. You know how you go to the doctor and they test everything?"

Ethan nodded.

"There might be a lot of waiting," Diehl added.

"I can wait." Ethan looked at him earnestly.

Diehl patted his head. "I know you can, son, but I need you to do something important for me, okay?"

"What?"

"You need to take care of Grandma here and go with her to the house, where Grandpa is waiting for us."

Ethan glanced at Mom. "Why do I need to take care of her?"

"Because Grandma is fragile, and you're the big boy of the hour."

"What about the next hour?"

"That's all included," Diehl said. "I'm going to bring Elisa home, and we should be at the house very soon, but between now and then you need to make sure Grandma is okay. Don't let her fall or do anything silly."

"Grandma's not going to do anything silly." Ethan made a face.

435

"I wouldn't put it past her." Diehl glanced at Mom, who was trying not to laugh.

"While you're at the house, help Grandma get Elisa's room ready for her, okay?"

"Don't you have a maid to do that for her?" Ethan asked.

Standing nearby, Earl chuckled.

"Grandpa is waiting for you," Diehl said. "The sooner we get out of this airport, the sooner we can have your sister back with us again."

"I miss Elisa."

"I miss her too. Now go." Diehl handed him over to Mom, who held the boy's hand tightly, as if letting go would spell disaster.

"Mom, we'll see you soon, okay?" Diehl said.

"Text me." Mom smiled before disappearing through the sliding glass door with Ethan and Dad's chauffeur. Trevor followed them out.

Diehl watched them go. Mom's words came back to his mind.

Manage your emotions.

Yes, Diehl felt relieved that Elisa was safe, but in what condition? The more he wondered, the angrier he became. If they hurt Elisa...

He prayed quietly for God to quell his emotions.

Diehl, Malik, and Miranda followed Earl to his parked rental SUV. Before he pulled out of the parking lot, Earl explained all that he knew about the situation.

"Hans Gray was the key," Earl said. "The words that Skye overheard at your mother's house and the conversation you had with him in the dining room both led us to this day."

Skye.

Diehl missed her more and more. He buckled his seat belt in the passenger seat.

"The Greyhound clue panned out then," Malik said from the backseat.

"Yep. And when Hans mumbled 'Romina,' that added some weight." Earl turned the car onto a street that Diehl was not familiar with.

"Romina?" It was a good thing that Diehl was buckled in. "I can't believe it. Why?"

"Sort it out later. I'm telling last night's story. So Hans didn't want to talk to the police at all. Still protecting his girl."

"That's where you came in."

Earl smiled. "Filling in the gaps is our specialty."

"What did Hans say?" Diehl asked.

"He had a thing for your nanny. It was lust at first sight, and they only had less than a week before Romina had to leave Seaside Island and take the two kids back to Hawaii."

"Well, in my own defense, I sent her and my kids to my parents' home for Thanksgiving, but I didn't go —as Malik would have told you," Diehl said.

"Hans and Romina got cozy that week," Earl said. "Shortly before you let her go."

"As I mentioned, we didn't need her service anymore," Diehl said.

"You're not admitting that you fired her because

she and Hans were frolicking on the private beach in the buff?"

"Did they?" Diehl glanced over his shoulder. Malik shrugged. "I had no idea. Was it at night? Did anyone notice?"

"Hans said no one saw them. Chef Pierre did not fire him. However, Romina thought that you somehow knew."

"Frankly, I don't care as long as they did not expose themselves to my kids," Diehl said. Then he went silent. "Wow. Malik, you sure you didn't know about it?"

Malik didn't say a word.

"Malik?" Diehl asked again.

"Well..." Malik cleared his throat. "I'm sorry. I only worry about the perimeters of Brooks Cottage and the guest house. Should I pay attention to what goes on at the beach beyond the dunes?"

"No, I suppose not."

"Besides, it was at night. And we're just now finding out because Hans confessed to Earl, who then told Detective Jeong."

"Should I even ask how you got a confession out of Hans?" Diehl asked.

"Better not ask," Earl said, stopping at the light. "Well, if Romina hadn't committed a crime, we wouldn't be discussing their midnight dalliance. The bottom line is that Hans felt he was responsible for causing Romina's marriage to fall apart."

"What does all this have anything to do with my daughter?" Diehl asked.

"After the divorce, Romina was destitute. She burned through money like an incinerator and accumulated some credit card debts. She has lived with the rich and famous for several years, and now can't live within her means."

"So she called Hans?"

"She blackmailed Hans. Said if he didn't help Elisa get away from the 'evil grandparents' that she would go to the police and report their tryst as a rape. At the same time, she gave the impression that she was still interested in him and would forgive him if he did that one thing."

"Mixed signals."

"He thought something didn't seem right, but Romina sweetened the deal by offering to pay his rent. Since he was desperately poor, he agreed to help her."

"Hans told you all that?"

"Last evening after he got off work." Earl yawned. "After this, I need to get some sleep."

"And you're driving right now." Diehl couldn't believe it. *Does Earl even know where the roads are?*

"I grew up in the metro area," Earl said. "I can find my way with my eyes closed."

"No, please don't do that." Diehl chuckled.

"I don't need much sleep. Don't worry about me. The point is, I told all that to Detective Jeong yesterday evening." Earl stopped at another red light.

"So... Instead of getting a legitimate job like everyone else, Romina decided to abduct my daughter?"

"It gets more interesting," Malik added. "Elisa

went with Hans because he was taking her to Romina."

"How? We watched all the security videos."

"Remember the carts and trolleys?" Malik reminded Diehl.

Diehl almost knew where Malik was going. "Yeah?"

"Elisa was in one of the tilt trucks, underneath tablecloths."

"No." Diehl's jaw dropped. "Did they drug her?"

"Hans told me that your daughter went willingly," Earl said.

Diehl's heart sank. Had he failed parenting class or something? He couldn't recall teaching Elisa not to go anywhere with strangers.

Well, Hans wasn't a stranger. He had been working for Chef Pierre for a few years, at least.

Neither was Romina a stranger.

The phone conversation that Elisa had with Romina a week before finally made sense. Somehow Romina must have convinced Elisa to get to a Greyhound station. And the only way out of Brooks Cottage without being noticed was in Chef Pierre's van—in one of his utility carts.

"Who drove her to the Greyhound bus station?" Diehl asked. "Hans?"

"Yep," Malik said. "The dishwasher suspected something and tried to warn Hans not to do it."

"He did it anyway—because of the threat from Romina, but also because he was probably still in love with her." Earl pulled in at Grady Memorial Hospital parking lot for visitors.

"Anything else I need to know before I see my daughter?" Diehl asked.

"That's all I know. I'm sure Detective Jeong will fill us in soon," Earl said as he parked the vehicle.

CHAPTER FORTY-FOUR

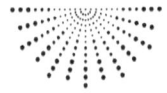

*A*s soon as Elisa saw Diehl walked through the door of the examination room, she started to cry.

She was sitting on the bed, looking quite disheveled and wearing a paper hospital gown. Her hair had been cut very short. She had scratch marks on her arms. She was barefoot.

"Shhh." Diehl wanted to hug her, but she pushed him away.

"You're not my dad." Her voice was sharp, like her mother's.

"I am too." Diehl sat on one of those rolling stools. He placed Elisa's tote bag on his lap. He was some distance away from Elisa to give her space, but close enough to let her know he cared.

She shook her head.

Diehl prayed. For the first time in his life, he found himself putting God first. Now that he had experienced the love of God—having been saved two days before—he felt more able to love his daughter, who might not have been his had God not placed her in his arms.

Diehl blinked as he recalled the day Elisa was born.

He leaned forward. "I held you when you were born. I changed your diapers. Your first word was 'Da.' And you burped all over my brand-new Italian silk tie."

He recalled his excitement of becoming a dad. Isobel had never said a word about who the father was. She let Diehl carry on being Dad.

And now, he was all they had left in this world.

Elisa curled her lips and frowned.

"I let you sleep in my bed when you were scared of thunder. I took you to Disney World." Because her mother had taken a vacation without her kids. Or Diehl, for that matter. "I bought you your first set of colored pencils. I made you chicken soup when you had a cold."

"You microwaved a can of soup," Elisa corrected him.

"Soup is soup."

"I don't think Chef Pierre would agree with you."

Diehl shrugged. "I was trying to say that I've been your dad, and I will always be your dad."

"My real dad is in Italy," Elisa blurted. "Romina was going to take me there."

"She abducted you," Diehl said.

"No. I took the Greyhound bus myself. Stop treating me like a child."

"You're only twelve."

"So?"

"If you want to go to Italy, why didn't you ask me?" Diehl wanted to understand his daughter.

"Romina said you're jealous because you're not my real father."

"She can't read my mind. Only God knows what I'm thinking," Diehl said calmly. "If you want to see Luigi, I will call him and make arrangements for us to meet."

Elisa didn't respond.

"You can't get there with Romina. She's not your mother or guardian. I'm the only one who can go with you to the passport office to renew your expired passport."

"Romina says we're getting new passports."

"You can't just get new passports from anybody, Elisa. It doesn't work that way."

"She lied to me? I don't believe you."

Diehl didn't want to miss the opportunity to break through to his daughter, since they were still talking. "If Romina is telling the truth, why did she have to hide? Why did you have to hide?"

"She said you would be angry."

"Why would I be angry? In fact, I would be sad, Elisa. And so would your brother, Ethan. We missed you so much."

Elisa folded her arms. Just like Isobel when she had been upset about something.

"What about Skye?" Elisa snapped.

"What about her?" Diehl wondered why her name came up.

"You like her very much. You're going to start a new family with her." Elisa's eyes filled with tears. "What will happen to Ethan and me?"

"Is that why you agreed to run off with Romina?"

"Maybe our real dad would take us."

Diehl didn't have the heart to tell her that Luigi was also married.

"Since Mom died, I feel so alone." Elisa's tears flowed.

"No, no. You're never alone. I'm here. God is here." Diehl looked around for tissues or paper towels but found nothing. He reached toward Elisa, but she swatted off his hand. She wiped her tears with her dirty hands.

Diehl prayed that the germs on her hands were harmless.

After this, Elisa would need a shower and a visit with a doctor to make sure everything was fine. His daughter was back now. Everything else, they could fix.

Correction: God could fix.

He watched his daughter cry. He knew she had to let it out. Poor thing.

But he could feel her pain of being abandoned by her mother while she had been alive, and now she was gone.

These kids were too young to have to endure such grief.

Diehl knew that he had grown attached to Elisa and Ethan. How could he have allowed the Bishops to keep them for one school year?

"Elisa?"

She didn't reply.

"I'm sorry I sent you and Ethan to Hawaii for the entire school year," he said. "After your mother passed away, I had a hard time. When your grandparents in Hawaii offered to take you to school, I thought it would be a good idea to have family around."

"It was fun there but..."

"You'd rather be home."

"I'm so angry with you, Dad."

Diehl waited to hear more.

"I had a hard time when Mom died, but at the same time, it was like we lost our dad too," Elisa said.

"I was working too much."

"Grandma Zeta said you don't care."

"She's wrong. I care. I just tried to work and not think about the fact that your mother is...uh..."

"Dead."

"Yes. I'm sorry I did you wrong. I pushed you two away because I didn't know how to handle my grief."

"We're all sad," Elisa said.

Diehl nodded.

"We spent Thanksgiving and Christmas without you, Dad."

What was I doing? "I failed, Elisa."

"And then to top it all off, you sent Grandma Rose to get us for summer break. You didn't go to Hawaii yourself. Even Grandpa Ned was there. But you weren't."

"I'm sorry. I was working and then I drove to St. Simon's a few days before you arrived."

"You were staying in Auntie Bling's beach house, not with Grandma Rose. Why?"

Diehl didn't want to get into how he could only spend a couple of days with his mom. He didn't like hearing all her complaints.

"I needed space," Diehl said. It was the truth.

"From us."

"No, no. I, uh, burned out at work."

Elisa gave him a funny look. "If Ethan was here, he'd ask if you were in a fire."

"In a way, I was in a psychological fire." Diehl drew a deep breath.

"What fire?"

"Never mind. God saved me from the pit."

"God? You never talk about God."

"I do now."

"Will God bring Mom back?" Elisa asked.

"No, but He can keep our family together." Diehl reached for Elisa. "Your brother and grandparents are waiting for you at the house."

"Not Grandma Zeta. I don't want to see her."

"Oh?" Something going on? Diehl recalled that Malik said the Bishops had left in the middle of the night.

"I heard her talk on the phone with Romina about new passports," Elisa said. "There were many children there, waiting for their photos."

"Photos?"

"We were getting our photos taken, like in a year-book, except this is for our new passports."

"New passports?"

Elisa nodded.

This was huge.

"Elisa, we always want to do what is right because God sees everything we do," Diehl said. "Tomorrow, the police will ask you more questions so that we can help all those children you saw, okay? We don't want her to take other children away from their parents."

"Romina doesn't do that. Other people did."

"Other people?" Diehl asked. "Adults?"

Elisa pursed her lips the way Ethan sometimes did.

Diehl made a mental note to mention all the above to Detective Jeong, who had given him some instruc-tions for the next day. Right now, he needed to get Elisa home.

He handed Elisa the tote bag. "Your shoes are at the bottom. I forgot a pair of socks, but oh well. Would you like to go home, Elisa?"

"Yes, Dad."

"Then let's go home."

CHAPTER FORTY-FIVE

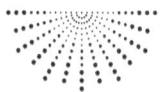

*B*izarre. Skye didn't know what to make of the news.

It was almost bedtime, and she was already in bed when Diehl called her on FaceTime to update her on the day's events. From the looks of the background behind him, he was sitting in his office chair in an enormous office. When asked, he said he was at home, where he would be working as much as possible to be near his kids.

"I know, right." Diehl shook his head. "Elisa went with Hans willingly. She climbed into the tilt cart, covered herself with a tablecloth, and let Hans drive her away from Brooks Cottage. Then she boarded the Greyhound bus on her own—with tickets paid for by Zeta via Romina."

"Your ex-nanny must have some power of persuasion."

"Well, the carrot on the cake was that she was going to take Elisa to see her biological father."

"In Italy. With an expired passport. Right." Skye almost laughed, but it was no laughing matter.

"Detective Jeong and the DHS agent in charge told me that you can't take a minor out of the country without parental permission, which was why they were at the underground passport office, trying to get fake mother-daughter passports plus other travel documents —like birth certificates and so forth. And how ICE agents found them in their child trafficking sweep at a place like that where forged documents were made."

From the news, Skye knew that the US Immigration and Customs Enforcement agents looked for victims of human trafficking all the time. "Who came up with this cuckoo plan? It would never work in this day and age."

"My former mother-in-law." Diehl cupped his face with his hands. "She makes my own mother look like a saint."

"I'm sorry."

"Me too. Now I'm waiting to see what they'll charge Romina and Zeta with. My lawyer is working with the prosecutors to see if they can come up with more charges than false imprisonment and the crime of kidnapping."

"Your lawyer in Atlanta?"

Diehl nodded. "Even though Elisa ran away— pretty much—on Seaside Island and got on the bus in Brunswick, she didn't meet up with Romina until she arrived in Atlanta. Romina picked her up in her car, and from that point on, Elisa was with her. Elisa told me she was scared a lot of times because she didn't know what was going on."

It sounded like there wasn't going to be a happy ending for Zeta Bishop. Skye didn't know her, but she hoped that Zeta would find the Lord and repent of her actions. "Glad God protected your daughter."

"Somehow Romina prevented anyone from touching Elisa. I think she knew in her heart something was not right—her nanny instincts—but she needed the money, being out of work. Fifty thousand dollars."

"One year's salary to some people." Skye shifted in bed. "You know what the Bible says. The love of money is the root of all evil."

"I've heard people talk about that verse. Where is it?" Diehl swiped his phone.

"Look in 1 Timothy 6 thereabouts." Skye waited.

"Here it is in 1 Timothy 6:10. 'For the love of money is a root of all kinds of evil, for which some have strayed from the faith in their greediness, and pierced themselves through with many sorrows.' Wow. That's a good verse to hang on my office wall."

"I remind myself that money is only a tool. I tithe to remind me that God comes first."

"Ten percent?" Diehl stretched.

"Minimally. But I give extra to ministry whenever the Lord places a need in my heart."

"Then you give a lot more than most people."

"I don't compare. Each of us has to answer to God individually."

"That's a good way to look at it." Onscreen, Diehl looked tired, exhausted. He also looked like he hadn't shaved in a day or two.

"Thank you for texting me throughout the day," Skye said. "It felt like I didn't miss too much, though I've been busy all day judging at the food festival."

Just as well, because Diehl had to sort out his family problems with his children without her interference. Perhaps after he had cleared the air, they could get together again.

If the Lord wills it.

Skye told herself to take everything in stride and not overthink the situation. What they had on St. Simon's Island was precious. Cooking breakfast in the same kitchen. Picnicking on the beach. Praying with each other. Attending church together.

If it was over, then it was over.

To Skye, the happy memories remained. She chose to remember the good times she had with Diehl. It was all she could do. There was enough stress at work that the last thing she'd want to do was to layer personal stress on top of her professional strains.

If Diehl didn't return to her, she would have to move on. All she asked was that he never said goodbye.

No goodbyes.

Diehl waved at the camera. "Earth to Skye? Are you there? Over."

Skye blinked away the tears, and looked back at the camera on her phone.

"It was sad. All those kids they found nearby," Diehl said. "The DHS is having a world of a time determining where the kids came from and where to send them back to."

"Were they certain Romina has nothing to do with them?" Skye asked.

"Well, she's not part of the trafficking ring, but she took Elisa there to get passport photos and fake foreign passports so that they could fly to Italy under assumed names. She's cooperating with DHS to try to get her charges reduced."

Skye could not believe that Elisa's former nanny would take money from the Bishops to do the evil deed. If Hans had not cracked under the persuasive pressure of one Earl Young, Elisa would have still been lost to the family.

"We all know it's not worth the fifty thousand that the Bishops paid Romina," Skye said. "Why do this when you could lose access to your grandkids forever?"

"To his credit, Wilson didn't know anything about it."

"How can a husband not know what his wife is doing?" Skye said it before she realized she probably shouldn't have. "You're saying that Zeta somehow has a secret stash of fifty-thousand dollars of cash lying around her pineapple plantation, unbeknownst to her husband of forty years?"

Diehl was silent.

Skye couldn't tell if he looked hurt or whether he was in deep thought.

"I'm sorry," Skye said. "It just came out."

"No. You're right. I should have been more aware of what Isobel was doing all those years."

"Diehl, I was talking about the Bishops."

"Like mother, like daughter."

"Don't let the dead of the past bury your present and kill your future. At my brother's wedding, the pastor said the marriage ends at death, 'until death do us part.' Isobel is dead. Your marriage is over."

"Is that scriptural? I know they say it at weddings, but..."

"Look it up."

"Okay." He swiped his phone. "Interesting. Here are two similar verses. I'll read the one in Mark 12:25. 'For when they rise from the dead, they neither marry nor are given in marriage, but are like angels in heaven.' So you are right. Until death do us part."

Skye thanked God that Diehl was growing spiritually. Diehl had mentioned in his texts earlier today that he had been listening to Pastor Gonzalez's past sermons as he exercised in the gym. He had also been enjoying the hymns on his sister's playlist.

Truly, Diehl needed to study the Bible more.

So do I.

"Are you going to stay in Atlanta for the rest of summer?" Skye asked.

"Pastor Gonzalez prayed with me this afternoon and he asked the same question. Said that if that's the case, I might consider taking the kids to Midtown Chapel, where they have grief counselors. Did you know that Midtown is a sister church to Seaside Chapel? Of course, you knew."

Skye nodded. "Seaside is also a sister church to Riverside Chapel in Savannah."

"Really?"

"Yep. My sister-in-law's parents attend Midtown, so you might see them. Her dad plays the harp in the orchestra."

Diehl looked at the screen, as if studying it. "Don't you want me back on St. Simon's Island?"

Of course, but...

Skye drew a deep breath. "I want God's perfect will to be done."

"What do you think is God's perfect will for us?"

"I don't know."

"I'm going to ask God to show us. Let's pray." Diehl closed his eyes and bowed his head.

It took Skye off guard.

"Dear Lord Jesus, we come before you at the crossroads of our lives. If we go this way, Skye and I will be separated. If we go that way, we would be together. Show us which road to take. In Your Holy Name, I pray. Amen."

"Amen." Skye was impressed. "If you go to Midtown, be sure to get into a good Sunday school."

"I'll miss our Sunday school class, though." Diehl sat back in his office chair. "And I'll miss you."

"You have to do what is best for your kids," Skye said.

"They can attend school on St. Simon's. Enrollment is ongoing at Seaside Academy. School starts the second week of August."

"You checked."

"Yes, I did. I have to weigh the pros and cons." Diehl leaned forward. "My problem is that our family business is stretched too thin across several industries. Either we consolidate departments or we sell part of the company. I don't know what else we could do. There's no way for Dad to manage two-thirds of it if I move to St. Simon's. I don't want him to have another stroke."

"That would be bad."

"Have you considered expanding Skye's the Limit to Atlanta?" Diehl asked suddenly.

Skye remembered her discussions with Sebastian. "My brother is opening new branches in metro Atlanta for Sage Café. He tells me that it's hard work and he's busy all the time. In a big city, the competition is tough."

"I'm sure you can handle it."

"It's a challenge, for sure, but I can only do so much. I suppose I can hire more chefs, but the cost of operating a business in Atlanta is higher than on St. Simon's. Also I love the atmosphere of a small beach town."

"I do too. If I could work there, I would in a heartbeat."

If.

"We're talking about hypotheticals here, Diehl. We got to know each other on your sabbatical—almost vacation—and now the reality is setting in that we must each go home when summer is over."

"What are you saying, Skye?"

"I'm saying summer is not over. Let's do what we need to do, and let God lead us where we need to go."

Diehl nodded. "I pray that God will lead me back to you. Would you like that?"

"Very much." Skye wasn't sure if she said it too quickly. She did not want to give Diehl the idea that the floodgates were open now that he was a Christian. At the same time, she had found herself falling in love with this man who used to come across to her as cold and uncaring—from a distance. Now that she had gotten to know him, he wasn't like what he had portrayed at all.

So yes, she would like God to lead him back to her again.

"That's what I want to hear." Diehl expelled a breath. "Have I asked you about your food festival?"

"No." In a way, Skye was hoping he wouldn't ask. He might find out that Jared Urquhart had shown up today in Miami Beach, having dropped in to see how his business partner was doing at the food festival.

"Selfish me."

"You had a lot on your mind." Skye couldn't blame him. Precisely why she hadn't mentioned Jared. She'd handle him without involving Diehl.

And also why she didn't mention her other business in Miami Beach. The meeting with her corporate lawyer and the Florida company she wanted to buy to expand Skye's the Limit all the way to Miami. To buy that business—if the option was still on the table—she'd have to sell her Saffron restaurant shares. Plus, possibly the piece of prime oceanfront land on Seaside Island that she had saved for her future family.

What family? She was all alone.

Oh well, life is life.

"You've been busy all day yourself. At least you don't seem to have food poisoning from all those experimental dishes you had to taste."

Skye chuckled. "The competition is getting tougher, and the cooks are getting better. Still, I'll be glad when it ends tomorrow."

"Once you commit to something, you do follow through, don't you?" Diehl asked.

"Isn't that expected? If I quit halfway, maybe I shouldn't have committed to it in the first place."

"Exactly."

"Why did you talk about commitment? Were you thinking of Saffron?" She was still the co-owner of the restaurant, whether or not she had lost her enthusiasm for the job.

"That didn't cross my mind. I was only thinking about the food competition, how you didn't bail out from judging even though you could."

Why was she thinking of the restaurant then?

Could it be because Jared was in town, always reminding her that if Jared had bought the entirety of Talia's shares, he'd have the majority ownership and would lord it over Skye?

"However, since you brought up the restaurant..." Diehl waited a bit, as if he was looking for the words. "How's that coming along?"

"You mean with Jared as a business partner?" Skye broached the subject. The name.

"Yes, I was getting to him."

"Let's just say he's all over the place." Skye didn't want to mislead Diehl, but at the same time she did not want to cause any additional worry for him, considering he had enough on his plate with Elisa and Ethan.

"All over the place, how?"

Uh-oh.

Maybe she should not have mentioned his name.

"Doesn't he have other businesses to do?" Skye asked. "I mean he's taking the restaurant business very seriously, even though I have more shares than he does."

"Who knows what Jared is up to. Just remember that he's very competitive."

Skye frowned. "Seb was right. On the flight here, he told me not to hang on to things. Here I am, hanging on to forty-nine percent of a restaurant I don't even want to deal with anymore. Why am I hanging on to Saffron?"

"Because it holds a memory for you, maybe?"

"Yeah? Of all the hard work my brother put into the restaurant for years."

"I looked it up the other day," Diehl said. "He poured blood, sweat, and tears into Saffron for his ex-girlfriend, right?"

"Talia. They wanted to do some business together."

"That relationship is over. It's no wonder he's done with it. Now he has moved on, being married to the love of his life." Diehl waved his hands around in front of the camera. "I'm speculating, of course."

"You might be right about my brother. He has moved on."

"So maybe you should too, particularly if you have no passion for the restaurant business."

"It's not my thing. I can be pressed into it, and I'll get it done, and do my best, but it's not something I'd choose to do—not for the rest of my life."

"How can I help?" Diehl leaned toward the camera.

"What do you mean?"

"Clearly, you have an issue with Jared. I've known him since we were both kids. I can tell you that he's tenacious. Has he offered to buy your shares?"

"No."

"Is he hovering?"

"Like how?" Skye's eyes widened.

"You said earlier that 'he's all over the place.' What did you mean by that?"

"I don't know."

"Skye, you don't want me to guess. I have a very active imagination."

"Do you?"

"Let me take a shot at this. I'll venture to guess that Jared is hanging out at the food festival."

Slowly, Skye nodded. "How can you tell?"

"Typical Jared. He's curious about you."

Skye was surprised at Diehl. His response tonight was more detached than his reaction to seeing her with Jared at the restaurant the other week.

"Should I be worried?" Skye asked. "He showed up out of the blue. Seb doesn't like the dude because he came on to Emmeline a couple of years ago."

Diehl cleared his throat. "Did Jared come on to you?"

"He wouldn't dare."

"Or you'll swat him with your frying pan?" Diehl laughed.

"I'd hate to ruin one of my expensive pans, and I've never used it on a person before."

"He'll have you arrested. Then I'd have to bail you out," Diehl said.

"But seriously, Diehl, I'm non-violent." Skye sat back in her bed and put her head on a pillow. "If you were in my shoes, what would you do? Sell your shares and walk away?"

"That would be my first thought. It's not worth the trouble."

Don't hang on to things.

Sebastian's words couldn't be louder in Skye's ears. She knew that was the right thing to do now. "Perhaps I'll send out some feelers tomorrow. See if any of my chef friends would want to buy a forty-nine percent share of an award-winning restaurant."

"If you can't find anyone, I'll buy it," Diehl said.

"Why?"

"Because I don't want you to be unhappy. My business manager can get rid of it easily. Jared won't be a happy camper, I can tell you, but business is business. Meanwhile, you can return to Skye's the Limit and sleep easy."

"Have you ever been in the restaurant business?" Skye asked.

"Never. But I'm just holding the ownership. I reserve the right to turn around and sell it to the highest bidder. Or if Jared wants to buy me out, he can."

"You'd do this for me?"

"Only for you."

"Why?"

"Because I want you to be happy in your career. There's nothing more time-consuming and body-wasting than to be stuck in a career you loathe. If a restaurant business is not for you, then you need to move on and find something you like to do—if you have enough funding to allow you to do that."

"If I sell my shares, I will have my savings back— although the parable of the buried talents comes to mind, where the servant digs a hole and buries his money and has zero investment profits to speak of."

"You're telling me that you emptied your savings to buy out your brother's shares of Saffron?"

Skye wondered how much she should tell him. "Let's just say that I sold my house—with my gourmet kitchen—and I dipped into some of my savings, but Seb sold me his shares at half price because I can't mess with my chef operating fund."

"Well, at least you didn't borrow money."

"No. But I won't ever do this again. I went into business with people who are not on the same page as I am—my belief that the restaurant should operate debt-free, for example. That sort of difference can cause problems. Not only that, one of my business partners is in London and couldn't care less, and the other business partner is breathing down my neck."

"Figuratively, right?" Diehl asked.

Skye shrugged. "He wouldn't dare touch me. My brother will beat him up with a rolling pin."

Diehl laughed, but he sounded nervous. "I've known Jared since high school. Please be careful with this guy."

"Okay. Don't worry. I told you my brother is with me."

"After the festival, when you return to St. Simon's, your brother won't be there. I'm not there either. I wish I could be there for you."

"God is with me, you know?"

"Right." Diehl drew a deep breath. "I didn't mean that He isn't."

"I'm not afraid of Jared," Skye said. "In fact, I feel sorry for the poor man."

"He's anything but poor, but I get what you're saying."

"He's just lonely, I think."

"That could be a bad moment. Don't help him. Don't think about him too much." Diehl's voice lowered. "I will pray that he will find a path away from you."

"What if he needs Jesus?"

"Then someone else can witness to him."

"You?" Skye asked.

"You want me to witness to Jared?"

"At least talk to him about Jesus," Skye said. "If the

Lord leads you to share Christ with him, he might be more willing to listen to an old friend. Besides, he would notice the transformation in you from lost to saved."

"I'll pray about it," Diehl said. "Meanwhile, stay away from him."

"Hard to do if he's my business partner."

"Well, I don't like it."

Skye tilted her head. "Are you jealous, Diehl?"

CHAPTER FORTY-SIX

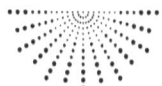

*J*ealous? Diehl buried his face in his palm, embarrassed at how he had handled the last question Skye asked him tonight.

Are you jealous, Diehl?

He had hemmed and hawed until his answer came back as diplomatic as a feral cat fighting back animal control out to take him to a kill shelter.

He couldn't believe he had told Skye that this was the twenty-first century and why would he be jealous if they were not married to each other?

What?

He closed his eyes and groaned. There was no comeback for his statement to Skye, which effectively ended their late-night conversation.

Yeah, he could always blame the time of day. He wasn't himself or something.

The tap outside his office door startled him. He

glanced at the clock on his laptop. It was way past eleven at night. He thought everyone was asleep.

"Who's there?" Diehl asked, as if it mattered. Actually, it was a lazy man's way of finding out without having to get out of his chair, go to the door, and see who was there.

Dad's cane appeared between the doors.

How much had Dad heard?

"I was getting some water," Dad said. "Mind if I sit a spell?"

"Sure." Diehl pointed to a plush armchair on the other side of the office.

"When this was my office, I had two sofas over there." Dad pointed toward the empty window area with his cane. "Parker and I would each take a sofa and we'd look out into the garden and talk business."

It was for that very reason that Diehl had moved both couches to another room in the house as soon as he bought the house from his parents. They sold the house to him because they retired to the Georgia coast shortly after Diehl's older brother passed away.

Parker had been the torch of Brooks Investments. A business genius, he kept Grandpa's legacy alive, and out-earned Dad and Grandpa combined.

Diehl had looked up to his older brother almost all his life. Parker married a beautiful and brilliant woman, whom he had met at Harvard Business School. With Riley, he had two kids. With her, he had taken Brooks Investments to new heights.

Every time Diehl looked at those empty couches Dad talked about, all Diehl saw were memories of

Parker laughing while Dad told jokes. The visuals in his mind were too painful for Diehl to relive every single time he walked into this house.

"You had a lot of furniture," Diehl finally said.

"Your mom went to many auctions." Dad's voice cracked.

Diehl wondered if Dad had also recalled his favorite son.

Yes, Diehl admitted it, he would always be the middle child. It wasn't that Dad would love him less than Parker, but Parker had come first.

"I kind of like it sparse."

"So it seems." Dad sat down in the armchair which Diehl had pointed to earlier.

"Are we just chatting or are we talking business?" Diehl asked.

"We should be able to just chat about life as father and son, don't you think?" Dad leaned his cane against the coffee table next to the armchair.

Diehl felt that Dad had aged a lot since the stroke. He had been able to walk Brinley down the aisle on her wedding day a few years ago, but would he be around to watch Brinley's child grow up and go to school?

"I worked hard all my life to get to a comfortable retirement, and then when I finally got there, a stroke happened and derailed my ability to enjoy life," Dad said. "I want to retire in peace, but I feel like I'm retiring in pieces."

Diehl sensed this was going to be more than a chat.

"If I could do it all over again, I would have tried to

enjoy life in my forties and fifties." Dad pointed a finger at Diehl. "I'm telling you, son. You're nearly forty now. Blink and you'll be sixty-five, wondering where all those dreams went."

Diehl nodded.

"What do you want to do, son?" Dad pointed to his own chest. "Deep inside your heart, what do you really want?"

I want to marry Skye and raise a family with her.

"What do you really want, Dad?" Diehl asked instead.

"Play golf and take my grandkids on vacation." Dad answered so quickly that Diehl suspected he had thought about it for a while.

"Do we need fifty-billion dollars to achieve that?"

"No."

"Then why are we hanging on to Brooks Manufacturing and Brooks Transportation? They are so outside what Brooks originally was about. At least Brooks Renovations is an offshoot of Brooks Properties."

Dad's eyes teared. "Because they were Parker's babies."

"I know. That's what makes it hard to let them go." Diehl came around the table and sat on the edge of it, facing Dad's armchair. "But you're retired and I've burned out trying to spin all these plates."

"He worked so hard on them. I don't want to sell anything."

That piqued Diehl's interest. "Has anyone offered?"

"Urquhart Enterprises."

Jared. Yet again. "Sneaky. He waited until I was away from the office to make you an offer."

"Do you want to know how much?"

"Does it matter? Let's see if we can keep Parker's legacy in the family," Diehl said. "If it doesn't work out, then we'll take the highest bid."

"How? You know that as soon as summer is over, we're back to where we were—you running all three subsidiaries." Dad had nailed the reality of the problem. "It's too much for one person to manage. Sucks the life out of you."

"What if we ask Riley if she wants in?"

"Riley?"

Diehl nodded. "Harvard MBA. Used to be VP of Sales at the manufacturing corporation Parker bought. So it's like going back to her old job, if she wants to. You don't look sure, Dad."

"Riley hasn't worked since Petra was born."

Worked?

For some reason, Diehl didn't like what he heard. "On the contrary, Riley worked more as a mother than she did in the corporate world. Don't you remember Parker singing her praises all the time?"

"I meant in a corporate office."

"It's overrated, Dad."

"She spent the last four years making pottery to display in her gallery that she owns. Sandpiper Gallery or something."

"That's because the kids need her the rest of the time," Diehl said. "If my wife had decided to stay at home and raise our children, I would have honored her sacrifice."

"Your wife partied away your money, Diehl," Dad reminded him.

"Not all wives are like that." Certainly Diehl hoped that Skye would...

Skye?

Was he getting ahead of himself?

"Riley is a recluse," Dad added.

"Was. She snapped out of her funk this year."

"I don't know..."

"Does a recluse decide to spend a month touring Europe?" Diehl asked.

"I don't know."

"All the reclusive people I know rarely leave their homes."

"Whatever."

Diehl cleared his throat. "The point is, Petra is now seventeen, and Zach is thirteen. I'd like to suggest that we ask Riley if she wants to get back into the corporate world."

"She might not," Dad said.

"She might." Diehl wondered why Dad was negative about Riley.

"She's been keeping up with company activities because she has Parker's shares." Even as Diehl reminded Dad about it, he realized he hadn't talked to Riley about this idea.

"Would they want to move back to Atlanta? Her kids would have to change high schools and find new friends."

"Remember how the kids were devastated when Riley moved them to their summer home on St. Simon's after Parker passed away? They missed their friends at their school in Atlanta. Now they get a chance to reunite with their old friends again."

"They're on vacation, right? Europe somewhere?" Dad seemed to have forgotten.

"Yes, touring the entire summer. I haven't kept up, but we can ask Brin when they're due back."

"Ah, yes, I seem to remember that now. They rented a chateau here and there, taking the train to places."

"Sounds fun."

"While the rest of us have to work." Dad grinned.

The same grin that Parker had inherited.

I miss my brother a lot.

If only Parker were alive to run Brooks Investments, Diehl could live wherever he chose and love whomever he wanted.

Diehl swallowed. "If you and I agree, we can ask Riley to think about it. She might want to think fast because it's June already, and school starts back up in August."

"If she says no?"

"Then I propose we sell the subsidiaries that neither of us wants to manage anymore. Or we hire a VP for each of them and see how long we can hang on to the business," Diehl said. "However, if she says yes, she can continue Parker's legacy."

That was all the argument Diehl had for asking Riley to join Brooks Investments as the CEO of the two subsidiaries her late husband had started. Would she be up to the task?

"If you bring up Parker's legacy, how could she turn us down?" Dad said. "Then again, when two people are in love, and one dies, the other might never get over it. Sometimes it could be hard for them to revisit old places. I'm not saying Riley is like that, but I know for a fact that she and Parker were madly in love with each other."

"Is it possible to love that much?" Diehl found himself asking.

"For sure. When my mother died, it affected Dad for the rest of his life. He thought of her all the time, and he saved all those musical instruments in her memory."

Diehl recalled how Grandpa Brooks had bequeathed those instruments to only Brinley, and not to her brothers. Eventually those violins and pianos would end up in a music museum that Brinley was still building.

Family had clearly been important to Grandpa Brooks. He had taken care of his only son well. Dad then passed on that family heritage to his four children, and hopefully eventually to his four grandchildren as well.

Could Diehl be the father that his children needed? What about in the here and now? They had spent one year of school in Hawaii, and now they would come back to Atlanta for the fall. However, if he could hand over two-thirds of the family business to

Parker's widow, Diehl could possibly move the rest of it to St. Simon's Island.

But how fast could they do this?

It was the middle of June. The next school year would begin in early August. Could he move his entire operation from Atlanta to St. Simon's Island in less than two months?

"If I only manage Brooks Properties, I could be location independent," Diehl said. "I could work on the beach."

"With technology, you can." Dad shifted in his seat. "The only reason I showed up in person at the office was to assure everyone working for us that all was fine with you. They were worried. I heard rumors circulating that you had a mental breakdown, ran off with a mistress, hid in rehab, et cetera. There were all sorts of speculations."

"It was nothing of the sort. I burned myself out overworking to try to get over Isobel's death."

"A grief counselor could have taken some of that pressure off."

"You're right, Dad." Diehl walked about the room. "You know, I'm glad I took time off. There is such a thing as life—before work, during work, after work. I have sacrificed my marriage, driven away my wife, and agitated my children in the process."

"Diehl, it's not your fault that your marriage fell apart. None of us saw the signs."

Diehl knew that Dad was trying to remind him of Isobel's sins. "We have all sinned, Dad. That's why Jesus had to die for the penalty of our sins."

Dad's eyes widened. "You..."

Diehl nodded. "I'm a believer of Jesus now."

"Since when?"

"Sunday night after church. Ivan led me to Christ."

"I thought you were a Christian already and that you were backsliding."

Diehl shook his head. "I don't know what I believed back then, but I showed no fruit."

"You sure didn't. I've been praying for you." Dad seemed happy. "Come to think of it, you do look calmer."

Diehl stood by the tall window where the couches used to be. "God is good."

"Are you attending Ivan's church?"

"Yes. In his Sunday school class as well."

"Going all in, huh?"

"All or nothing." Diehl walked back to his desk.

Dad slapped the armrests and got up from the armchair. "We'll talk some more in the morning. I'm going to bed."

"What about the water you came downstairs to get?"

"I'm not thirsty anymore." Dad waved him off. "What are your plans tomorrow? Will you be at the office?"

"No. I'm supposed to take Elisa for a forensic interview."

"Interesting. What for?" Dad asked.

"There are actually two sets of interviews. The DHS wants to know what she saw at the underground passport center because she said there were other kids there. ICE agents are hunting for human traffickers."

"Seems like a lot to put a twelve-year-old through."

"I know." Diehl credited God for giving him strength. "We got Elisa back. Many other parents haven't gotten their children back. If Elisa saw anything, she might be able to help those kids they found."

"Do we know all that's been happening?"

"Not really. Detective Jeong assured me that once he has more information that he can share with us, he will. He also wants to talk to Elisa. Whatever she can remember might help convict Romina and Zeta."

Dad shook his head. "Unbelievable. I can't imagine what Zeta was thinking when she put her own biological granddaughter at risk just to meet a need."

"This world is sinful." It was all Diehl could say.

"Which station are you taking Elisa to tomorrow?"

"Not a police station. I think it's at the Georgia Center for Child Advocacy, where a forensic interviewer will be talking to Elisa. I won't be allowed in—I suppose they don't want me to influence her responses —so I'll bring a laptop to work."

"How long is that going to take?"

"They told me it'd be a couple of days. I'm guessing I'll be here until this weekend."

Dad looked disappointed.

Somehow, Diehl had a feeling Dad didn't like office work anymore, even though he had been CEO of Brooks Investments for many years.

"I'll be praying for Elisa," Dad said.

"Thank you." Diehl watched Dad shuffle out of the office.

He waited until Dad was out of sight before he logged in to his laptop. He wanted to write down the pros and cons of having his sister-in-law take over some of the workload.

Then he remembered how Skye prayed.

"Lord, if this is Your will for the family business, then let Riley be positive about being CEO for two of the subsidiaries. If she could do that, I would like to move Brooks Properties to St. Simon's Island. If it's Your will for me to be with Skye, I pray that it will all work out nicely. And please somehow get rid of Jared or keep him far away from Skye."

He added a few more prayers for his children, especially Elisa with her harrowing experience, and for his parents, who were getting older too quickly for him to keep up with.

He then went back to praying for Skye. He hoped that his offer to buy out Skye's majority share of Saffron on Jekyll was the right thing to do. He wouldn't have to do it if Skye found a buyer first. Either way, she could go back to focusing on Skye's the Limit—what she said she'd rather do.

And it would get Jared off her back.

Diehl told himself he would never again ask Skye if she would consider moving to Atlanta. She was happy partly because she was where she needed to be. If he persuaded her to leave the islands and the coast, she might lose her happiness.

Or could she?

Still, it was a big sacrifice to expect her to make.

Perhaps she didn't have to do that if he made the sacrifice instead.

Diehl tried to keep his feelings in check, but he knew that he'd do whatever was necessary to be with Skye, even giving up two-thirds of the company to his sister-in-law.

Was this true love?

Whether it was or not, it made sense to him.

He recalled something similar that Brinley had done a few years before. She lost interest in the corporate world and wanted to manage only Brooks Renovations, restoring historical properties on the Georgia coast. Even though the work was arduously long-term and the profits were nothing like the other Brooks subsidiaries, Brinley was happy.

I want to be happy too.

But not at Dad's expense. Diehl would rather sell parts of the family business than put Dad back to work again twenty-four seven, knowing that was what Dad would do at the office.

Somehow Parker and Diehl had inherited the gene of workaholism.

It could kill them all.

Parker had coped by drinking his stress away, something that he had passed on to his brother.

Diehl knew he could never go back there. Now that he had a new life in Christ, his perspective must also change. He knew that much.

With great shame, he recalled that Saturday morning when Skye had found him sprawled out in the living room of Brinley's beach house, surrounded by empty bottles. He remembered reaching out to Skye and asking her to stay with him because he had felt so lonely and abandoned.

Without making any facial gesture of disgust at his hangover, and in an even-keeled voice, Skye had said something profound to him at that time—but now it all made sense.

Once you belong to God, He does not leave you nor forsake you.

Now, without Skye with him physically, he still felt the presence of God.

So this was part and parcel of what it meant to be saved. God was with him always.

I get it now, Lord. I get it.

CHAPTER FORTY-SEVEN

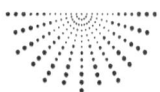

The Southern Sunshine Food Festival baked in the noonday Florida sun on Miami Beach, multicolored awnings and beach umbrellas on booths providing little relief from the temperature hovering in a humid upper eighties. Waves of sea breezes offered no respite to Skye, who wore a sleeveless dress and was slathered with plenty of sunblock.

Jared Urquhart had somehow found her in the crowd because he no doubt knew that she was judging booths today. All he had to do was walk from booth to booth until he ran into her.

"It's hot today, isn't it?" he announced, his Chopard sunglasses reflecting sunshine. He was wearing a Hawaiian shirt over cotton shorts and a pair of sandals. All designer brands of some sort, but they didn't impress Skye.

She tried to ignore him as she filled out the judge's rubrics on her iPad.

Jared followed her to the next booth. "You don't have to sell your shares. We work well together."

Ah, he was referring to Saffron on Jekyll.

"I thought I mentioned it." Skye drank from her water bottle. The water was almost gone. "I bought my brother's shares as a favor to him. I thought that if he ever wanted them back, there they are. However, he has moved on."

"You're doing well, though."

"It's not what I want to do. Why don't you buy my shares?" Skye asked.

"No."

"Then I'll sell them to someone else. Don't say I didn't give you first dibs."

Jared looked like he didn't take her seriously. "To whom would you sell?"

"I'll ask around," Skye said. "If there's no one, then Diehl will take it off my hands."

"Diehl Brooks?" He lifted his sunglasses. "You're lying."

"Am I? Call him yourself." Skye checked her iPad to see how many booths she had to visit. Eleven more. Well, it was time to keep going.

Before she reached the sushi booth, she heard Jared speaking on his phone.

"Since when are you in the restaurant business?" Jared asked someone on the other end.

"I am now." The fact that Skye could hear Diehl meant that Jared had put him on speakerphone.

"Why?" Jared asked in disbelief.

"What concerns Skye concerns me," Diehl said.

"You two dating?"

All around them, the crowd thickened. Skye was listening with one ear, but her attention was divided now that she had picked up a spicy vegetarian sushi roll that tasted like a corn tamale gone wrong. Someone was trying to be clever about using anything else but rice for the roll.

Then again, she could see the intention of the chef —or cook—to try to make a sushi roll outside the box. Skye tried to be benevolent in her rating, adding a few mercy points for thought.

When she stepped out of the booth into the hot sunshine, Jared was still on the phone with Diehl.

"Did you call me up to question my personal life?" Diehl asked for all of Miami Beach to hear.

"Just checking on my business interests." Jared didn't seem to care that they were in public.

"Let me talk to Skye."

"Sure." Jared lifted the phone to Skye's face.

"Hey," Skye said softly, the spicy tamale stuck in her throat. She drank some water to wash it down. That was the end of the water in her bottle.

"Hey, babe."

Babe?

Skye had never heard Diehl call her that. He must be putting on a show for Jared.

"Are we still having dinner Thursday night?" Diehl asked.

Dinner? Skye didn't recall being invited to dinner. The plan was to wrap up the food festival at noon, pack up, fly out of Miami at two-ish, arrive at the

Atlanta airport at four-ish, and drive home to Athens with Sebastian to visit with him and his wife for the weekend.

"Yeah." She played along. She'd unravel it later, whatever the game was that Diehl had in mind to push back Jared.

"I'll pick you up at the airport," Diehl said. "I'll have my assistant, Jodie, call you to get it on my calendar or I'll end up being late."

"Okay." Clever man. Diehl had no idea when Skye's flight would be. By asking Jodie to call her to confirm the plans, he would actually be getting the information for the first time.

"Ask your brother if he wants to come to dinner too," Diehl said.

"I will."

"I'll take you to Athens on Friday," Diehl added.

Jared sighed.

What was that about? Was Diehl implying that Skye would be staying overnight in Atlanta on Thursday before going to Athens on Friday? *Why, yes.*

My reputation.

"I'll stay at my usual hotel," Skye said. Whatever that hotel was. She hadn't made any reservation anywhere.

"I'll show you my new vehicle." That must have been thrown in for effect.

"What new vehicle?" Jared yanked the phone back from Skye and tapped off the speakerphone.

Skye rolled her eyes as she swiped her iPad and went to the next booth.

Bad news: Jared was still right behind her.

He came alongside her. "I apologize for not believing you."

Skye barely nodded.

Forgive me, Lord, for the ruse.

"So what do you think?" Skye asked. "Buy my shares and run the restaurant yourself, or Diehl is your new business partner."

"I do like the idea of an anchor investment." Beads of sweat popped out on Jared's forehead.

Skye stepped into a booth and stood in the shade. Someone handed her a small bottle of water. "Two, please."

She handed one to Jared.

Jared rolled the cold water over his forehead. "Saffron is doing well. Great food. Super chefs. Never an empty seat."

"There you go." Skye tried a piece of teriyaki chicken. Too salty.

Jared picked up a sample too, and winced as he chewed his chicken slowly. "I don't like dark meat."

"But you still ate it."

"I like the saltiness."

"If you were to rate it from one to ten, where would it be?" Skye asked.

"Eight," he said without hesitation.

Skye had rated it at four on account of the crazy amount of salt. She wondered if they had used a store-bought teriyaki sauce and then added more salt. That could explain it, but it was not her job to ask. The rules of the booth competition included zero questions.

Just go to each booth, taste the food, and hope your stomach won't revolt.

Skye wondered if this would be the last time she would judge at a food festival. She'd rather not have the pressure of having to perform. That was why she hadn't entered a single cooking competition since Sebastian married and moved to Athens.

The next stop was another sushi booth. It was probably a good idea for an outdoor festival like this because visitors and beachgoers could simply treat sushi as finger food.

Jared was still tagging along, though his interaction with Skye had become less personal and more like they were casual acquaintances. He let his guard down and stopped behaving rich and spoiled.

Jared put a dollop of bright green wasabi on his sushi. His eyes flared.

Skye laughed so hard she nearly dropped her iPad onto the sand beneath their feet.

His tongue was out and he looked for water. He ran to the next booth where they gave him ice-cold coconut juice.

"Y'all are brilliant," he told them after his second cup.

Skye sampled a lychee drink. Tapped in the score and moved on. She couldn't get Jared to stop tagging along, and she had a limited time to finish her judging round, so she just took it all in stride.

Jared handed Skye a can of coconut juice.

"Was it all canned?" She hadn't noticed when she was at the booth.

"Some are canned, but the ones you judged were made right there at the back of the booth—except the lychee fruits."

"Okay. Good." She shook the can to get the coconut flakes mixed up. Then she pulled the tab to open the can. It was refreshing and cold. "Thank you."

"I aim to please."

"So you bought Sebastian's share of Saffron to save him from Talia's talons." Jared wiped his forehead on the back of his hand.

"Talons?" Skye asked. "That's not a nice thing to say about the mother of your child."

"It's the truth."

"Have you ever said that in front of her?"

"I don't recall. Haven't seen her in months." Jared shrugged, like he didn't care. "It's not like I fly to London all the time."

"I thought your mom wanted her grandchild to grow up on Seaside Island."

"That was before Dad died. That changed everything. Now, Mom likes having me around at the office —she still grieves—so I don't have time to visit Talia."

"Or your daughter, Jewel?"

"Don't judge me."

"I'm not and I'm sorry. We're having a conversation. You asked about Diehl, so I asked about Talia."

"Touché." Jared followed Skye to the next booth. "Mom said that a child needs her father. That's such a traditionalist statement, you know."

"Is it? A child also needs her mother, but we never say that is traditionalist, do we?"

Jared nodded. "Okay. I concede that children need their parents."

"You could fuel up and fly to London anytime," Skye said.

"I don't think she wants to see me, to tell you the truth. We had a falling out while she was pregnant."

Skye did not want—or need—to know what the falling out was. It was none of her business. "I'll pray for you and Talia."

"Pray? You're one of those religious freaks." Jared laughed. "Sell me your shares already before you exorcise me or something."

"You watched too much TV growing up, didn't you?" Skye stopped at the next booth. "I'm just a Christian, Jared."

"Then you're super religious."

"Not all Christians are super religious. Am I?"

"You tell me," Jared said.

"Then I rest my case. If I have to tell you, then I'm not showing it." Skye picked up a small paper-boat container of tamale and a plastic fork. She thought it was not spicy enough.

"A bit oily." Jared spat it out.

"But the beef is well-seasoned." Except for the spiciness. Then again, not everyone liked spicy tamales.

Jared threw the trash away for both of them.

"You seem to know food," Skye said.

Jared nodded. "Growing up, my parents liked to visit restaurants. Mom still does."

Skye knew about Marguerite Urquhart and her

frequent visits to Saffron on Jekyll, especially back when Sebastian ran the restaurant.

"We had a private chef at home, but we also ate out a lot," Jared said. "If I didn't have to work in the family business, I might have been a food critic."

"Saffron is up your alley, then."

"Totally. If I could buy all of Talia's shares, I would. At this point, she's holding back and won't sell the rest of them to me."

"How about my shares?" Skye tried not to get her hopes up. She had mentioned it earlier, but he hadn't reacted. "Seriously."

"I'm thinking."

"I own forty-nine percent. Add that to your twenty-five point five."

"Let me think about it and get back to you. Talia might be pleased, because I think she'd rather I buy you out than work with you. She's probably even more jealous than Diehl."

So Diehl's jealousy was noticeable? Skye wished she could tell Diehl right now that there was nothing for him to worry about. She had no interest in anyone else.

"Say, how do you get along with Diehl?" Jared asked.

"Why do you ask?" Even though it had only been a few weeks, Skye felt like she had known Diehl for a few years since his sister joined Treble Trio and they started to pray for one another's families.

"Maybe I can get some tips on how to manage Talia?"

"Manage?" Skye stepped into the shade. "Maybe that's one of your problems."

"What do you mean?" Jared looked baffled.

"You manage employees, Jared, not the mother of your child. She's not your subordinate. She's your equal."

Jared stood next to her. "Maybe you can talk to Talia."

"I'm not a marriage counselor."

"She and I are not married."

"Still, you have a family now—a child, at least."

"Talia doesn't look at it that way. She's dating again."

"Like I said, I'm not a counselor. I'm just a chef, Jared. However, if you want, I could ask Pastor Gonzalez."

Jared shook his head. "I only go to Seaside Chapel if someone dies or someone gets married."

"Christmas?" Skye asked.

"I'm usually with my Mom then. We try to keep our family reunion every Christmas so she won't miss Dad that much."

"Does she still split her time between Seaside and Urquhart Island?"

Jared nodded. "Yeah. Dad bought that island for her."

"That sounds nice." Skye could never imagine having her own little island. The Urquharts had tried to buy Seaside Island, but the residents wouldn't hear of it. Soon after that spat with the locals, the Urquharts found a smaller island on the gulf side of Florida.

"I wish Talia would come home one of these days, but it would take a miracle for her to spend Christmas with the Urquharts."

"God is in the miracle business," Skye said.

"Is He?"

"Absolutely. All the time."

Skye thought she could use a miracle about now. She wished that Jared would stop following her around. Or if he had to stick to her, he might as well carry a parasol over her head to protect her from the South Florida heat.

CHAPTER FORTY-EIGHT

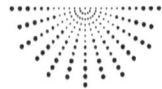

The sun was blazing hot, and Skye reminded herself not to attend any future outdoor food festivals in the middle of summer. Rivulets of sweat poured out of her head. She saw a booth with a spinning fan and made a beeline for it. Unfortunately, a crowd of people had the same idea.

"Cold water for a weary soul?" someone said.

Skye recognized that voice. She spun around.

Watt Watanabe in an orange sherbet shirt, signature fluorescent-green tennis shoes, and with his arms around a woman who was no more than twenty-five years old.

Skye hadn't realized that Watt had a granddaughter. She thought that Watt and his now deceased wife were childless.

"What brings you here to Miami Beach?" Watt gave Skye a bear hug.

"Watt did," Skye deadpanned.

Watt laughed. He had the same laughter that Skye remembered from years past when Watt and Uncle Miller used to hang out on St. Simon's Island. They both had their own cooking establishments, but while Sebastian had followed Uncle Miller into the restaurant business, Skye had preferred the professional personal chef service company that Watt owned.

Watt had given Skye her first start in the business in Savannah right after she graduated out of cooking school. It had only been for one Christmas season when Watt's for Dinner was small, but it was enough experience to motivate Skye to register her own LLC and eventually a corporation.

In fact, Watt had also gifted her with seed money to get Skye's the Limit going. While she had returned it years later after receiving an inheritance from Uncle Miller's estate, Skye never forgot the kindness and generosity of her uncle's friend.

How could it be that they had lost touch in the last ten years?

"It's been a while," Skye said, regretting how time had passed by. "When was the last time I saw you?"

"I don't remember, but you look great." Watt stepped back to assess Skye. "Your company doing well?"

Skye nodded. She didn't like to talk about company business in public—although she had broken her own rule within the last hour discussing sales with Jared.

Speaking of Jared, where had he gone? Skye glanced around and spotted Jared talking up a pretty redhead at another booth.

"Skye, meet my girlfriend, Anastasia," Watt said. To the young lady, he said, "Love, this is Skye Langston, the granddaughter of my best friend from cooking school, Miller Langston."

Love? Oh sorry. Not granddaughter.

"Nice to meet you." The young woman in spaghetti straps and too-short shorts handed Skye a bottled water. It looked cold with condensation on the outside.

"Thank you." Skye twisted the cap open and drank half the bottle. "You're a lifesaver."

"She is, for sure." Watt held Anastasia tighter and planted a noisy kiss on her cheek. "We're moving to St. Thomas to live on a yacht."

"You are?" Shocked, Skye didn't recall Watt ever mentioning yachting while Jessica had been alive. They had been a down-to-earth couple who worked around the clock, built Watt's for Dinner from the ground up in Savannah, then moved their company to metro Atlanta, where their revenues went through the roof.

"Since Jessica's been gone, I don't have the energy left." His voice was tinged with tones of regret.

"Are you managing Watt's for Dinner from the Caribbean seas?" Skye was curious, more than anything else.

"Absolutely not. I'm retiring, Skye. Watt's for Dinner was more Jessica's thing. Without her..." He cleared his throat. "Anyway, I waited too long to enjoy myself."

He pointed a finger at Skye. "Don't drive yourself to the ground. Make time for your loved ones, for a family. One big thing I always regret is how Jessica and I didn't have time for children."

"We're going to change all that," Anastasia said. "Three months on a yacht should do it."

Skye didn't know whether to laugh or cry. She barely remembered how old Watt was.

Watt nodded. "Yep. We're leaving next week. Do you want to buy Watt's for Dinner?"

"What?" Skye's jaw dropped.

"Watt, you mean?" Watt wiggled his eyebrows. "I'll sell it to you for what you can afford."

"Why?" Immediately, Skye's mind began to calculate how much she would profit from the sale of her restaurant shares. If she needed more money, she could sell the piece of land she'd been hoarding on Seaside Island for who knew what.

"At my age, I can't keep up with my chefs. I've downsized it to what I can manage, but I can't be running around like I'm thirty anymore. I've got my American dream. Now I'm going on a permanent vacation." He pointed to his hips. "These hips can't take it."

"What are you saying?" Skye asked.

"I was going to move my office out of Alpharetta to Cobb County or somewhere with lower taxes, but I decided I don't want to deal with the corporate life anymore. Take it off my hands. In fact, if you don't buy it, I'll will it to you." And he kissed Anastasia again. "She doesn't want any of it. She just wants cold hard cash."

Skye was speechless.

"I'm talking to you, Skye," Watt said. "Say something."

"Are you drunk?"

Watt laughed. "Nope. Haven't had a drink since breakfast."

"Did you just make me a business offer right in the middle of a food festival?" Skye asked.

"We didn't run into each other for nothing. I was waiting for a sign from heaven."

"You don't believe in heaven."

"My own heaven is waiting for me on St. Thomas." Watt let his girlfriend go. "Love, go mingle. I need to talk to Skye about business for a minute."

"Before I go, let's get a photo." Anastasia whipped out her hot pink phone and snapped a photo of Skye and Watt. Then she wandered off.

"Let's go over there a minute." He pointed to a clearing where there were some makeshift picnic tables and benches, all occupied.

"I'm still judging."

"You're taking a break."

When Skye saw Watt limp, she didn't have the heart to say no. "A few minutes."

"That's all I need." Watt led the way. "I turned eighty-eight in December."

"Eighty-eight. Wow. Did you get the birthday card I sent?"

Watt nodded. "You're the only one who wishes me a 'Happy Seventieth Birthday!' for the last eighteen years."

"That was because I forgot your age and didn't want to get it wrong."

"You made my day and I never forget a good deed —even after years." He turned solemn. "I also never forget regrets and mistakes. This elephant memory I have is a curse."

Quietly, Skye prayed for God to comfort her uncle's old friend.

"You probably don't know this, but after cooking school last century, I made some poor decisions and ended up a pauper." Watt stopped in the middle of the clearing in between the booths and picnic tables. Foot traffic flowed around them. He grabbed his hip. "Your uncle gave me a job for a while in his kitchen. Do you recall?"

Skye had to dig back into her memories a long way for that. "I remember Uncle Miller saying that you were his best friend from cooking school."

"Was that all he told you?" Watt smiled. "He was the best friend anyone could ever have. He gave me a hundred thousand dollars in operating funds to start my own personal chef business in Savannah. That was how Watt's for Dinner was born. And he never asked for a dime back."

"I had no idea."

"Now you know. I didn't say anything to anyone, but Jessica knew—I told her after we married. Years later, when I turned a profit, I didn't give any money back to Miller. In fact, when I opened my new branch in Atlanta, I lost touch with Miller. I'm sorry I wasn't there when he died. I figured Irma had enough money from the restaurant to take care of herself."

"She sold the restaurant, fell ill shortly thereafter, and passed away in her sleep." Skye felt she had to say it, even though Watt probably remembered.

"The glory days were no more. You and your brother were in college."

"They did leave Seb and me something to start our careers after college and chef school." Skye was grateful for the inheritance. "Seb went into the restaurant business and I became a personal chef. We both also ran a catering business for some years."

"You became a personal chef because of my influence." Watt drew a deep breath. "I'm sorry I wasn't there for you. I named you in my will, you know?"

"What?"

"Stop saying that, Skye."

"You're unloading a lot of information on me, Watt," Skye said. "Are you sure it's not heatstroke or something?"

"I'm not babbling. I called Sebastian and found out where you were going to be this week."

"No wonder. See, I knew we didn't just run into each other."

"Anastasia thought we'd make a vacation out of this, so after tomorrow, we're going to drive down to Key West and rent a yacht. Practice run."

"Sounds like an expensive vacation."

Watt shrugged. "Do I look like I care? I want to cash out and spend every dime."

"Isn't that reckless?"

There was a twinkle in Watt's eye. "That's what Miller would've said if he were right here. You take after your uncle so much."

Then he turned solemn. "You're my favorite Langston kid, you know. I like Seb too, but I always thought that if I ever had a daughter, you would be exactly who I envisioned."

"That's sweet of you." Skye sniffled. "Don't make me cry."

"I'm about to make it sweeter. I don't trust those large corporations buying me out and running my personal chef business. I'll sell it to you at a price you can afford. I have loyal clients north of Atlanta, and I'll rest easy on my new yacht knowing that Watt's for Dinner is in good hands."

"I'm not overflowing with ready cash right now." Not after she bought Saffron. Well, there was that piece of oceanfront land she could sell if she needed money, although she wondered how long it would take to sell it.

"I heard about Saffron through the grapevine." Watt lifted a hand. "Don't ask me how. Suffice to say that if you sell your shares of Saffron, you could buy out my Atlanta business."

"What about your Savannah branch?"

"Sold it last week on a handshake."

"Do they still do that sort of thing anymore?" Skye asked. She was sure she'd need to call her corporate lawyer and accountant. It wasn't going to be on a handshake.

And she would need to look into the finances and profitability of Watt's for Dinner. If Watt had neglected it in any way, she might not want it. "When was your last audit?"

"Now we're talking."

CHAPTER FORTY-NINE

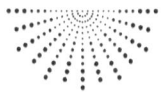

iehl left the office at three o'clock to pick up Skye at the Hartsfield-Jackson Atlanta International Airport domestic terminal. Her flight from Miami was on time, and she arrived promptly at 4:12 p.m. He rushed to baggage claim, and found Skye and her brother waiting for him.

Diehl shook hands with Sebastian, who was at least a couple of inches taller than he was, but he still looked the same as Diehl had remembered him from past catering events at Brooks Cottage and its adjacent guest cottage.

"How's Elisa?" It was the first thing Skye said to Diehl, even before a hello.

"She finished her interviews. She's at the house, safe and sound." Diehl reached for her hand. "Mom is hovering over her. Malik sent two security personnel to stay with both Elisa and Ethan around the clock. He's upgraded the security system in the house."

Skye nodded. "How is she emotionally?"

"Confused, I think." Diehl was taking a guess. "After the CAC interview is over, she's going for counseling. Pastor Gonzalez recommended someone at Midtown Chapel."

He waited for Skye's reaction to his mentioning a church in Atlanta and not on St. Simon's Island. She didn't say anything as the luggage carousel began to move. Perhaps she was compartmentalizing again.

When he and Sebastian pulled off multiple suitcases and Skye identified hers, Diehl knew they had a problem.

He had brought his 1964 Ferrari 250 GTO to show her—because he had said he'd do so on speakerphone in front of Jared and must now deliver on his promise. Now he realized that the vintage sports car didn't have enough trunk space.

"Uh-oh. I brought a small car." Diehl stared at Skye's two large teal-colored suitcases. That, plus her backpack. And her guitar in a case.

Oh boy.

"I know, right." Sebastian laughed. "I told her to pack light. It's only for a week."

"A long week," Skye protested.

"Fortunately, there's an easy solution. I'll take Skye's stuff with me back to Athens in my truck," Sebastian offered. To his sister, he said, "You might want to get what you need out of your suitcases if you're staying overnight."

"You mean like in a hotel somewhere?" Skye asked.

Diehl thought she looked lovely with her hair up and her face and arms tanned. She was wearing a somewhat crinkled T-shirt that said "Miami Beach," a pair of denim shorts, and a pair of hiking boots.

In other words, she was casual. Diehl mentally scratched off the five-star restaurant he had in mind, for which they had to at least halfway dress up.

Since he had come directly from his office, he was still wearing the button-down striped shirt he had on all day, and a pair of matching charcoal pants. He had changed into loafers, but nothing he had on was casual.

"A hotel, of course. Is there anywhere else you'd stay overnight?" Sebastian eyed Diehl.

"You sure you don't want to have dinner with us?" Diehl asked Sebastian instead.

"No. I've been away from my wife since Sunday. That's a long time. I need to get back to her," Sebastian said. "We were going to have dinner at my house tonight. You're welcome to join us."

"Thank you for the offer, but I have an idea for you," Diehl said. "Athens is a little more than one and a half hours, whichever main route you take. If you leave now, you'll get there around six o'clock. How about taking your wife out to dinner tonight at some-place nice? Meanwhile, I'll take Skye to dinner, and then I'll drive her to Athens after dinner tonight."

Diehl turned to Skye. "Then you don't have to unpack your suitcase in an airport. It's a hassle just to stay one night in a hotel when Athens is that close."

"What about Elisa and Ethan? Will they miss you this evening?" Skye asked.

"My parents are in town and staying with me. Mom is all over Elisa. The house has twenty-four-hour security. I think they will be fine. If we finish dinner by eight, and I get you to Athens by nine thirty, I'll be back home by eleven. I usually don't go to bed until midnight. Then you get to ride in the car I told Jared about."

Oops.

He didn't want to mention Jared's name, but it came out.

Skye wrinkled her nose. "I don't care what kind of car you have."

"I know, but I told him..." Diehl wished he didn't have to show off to Jared—who wasn't even here—but he had given his word.

And perhaps that had been a mark on him his entire life. Maybe he should have broken his word from time to time—it might have saved him from all those years of woe with Isobel, rescued him from a job he was stuck at, and opened up new worlds he had no time to explore beforehand.

Skye touched Sebastian's arm. "You can trust him with me."

"And her with me." Diehl grinned.

"Well, if I hadn't known you before this, Diehl, and if you hadn't gotten saved, I would have said no way. But you two go have your dinner somewhere, and we'll see you tonight. And hey, great idea for me to have dinner alone with Em." Sebastian turned to Skye. "Not that I don't love you, my baby sister."

All that sorted out, Diehl walked with Skye to his

Ferrari, which was parked in the hourly parking lot across the drop-off lanes at the airport. Skye only had her crossbody purse with her as she left her backpack with her brother back at the luggage carousel.

When they reached the sleek midnight blue sports car, Skye's jaw dropped. "What is this cute thing?"

This "cute thing" had cost Diehl a fortune at an auction he shouldn't have gone to with Dad. Diehl had bought it on a dare. And then realized that Dad had won even though he bought nothing.

Never be afraid to walk away empty-handed, son.

It was the advice of a lifetime, but it was too late. The auction was over and Diehl was stuck with yet another car that would go into his garage for occasional fun.

In fact, his mechanic would drive these vehicles more than he had time for.

"Truth be told," Diehl said as he unlocked the car and helped Skye into the passenger side. "I miss my Ford pickup, which is still parked in Brin's beach house garage."

"Is that who you really are? A pickup truck guy?" Skye asked. "Or is this sports car a side of you we don't know about."

"This car is so that I could keep up with the Joneses." Truthfully. "The pickup and life on the coast, that's what I want to be."

"The real you?"

"The real me doesn't care what vehicle I drive. The real me just wants to be with you and only you." Diehl lifted Skye's hand to his lips and gently kissed it.

He closed the door and went around the car to the driver's side. He could feel his heart beat faster than usual. Never had he felt this way toward any other woman in his entire life.

More than ever, he was sure that she was the one.

After he turned on the ignition, he reached out to hold Skye's hand. "You're really here."

"I gather you missed me."

Diehl nodded. "I've never missed anyone this much in my life—and I hate to say this, but not even my kids, though I thank God we got Elisa back in three days. Isn't that a miracle?"

"God works miracles all the time." Skye squeezed his hand. "Don't you need two hands to drive this car? It looks kinda old and fragile."

Diehl chuckled. "Before we leave this place, shall we decide where to go eat?"

"I don't care as long as I'm with you—but I don't want anything exotic. I've had enough surprises this week."

"Okay. No surprises. And somewhere casual."

"Yes, please, considering what I'm wearing. I'm glad the flight was no more than two hours long, but we did have to wait at the airport."

Diehl nodded. He hadn't traveled commercial in decades, if ever. He wasn't sure what he had missed.

"Shall we pick a random restaurant?"

"No, not random. That sounds unpredictable," Skye said.

"You don't like surprises?"

"Oh, I'm okay with surprises. I'm saying that I just

got off the plane, so I don't want to drive all over town in Atlanta traffic looking for a restaurant. I've had adventurous food all week."

Diehl appreciated Skye's honesty. She didn't try to please him. She spoke her mind. And she didn't seem to care about his sports car.

"How about comfort food?" Skye asked. "Barbecue, maybe? I haven't had brisket in forever."

"I haven't had ribs in months. I know a place in Buckhead."

"Let's go."

And so that was how billionaire Diehl Brooks drove his forty-million-dollar 1964 Ferrari 250 GTO to a woodsy, greasy, outdoorsy barbecue joint where a platter cost only fourteen dollars so that his girlfriend of three weeks—or had it been four weeks?—could have the best beef brisket in town.

CHAPTER FIFTY

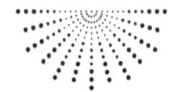

The service was fast and they were saying grace for their hot meal and eating by 5:30 p.m. Diehl thought they had plenty of time to talk in the restaurant before the usual crowd filed in, but first, he was busy eating ribs and making generous use of the roll of paper towel on the table.

"I never pegged you as a barbecue sort of guy." Skye squirted more sauce on her chopped brisket.

"I eat anything. Food is food." He wiped his fingers yet again on some clean paper towel. The pork fell off the bones, but eating ribs was messy—a different kind of messiness than eating boiled crab legs or crawfish.

"You better wash your hands really well before you touch the steering wheel of your fancy little car," Skye said.

"For sure."

She hadn't asked him how much it cost. And Diehl didn't say.

Truth be told, he'd sell every car and house he owned and give up the family business if he could be with Skye. He realized now that he loved her.

"Is it possible to fall in love quickly?" Diehl asked.

Before Skye could answer, the server came by to refill their tea and water, and to ask if they wanted anything else.

"I'm fine," Skye said. "These hush puppies are great. Love the bits of jalapeños in them. Compliments to the chef."

"I will tell him. Thank you."

After she left, Diehl waited for Skye to answer his question.

"You mean us or in general?" Skye asked.

Apparently, she had not only heard his question, but she had given it some thought.

"I guess both?" Diehl said. "When my sister met Ivan, they were casual friends for one year—on and off —before they met again in a new light. She said it was somehow different that time."

"So they knew each other before. I'm trying to think how my brother met Em—I mean Emmeline, since you don't know her. She's my best friend—was anyway until my brother came along, and now he's her best friend. My brother... Do you really want to know how it happened for them?"

"Sure. We're just analyzing relationships. Just between us." Diehl drank more water as he watched Skye drink her unsweet tea. He hadn't ordered any tea because this place made sweet tea too sweet and unsweet tea too bitter. Other than that, they made the best ribs and brisket.

"My brother was engaged to Talia a few times. Every single time, she'd break off with him, run off to other men, break up with them, and return to Sebastian. You'd think he'd get the pattern. Oh no, he still thought that Talia was the one. Then he asked me—his own sister—to help him get Talia back. I said no."

"You said no." Diehl smiled.

"I told him to move on. Talia refused to go to church with him, so right away, they had that divide. And blah blah." Skye finished her tea. "Instead of listening to my advice, my big brother—whom I love to death—asked my best friend Emmeline behind my back and paid her to be his rent-a-girlfriend for the summer."

"Paid escort?" Diehl spluttered on his water.

"What I said. Trust me, it's all clean—they're both Christians. My brother promised to help find her brother, who had vanished some years ago. They faked a relationship so that Seb could win back Talia."

"I gather it ended well since they're married now."

Skye nodded. "In the process of helping each other, they fell in love. So that's not love at first sight for you."

"What about us?"

"Us?" Skye went quiet. "What do you think?"

"When was the first time we ever saw each other?" Diehl tried to recall when Sebastian first catered luncheons and dinner parties for his parents at Brooks Cottage.

"It was before your parents hired Chef Pierre," Skye said. "Seb had a catering business then, and I just graduated out of chef school—wow. That was at least ten years ago."

"Has it been ten years? I remember your brother more than I remember you."

"I was working at Sage Café at that time as chef de cuisine, so I didn't go to the catering venues unless Seb needed me to fill in for someone. I think we had a few Christmas dinners at Brooks Cottage—before they bought the house next door—where I saw you. You were with friends, but your wife was not with you. That's all I remember because I was busy in the kitchen."

"Isobel rarely went with me to Seaside Island. If she ever did, she would stay at The Priory and not at Brooks Cottage. It was awkward. I don't mean to dredge anything up or put her in a bad light—though I suppose I just did, and for that, I apologize."

"Don't worry about it. We're being objective about our past history as a matter of analysis," Skye said.

There she went again, compartmentalizing things. Diehl found it fascinating that Skye hadn't shown any shred of jealousy.

As for him, he wanted her for himself exclusively.

"What about your kids?" Skye pushed her plate to one side and wiped her hands with a paper towel. "I don't recall seeing them around at the dinners and luncheons."

"They were always with nannies. That was Isobel's wish that the kids would not be attached to us.

That way, we could do adult things or take vacations without a bunch of kids clinging on to us."

"That's sad. Poor kids."

Diehl realized that he didn't feel that way anymore. "When I got saved, I saw how precious my kids are. If I were to do it over, they wouldn't have nannies. They'd have me."

"They're older now, so they might not be as needy —although I remember a sermon that Pastor Gonzalez preached a few years ago in which he said that teenagers need their parents more than we realize."

"Really?" Diehl hadn't put too much thought into it.

"I'm just telling you what he said. I have no experience of my own."

"Well, Elisa will be thirteen next year, so I better pay attention. Could you send me the link to that sermon? I need to hear it."

"Sure. Remind me later, okay? I don't want to touch my purse with my sticky fingers." Skye wiggled her fingers in the air. "By the way, there are many godly parents at Seaside Chapel who are ahead of you in parenting teens and college kids, so you might get some good advice from them too."

"Good idea."

"If you ever go back to St. Simon's, you might talk to the pastor about it and he'll point out some godly fathers who can provide wise counsel. Iron sharpens iron, you know."

"I've heard of that phrase."

"It's in the Bible." Skye realized she had reached

into her purse with her sticky fingers. "Aargh. Let me go wash my hands and I'll look up the verse for you."

Diehl also took the opportunity to run to the men's restroom. When he returned, the server had brought them the dessert menu. He was debating between peach cobbler and pecan pie when Skye returned, texting on her way.

"Seb texted to say he arrived safely in Athens and asked how dinner was." Skye sat down. "He's waiting for Em to get ready so they can go to a seafood restaurant."

Something about that idea made Diehl all warm inside. A simple dinner out with the one he loved meant all the world to him—more than luxury vacations, new fast cars, and expensive jewelry.

Ah, why did he compare Skye with his deceased wife? Skye was nothing like Isobel. While Isobel lived from party to party, drink to drink, burning holes in their fortune, Skye was down-to-earth, practical, and sensible.

Here they were, having a pleasant dinner without it erupting into a big fight and different bedrooms afterward—as it had been for years with Isobel. If she didn't get her way, there would be a price to pay for months on end. Isobel never forgave a grudge. She carried them around with her for years, like precious little cargos.

"What's on your mind?" Skye smiled. "Something amiss?"

"No, no. I was thinking of how..." His voice cracked. He wanted to be stronger, but it hit him at his rib cage. He cleared his throat. "About how nice it is to have a pleasant dinner conversation."

"Shouldn't this be a normal thing?" Skye asked. "Stress makes digestion harder."

"Not just physiologically, but I haven't had peace of mind until I got saved. Now I see all the things that are possible. Like a nice dinner with someone I love."

Diehl waited for her reaction.

She sat there, looking at him.

"Have I ever told you that?" Diehl asked.

"No."

"I have thought of it for a while."

"Three weeks?"

"I realized it last week." Diehl kept his voice down. "Whenever we weren't together, I wanted to be with you."

Crowds of people were being seated all around them.

"Let's vacate. Someone's probably waiting for this table." Skye waved to their server, who seemed to have forgotten to drop off the check.

"What about dessert?" Diehl asked.

"I'm on a diet. I ate too much this week."

"You still look good."

"Wait until next week." Skye chuckled.

When the server came over, Diehl reached for the check. "Let me take that."

"I'll get the tip." Skye unzipped her purse.

"No. It's on me."

"Then let me pay for gas," Skye said.

Diehl looked up. "I have a full tank."

"I need to do something."

Diehl found it interesting that Skye wanted to pay for something. Didn't she realize that he didn't need any help at all? This dinner was nothing to him. The entire cost of dinner was way below any tip he had given a server in the last year he'd gone out to meals with Dad or a colleague. And yet, it was the best dinner conversation he'd had in a long time.

The company made all the difference.

"No, you don't." Diehl signed the check. He tipped the server over twenty percent. She went away happy.

Diehl walked Skye to his Ferrari, parked in the back of the restaurant. It had no valet parking, but even if it did, Diehl did not want anyone to touch his car other than himself and his mechanic, who had to take it out for a spin every now and then whenever Diehl was too busy to drive it anywhere.

The gentleman that he was or wanted to be, Diehl opened the passenger side door for Skye.

Before she got in the car, she touched his arm. "Thank you for dinner. That was sweet of you."

"Good food, good company. I meant everything I said." He waited, wondering whether she would let him kiss her.

She didn't seem to encourage him either way, so he reached for her. She rested her head on his shoulder and wrapped her arm around his waist.

"I missed you all week," she sort of mumbled.

But Diehl heard every word.

"I missed you too."

She stepped back. "Nothing like talking face-to-face, is there?"

"No. I'm happy you agreed to have dinner with me." Diehl still held her hands. "I'm sorry you found out about the invitation the same time Jared did."

"I'm glad you did that because it drew the line for him. You rescued me. My hero." She smiled. "Now let's stop talking about other men. I know you want to kiss me."

Diehl replied by proving she was right.

Afterwards, he threaded his fingers through her hair, accidentally loosening the ties on top of her hair. "Oops."

Skye's hair cascaded onto her shoulders in large waves. There was only one other time Diehl had seen her hair down. It was at her restaurant on Jekyll Island.

"You have beautiful hair." His lips found hers again.

And Diehl knew he wanted to be with her—and only her—for as long as God would let them be together. A lifetime, he hoped.

They stood there for a while in each other's arms, just as the sun started to dip above the tall trees in old Atlanta in this corner of Buckhead. Around them cars came and went, people walked to and fro.

"We should let other people have our parking spot," Skye said.

"Sensible Skye," Diehl whispered into her hair. It smelled like citrus and rain. He kissed the base of her ear, and noticed that she did not have any ear piercings.

He made a note to himself not to buy her any pierced earrings.

Other than that, he'd buy her the world if he could.

And yet, what he knew about Skye so far told him that she wouldn't want him to do that. She probably wouldn't mind if he gave to charities in her name.

Like that reward money for finding Elisa. He had written a check to Seaside Chapel for thirty thousand dollars. It had been Skye's vigilance that led to useful tips for the police. And yet, she didn't want a dime of it. In fact, she tithed it all to the church for ministry work.

Selfless Skye.

This is definitely the woman I want to marry.

CHAPTER FIFTY-ONE

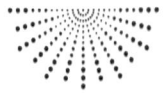

There were several routes to drive to Athens from Atlanta, depending on where Skye happened to be. When they got in the car, Diehl asked her for suggestions when the dashboard GPS showed several routes.

"I've been to Athens, but it was a long time ago. Once or twice, tops," Diehl said. "I went to a Georgia Bulldogs football game. And to dinner at another time."

"Before my brother moved there, I'd been to Athens several times. However, even though my brother lives there for now, I don't go there much." She pointed to the screen on the dashboard, to the route that would take them to Interstate 85 and Highway 316. "It says that we'll be there in one hour and sixteen minutes if we take that route, give or take."

If she were at Emmeline's parents' home in Roswell, she would take the northern route on Interstate 85 through the small towns of Braselton and Jefferson. However, if she were coming directly from the airport, she'd drive on Interstate 20 and go through Walnut Grove and Monroe.

"Then we can talk more on the way." Diehl put the car in reverse and backed out of the restaurant parking lot.

Skye nodded. She felt tired from a long week, and that tea she drank at the barbecue place was a little light on the caffeine. She didn't want to fall asleep while Diehl was driving, though. He wasn't her chauffeur. This was a road trip.

"I guess this car only looks old—I mean, classic—from the outside?" Skye asked. "You have GPS in here. I gather it's not the original."

"Not in 1964."

"Wow. I don't think I've ever been in a vehicle this old—oh wait. Brinley drove us around in Ivan's old 1946 Chevy truck once. It belonged to his grandpa."

Skye's phone buzzed. She checked. Frowned. "Excuse me. I have to answer this text. Chef Joseph cannot find the saffron and vanilla beans I bought for him last week."

Diehl nodded.

Skye texted quickly so that she could get off the phone. "I could turn it off."

"No. You might have emergencies."

"I hope not. I'm too tired to put out fires tonight." Skye chuckled.

"Tired? I'm sorry. Was dinner too long?"

Skye touched his arm. "Why are you apologizing again?"

"I don't want to be blamed for anything."

"Why would I blame you for a long week of cooking in the sun, judging dishes in the sun? That was all me and none of you," Skye said. "I admit I'm worn out and could use a vacation, but I can't afford to unless I sell my shares to Saffron and hire more chefs for STL."

"Is that right?" Diehl seemed surprised.

Skye wondered what he had heard about her businesses.

"Don't burn out like I did." Diehl drove through light traffic—because rush hour was over. "Anything I can do?"

"Pray that God will give me wisdom to say no to too many things." Skye leaned back.

"That's a good prayer for me too. What else can we pray about?"

Skye was impressed at Diehl's personal spiritual growth. "Maybe I should write them down to remind us."

"Good idea. Send me a copy of it."

"Okay." Skye swiped her phone. "Wisdom for us about decisions at work. Other prayers? How's Elisa doing psychologically?"

"Pastor Gonzalez called Midtown Chapel, and they sent over a grief counselor for both Elisa and Ethan. That way, Elisa won't feel singled out."

"That's good. Did she finish those meetings you were talking about?"

"The sessions at CAC?"

"Yeah. I'm not familiar with it much, and keep forgetting it's called the Child Advocacy Center. But it does make sense. When is that over?"

"Tomorrow at one o'clock. They will record everything so that Detective Jeong can have a video copy for his investigation on St. Simon's."

"Makes sense. Then they don't have to interview her multiple times."

"Exactly."

"What questions do they ask her?" Skye was curious.

"I don't know. They don't tell me when I ask. I go with her because she wants me there, but they won't let me in the interview room, so I sit in the lobby and try to get some work done," Diehl said. He turned on his blinker, and he now drove in the middle lane of Interstate 85. "However, Detective Jeong said that Elisa has been helpful to the DHS because she saw things at the places Romina took her."

"That's amazing."

"I know, right. When I was twelve, I don't remember helping with national security. Did you?"

"I was learning how to make sandwiches," Skye said.

"I probably played too many video games at that age." Diehl chuckled. "Elisa is growing up fast. She's strong and sure. She told me yesterday that when she grows up, she wants to be a policewoman."

"When you were a kid, what did you want to be?" Skye asked.

"I wanted to be like Grandpa Brooks. He did nothing all day long except walk on the beach and check on his collection of violins and pianos. Somehow money grew on trees."

They laughed.

"You?" Diehl glanced over at Skye.

Outside the car, the sun had almost set. Through the side rearview mirror, Skye could see red and vermillion bands across the sky behind them as they drove eastward toward the college town of Athens.

"I wanted to cook," Skye said. "I dreamed of a beautiful kitchen, and there I was in the kitchen, cooking."

"That's all you ever wanted to do?"

"Once I got in the youth group at church as a teenager, I started getting asked to babysit. The pay was good, but most of all, I loved those little babies. I started wanting...uh..."

Too much information.

Skye looked away.

"Skye?"

"I thought that as soon as I finished school, God would send me the man He wanted me to marry, and we'd have lots of kids." Skye shook her head. "I was such a dreamer."

"Were you? Wanting to be a mother is a noble thing."

"I didn't want to bring it up, but I've had boyfriends in my life, you know, and none of them worked out."

"That's because they were all wrong for you." His voice sounded certain.

"Really?"

He rubbed her hand with his palm. "I'm sure because God prepared you for me."

"Are you sure?"

"You have no idea how sure I am. Remember back at the restaurant, I asked you if you believe that people could fall in love quickly?"

Skye nodded. "We never got to the end of that, did we? We talked about how our siblings fell in love, but that was it."

"I didn't tell you how Parker fell in love with his wife, Riley. They were on a canoe trip in the Okefenokee. Singles retreat out in the middle of mosquito land. Can you believe it? Parker fell in the crocodile-infested swamp, and she pulled him out. She did have help from the other singles, some of whom were in rowboats, but still..."

"That sounds...romantic."

"When he got in the boat, Riley scolded him for not wearing his life jacket. He told me he was puzzled because a total stranger—who didn't know his name—was mad at him for not wearing a life vest. He was in love with her from that point onward."

"Seriously?"

"Yep. They dated for two years, he proposed, and they were married for eighteen years, before he went deep sea fishing and drowned in the ocean trying to rescue his adopted daughter who fell overboard."

Skye blinked. She knew how Parker had died

because Brinley had told them about Riley Brooks, the grieving widow. Riley had not remarried even though Parker had been gone for a number of years.

Skye wondered what it felt like to be a widow in her early forties. So young. Alone so soon.

"Interesting. I didn't know their love story." Skye couldn't say that Parker had been reckless for not wearing a life jacket while boating. Skye herself had been on pontoons without a life vest.

"Parker fell in love with Riley the first day they met," Diehl said. "He never stopped loving her until the day he died. I know that because he was going to return from the fishing trip the next day—one day early—to surprise Riley with an anniversary gift. He didn't get a chance to deliver it himself."

"What gift was it?"

"He bought her a new house in Atlanta."

"Without her knowing? A house?" Skye wondered how such a gift would work. It could never work for her because she would want to design her own kitchen.

"Parker knew Riley so well that he put in everything that she would want in the house. The only person he told about the house was me."

"So you had to tell her."

Diehl nodded. "I had the key to the house. I was also the executor of his will."

"Six years ago. That must've been traumatic."

"His body was lost at sea. Never found. Neither was his daughter's." His voice cracked. "Parker and Riley loved each other so much, and yet their marriage ended when they were both in their thirties."

Skye almost asked him to talk about something else, but she realized that he needed to talk about it now.

"Because God is with me now, I can look back and talk about it," Diehl said.

"Did Riley like the house?"

"She loved it, but she never moved in. It's still there, several streets away from my house. It's still empty. She wouldn't sell it, and wouldn't live in it. It was all paid for."

"Interesting."

Skye didn't realize they were already on Interstate 316. The traffic lights were bright in the dark night. Somewhere overhead, she heard thunder.

"Was it supposed to rain tonight?" Skye swiped her phone. "Uh-oh. Thunderstorm tonight."

"In Athens only?" Diehl asked.

"Between Atlanta and Athens." Skye didn't like bad driving weather. Especially tonight after they'd had a good time together. She was on the mountaintop and did not want anything dangerous to happen.

"I'll drive slowly." Diehl squeezed her hand. "Let's pray for safety."

Skye nodded, wrapping both her hands around Diehl's hand as he prayed. "Keep your eyes on the road."

"Yes, ma'am." Diehl smiled. "Lord Jesus, we know that You are with us. Never have I been more sure now that You are with us. Protect us as we drive to Athens. Keep Skye, Sebastian, and Emmeline safe in Athens.

Protect me as I drive back to Atlanta. Keep the storm away from us if at all possible."

He was about to close the prayer when Skye decided to add on to it.

"And Lord, we lift up the prayer requests we have this evening, but first we praise You for bringing Elisa home safely to us. Thank You that she was unharmed. Although Romina took her into harm's way, she also protected her all the way until the police found her. I pray that Zeta Bishop would repent of her sins. She has no idea what could have happened to her own granddaughter. I pray that as Elisa is being interviewed by the forensic people, that You will give her strength. Someday, may Elisa and Ethan also know Jesus as their personal Lord and Savior."

"Amen," Diehl said.

"I'm not done," Skye said.

"No?"

"We haven't prayed for the first thing on our list. Wisdom, remember?"

"Go ahead."

"Dear Heavenly Father, we need Your supernatural wisdom regarding our businesses. We have decisions to make at work that could build or tear down the companies. Surround us with wise people who know what they're doing and have our best interests in mind. Show us where we need to step forward, and where we need to retreat. Catch us when we fall. Lead us with Your perfect peace. In Jesus' name, I pray. Amen."

"Amen again," Diehl said. "I like that. 'Catch us

when we fall.' God is amazing. If I had Him all those years, I wouldn't have had such a hard time."

"Work is always hard."

"True."

"Do you give yourself a day off?" Skye asked, knowing that she gave herself the weekends off.

"I do now. I try not work on weekends, like you."

"It's Friday tomorrow, still a workday," Skye said. "And yet you're driving to and from Athens."

"I want to. It's going to be okay. One more day of work and I'll be spending the whole weekend with my kids."

"Are you usually busy at work on Fridays?"

"Tomorrow, I am. I have a meeting at nine o'clock." He paused a little. "This is hush-hush for now."

"Then don't tell me the details," Skye said.

"I can tell you that since my brother passed away, Dad and I have been stretched too thin trying to manage the three of four subsidiaries of our family business."

"That's a lot of work, it sounds like."

"The fourth subsidiary is doing well. Brooks Renovations."

"The one Brinley is running."

Diehl nodded. "It's the only one on St. Simon's. The rest of them are in Atlanta."

"Your dad's retired, isn't he?" Skye tapped on the keyboard on her phone. *Pray for the Brooks businesses.*

"Yes, although for the last three weeks, he has been back at the office because of me."

"How can anyone blame you?" Skye asked.

"You're just one person, running three companies, pretty much."

"Well, I burned out."

"I would too."

"It's nice of you to understand."

"We both run businesses," Skye said. "As a Christian, I need God's wisdom to make sure I don't do anything stupid and lose my company. Sometimes we have to make tough decisions, like selling something."

Diehl nodded. "Interesting you should mention that."

"Your mental health and your family are not worth sacrificing just to secure another million—or billion."

"Right."

"Maybe it sounds like tough objectivity, but now that I realize Saffron is stretching me too thin, I know I have to let it go. I don't feel bad anymore, even when I recall the days my brother was all excited about the restaurant." Skye chuckled. "Oddly enough, it means nothing to him at all whether I sell or don't sell my shares."

"He has found something—someone—else more important."

Traffic was light but the night was dark and cloudy. Rain began to fall all around the car. The windshield wipers cleared away some of the rain.

Skye prayed silently for their safety.

Driving through the rain, Diehl hummed a tune.

"What was that hymn you sang to me last weekend?" Diehl asked.

"Which one?"

"Something about God's amazing love?"

Skye began singing a line or two.

"Yes, that one," Diehl said.

"Did you know that Charles Wesley wrote the words in 1738, the same year he was saved?" Skye asked.

"Really?"

Skye nodded. "Two years before that, he visited Savannah and St. Simon's Island in 1736, where he preached in a church service at Fort Frederica."

"I didn't know that."

Skye started singing the first stanza of the hymn.

> *And can it be that I should gain*
> *an interest in the Saviour's blood?*
> *Died He for me, who caused His pain?*
> *For me, who Him to death pursued?*
> *Amazing love! how can it be,*
> *that thou, my God, shouldst die for me?*

When she finished, Diehl said, "Teach me the words."

For the rest of the way to Athens, they sang a duet until Diehl had half the song memorized. The rain outside kept falling, but the thunder was far away now.

In spite of the rain, the small college town was bustling with umbrellas and ponchos everywhere as people—students, residents, visitors—milled about, running from car to restaurants and vice versa, walking here and there at nine thirty at night.

"Yes, that way." The GPS in the car suggested the

same route she would take. "Sebastian traded his house by the marshes on St. Simon's for a small apartment in Athens so that he could pour the rest of the funds into Sage Café Athens. I don't know what the appeal is, but he's opening another Sage Café in Buckhead next year."

"Let me know as soon as he does because I'll tell everyone," Diehl said. "Lots of people in my office eat lunch in Buckhead."

"Thank you. He'd like that."

The rain started again, with the rumblings in the sky and bolts of lightning.

"Are you and your brother very close?" Diehl asked as he turned into the parking lot of a large apartment complex.

"Yes. Well, I should say *were*—because he's married now. God sent the perfect woman for him. Before he married, my brother and I did a lot of businesses together—restaurant, catering, cooking for clients. Then we branched out into our own different interests, but from time to time, we still do it together." Skye pointed. "Look, someone's leaving."

The rain fell in sheets.

Slowly, Diehl eased into the empty parking spot.

"Let me see if I have an umbrella." Diehl reached in between the seats to the back. "Uh-oh. I must not have thought of putting one in here."

"Let's just make a dash for it. See the green awning over there?" Skye pointed. "That's our entrance."

"How about I drop you off?"

"We're already parked. If you leave, someone else will take this spot."

"Well, all right."

"We can always dry off. Ready?" Skye put her hand on the door handle.

"Let's go." Diehl jumped out of the car and locked the door.

The rain poured all around them like a waterfall as they held hands and ran toward the entrance.

"I see why you're wearing hiking boots," Diehl said. "My loafers are useless in this rain."

Soaked through, they reached the awning. Skye laughed. "It feels like we fell into a pool."

"It does." Diehl reached for Skye's face and pushed away a strand of hair stuck to her cheek. His eyes were on her lips. "Do we have time?"

"We make time." Skye lifted her lips, inviting.

Diehl accepted the invitation.

CHAPTER FIFTY-TWO

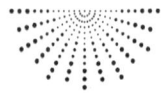

*D*iehl watched Skye bury her face in a throw pillow as Sebastian went on and on about their teenage years living with their aunt and uncle on St. Simon's Island. Emmeline was laughing her head off and her face had turned red.

"Stop it, Seb!" Skye's voice came from behind the pillow. She was sitting on the rug on the floor in front of a couch on which Emmeline was rolling in laughter.

Across from the rug, Diehl stretched out in a recliner, wearing Sebastian's Georgia Bulldogs T-shirt, gym shorts, and socks. His clothes were in the dryer somewhere down the hall.

Outside the apartment windows, the rain continued to pour, peppered regularly by thunder and lightning. It wasn't going to let up, but Diehl wasn't in a hurry. He could drive home slowly in the rain and he'd still get there by midnight.

He smiled as he recalled how they had kissed briefly outside. It was spontaneous, but he felt he could open up to Skye more than anyone else in the world.

In fact, he didn't want anyone else.

His conversations with his Sunday school teacher at Seaside Chapel helped him to see his past and present in perspective. Matt had told him that there were things he hadn't understood in his twenties that he could begin to see now that he was older.

Diehl had carried some emotional baggage in his life that God was lifting off his shoulders day by day. He had to let his brother go. And let Isobel go.

Then he would be free to love Skye.

"And then when we were in eleventh grade, Skye fell in love," Sebastian said.

"Nooo!" Skye rolled over on the rug, her face still covered by the pillow.

"You can't hide forever, sis!"

"How would you like it if I told your stories?"

"They're too boring." Sebastian wiggled his eyebrows. "Yours, on the other hand..."

The dryer buzzer went off.

"Excuse me." Diehl got up from the recliner and padded to the hallway. If his clothes were dry, he'd be out of there in five minutes.

"Are you leaving now?" Skye asked. Her hair spread out on the rug. Her floral pastel pajamas made her look dreamy lying sideways. She seemed more comfortable around him now.

Diehl choked up, wondering how he could drive

away alone tonight without Skye. "Just checking on my clothes. They could be dry by now."

An alert went off on someone's phone. Sebastian picked it up from the side table, so Diehl assumed it was his.

"There's an electrical storm warning until three in the morning," Sebastian said.

Skye sat up. "It's not safe to drive home tonight, Diehl. Stay until morning?"

"Looks like the rain is supposed to stop around five," Sebastian added. "If you need us to wake you up, we will."

"Five?" Diehl asked. If he left at that time, he'd get home at six thirty to shower and eat breakfast. His meeting with Dad and Riley wasn't until nine. There would be plenty of time.

"If you don't stay, Skye will be worried sick for the next two hours until you get home—if you get home," Sebastian said.

Diehl wasn't sure if he was kidding. He glanced at Skye, who did not refute her brother's statement.

"They have a guest room with its own bath," Skye said. "You can sleep there. The bed is soft and feathery."

Having been a good listener, Diehl knew for a fact that there were only two bedrooms in this apartment. If he took the guest room, where would Skye sleep?

"This couch is fine." Diehl pointed. "All I need is a pillow and a blanket."

Lightning lit up the windows, followed by peals of thunder shaking the old building. A loud crackling sound was soon followed by crashes and the noise of car alarms going off.

Skye went to the window. "Wow. A tree fell on the vehicles!"

What? Diehl rushed to her side. "Where did I park?"

"On the other side of the building," Skye said.

"Whew." Not that he didn't have insurance for his overpriced classic Ferrari, but he didn't want the hassle of having to rebuild or replace a totaled car.

Standing this close to Skye made Diehl long to be with her even more.

"That's a big old tree. I hope no one is hurt." Skye peered.

Diehl looked in the same direction. People were out there with their flashlights. The vehicle alarms continued blaring.

Skye reached for Diehl's hand. "I don't know if we can sleep through that din, but better in here than driving out there. No matter how great a driver you are on the highway, other people might not be as careful."

"True," Sebastian said. "We have a spare tooth-brush—unused—and new tubes of toothpaste—gifts from the dental office—and I can get up early and make you Belgian waffles."

Skye's jaw dropped. "You didn't offer to make me waffles."

"I made you plenty of waffles in your lifetime," Sebastian said. "And they're great waffles—unlike the ones Thaddeus tried to make for you."

Skye's eyes flared.

"Who's Thaddeus?" Diehl asked.

"Her first boyfriend," Sebastian said. "Eleventh grade, as I was trying to tell you, before the tree fell."

"A sign to tell you to shut up," Skye snapped.

"Thaddeus." Sebastian stepped back, away from the window, just before the lights went out. "What in the world?"

Quickly, four cell phone flashlights appeared in the dark apartment.

"We sure picked a perfect time to visit," Skye said. "Do you have real flashlights?"

Emmeline nodded. She made her way to the kitchen pantry, where she retrieved two flashlights and a lantern.

Diehl realized he was still holding Skye's hand.

"Thanks for the invitation. I think I'll stay the night," Diehl said.

In the dim light, with her hair down, she leaned against his shoulder. He wasn't sure why she did that, but he liked the proximity.

Skye's phone rang. "Avery. I have to take this call."

She left the living room, but turned back. "Diehl, better check the dryer and hang up your clothes so they aren't wrinkled in the morning."

Diehl liked to hear Skye call his name.

When he returned from the dryer alcove, his phone in front of him as a flashlight, Sebastian had placed a pillow and a folded blanket on the couch.

"Are you sure you'll be okay?" Sebastian handed him a toothbrush and a tube of toothpaste, both still in their boxes. "I have a cot that might be more comfortable. It's longer."

"No need to go through all the trouble. It's only for one night. Thank you for having me here. Saved me money for a hotel."

"Wait till you eat his waffles." Emmeline walked by. "No five-star restaurant can top them."

"She says that because she's my wife." Sebastian kissed her in front of Diehl.

It made Diehl long for his own.

Speaking of whom, he didn't see Skye anywhere.

Is Skye mine, though?

"Since you're on the couch, Skye is in the guest room, so you might want to take turns with her using the bathroom. Her room is past the washer and dryer," Emmeline said. "She's in there right now, chatting with Avery on the phone. It could be a while."

"I'll just brush my teeth at the kitchen sink, if you don't mind," Diehl said.

"Not at all. Let me know if you need anything else." Emmeline smiled.

She had a warm smile, a quiet voice, and a pleasant attitude. Diehl wondered how she ended up being a rent-a-girlfriend for Sebastian. It showed that sometimes it was impossible to know people just by how they looked.

After brushing his teeth, Diehl settled down in the dark living room. He propped up the pillow to one side of the couch so that he faced the window. He had slept on couches at the office, so it wasn't like he couldn't get comfortable.

Outside he could still hear distant car alarms, but thankfully not from the parking lot outside this side of the building.

Every so often, the dark sky would light up with flashes of lightning in the midst of the pouring rain. It was a great idea to wait until morning.

He texted his parents to tell them about the electrical storm. He told them that he'd drive home in about six or seven hours. And no, he wouldn't miss the meeting with Riley at nine in the morning. If he had to, he'd call in remotely.

He pulled the blanket over his entire body. It was a long blanket, longer than his six-foot-two frame. Sebastian was taller than he was by an inch or two, so this blanket was probably his.

He swiped his phone to his Bible app and read a few Psalms. The week before, he had been camping out in Galatians, but today, he knew he'd fallen behind in his Bible reading to keep up with the Monday morning men's Bible study group. He wondered when he might return to St. Simon's Island.

As soon as possible, he prayed.

He had been away from Seaside Chapel for a week, and on Sunday, he'd probably end up at Midtown Chapel—unless he livestreamed the sermon from Seaside Chapel.

Diehl texted Skye to wish her goodnight. He was closing his eyes to get some sleep when the screen flashed.

> Skye: Sorry about my brother. He likes
> to tell stories.
> Diehl: About Thaddeus? Did he give you
> your first kiss?

Silence. Diehl regretted asking it. He would rather talk about something else, but he was curious. Too curious for his own good. Within seconds, Skye replied.

> Skye: A long time ago.
> Diehl: First love?
> Skye: Looking back, I don't know. Those
> teenage years.
> Diehl: Puppy love.
> Skye: Probably. We broke up in my
> senior year. He wanted something to
> celebrate the prom that I could not
> give him.
> Diehl: Jerk.
> Skye: I told him what he wanted is only
> reserved for my future husband and
> no one else.
> Diehl: Oh.

Skye reminded Diehl of Brinley. Grandpa Brooks had made Brinley take a vow of purity in exchange for a special wedding gift that he said God would give her. Turned out it wasn't his collection of old violins and pianos. It was something more than that, beyond Brinley's wildest dreams: a godly husband.

Could I be a godly husband to Skye?

> Diehl: Pastor Gonzalez says that inside every one of us is a heart wanting to be loved.
>
> Skye: I heard that sermon before.
>
> Diehl: Then you remember that once God loves us, we can love others.
>
> Skye: What are you getting at?
>
> Diehl: God has loved me. With God's love, I can love you. I may be imperfect, but Christ is perfect. His love is what I give to you. Together we can help each other through the journey of life.

When Skye didn't reply right away, Diehl got concerned. Then he felt a movement nearby. He glanced up to see Skye leaning over his face and planting a quick kiss on his lips.

"I just want to say good night," she whispered in his ear.

"I didn't hear you."

"The storm outside is louder than my footsteps."

Diehl threw back his blanket, and tapped the flashlight on his phone. He placed it on the coffee table. It cast a silvery glow around them. He was up on his feet, wrapping his arms around Skye. They stood there for a while, enjoying each other's warmth.

His lips swept across her cheek before he remembered that they were not alone in the apartment.

Behind that wall over there, Sebastian and Emmeline might still be awake.

"What time do you plan to get up in the morning?" Skye asked softly.

"I need to be at the office by eight forty-five for the first of several meetings," Diehl whispered. "Working backwards, if I get up at six and leave thirty minutes after that, I would be able to get to my house and change by eight with plenty of time to get through Atlanta traffic."

"Then we could have breakfast at six o'clock."

"Is that too early for you? I can go to a drive-through on the way."

"And miss my brother's Belgian waffles?"

"Will he be offended?"

Skye shrugged. "It's on the Sage Café menu."

"Never had it."

"Then you have no idea what you're missing."

"All right. You've convinced me. I'll stay for breakfast." He nuzzled her hair. Her shampoo smelled like fresh rain. "I wish we could sit a while and talk."

"We could sit in the kitchen for a few minutes, but I'm going to bed. I came out to the kitchen to get some water and I had to wish you a good night." Skye walked toward the open kitchen.

"How did you know I wasn't asleep?" Diehl followed her with his phone acting as a flashlight to lead the way. Outside the storm was still raging.

"You just texted me."

Diehl chuckled. "Yeah, I forgot."

"See. You're tired. You really need to get some

sleep." Skye opened the refrigerator. She picked out a bottled water.

Diehl did the same. He had brushed his teeth and wasn't about to do it a second time if he drank anything else other than water.

"If you sleep now, you'll only have six-and-a-half hours of sleep," Skye said. "Then you have to drive home to a meeting."

"Yeah. The meeting is important. It could remake or break the company."

"Remake?" Skye asked.

They were still keeping their voices down, although the loud thunder and rain outside would have masked their conversation.

"I can't say anything now because it could go either way." Diehl twisted the cap of the water bottle. "When things are clearer, I'll tell you."

Skye nodded.

"You're not upset I'm not telling you things?" Diehl asked.

"While I am curious, I trust God for His timing. If it's something I need to know, then at the right time, I will know. If it's something I shouldn't know, why should I pry?"

"It's something I want to tell you, but now is not the time."

"Then at the right time, we'll have another talk. For now, we keep praying for God to give us wisdom in our businesses."

Diehl nodded. "I like your confidence."

"Remember the verse we heard at the Fire Pit Service a few weeks ago?"

"Remind me." He noticed that Skye didn't mention who preached that evening.

"Philippians 4:13 says 'I can do all things through Christ who strengthens me.' There's no other confidence for me except in Christ alone."

"Always a good reminder to focus on Christ."

CHAPTER FIFTY-THREE

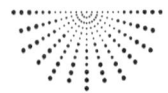

Sebastian's Belgian waffles were better than any of the five-star restaurants that Diehl had ever eaten in around the world, but he only had fifteen minutes to eat them hot or take them to go cold.

While Diehl enjoyed Sebastian's company as well as Emmeline's, he was disappointed that Skye had slept in. He wanted to kiss her goodbye, but not in front of her brother, and not if she hadn't given him permission to enter her bedroom. He'd have to text her later.

Diehl thanked God that he left Sebastian's apartment promptly at 6:30 a.m. because it took a while to get out of Athens. The storm had passed, but downed trees were everywhere. Old oak trees that had seen the growth of the city for decades, perhaps at least a century, were either still on the roads or moved to the side to allow traffic to go through.

His Ferrari GPS worked overtime to recalculate

alternate routes for him so that he would be able to get to the office on time. Forget going home to change.

He called Mom, asking her to go to his closet and pick out a shirt, a pair of pressed pants, socks, and briefs. Oh yes, a belt and matching dress shoes.

"Please ask Dad to bring them to work and leave them in my office," he added.

"Is everything okay?" Mom asked.

"Yes. I texted you last night." Diehl spoke into the phone that was docked in his car. By the time he reached the office, the phone would be fully charged.

"I got it. You were caught in an electrical storm in Athens and stayed overnight at Sebastian's apartment."

"Right. You should have seen the damages. Trees are down everywhere. In fact, last night, a giant tree fell across the parking lot. Good thing my car was on the other side of the building."

Mom sounded shocked. "Good thing you were not in the car."

"Right. God protected us all."

"Maybe He did," Mom admitted.

It did Diehl good to hear Mom mention God in a positive light. Perhaps there was hope yet for her to have the peace of God in her.

"I better let you go. I want to go back to bed—after I pack your clothes for you and put them in a garment bag."

"Maybe you could give the garment bag to Murray. He won't forget to take it to the office."

"Good idea. Okay." She yawned. "Bye. Drive safely. Have a good meeting, et cetera, et cetera."

After Mom hung up, Diehl found himself talking to God.

"Siri, start reading Galatians 1 audio," he said after he prayed. He'd have to check with Matt where they were at in the men's Bible study, but there were only six chapters in Galatians. He was sure he'd hear the entire book by the time he reached Atlanta traffic.

Before he reached Atlanta, he had gone on to listen to the next book of the Bible, Ephesians. By the time he navigated through heavy rush hour traffic to get to his office in midtown Atlanta, he had gone past Ephesians and Philippians, and all the way into Colossians, the next book.

The longer rush hour was, the more books of the New Testament filled the car.

Diehl felt like a sponge, and yet he knew he had to re-read almost all of what he had heard. God's Word was deep and wide, for sure.

When he pulled into the parking lot of Brooks Investments, it was almost nine o'clock. He had a couple of minutes to change—or not.

He walked straight into Dad's office, wearing everything he had worn the day before. The shirt was slightly wrinkled. Even though he had hung it on a hanger as soon as it came out of the dryer in Sebastian's apartment the night before, he had worn it on the hour-long drive from Athens this morning. He opted to roll down the windows and roll up his sleeves, adding more wrinkles.

"You look slightly untidy," Dad said. "Didn't shave this morning, did you?"

Diehl snapped his fingers. "Forgot to ask Mom to pack my razor. Then again, even if she did, I didn't have enough time to change when I got into the office."

"You look like you've been through a storm." Dad laughed as he logged in to his secure video conference account. The screen on the wall displayed a split screen.

Diehl sat down on one end of the sofa and Dad sat down on the other end. The camera pointing their way displayed them on one side of the screen. The other side was still dark.

"Ready when you are, Riley," Dad said.

"I'm here. Let me get set up," Riley replied.

"Here where?" Diehl asked as the screen showed Riley at a table in a sitting room of some sort. She had all the curtains closed. Her hair was cut short, and she looked older and worn out.

Diehl wondered if Dad had been right about Riley not wanting to get back to the corporate world.

"Berlin," Riley said. "This is the last leg of our tour. Then we fly to Houston to see my parents."

"Nice to see you out and about," Dad said.

"Life goes on." Riley looked a bit sad. She drew a deep breath, as if pulling up her imaginary bootstraps. "How are you, Diehl?"

"Better than ever," Diehl said. "Thanks for asking."

"How are your kids?"

"Adventurous." It was the only word Diehl could think of. "I'll have to tell you later about them. Long stories. Painful to tell."

"Phases." Riley nodded. "This too shall pass."

"True."

"Hello, Ned. I didn't forget you." Riley smiled.

"Of course, you didn't," Dad said. "You're only my favorite daughter-in-law."

"Your only one."

For now. Diehl tapped his iPad.

"The kids are watching a movie in the living room so if you hear loud noises, you know what that is." Riley adjusted something or other on the table. "So what brings us to the table today?"

Diehl prayed there would be peace between Dad and Riley. Those two hadn't always gotten along, not even when Parker had been alive.

For the new Brooks future to work such that Diehl could move to St. Simon's Island and be with Skye—if she would have him—someone had to take some of the burden off him.

"Let's just get to the bottom of it," Dad said. "Diehl is burned out."

Diehl pursed his lips. He didn't know whether that was a good start to the meeting, but it wasn't kind. Here he was at forty years old and burned out.

"Diehl?" Riley asked, as if she did not believe Dad.

"I was," Diehl said. "I came out of it with a new perspective on what I want to do with the rest of my life. I believe I am overworked running three subsidiaries of Brooks Investments. We want to know if you would be willing to continue Parker's legacy by managing the subsidiaries he started, considering you're invested in the stock options for those two."

"Brooks Transportation and Brooks Manufacturing," Riley said.

"Precisely." Diehl tried to read her facial expressions, but there were none.

"I don't want to be negative or anything, but Parker shouldn't have acquired Brooks Manufacturing," Riley said. "I advised him against it, but Parker was Parker, as you know."

"Yep. Parker was Parker," Dad echoed. "I still miss him."

"We all miss him, Ned." Riley sat back on the sofa. "Thing is, if you list all the subsidiaries, you can see that manufacturing is unrelated to the rest of what the Brooks family is best at. You have real estate, renovations, restorations, properties. Transportation is somewhat related because you need to transport building materials. But manufacturing?"

Dad and Diehl nodded at the same time.

"You might not know this, but Parker admitted to me that Brooks Manufacturing was a mistake. It stretched him to the point of no return."

"No return?" Diehl asked. "What do you mean?"

"Your perfect brother was so stressed out that he was drinking every night. How did that help his mental faculty in the morning?"

Diehl never thought Parker had been that bad off.

"Nine years. Now you tell us?" Dad asked. His voice was snappy. It meant he was angry.

Perhaps he was angry that his firstborn son's good reputation was being sullied now by his widow.

"I'm telling you the truth." Riley pointed to Diehl.

"Your brother burned out many, many times over. He never lifted a fist at me, but often, I had to take the kids to my parents' house so that they did not see him in that state of drunken stupor, cussing out the Brooks family name, and blaming himself for expanding the family business too quickly."

Diehl placed his iPad on his lap. He didn't know what to say or think.

Poor Parker.

"The night before he went deep-sea fishing with his buddies, he was drunk out of his mind," Riley said. "I told him not to go. Told him not to take Anna and Petra. He wouldn't listen. Said that a couple of his friends were bringing their wives and kids, so our girls would have company. The next morning, he looked sober, so I let the girls go with him. I stayed home with Zach."

"They were celebrating something. I forget what," Diehl said.

"One of his friends in the boat had just gotten a new job as CFO of MacPherson," Riley reminded him.

"No way." Dad grunted. "Bruno MacPherson?"

Diehl hadn't heard that name in a long time. "MacPherson Enterprise went under a while ago now."

"Right." Riley nodded. "But before they did, they sent Parker's best friend and drinking buddy to loosen up Parker's lips and tell them how to take over Brooks Investments."

"Nine years," Dad repeated. "Nine years, Riley. You kept the secret from us?"

"They failed, didn't they?" Riley started to smile now.

"How?" Diehl asked.

"Because I took care of it," Riley said. She seemed relieved that she had finally confessed.

Dad snorted. "You? You were a recluse for a long time after Parker died."

"Was I?" Riley drank water—or what looked like water in a goblet. "It took me a few million dollars of money that Parker left me to hunt Bruno down. He had gone into hiding. But I had to know what he made Parker tell him on the boat."

Diehl and Dad glanced at each other.

"You went hunting?" Diehl held his breath.

"Sometimes, but most of the time, I hire people to do it."

"Now we know." Diehl expelled a breath.

Dad chuckled. "So you were the one who brought down MacPherson."

Diehl could see that Riley's reputation with Dad had skyrocketed.

"Someone had to do it. He was stealing intellectual properties from Brooks Investments under your noses, and I could not let my husband die in vain."

"But all those pottery pieces at Sandpiper Gallery..." Dad bleated. "I thought you..."

"I made them. Why? Can't I have a hobby?" Riley asked. "I prefer plates but these days I just make bowls."

Diehl smiled. "And here we thought you were just a stay-at-home mom."

"That's my favorite job." Riley sighed. It was as though the secret was finally out and she was relieved.

Diehl's bet on Riley seemed to be paying off. "If I am hearing you right, you're recommending that we sell Brooks Manufacturing."

Riley nodded. "It does us no good. Each of us needs to find time to spend with our families, right? Ned, don't you want to see your grandchildren more?"

"And play lots of golf," Dad said.

"There you go," Riley said. "After Parker died, I asked myself one question over and over: what could he do with a hundred billion dollars that he couldn't with ten? His dead body was swallowed up by the ocean. What good are these billions?"

"Same," Diehl said. "I burned out. I'm not going back there."

"I propose we sell Brooks Manufacturing. I don't mind running Brooks Transportation if Ned helps me. I know you want Brooks Properties, Diehl."

Diehl nodded. "Real estate is where I want to be."

"Brinley has Brooks Renovations on St. Simon's. It's the smallest, but you know what? She is the happiest among us."

Diehl glanced over at Dad. He was in deep thought.

"Dad?" Diehl asked.

"I'm not asleep." Dad grinned. "I'm trying to figure out how to make this work."

As they all waited, Diehl prayed for God's wisdom. He tried to remember what Skye had prayed the day before on their drive to Athens, but all he could recall was one sentence.

Catch us when we fall.

"Let's do this," Dad finally said. "We'll take a bit of time, think about it, and regroup. Riley, how long are you going to be in Houston?"

"We were thinking through July, but I can leave the kids there and go to Atlanta if we want to have a face-to-face meeting. I can fly back and forth between Houston and Atlanta in July," Riley said. "However, we have a catch..."

"Uh-oh." Diehl glanced over at Dad.

"Let's hear it," Dad said.

"Petra will be a senior at Seaside Academy this fall," Riley said. "I hate to take her out of there and move her to Atlanta, you know? I've already enrolled both of them—and paid in full—for the fall semester, so once school starts in August, I can't commit to anything until the end of the school year in May."

"Right. I forgot." Dad thought for a minute. "Now I vaguely remember Rose saying something about a graduation party. She talks a lot and sometimes I miss important dates."

"I'm sure she'll remind you. Rose is our calendar girl." Riley laughed. "The bottom line is that I don't want Petra's life disrupted. She's trying to make college decisions, is busy with her dual enrollment classes, and her senior class has lots of events going on. It's almost like she has to find time to study. I can't add a big move to her plate right now."

Dad turned to Diehl. "What do you suggest?"

Diehl quietly asked God for wisdom. "What grade is Zach?"

"Entering eighth," Riley said. "When Petra goes to college one year from now, Zach will enter high school."

"Next summer is your best transition time," Diehl said.

"Looks like it. How about you?" Riley asked.

"I've already registered my kids for school in Atlanta, but if I can move to St. Simon's by July, I can transfer them to Seaside Academy in August when school starts."

"So you're thinking of moving Brooks Properties to St. Simon's?" Riley asked.

"If possible." Diehl closed his iPad cover.

"Then you need to know that they changed their deadline to the end of June."

"What? They used to have rolling admissions."

"The website is outdated. Get on their mailing list if you don't want to miss the deadline."

"Thanks, Riley. Appreciate that information." Diehl thought about it. "So we have a dilemma. I want to move my kids to St. Simon's this summer. Riley can't move back to Atlanta until next May."

"Looks like I'm the variable here, which might work out," Dad said. "I think I need to be here to get the best deal for Brooks Manufacturing."

"So you'll put it on the market?" Riley asked.

"We're a family business so I decide what goes and what stays," Dad said. "Since nobody wants to handle manufacturing—why on earth did I let Parker expand there?—we'll sell it and split the profits across the three remaining subsidiaries."

Diehl nodded. "Hopefully we can sell Brooks Manufacturing soon."

"While keeping Brooks Transportation running in Atlanta until Riley moves here," Dad said.

"I can shadow you," Riley said to Dad. "Hopefully, I'll learn the ropes in eleven months."

"Eleven months," Dad repeated. "Let me ask Rose if she'd like to stay in Atlanta that long."

"I'll sweeten the deal," Diehl said. "You can stay in my house rent-free. If you bring Chef Pierre with you, Mom can still have her Christmas dinners. Isobel designed the house for entertaining, as you know. Mom doesn't have to fly everyone to Brooks Cottage, and thereby saving you money."

Dad laughed so loudly even Diehl was startled. "Since when does your mother save me money? If she saves it in jet fuel, you can be sure our parties are going to get more lavish and over the top."

"Well, if my house is too small for Mom's dinners, then she could always rent bigger buildings in town, like the historic Swan House or the giant Atlanta Aquarium," Diehl said. "It's only for eleven months. School will be out in May, and then Riley will move to Atlanta, right? When she does, you can finally retire to St. Simon's."

Even as he said it aloud, something still didn't feel right to Diehl. He couldn't put his finger on it. It seemed that the more prudent thing to do was for him to stay in Atlanta until May, when he and Riley would swap cities.

Dad could come and go as he pleased. That would take pressure off him and Mom.

"That's the plan—if you want me to do this." Riley nodded. "That's how it goes when we have school-aged children. Our careers might revolve around them, like it or not."

Diehl didn't counter her with his own thoughts, that he wanted his career and life to revolve around God's plans instead of man's plans.

What was God's plan for his life?

Diehl was surer than ever that it included Skye.

He was also certain that if he missed his opportunity with Skye, he might never be able to love a woman this much again.

At the same time, he was fully aware that Dad was winding down. Mom had told Diehl over time that Dad wanted to retire full time, although he kept leaving the golf course to keep an eye on Diehl and the company. Now he would have help with Riley.

Her kids were older than Diehl's. She could commit more time to the company.

Diehl's kids were younger and required more supervision. Therein was the problem. If he moved his kids to St. Simon's Island now—living on the neighboring Seaside Island—he would be a single dad with a full-time job. In the first year, he'd be busy transitioning Brooks Properties to its new office on St. Simon's. Who was going to watch his kids? Mom would be in Atlanta. Brinley would have her own baby to care for.

Diehl would have to hire a nanny.

Lord, what do I do?

It seemed to Diehl that setting aside what his heart wanted, the logical thing to do was to sell Brooks Manufacturing, but keep the rest of the company where it was—mostly in Atlanta—until Riley could move to Atlanta and take over from Dad.

Could Diehl endure the eleven-month-long separation from Skye? Still, he knew he had to do the right thing, even if it meant personal pain.

Dad sighed. "Does anyone have anything else to add before we adjourn the meeting?"

"This is a major tectonic shift in our family business," Diehl said. "Why don't we pray over it this weekend and see if we missed anything?"

"Good idea." Dad looked at the screen on the wall. Riley nodded as well. "I'll call Xavier. His legal team can get started on the transition."

"Tell him to send me something I can sign," Riley said.

After Riley hung up, Dad didn't leave the office. He sat there at the same spot on the couch.

"I'm going to miss this place," Dad said. "I remember the day when my father moved Brooks Properties to Atlanta, subsequently putting it under the Brooks Investments banner. I was so excited about working for him. However, I had just met your mom at the commencement—can you believe it, the last day at college? She graduated with a bachelor's in art history, and I had my MBA. She was heading to Boston, and I was heading to Atlanta."

"How did you make it work?" Diehl asked. He couldn't remember the last time Dad had told the story.

"We didn't. We didn't meet again until several years later at a fundraiser for UGA."

"I remember now, but you rarely talked about those years."

"It was tumultuous. I knew she was the one, and yet she wasn't the one yet, you know?"

"How did you know she was the one?"

"It was love at first sight." Dad smiled.

"Is there such a thing?"

"Of course. Just ask around. I knew I was going to marry Rose the first time I ever saw her."

It had taken Diehl a few weeks to know his own feelings for Skye. How could Dad's love for Mom be instant?

"Fifty-two years," Dad said. "Could have been longer, but we lost several years chasing careers."

Why was Dad telling him all that?

"We can't go back, Dad."

"I know. But I got the girl." He chuckled. "My advice to you, Diehl—now that we're both Christians— is to seek God's best for you and Skye. If you're meant to be, you're meant to be, no matter how long it takes. I don't want you to put your career above love, and certainly not above Christ."

"I'll pray about it."

"Good answer, son."

"In that case, probably the best thing for me to do is stay in this building until Riley gets here," Diehl said.

"That's a switch."

"Because of our conversation with Riley, I realized that the transition would be smoother if we leave things in place while you train Riley to run this office."

Dad nodded. "Seems like a simple solution."

"I let my emotions get in the way," Diehl admitted. "I want to rush back to St. Simon's ASAP."

"Me too, for other reasons. Golf, for instance."

They laughed, but Diehl could see the lines relaxed on Dad's face. He knew then that he had done the right thing—though Dad would have supported him either way.

"What about Skye?" Dad asked.

"If Skye loves me, she will wait for me. She's also her own boss and understands that we have to make hard business decisions sometimes." Diehl prayed that he was right about Skye.

Would she wait for him?

CHAPTER FIFTY-FOUR

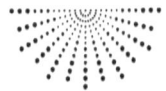

"*D*id you make it to all your meetings?" Skye asked on the speakerphone. She was stir-frying some shrimp and vegetables as a pot of rice boiled away on another burner.

"Yep, all three of them," Diehl said over FaceTime.

Skye could see his face on the small phone she had propped up against the refrigerator wall that was next to the quartz counter by the stove.

Sebastian's kitchen was small, but he usually cooked at the restaurant, so there was no need for a fancy kitchen here. Tonight, Sebastian was filling in for a chef who had called in sick. Emmeline was at a harp recital downtown.

Skye would have gone, but she wanted to catch up on work. She decided to eat in. Next thing she knew, it was past eight o'clock before she started dinner.

"You're eating dinner late," Diehl said. He was in

the same old T-shirt Skye first saw him in the Friday he arrived at Brinley's beach house.

"Time ran away from me. I was going to cook an hour ago, but here I am. I could still be eating dinner when Seb and Em get home."

"Maybe you're away from home, and it feels like a vacation."

"A working vacation, at least. Yeah. Maybe." Skye stirred the rice in the pot. "Has Detective Jeong called?"

"I was going to tell you that he came to the office this afternoon. He was heading back out to St. Simon's."

"What did he have to say?" Skye turned down the stove and put a cover over her shrimp dish.

She moved the phone to the island so she could sit on a barstool and take a break from standing. She propped up the phone in front of a candle jar.

"They arrested Zeta Bishop and charged her with a criminal conspiracy to commit kidnapping," Diehl said. "She masterminded the whole thing, according to Romina."

"Everyone confessed?"

"Not all. The investigation is ongoing," Diehl said. "Elisa is done, though. They asked her everything they needed in two days of interviews. That way, they don't have to make her recall everything all over again."

"Will they charge those people for crimes in both cities?"

"Well, Romina talked to Elisa on the phone while Elisa was still at my mother's house, so that's where

Romina had control of the victim. Romina was like a mother figure to Elisa—since Isobel and I were gone all the time."

"So the crime began on Seaside Island, which is under the jurisdiction of the Brunswick and Golden Isles Police Department."

"Right. The District Attorney there could file charges against Romina and Zeta. However, the case is stronger in Atlanta because Romina was caught with my daughter—in the middle of an ongoing ICE sting. At least that's what my family attorney told me."

Skye breathed a sigh of relief. "Thank God Elisa is safe."

"Indeed."

"Hans helped Elisa get out of the house and he drove her to the bus station. What's he going to be charged with?"

Diehl nodded. "He is a party to the crime. Now I found out that Zeta gave him three thousand dollars in cash that night."

"Ruh-roh. So it wasn't all love."

"Well, he was behind on his rent."

"Did Chef Pierre fire him?"

"Yes. Now he's even more behind on his rent. Plus, he's in trouble with the law."

"He confessed to his part. So maybe the judge will take that into consideration?" Skye got up to stir the rice one more time. It was almost done.

"I don't know. Frankly, I'm just letting my attorney sort it out. He gives us the daily briefs."

Skye turned off the burners. "Makes me think that

your ex-nanny and mother-in-law hadn't thought through this entire mess."

"I think they were desperate. Romina needs money and Zeta wants custody of her grandchildren."

"How's kidnapping going to further their cause?" Skye found a bowl. She put a dollop of rice in the bowl and a generous helping of shrimp and vegetables on top.

The asparagus and carrots and zucchini in light curry sauce washed over the jumbo shrimp and seeped into the jasmine rice. Skye's stomach rumbled.

"I should let you eat," Diehl said. "Sorry to interrupt your dinner."

"No, no. Let me say grace and you can continue telling me about your day." Skye bowed her head and thanked God for the safe return of Elisa. She prayed for justice for the criminals. She felt sorry for Zeta. And she thanked God for her food.

When she opened her eyes, Diehl was drinking mineral water and staring at her.

"That shrimp bowl looks delicious," he said.

"It's a very simple dish. You can cook it."

"When I get back to St. Simon's, show me."

"Okay." She did not ask him when he would return to the Georgia coast. She wanted to know, but she didn't want to ask.

"I hope to get back to St. Simon's at some point," Diehl added.

Skye chewed her food slowly and didn't say a word.

"Maybe sooner than later."

She nodded. "What are you trying to tell me, Diehl?"

"Uh... Well, I think my dad needs me at the Atlanta office, but I'm not sure. My sister-in-law is joining the company, but she can't do it until May, when her daughter finishes high school. That leaves eleven months when my Dad would juggle three subsidiaries."

"I thought Brooks Investments has four."

"We're selling one."

"Nonetheless, it's a lot of work for someone who is still walking with a cane three years after his stroke." Skye speared a shrimp with a fork.

"He looked tired today."

Skye nodded. "Have you prayed about it?"

"Yes, but I need to pray more," Diehl said. "I have something in mind but I'm not sure whether that's the best way to go."

"Don't tell me what it is. Let's hear the options first."

"Options?"

"I'm a businesswoman too. If you want to bounce ideas off me, I can be a third opinion."

Slowly, Diehl smiled. "I'm in love with you."

"Options?" Skye steered him back to the topic.

"Just between us?"

"The only person I can tell is God. I hope that's the same if I ask you for your opinion about my career or company. Like the Jared situation."

"Yeah." Diehl's eyes brightened. "As mentioned, we're down to three subsidiaries. Brin is handling

Brooks Renovations. I'll take Brooks Properties home to St. Simon's. In one year, Riley will run Brooks Transportation. Until she moves to Atlanta, I don't know whether it's a good idea to leave Dad in Atlanta until the transition."

"Wait. What did you just say about Brooks Properties?" Skye asked.

"You heard me. If Brin can run Books Renovations from her Brunswick office—and work at home most of the time—why can't I?"

"So you fell in love with island life." Skye chuckled. "That happened to me a long time ago. That's why I never left."

"I fell in love with you."

"Don't make me cry, Diehl. I'm happy to hear that we might be together again, but the question is always when. God's timing is perfect." Skye blinked. "We both have work to do. Tell me about your dad."

"Ah, like I said, he looked tired and worn out today. I don't think he's a hundred percent since the stroke. I know he's walking and talking and looking all fine, but I'm thinking of the physical stamina he needs to run the company."

"You need to be there with him. It's the right thing to do. He's your dad. He needs your help."

"Until we sell Brooks Manufacturing," Diehl said.

"Or until Riley goes to Atlanta."

"Eleven months."

Skye nodded. "It's not like it's eleven years."

"That reminds me of my dad's story. He told me today that he fell in love with Mom at first sight but they didn't see each other again for several years. It was such a difficult thing for him that he blocked that out of his memory."

"What did they do in the intervening time?" Skye asked.

"Work, work, work. Then one day, during a fundraiser at their alma mater, they ran into each other. They remembered each other, and started to correspond again."

"Correspond?"

"Letters. No emails back then."

"How romantic."

"You know, he kept all her letters," Diehl said. "I asked Mom this evening at dinner whether she kept his letters too. Unfortunately, she said she lost them in one of the many Brooks Cottage renovations."

"Oh, that's too bad."

"Yeah. I would have liked to have seen what my dad wrote all those years ago."

"Have you checked Brinley's music vault? Maybe your dad put them in there."

"Hmm. I'll check. Dad didn't say a word about it at dinner." Diehl tented his fingers together. "So you think I should stay here for eleven months to run the company with my dad until Riley can move to Atlanta and take over."

"Pray about it. Does it make sense to you?" Skye finished her shrimp bowl. She decided not to get seconds.

"I'm leaning that way."

"But?" She put the empty bowl in the sink. "Keep

talking. I'm looking for two containers to put away my shrimp and rice."

In between the opening and closing of cabinet doors, Skye heard Diehl talk about his relationship with his dad.

"Dad worked all his life to pass on the company to Brinley and me. If Parker were alive, he'd probably get the lion's share. However, he's dead."

"What about your sister, Zoe?"

"She cashed out. Asked for the inheritance in one lump sum. She's not coming home from Paris," Diehl explained. "With Brin busy with renovations, I have a feeling that Dad wants me to handle the rest of the family business after he's gone. I'm glad Riley came onboard so it's not all on me."

"That way, you don't have to sell Brooks Investments." Skye put away the leftovers in the refrigerator and decided to do the dishes after she finished talking with Diehl.

"Exactly. Dad's super happy."

"You know, I'm glad Sebastian and I were able to spend some years with our aunt and uncle." Skye sat down at the island with a glass of water. "We made good memories, the four of us."

Diehl nodded.

"Every now and then I have a question that I thought my aunt would know the answer to, but she's gone. I can't hug her anymore. I can't see my uncle laugh. I can still hear his laughter in my mind and memory, but he's not here anymore."

"Someday, Dad will be gone," Diehl said.

"And we don't know when. Perhaps for such a time as this, your job is to encourage him. I don't know. You need to pray and ask God about your role," Skye said. "After my uncle died, my aunt was never the same again. We tried to spend time with her, but we were busy with college. She passed away a few months later, just when we were about done with school."

"That's sad."

"They were both saved. They're in heaven now. Thank God."

"What about us?" Diehl leaned toward the camera. "The Bible says that we're not promised tomorrow either."

Skye wiped the island with a damp dishrag. "Well, there is a time for everything. A time to work, a time to rest. A time to be apart, and a time to be together."

"Is that in Ecclesiastes?" Diehl swiped his phone.

"I mixed it all up. Look up chapter three."

As Diehl read Ecclesiastes 3:1-8, Skye listened to his calm reading voice and wished she could record it to listen to it again later.

To everything there is a season,
  A time for every purpose under heaven:
  A time to be born,
  And a time to die;
  A time to plant,
  And a time to pluck what is planted;
  A time to kill,
  And a time to heal;
  A time to break down,

And a time to build up;
A time to weep,
And a time to laugh;
A time to mourn,
And a time to dance;
A time to cast away stones,
And a time to gather stones;
A time to embrace,
And a time to refrain from embracing;
A time to gain,
And a time to lose;
A time to keep,
And a time to throw away;
A time to tear,
And a time to sew;
A time to keep silence,
And a time to speak;
A time to love,
And a time to hate;
A time of war,
And a time of peace.

"I guess 'A time to embrace, and a time to refrain from embracing' applies to us," Diehl said. "Do you think it's a good thing to be apart?"

"We're not apart all the time. We'll call each other every day, if you want. We'll see each other when we can."

"What if our love grows cold?"

"Are you a poet now?" Skye asked. "If our love grows cold, then we're not meant to be, are we? I would think if we love each other, our love will only grow stronger."

"Good point. This is yet another test."

"We can look at it that way," Skye said. "You have to consider the fact that your children and your dad need you. Once their hearts are settled, then we can work on each other."

"Skye?"

"I'm right here." Skye wondered why he called her name.

"You're the strongest woman I know."

"Is that good or bad?"

"It's good. It means if something happens to me, you'll be okay."

Skye felt alarmed. "What are you talking about?"

"I mean that if we break up or something, you'll be okay."

Skye shook her head. "No, I won't be."

"Then stop compartmentalizing your emotions," Diehl said.

"What do you mean?"

"I believe that if we don't see each other for a while, you'll be sad. We'll both be sad. But you're trying to put your emotions in categorized boxes—like labeled spice containers—so that you'll go on day by day," Diehl explained. "If you don't face your emotions, then someday the floodgates will burst open."

"Face my emotions?"

Diehl nodded.

"Well, Dr. Diehl, how come you know so much about my heart?"

"Because I've seen it. You're kind, generous, compassionate. You don't judge me or tell me what to do. You care more about where I am spiritually than how I'm doing temporally." Diehl paused. "And yet when it comes to your own self, you're tense and you don't show it."

"Show what?"

"Your feelings for me. I need to know where I stand with you."

"I think I'm where you are?" Skye said quietly.

"I want to hear it directly from you, in your own words. I don't want to hear *ditto* or *same here*."

Voices outside the apartment interrupted Skye's thoughts. Keys jangled as the front door unlocked.

"My brother and Em are home," Skye said. "Let's talk later."

Diehl sighed and nodded. "Okay. Call me any time."

CHAPTER FIFTY-FIVE

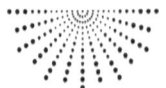

he next few weeks were so busy for Diehl that he had no time to continue his conversation with Skye.

Let's talk later.

It had been the last thing Skye told him that Friday night when she was still in Athens, Georgia, visiting her brother and sister-in-law.

The weekend zoomed by with Diehl back at the office on Saturday—something he needed to stop doing if he were to have a semblance of a life outside the office—and with both of them attending churches in different cities on Sunday.

After church at Midtown Chapel, Diehl left his kids with Mom while he and Dad returned to the office to hammer out the details of how they were going to split the profits for Brooks Transportation. Dad wasn't about to hand the subsidiary over to Riley a hundred percent.

And on and on.

The first week of July was busier than any other week because of the day off in the middle of the week, thereby causing Diehl to have to work extra on the other days when potential buyers of Brooks Manufacturing came to call. Everyone was relieved they were getting rid of that subsidiary.

By the end of that week, Diehl was beginning to feel sapped of strength. No amount of gym time was going to restore that. Something was missing in his life.

He had God now. Didn't that mean he had everything?

Yes, but even Adam had a companion.

Was he lonely?

Diehl had kept busy taking his two kids to church at Midtown Chapel. They also had day camps at church, which Ethan enjoyed tremendously once he found out that Midtown was a sister church to Seaside Chapel back on St. Simon's Island.

Mom somehow got recruited to help with midmorning snacks. Diehl was happy that Mom had made some new Christian friends her age, although some of them were shopaholics like she was.

As for Elisa, she started to like her music camp in which she was learning to play guitar. Diehl was surprised she had chosen that instrument—what Skye played. Diehl also took her to grief counseling once a week, something that Ethan didn't want to participate in for some reason.

Two kids with two different minds.

On top of trying to be there for his kids, Diehl

had to make time for his sister-in-law, who showed up for one week to sign papers, talk to the interior designer about her new office space, and figure out what Dad wanted her to do with Brooks Transportation.

Fortunately, Diehl didn't have to provide Riley with training. That was Dad's department. However, Dad liked to have Diehl with them when they discussed the goals of the company.

There went another week.

The routine continued until Diehl received a text from Skye toward the end of that week, saying that Jared Urquhart had bought her shares of Saffron on Jekyll.

"Celebrate with me," the voice recording said.

Somehow, Diehl could not. The thought that Jared spent more time with Skye than he did bothered him that entire day, then the whole weekend, and Monday, and now Tuesday.

Alone in his office with the door closed on this quiet afternoon, Diehl listened to her voicemail again.

Her voice was calm and sweet. He could detect no malice in it. Why would there be? Skye was simply inviting him to celebrate with her. However, Jared was involved, and Diehl felt bitterness on his tongue. If he replied to Skye, he was afraid he'd say something embarrassing.

Something that showed how jealous he was of the men around Skye.

Compared to Jared, Diehl hadn't done as well. Earning less than the Urquharts was one thing. Jared spending more time with Skye than Diehl was another.

And yet, he recalled once again their conversation on FaceTime that Friday night a couple of weeks before. What she had said bothered him.

You have to consider the fact that your children and your dad need you. Once their hearts are settled, then we can work on each other.

Diehl wondered why they could not be worked on simultaneously. Couldn't he manage his children, work with Dad, and still love Skye at the same time? Why did she have to compartmentalize everything into their little spaces?

"The solution to the problem is to meet and hash it out," Diehl said to an empty office.

He pressed a button on his phone to call his administrative assistant. She knocked on the door.

"Come in," he said.

Jodie entered with a large tablet in her hand. She was in her fifties, twice married, four children between the two marriages, and now filing for divorce proceedings against her second husband, who had run off with a motorcycle chick he had met in his last cross-country vacation without Jodie. Somehow in the middle of her muddled life, she had put three kids in college, with one more on the way. The last child had a full scholarship to a college of his choice.

From time to time, Diehl wanted to pay off all of Jodie's children's student loans. He hadn't done it because he wasn't sure if that would be helpful to the fiercely independent woman.

"Yes, Mr. Brooks?" Jodie sat down in a chair on the other side of Diehl's desk.

Diehl rolled his eyes. "You know that's for my father only and you still say it."

"Someday, you'll be the only Mr. Brooks around here—at least while I'm still alive. Besides, Mr. Diehl doesn't have the same impact, like you're wheeling and dealing. You know, Diehl and deal?"

A straight talker, this woman.

Why Diehl could never fire her. However, she had said she wouldn't relocate to St. Simon's Island ever, so Diehl knew he was about to lose his able assistant of twenty years. She had been at Brooks Investments so long that he had started to consider her an older sister.

"Remember when you first started working here?" Diehl asked.

Jodie nodded. "Five months pregnant with my third child, and suddenly a single mother. You gave me a receptionist job because I can talk to people with a smile on my face no matter what my own personal circumstances look like."

"It was temporary, but you proved yourself invaluable."

"I worked my way up. Did you call me here to offer me a new pay raise or a Christmas bonus?"

"It's still July," Diehl said.

"This week is the last full week of July." She swiped her tablet to display a large clock. She showed it to him. "FYI, your kids start school in two weeks."

"What?" Diehl blinked. "What happened to summer?"

"Summer is gone, Mr. Brooks."

Is Skye gone too?

"We're closer to Christmas than ever before."

"No, we're not."

Jodie leaned toward the desk between them. "Many of us are anticipating that management is working on our Christmas bonuses."

"On that cheery note, let me ask you if these are done." Diehl scrolled up the notes he had been jotting down on his iPad. "Riley's new office?"

"Emptied out for her to fill in."

"Good." Diehl wondered how Riley was adjusting to the thought that she would be occupying Parker's old office.

He moved on. "Have you confirmed my meetings next week with the potential buyers of Brooks Manufacturing?"

"You don't have to micromanage me as you have done the last twenty years," Jodie said.

"Yes or no?"

"Yes. I also resolved some scheduling conflicts with some of the meetings because your dad wants to meet a couple of them at the golf course instead of here in the office, and two of them canceled."

"Reasons?"

"None, sir. I tried to pry—I mean, ask."

"And?"

"Being friends with their administrative assistants helps."

"And?" Diehl was getting impatient.

"In both cases, there have been unconfirmed Urquhart sightings."

"Jared. He must have found out that we're selling Brooks Manufacturing. What could he be thinking?"

"That Brooks Investments is in some sort of financial trouble. Mr. Urquhart is known as a vulture."

"More like a buzzard." Diehl leaned back in his chair.

"Do you want me to schedule a meeting with the buzzard, sir? For the kill?"

"Nah. His office will give you the runaround. I'll call his private line myself." Maybe he could congratulate Jared on his newly acquired position as the majority shareholder of Saffron on Jekyll.

"Anything else, sir?" Jodie asked.

"That's all."

"You forgot something."

"Oh?" When was the last time he had forgotten anything important?

"Flowers for your girlfriend."

Diehl stared at Jodie. "I don't know."

"Yes, you do know, Mr. Brooks."

With that, Diehl knew that his trusted assistant was about to spill into her "if you asked me" routine. He waited.

"Do you know how my two husbands lost me?" Jodie asked.

"Incompatibility?"

"Nope. That was the fun part. The problem was time. They never had time for me. I don't know why I kept finding men who wouldn't spend time with me before or after work—except to produce children."

Diehl wasn't sure if he wanted to hear any personal stories.

"This is not personal," Jodie said.

Whoa. She read my mind.

"This is about the health of the company your grandfather started—that's paying my salary and the salaries of hundreds of other people. If you go down, we go down. When you burned out in May..." Her voice trailed off. A second later, she steeled herself. "I thought we were going to lose our jobs."

"No, that wasn't going to happen."

"Thank God—if there is a God."

"There is." Diehl smiled. "It was a good thing that I took a couple of months off. I found God—and His only begotten Son, Jesus. My life has changed. It's all different now—my perspective, point of view, purpose, plan. All different."

"Then why are you working yourself to the ground again?"

Good question. "Well, I'm trying to focus on work..."

"At the expense of your own personal welfare?"

"We're at a crossroad here."

"Is your God not bigger than your crossroad?" Jodie asked.

Diehl was stunned. Coming from a non-Christian, the question was theologically profound.

"Send her flowers," Jodie repeated.

"Skye?"

"Is there another?"

"No."

"Then why haven't you sent her flowers or chocolate or something? Do you even know what she likes?"

To be honest, Diehl didn't.

"Let me call her office and ask her assistant."

"She doesn't have an assistant."

Jodie let out a groan. "No wonder."

"No wonder what?"

"She's busier than you are."

"Is she?"

"You have me. I do all your administrative work. Who does all her office work?"

"She does, I think."

"She just sold her shares of Saffron—word gets around whenever it has anything to do with the Urquharts—and all she is doing now is managing her personal chef business."

"Right."

"Wrong, Mr. Brooks." Jodie swiped her iPad and showed Diehl a news article. "Don't you read regional news from time to time? I just read in the cooking section of the newspaper this morning that Skye's the Limit just took over Watt's for Dinner, another personal chef company, about the same size, but operating primarily in... Guess where?"

Diehl raised his eyebrows. "How would I know? I don't read cooking news."

"Alpharetta."

No way. In the northern metropolitan Atlanta?

Could God be this good to him?

"For real?" Diehl almost fell off his seat. "When?"

"A few days ago. Apparently, Skye's the Limit and Watt's for Dinner have been in talks since Watanabe ran into Skye at the Southern Sunshine Food Festival on Miami Beach. Scroll down and you'll see a photo from the food festival recently, with Skye and Watt."

A food festival. Skye hadn't said a word about how busy she had been. "She told me she was judging all week."

"It takes you ten seconds to put your signature on a piece of paper."

"True, if you have a good lawyer."

"She has a good lawyer. Trevor Dell."

"My sister's corporate attorney."

Jodie scrolled down the article. "She's still contemplating whether to keep the name Watt's for Dinner for the Atlanta subsidiary. Its parent company, Skye's the Limit, will remain headquartered on St. Simon's Island. Her company just doubled its value."

"Where did she get the money to buy another company?" Diehl was embarrassed he had asked aloud. Beyond the restaurant shares, had she sold the piece of prime oceanfront land on Seaside Island? He hoped not. "Why didn't she tell me anything?"

"I'm speculating here, but I wonder if she didn't tell you because if it fell through, no one would be disappointed. Or maybe she didn't want anyone to think you had anything to do with it. An independent woman, you know?"

I'm not needed. But am I wanted?

"I'm a liability. No wonder she compartmentalizes everything. I don't know her much, do I?" Diehl asked.

"You don't know her at all."

"Forward me the article, please."

"Already done."

"Thank you, Jodie. Please close the door on the way out."

"Will do."

After Jodie left, Diehl opened his email and read the entire article himself. There was one photo of Skye in a pair of sunglasses at the food festival. She was standing next to two other people. One was her brother, but who was the other man? He read the caption.

Watt Watanabe, owner of Watt's for Dinner personal chef service, was eighty-eight years old and decided it was time to finally retire after his wife passed away following a long illness. An old friend of Skye's uncle, Miller Langston, he had refused to sell his business to anyone but Skye. The actual sale price was undisclosed.

"I wonder if Skye got a deal." Diehl started to get curious. He glanced at his watch. Five o'clock and not a moment too soon.

He was staring at the photograph of a casual Skye in a pretty dress doing the thumbs-up sign with Watanabe—who looked old enough to be her grandfather—when he spotted someone in the background, among the crowd.

Diehl enlarged the photo. It was grainy but he could spot that stance any time. There, in the front row of the crowd, eating a corn dog or something on a stick, was none other than Jared Urquhart.

CHAPTER FIFTY-SIX

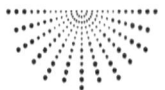

*D*iehl was about to send a congratulatory text to Skye when Dad appeared at the door. "Ready to go home?"

Diehl nodded as he stared at the old message from Skye.

Celebrate with me.

She had wanted to share her good news with him, but he had been too busy. And when he had a bit of time, his jealousy of Jared got the better of him.

Jared seemed to have weaseled his way to Skye's side. If Diehl didn't act fast, Jared might worm his way into Skye's heart. It would be worse than his appearing in the background of a photograph with Skye in the foreground.

Luigi had stolen Isobel from Diehl when he had no time for her.

He wasn't about to let someone else steal his new love.

"Diehl?" Dad asked.

"Ready." Diehl closed his iPad, and looked around for his satchel.

"Something the matter?" Dad stepped inside his office.

"Let's go home."

"Murray can wait. He's listening to the five o'clock news anyway." Dad sat down in one of the armchairs facing the couch. He used his cane to tap the couch, asking Diehl to sit there. "Talk to me, son."

Almost forty years old, and he couldn't handle his own problems.

Perhaps being married to Isobel and having kids too early had robbed him of time to fall in love. Really fall in love.

Now he didn't know what he wanted—

Yes, I know what I want. But...

"I can't have her, Dad." Diehl dragged himself to the couch. When he lay there, he remembered the day Skye had found him drunk out of his mind—before Elisa was abducted.

To be sure, after he was saved, he hadn't drunk a single drop. Not even when Dad and Mom invited him to join them. Sure, he sat with them in Isobel's "drinking room" but all Diehl had that evening was mineral water.

His old desire for alcohol had vanished. God had removed it from his system. He had no desire to touch another drink.

And yet.

"I don't want to inflict the stains and sins of my

past life on her." Diehl kicked off his shoes. "She is so beautiful and pure, and I don't know how to love her."

"The woman you spent the night with a month ago?" Dad asked.

Diehl placed an arm on his forehead to block the ceiling lights. "We didn't spend the night—not technically. I slept on the couch, and she was in the guest room. Her brother and sister-in-law were in another room. It was all clean. God was our witness."

"Did you kiss when no one else was around?" Dad wiggled his eyebrows.

"Dad, I'm not a teenager."

"I'm trying to assess how strongly you feel about her."

"I want to marry her, but I can't. I have no record to show for. I failed in my first marriage. How can I love again?"

"Oh, I see. You are afraid your past will mess up your future."

"I guess that sums it up."

Dad was quiet for what felt like a long second. "When you got saved last month, what did you think God did with your heart?"

"I have a new heart, a new life in Christ."

"So love her with your new heart," Dad said. "You're a new man in Christ now."

"How?"

"Did you hear what I said? New man in Christ. Not in yourself, but in Christ." Dad logged in to his phone. "Let me read a verse to you that Argo Perry read to me after he led me to the Lord. 'Then He who sat on the throne said, "Behold, I make all things new."' Revelation 21:5a."

Diehl nodded. "I believe it, but I don't feel it."

"Walk by faith, son, not by feelings."

"I still feel drawn to Skye, but I can't go to her. I can't call her. I can't reply to her text. I feel so inadequate."

"I just read to you Revelation 21:5a. Didn't you hear me? You're not the old self you used to be. Skye does not have to put up with the old unsaved self that you were. That life is gone. She can love the new you."

Diehl's eyes stung. It wasn't the ceiling lights.

"I want to be the best man for her," Diehl mumbled.

"You're farther along than I was the first year I got saved."

"Were you in a Bible study right away?" Diehl asked.

"I went to Argo's Sunday school class. And yes, we read the Bible, but I didn't go to his midweek prayer group or even to the Wednesday night outdoor service."

"The Fire Pit Service?" Diehl remembered holding Skye's hand in one of those.

"Yeah. I guess that's what they call it."

"Ivan got me in the men's group, and we meet every Monday morning. I miss that, being here."

"Only ten more months, son, and we'll both be back on St. Simon's," Dad said. "Look ahead."

"In ten months, Skye might be gone."

"Gone where?" Dad asked.

"I mean, she might have found another person."

"Or she could be married to you."

"So soon?"

Dad nodded solemnly. "Love is love. You can't hurry it. You can't stop it. You just have to let it flow like a river."

"I don't know where this river flows," Diehl said.

"Then pray about it," Dad said. "God will show you."

"Show me, Lord." Diehl blinked. "I love her so much."

"Have you told her?" Dad asked.

"Several times."

"How did she respond?"

"She doesn't show it as well as I expected."

"What do you mean?"

"She compartmentalizes everything. I found out today that she's been so busy..." Diehl sighed. "I have asked too much of her."

"If she really loves you, it will eventually show." Dad lifted a finger. "Mark my words. One of these days, it's going to come out. She can't compartmentalize love forever."

"Meanwhile, what do I do? My heart is aching."

"Well, if I were you, I'd figure out how to be in every single compartment so she sees you all the time."

"You would?" Diehl nearly laughed.

"Yeah. Why not? Out of sight, out of mind, right?

Give her the opportunity to tell you she loves you—or not—by being everywhere."

Could Diehl take that advice? He wasn't Jared—the guy who was in-your-face everywhere. However, he appreciated Dad sitting down with him and listening to his problems. "I'm going to think about what you told me. Thanks, Dad."

"More importantly, you need to do some forensics on your life. Pastor Fizz at Midtown helped me sort through some issues I had—baggage from my past—so if you want a good counselor, he's it."

"What baggage from your past, Dad?"

"Nothing that concerns you." Dad reached for his phone. "I just emailed you his direct number. Call him any time. He might be free tomorrow because I canceled my appointment with him at eleven o'clock.'"

"Why did you cancel?"

"Golf."

"Seriously, Dad?"

"Tournament this weekend."

"Tomorrow is only Wednesday. Last I checked it's not the weekend." Diehl tried not to laugh.

"Preliminaries." Dad used his cane to prop himself up. "Your mom and I will watch the kids whenever you need some alone time with Skye."

"I appreciate that. Skye and I have a lot to talk about."

"Well, that too." Dad chuckled. "Don't you worry about Brooks Investments. It's going to be just fine. Your suggestion to bring Riley in is brilliant. Already

JAN THOMPSON

she has found ways to improve the system to be more efficient. Twenty-first century, here we come."

Diehl didn't have the heart to tell him that they were already well into the century.

"Have you heard from Mark Gill?" Dad asked.

"This morning. I forgot to tell you." Luigi Bellini had signed away his rights as father to the kids. It had cost Diehl a lot of money, but he didn't care. "Mark suggested I formally adopt Elisa and Ethan so we don't have any problems later on."

"An overkill, in my humble opinion. Your name is on their birth certificates. But if Mark says so, do it."

"Just in case, you know."

"You really want those kids, don't you?"

Diehl nodded. "It's not that they don't have anywhere else to go, but they're my kids."

"Your uncle did something like that years ago," Dad said. "Except he adopted his sister's kids after she died of cancer."

"I remember that."

"In the same way, God adopted you and me into His family as His own." Dad swiped his phone. "Here it is. 'For you did not receive the spirit of bondage again to fear, but you received the Spirit of adoption by whom we cry out, "Abba, Father." The Spirit Himself bears witness with our spirit that we are children of God, and if children, then heirs—heirs of God and joint heirs with Christ, if indeed we suffer with Him, that we may also be glorified together." That's from Romans 8:15-17."

"Isn't there another similar verse?" Diehl had

listened to some of Pastor Gonzalez's old sermons while sitting in Atlanta traffic. He had bookmarked the verse on his phone. "Galatians 4:4-7 says, 'But when the fullness of the time had come, God sent forth His Son, born of a woman, born under the law, to redeem those who were under the law, that we might receive the adoption as sons. And because you are sons, God has sent forth the Spirit of His Son into your hearts, crying out, "Abba, Father!" Therefore you are no longer a slave but a son, and if a son, then an heir of God through Christ.' That describes us."

"Praise the Lord," Dad said, sounding more and more like Argo Perry each day. That elderly gentleman had punctuated many conversations by praising the Lord.

"I feel sorry for Zeta, though." Dad put away his phone.

Diehl didn't want to be reminded of his former mother-in-law. Detective Jeong had informed them that they charged her with interference of custody, but it was only a misdemeanor. The District Attorneys in Atlanta and St. Simon's Island had negotiated a way for her to serve her sentence in her home state of Hawaii.

As for a restraining order against Zeta, Diehl didn't have the heart to do that to the seventy-something-old woman, who had already lost her only daughter, Isobel. However, Zeta would not be allowed to speak to or be with her grandchildren without the presence of someone approved by Diehl, such as the two new bodyguards whom Diehl had hired to be with Elisa and Ethan around the clock.

Still, that would be a long time coming since Zeta's husband promptly had a massive coronary in the midst of her kidnapping plan gone awry. If anything, Wilson's heart attack had caused the court to be compassionate toward Zeta.

"Everything is fine now." Diehl patted Dad's shoulders as they walked out of his office together, father and son. Diehl had no idea how much time he had left to spend with Dad and Mom. He hoped to make the best use of whatever time they had left with one another.

"Fine, but not normal like before." Dad shook his head. "Even Chef Pierre had to find a new sous chef."

"I do feel sorry for poor Hans Gray. He had an opportunity to rise in a difficult career, and he threw it away." Diehl locked his office door. He wondered why he did that when the housekeeping people had the master key.

"I'm sure he'll find work somewhere. What did they charge him with?" Dad asked.

"Party to the crime. To Hans's credit, he helped the police to nail Romina, so they dropped the charges against him, but Chef Pierre fired him anyway."

Dad nodded. "I don't want him anywhere near our family ever again."

"Don't worry." Diehl glanced at his watch. He wondered what he could say to Skye after dinner tonight when he called her to congratulate her on the acquisition of Watt's for Dinner.

So far, their twice weekly conversations had only scratched the surface. There was so much more that Diehl wanted to talk to Skye about that he couldn't do over FaceTime.

He had to find time to see her in person.

But when?

CHAPTER FIFTY-SEVEN

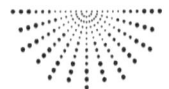

*J*n the middle of a hot August month, Brinley's baby arrived on time at over nine whopping pounds. Avery had been to the hospital twice in two days, and Skye had gone once on Wednesday. When Skye was there, she found herself surrounded by Brinley's parents and her other friends whom she didn't know, and she felt out of place.

Missing at the hospital were Diehl and his kids.

Skye hadn't realized how much she missed Diehl until she saw Brinley again this week. The brother and sister had some semblance in looks—the same smile, for example.

As a gift, Skye sent over Chef Joseph for three weeks. Brinley could easily pay for his services, but Skye wanted to do this as a baby gift—on top of the baby shower gifts she had bought her friend.

By Friday, Brinley was back in her own home, and Skye had a relatively long day at work evaluating

Watt's for Dinner chefs to see if she might eliminate waste and increase efficiency. Even though Watt had amassed for himself some sixteen chefs, Skye had yet to meet them all. She'd have to make a trip to Atlanta for this.

She had talked to Chef Joseph about becoming her Vice President in the Atlanta branch of STL. It was a shame that she might drop the name Watt's for Dinner, but truth be told, they cooked more than just dinner. STL seemed like a better fit since the sky was the limit.

At four o'clock in the afternoon, Skye headed to the grocery store down the road before rush hour hit the little island—nothing like rush hour in Atlanta, but still, there was traffic nonetheless. She had just gotten into her car and put on her seat belt when Avery called.

"Stop," Avery said on the phone.

"What?"

"I know what you're doing and you'll just burn yourself out."

"What am I doing?" Skye asked.

"You're going to be anti-social tonight and cook in your test kitchen into the wee hours of the morning. Am I right?"

Gillian must have told her of Skye's plans.

Avery's cousin was a godsend when Skye desperately needed an administrative assistant in her new office space to take phone calls from potential new clients—now that STL was in the news—and do some other office work for Skye. However, Gillian needed to learn not to tell her cousin about everything that went on at the STL office.

"Let's go see Brinley," Avery suggested. "She's done feeding her baby, and she has an hour or so maybe."

"Do you know everyone's schedule?" Skye laughed.

"Just yours and Brinley's."

Skye felt justifiably reluctant to see Brinley twice in a week. "Brinley needs to rest. Let's go next week."

"No. It has to be today."

"Why?"

"Because it's Friday."

"I can't." There was no way. "Fall is coming, and around this time of year, I test new menus. Next week, I'll be in Atlanta meeting Watt for dinner—no pun intended—where I'll meet his chefs. I'll bring Chef Joseph with me because I think he'll make a good VP for me in the Atlanta area. So this is my last weekend left to update the menu."

Could she cook several dishes tonight? Well, since she didn't have a date for Friday night, why not? Since she had asked her chefs to suggest recipes, she felt obligated to test them herself before she made other chefs cook them.

Avery sighed. "Sometimes you're something else. It feels like I have to push you to do something, like you have perpetual inertia to sit in place."

"What are you talking about?"

"I'm talking about rest and self-care," Avery said. "You've been working non-stop for the last three weeks in your new company, and Gillian told me that you were in the office before she arrived and you were still in the office after she left for the day."

"Gillian needs to know where her boundaries are with company matters," Skye said.

"Don't blame her. I asked. I pried it out of her."

"You could've asked me yourself."

"Would you tell me that you're working twelve to sixteen hours a day to make the business merger work?"

"Well..."

"See, I know you wouldn't. You used to take weekends off, but now you're working on Saturdays and after church on Sundays," Avery continued. "As your best friend, it's my obligation to be honest with you. You need time off."

"You're my best friend now?"

"I hate to break it to you, sister, but I'm your only friend left." Avery grinned. "When was the last time you went to the ladies' night out that Olivia organized? And you skipped two women's Bible studies in a row."

Skye cringed. She had spent more time at her test kitchen sorting out new recipes and menus than she had studying her Bible. "Yes, it sounds bad. But STL..."

"STL is a job, a company. It's not your life."

"I put a lot of my savings into it."

"You sold your shares in Saffron and Watt gave you a deal on his company."

"Well, a sale is a sale."

Avery shrugged. "It's past four o'clock on a Friday

afternoon. I'm heading over to Brinley's house. How about you meet me there?"

"Nope. I have to get the menu done. Sorry. Tell Brinley I said hello." Skye turned on the car ignition. "I'll talk to you later, okay?"

"All right. Don't say I didn't try." Avery sounded disappointed.

Skye let her go. She backed out of the small office complex, where the other car belonged to Gillian, who stayed at the office until five o'clock.

Before Skye knew it, she was at Seaside Organics. Pushing a cart down the aisles, she smiled as she remembered that Sunday afternoon in June when Diehl surprised her by showing up to help her shop for groceries. It might seem mundane to other people, but to Skye it was a memory she would cherish forever, even if they did not come together ever again.

I miss you, Diehl. I miss you so much.

Skye had no idea why she couldn't tell Diehl the truth. On the other hand, he had indicated with his attention and kisses that he loved her. Not only visually, but he had texted her—and she screenshot and saved it on her phone, and memorized his words.

With God's love, I can love you. I may be imperfect, but Christ is perfect. His love is what I give to you. Together we can help each other through the journey of life.

It would be a wonderful wedding vow—for some couple out there.

From that statement, Skye was convinced that

Diehl was a true believer in Christ and that Diehl loved her.

How could she love him back? She had never been with any man intimately in her life. Her past boyfriends had kissed her and held her hands—like Diehl had done several times—but she had remained a pure Christian woman all her life, wishing for the day when God would bring to her doorstep a Christian man who would love and cherish her the rest of her life, and be the father of her children.

Diehl was further along than Skye. He had so much more experience in life and love—having married before, although twice to the same woman. Thirteen or fourteen years of marriage. That was a lot of experience.

Also, he had kids. Whether they were biologically his or not, he was raising them as his own. Compared to him, Skye had zero knowledge in that department. She had tried to talk to Elisa the other day—before she was abducted—but Skye knew it was nothing like real parenting. Ethan was easier to deal with since he was always bright-eyed and bushy-tailed. But Skye hadn't been there from the beginning when they were still infants.

Thirty-four and single, Skye felt that God had kept her this way for a reason. Perhaps a special someone would come along and sweep her off her feet...

Seriously?

Skye sighed all the way to the seafood section, where she picked up a generous filet of Icelandic cod for her new test dish. Next to the fish was a mound of shrimp with heads, tails, legs all attached.

"Are those fresh?" Skye couldn't believe her eyes.

"Yes," the fishmonger replied. "Caught this morning."

"Give me ten pounds." An overkill, perhaps, but she could binge on shrimp and put it in everything. She remembered how Aunt Irma would sneak shrimp into stir-fried vegetables, soups, salad, fried noodles, whatever she could "stick shrimp in," as she would say.

"It won't be a lot once you peel off the shells."

Skye agreed with the fishmonger. "Please put them in a bag of ice."

Skye began to think of all the new shrimp dishes she could conjure up for STL. Her mind was going a mile a minute, but she felt relaxed. Yeah, cooking was therapeutic for her—just as playing the guitar and singing also were.

Cooking was easier than playing the guitar or singing because Skye could cover up mistakes in the kitchen, even while cooking for someone. She could get creative and come up with a variation of the dish, and it would still work.

If she hit the wrong note while singing at church or messed up on her guitar chords, the microphone would broadcast it to the ends of the church building, and she would be embarrassed. Not that it had happened often. In fact, she had almost always given a "perfect" performance at church.

That was because she practiced a lot for days and weeks.

Almost like what she was doing this evening. Practicing making these dishes. If she could cook them well, then her chefs could too. The happier their customers, the more they would tell others about STL.

Skye was on the other side of the store in the bread section before she realized she had forgotten to buy some beef bone broth. The small amount was only for tonight's test menu. If the dish passed her test, she'd ask Marlo to cook their own bone broth from scratch. Right now, she had chicken broth stored up at the Sage Café freezer, but not beef.

Even though cooking was easy, she wished she had someone she could invite to taste the food. Gillian had other things to do. Brinley just had a baby. Avery was busy tonight. Skye wondered how objective she might be tasting and rating her own cooking.

Then again, she cooked alone most of the time. No one else needed to know the dishes that did not turn out—that she had to either eat them herself or throw out because they were absolutely inedible.

Yep, I've had some of those.

By the time Skye wandered to the checkout, it was past five o'clock and she had bought more ingredients than she had wanted to in the first place. She blamed the shrimp, but her mouth was watering at the thought of shrimp curry tonight. It was meant to be when she saw fresh lemongrass in the vegetable department. Which led her to pick up some tamarind and coconut milk, and next thing she knew, she wasn't going to cook cod tonight.

She had no idea how time ran away from her, but

she loved walking around the grocery store. This was her safe space, her happy place, where she didn't have to think about how lonely she was and how she loved a man she dared not have.

Diehl.

Being alone with her own thoughts, she could admit to herself that she was afraid to love Diehl. He was too much for her. Too rich, too experienced, too fast, too soon after his wife had died. Somehow, he had known within weeks that he loved her. As for her, she needed time to process the idea, just in case she didn't know what she was getting into.

Yeah, she was afraid to tell him that she loved him.

So she put him in a little compartment and set him aside.

Perhaps she was so used to separating all her emotions so that she could function and run Skye's the Limit—and now the expanded STL—that she had sacrificed her own personal life for the pursuit of...

Pursuit of what? Self-sufficiency?

What was she trying to prove? And to whom?

Those thoughts filled Skye's mind as she loaded her car with four hundred dollars of experimental groceries. After she pushed the empty cart back to the store, she returned to her car and prayed that everything she cooked tonight would be worth the money she just spent.

Even from childhood, she had been taught to watch her spending.

She hoped that her wandering mind in the store had not caused her to buy food that she didn't need.

How many dishes was she going to cook tonight to impress Uncle Miller's old friend?

Maybe too many.

Traffic toward the marina flowed around Skye as she made her way back to her rental condominium overlooking the river. She had a few hours left before sunset. Maybe she could eat a late dinner while watching the sun vanish over the Georgia horizon.

Alone.

It shouldn't be the reason for her to date again—but how could she date again when her heart was taken and then left in limbo? Her relationship with Diehl seemed to be on hold because both of them were too busy and far apart geographically to be together.

Perhaps it had been a summer fling after all.

Skye sniffled. She had been afraid of that.

Still, his touches and kisses would remain in her memory forever.

When she turned the corner into her condo parking lot, she stepped on the brake in a hurry. Someone else's vehicle had parked in one of her two reserved spots.

A charcoal-colored pickup truck.

There must be many of these.

Probably a new resident who hadn't figured out which spots were reserved for whom.

Slowly, Skye eased her car into the remaining spot, which was by the curb. She popped the trunk of her car. When she got out of the car, she saw him.

Dressed casually in a T-shirt, a pair of shorts, and flip-flops.

"Diehl." Skye nearly wept, but she did not. She was stronger than to burst into tears at the sight of a man she hadn't seen in almost a month. Video calls and text messages just weren't the same as in-person meetings. "I thought we were going to talk tonight."

"In person this time." In a few quick steps, he stood in front of her, his fingers brushing against her jawline and then weaving into her hair.

"You weren't going to my sister's house tonight, so here I am." Diehl hugged her and rubbed her back with his warm hands.

No wonder Avery had been insistent that Skye drop everything this afternoon and go to Brinley's house. Did that mean Avery had finally approved of Skye's relationship with Diehl?

"I wondered when I'd ever see you again." Skye felt she could stand here forever with this man. He was warm and comfortable. "Where are your kids?"

"Having dinner with Brin. After dinner, my parents will take them back to Brooks Cottage for the night."

"So you're staying there this weekend?"

"Yes. Elisa brought her homework to do since she has an assignment due on Monday in English class. Ethan..." Diehl shook his head. "That boy also has homework due on Monday. I suspect he deliberately left his backpack at home when we left the house for the airport."

"So you'll have to go home sooner than later so he can get his homework done."

"After church on Sunday. I want us—you and me and the kids—to go to church together on Sunday."

"I'd love that. What a nice weekend this is turning out to be—except for Ethan's homework." Skye slid her hand around his neck and pulled his face gently toward hers, raising her lips to his. She kissed his chin —smooth and clean-shaven. She kissed the edge of his lips where a smile had formed.

She waited for him to respond.

She didn't have to wait long. His lips were warm and tasted like honey lip balm.

Their kiss was full of hope and possibilities. Neither of them seemed to want it to end, but Skye pulled away. "I need to get the perishables to my fridge."

"Yes, ma'am." Diehl started taking grocery bags out of the trunk. "Anything fragile or breakable I need to be aware of?"

"Just keep everything upright and don't drop any bag."

"Okay." He seemed very careful with each bag, as if every one of them carried a dozen eggs.

"Thank you for helping me carry the groceries," Skye said.

"Happy to do it."

"How did you find me? Did Avery give you my address?"

"Brin did."

"Why?" Skye picked up the remaining grocery bags and put them on the ground.

"I'm entering your world," Diehl said. "Don't compartmentalize me anymore, Skye."

"Excuse me?" She closed the trunk and locked the car.

"I don't want you to put me in a little box to one side. I want to be in your whole world, and I want you in mine."

Skye glanced to her left and right to see if anyone else was around. No one was. They were alone, walking to the elevator that would take them to her rental condominium upstairs.

Diehl's eyes were on hers. "Do you miss me?"

"More than you know." Her voice cracked.

"I figured. I miss you too, but I was afraid to see you," Diehl said—almost nonchalantly like it was normal for him to talk about fears.

Afraid?

"We all have fears." Before Skye could say more, the elevator door opened and a family carrying pool noodles spilled out.

Diehl used his foot to hold the door open for Skye to enter the elevator after the family had vacated it.

Skye pressed the third-floor button, and then they were alone. She wanted to ask Diehl what he was afraid of—because she had fears of her own—but this wasn't the place, and she was feeling emotional.

"When did you get in?" Skye asked instead.

"This afternoon."

"How did you know I was in town? I almost went out of town for a meeting—ah, never mind. Avery's very close cousin works for me. She knows my schedule."

"Atlanta, right?"

"You heard about the merger."

Diehl nodded. "Congratulations. Were you going to visit me when you got to Atlanta?"

"I was going to surprise you at your office. Thought you might give me a tour."

"Sorry to spoil it for you by surprising you first."

The elevator door opened. Diehl followed Skye to the end of the hallway.

"I'm glad you're here," Skye said.

"Have you thought of me in between our phone calls and FaceTime?"

Skye nodded.

"Not nearly enough, are they?"

"No. Maybe we need to be more organized..."

"So we can see each other more often than once in a while," Diehl said. "We have to make this long-distance relationship work. Which one of us is more flexible?"

"Neither one of us is."

"Except on weekends, but not nearly enough." Diehl smiled. "I'm glad you have an administrative assistant now. If they're proficient and organized, they will save you a lot of time. Otherwise, they can be a nightmare."

"I hear you. That's why I did all my own work when STL was by itself. Thing is, I was spending all my waking hours doing office work into the night. I do have an accountant, but he doesn't answer phone calls or write evaluation reports. Basically, my company grew beyond my ability to juggle all the roles myself."

They put the grocery bags on the floor outside Skye's condo to give their arms and wrists a break.

"I miss my house." Skye unlocked the door. "I usually parked outside the kitchen."

"So buy a new house."

"That crossed my mind, but I couldn't decide on the type of beach house I like. I didn't want to spend three thousand dollars a month renting an oceanfront condo. So here I am watching sunsets by the river while buying time to decide where I want to live." Skye reset the alarm.

"Are you inviting me to dinner?" Diehl grinned.

"If you help me cook."

CHAPTER FIFTY-EIGHT

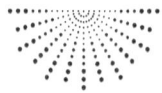

$\mathcal{D}$iehl followed her into her condo. "Do you always put me to work? Last time, I cooked breakfast with you. Now we're doing dinner."

"Dinner is harder." Skye locked and bolted the front door, and led the way to the kitchen. She put her grocery bags on the floor.

"Why the floor?" Diehl asked.

"The bags have been in a grocery cart. I don't know what's in the grocery cart, and I don't want any germs from there—and also from my trunk—to get on the counter where I prepare food."

"Such a thing never crossed my mind."

"Well, you don't have to cook much." Before she put away the groceries, she washed her hands.

Diehl followed. He wiped his hands on the kitchen towel that Skye gave him.

He watched her put a pot of water on the stove. "What's that for?"

"Rice. I was going to cook shrimp curry. Are you okay with that?"

"Sure. I'm game for new dishes. I don't remember the last time I had shrimp curry." Diehl followed Skye back to the bags of groceries on the floor.

Skye took the items out one by one and put them away, with Diehl assisting, asking where everything went, and being careful to put things in the right places.

"You're helpful," Skye said.

"I don't want you to be angry with me later when you can't find this or that."

"You're the first b—uh, person to tell me that."

Diehl stopped in his tracks, still holding a head of broccoli in his hands. "Say it, Skye."

"Say what?"

"What you were about to say."

"Which was?"

Diehl didn't frown. He looked straight at Skye. "You almost called me boyfriend, but you were afraid to because our relationship has been fast and furious, and our time is split between two cities. We're an item, and yet how could we be if we're not together every day?"

Slowly, Skye nodded.

"You were in my world last month, and now I want to be in your world."

"You keep saying that. What does it mean?" Skye washed her hands again and continued putting away the groceries.

"Well, prior to June, my world was in Atlanta and your world was here. We knew who each other was—in passing or because my sister prayed with you about me. However, when I came to stay at Brin's beach house, our worlds collided, and I...fell in love with you."

The bottle of bone broth slipped out of Skye's grip. Diehl caught it, and put it back in her hands. He felt pretty good about his quick reflex—especially with only one hand free. Thank God the bottle didn't hit the floor first.

"You feel the same way about me, don't you?" Diehl asked.

Tears pooled in Skye's eyes. "I miss you every time we're not together."

"You love me too."

"More than I can say."

"I figured." Diehl handed her the bottle of broth to put away in the refrigerator. "Which begs the question: why haven't we moved forward?"

The water boiled, interrupting their conversation. Skye put a plastic bag of something in the sink. It turned out to be shrimp—heads and tails and all.

"Do we have to peel and devein those shrimp?" Diehl asked, thinking it could take all night.

"I'm just cooking a couple of pounds of shrimp. The rest, I'll figure out tomorrow." Skye put away the rest of the meats in the refrigerator.

"Putting away groceries takes forever," Diehl complained.

"I usually listen to the news or a podcast when I do

this." Skye cleared some of the bags, folding her reusable shopping bags.

Diehl asked where the fruits went and Skye pointed to the fruit drawer in the refrigerator. "Do you know of a Pastor Fitzpatrick—better known as Pastor Fizz—at Midtown Chapel?"

"Never heard of him." Skye put on a pair of disposable gloves, and started dividing up the shrimp in the sink. She bagged some of them and put them in a stainless-steel mixing bowl before she put them in the refrigerator. "To be fair, I only visit Midtown whenever I'm in Atlanta, but I haven't had time to get to know the church."

"He's the head of the counseling department at Midtown," Diehl said. "He said he'd meet me one Wednesday night at the midweek service, and next thing you know, I've been in his office twice a week for the last two weeks. He's been helping me sort through my past and how I got here."

"That's good. We all have pasts we need to figure out. I still miss my parents—but I miss my aunt and uncle more. And they've all been long gone. They will always affect me."

"I miss my grandpa too, and yes, he had an impact on my life." Diehl stared at the bowl of shrimp with eyes and legs pointing at him. "You need any help with that?"

Diehl hoped Skye would say no. He wasn't up to peeling shrimp.

"No need."

What a relief. "How else can I help?"

"You can wash and cut some vegetables for a side dish. I bought some squash and zucchini."

"I can do that. They don't have bulbous eyes."

Skye laughed.

"Wash all of them?" Diehl asked.

"Yes, I have other vegetables for tomorrow." Skye pointed to the sink by an empty bar. "Use that sink. I've got shrimp in this one."

Diehl was disappointed at being banished to another corner. He wanted to be with Skye—standing next to her.

"I can still hear you from here," Skye said. "The kitchen is not very big."

"It's tiny," Diehl said as Skye pointed to colanders he could use to rinse the vegetables.

"Yeah. Too small for a test kitchen. I don't test new dishes at Sage Café on Friday nights when their kitchen is busy."

"Makes sense. Why not get a bigger place for yourself?" Diehl washed the vegetables but wasn't sure what to do with them.

"I have one piece of land but I haven't decided what to build on it. They won't let me park an RV there."

A recreational vehicle?

Diehl almost laughed. If it was the land he suspected, there was no way she could build a house smaller than three thousand square feet on that ocean-front property. The covenant association wouldn't allow it.

"I'm just kidding." Skye laughed. She rinsed the shrimp she had peeled.

"I almost believed you." Diehl carried the vegetables back to the island counter. He realized he had left a trail of water on the floor. He looked around for a rag.

Skye pointed to a closet. "There's a mop in there."

When Diehl returned, Skye was stirring rice in a pot of briskly boiling water. "I hope you like brown rice."

"I like all types of rice."

"Me too." Skye put two chopping boards on the island and took out two knives.

"Those look sharp." Diehl made quick work of mopping the floor, and then he returned the mop to the closet.

"Sharp knives are the safest ones in a kitchen," Skye said. "Please wash your hands so we can cut some vegetables."

"Again?"

"I wash my hands all the time in the kitchen."

When Diehl came around the island, Skye was washing some odd-looking things in a bowl. Leaning to see what they were, Diehl pecked her on the cheek.

Skye smiled. "So what did Pastor Fizz tell you—if it's something you can talk about."

"Only you because it affects us."

"Oh?"

"I have failed in past relationships—as you well know, considering I just found out today that my sister told you everything about my sorry life."

"Well, not everything." Skye stirred the rice again

and turned the heat to medium before she partially covered the top.

"Just about," Diehl replied. "You knew about my bizarre marriage, the children who are not biologically mine, and my career that nearly killed me. You also saw me all hungover…"

Skye put a finger on his lips. "Shh. It's over. In the past."

Diehl held her hand over his heart.

"You weren't saved," Skye said. "You did what you knew to do to the best of your knowledge without God's help."

"True. And my first wife wasn't saved either. Between the two of us, we made a mess of things. And when times got tough, we hit the bottle."

"You've told me that before," Skye said. "There's no reason to repeat what you said. Besides, your wife has been dead for more than a year. Your marriage to her ended when she died."

"I guess I want to remind myself how far I've come." Diehl reached for Skye. He held her hand. "God is putting an armor of protection around me for our sake."

"And the sake of your children."

Skye put a squash on her chopping board and showed him how to bias slice the squash after cutting off the ends.

Diehl tried to follow to the best of his ability. His squash slices were uneven.

Skye handed him another squash. "Please slice up all the squash. And the zucchini the same way."

While Diehl cut up the vegetables, Skye moved on to her bowl of strange roots.

"What's that?" Diehl asked. "That doesn't look like ginger."

"No, it's turmeric." Skye lifted the root in the air.

"It looks like an orange cocoon."

"It does not. You're used to dried turmeric, right? This is where it came from."

Skye chopped up the turmeric and put it into a small container. Then she showed Diehl another root. "This is ginger."

"I know ginger."

Skye moved on to cut up what looked like green sticks.

"What are those sticks?" Diehl asked.

"Lemongrass stalks." Skye sliced off the root base and lifted it to Diehl's nose. "What do you think it smells like?"

He took a whiff of it. And kissed Skye's fingers. "Lemony."

Skye retracted the lemongrass and made a face. "You're contaminating everything!"

She washed her hands and the lemongrass stalk in the sink again as Diehl laughed.

"We're the only ones eating them tonight," Diehl said as Skye minced up the bulbous part of the lemongrass.

After chopping up ginger, onions, and garlic, Skye opened a tub and showed it to Diehl. "This is tamarind. I'm going to squeeze the meat and put it in the shrimp curry."

"What does it taste like?"

Skye found a small teaspoon and scooped up a sample for Diehl to try.

He smacked his lips. "Slightly sour. Interesting."

"They grow on trees in the tropics," Skye said. "I'd love to plant a tamarind tree, but the climate here won't support it."

"Unless it's in a greenhouse."

"A big one."

While Skye heated up the pan for the curry, Diehl finished cutting up the zucchini and squash. However, there wasn't enough room on the stovetop. The burners were too close to one another, so he had to wait his turn.

"I'll need you to show me how to cook the vegetables," Diehl said.

"When the rice is done—shortly—we can use that burner for the vegetables." Skye pointed to her array of spices on the counter. "What's your heat level?"

"Very hot." He laughed.

"You want me to put the hottest chili into the curry then?" Skye asked.

"Oh, that. Mild to medium. I can't do too spicy." Diehl watched Skye heat up avocado oil in a frying pan. Then she sautéed garlic, onions, turmeric, ginger, and spoonfuls of dried spices. "What are those?"

"I've got curry powder, cumin, coriander—the usual spices—and whatever else I can find from my spice cabinet—maybe cardamom, fennel, and paprika." She stirred them. "Be warned, we don't have an outside vent in this kitchen, so the smell of curry might fill the entire condo."

She sighed. "I sure miss my old house. Oh well. Life goes on."

At this point, Diehl wanted to buy her a new house with everything in it, but all that came out of his mouth was: "Do you want me to open the windows?"

"Turn off the AC first. Thank you."

Diehl wandered around to find the thermostat. He glanced down the hallway to a bedroom, which he assumed was Skye's room. The door was open. There was a bed with a teal comforter on it. A closed Bible was on top of the comforter. Next to the bed was a side table with a small vase of what looked like fresh flowers in it.

Send her flowers.

His administrative assistant's words came back to haunt him. He made a mental note to have fresh flowers delivered to Skye from now on.

When he returned to the kitchen, Skye's back was facing him. She was busy stirring rice and the shrimp curry. Diehl had to move a couple of small dining table chairs in order to reach the lone window. The sliding glass moved vertically but it was tight. Then he walked over to the double French doors that led to the porch.

The French doors reminded him of Brinley's beach house—both the first and second floors where his bedroom balcony was. Brinley still intended to sell the house, but Diehl did not want Skye to buy it and live in a house that other people designed. He wanted to build her a house that she wanted.

He wanted to do that and more.

Back in the kitchen, Skye removed the pot of rice from the stove. She turned up the burner and heated a frying pan on it.

"I'm putting just enough olive oil to coat the pan." Skye showed him. "Then when the oil has heated up some—not too much—we can put in the squash and zucchini."

Diehl nodded.

Skye glanced at him. "What's the matter?"

"I forgot to bring you flowers," Diehl said.

"Does it matter?" Skye smiled. "You brought me kisses."

Diehl eyed her lips again, but Skye shrieked.

Smoke was rising from the empty pan.

"Too hot. What did I say?" Skye turned the burner down. She dumped all the zucchini and squash into the pan. They made a loud sizzling noise.

Skye stirred and tossed the vegetables.

"How did you know they'd fit?" Diehl said.

"Once you've cooked for a while, you'll figure out how much."

"Just like those spices. You hardly measured."

"I eyeballed them." Skye handed him a wooden spatula. "Stir it every now and then."

When Diehl looked up, Skye was heading toward the screened-in porch.

"It's still humid outside." Skye turned on the fan. "Do you want to eat out here with the ceiling fan on and watch the sunset or do you want to eat inside?"

"Sunset." Diehl didn't hesitate. "It'll cool down soon."

Skye set the dining table on the porch with a tablecloth and two place settings. "At least the screen will keep the mosquitoes out."

"Is this the top floor?"

"Yes. But someone else has the rooftop deck. I got this corner porch." Skye came inside and wiped down the island counter. "How are the vegetables?"

"I'm still stirring them."

Skye sprinkled some salt and pepper on the zucchini and squash. "Since the curry is strong, we'll just make these side veggies as plain as possible."

She poured a small cup of water into the pan, and it made another loud sizzle. She quickly covered it with the lid to contain the steam. "We'll check it in a couple of minutes."

She stirred the curry. Using a clean spoon, she scooped up a small amount of curry for Diehl to taste. "Be careful. It's hot."

Steam was rising from the spoon. Slowly, Diehl tasted it. "Not too spicy. I'm okay with it."

"Then dinner is almost ready." Skye opened cabinets where the plates and serving platters were. "The nice thing about a small kitchen is that everything is right here."

"Are the rest of your kitchen things in storage?" Diehl asked.

"How did you know?"

"I guessed. As a chef, you must have more than these things."

"Well, I've collected platters and dinnerware, but really, I repeatedly use the same frying pans." Skye put three serving platters on the island counter. "Two years of keeping things in storage reminded me that I can do without so many things in life."

Diehl nodded. "Fourteen years with a family in my house in Atlanta told me that I don't need such a big house."

"I don't need a big house myself. I need a functional house."

Diehl took the dinner plates from Skye. "Someday, I'll build you a functional house."

"You will?"

"Yeah. Brooks Properties buys, sells, and builds both commercial buildings and residential homes."

"Are you trying to advertise something to me?" Skye chuckled.

Diehl tried to laugh it off, but in his mind, he wondered where they would stay for the rest of their lives together.

Skye transferred curry, vegetables, and rice onto their platters.

Diehl took them out to the table on the porch.

"Mineral water or spring water?" Skye asked.

"Spring." Diehl came back inside for the silverware as Skye filled their goblets with water.

"All we need are candles," Diehl said.

Skye tilted her head. "I never pegged you as being that romantic."

"Candles are not too romantic. I mean, we had them at five-star..." He stopped himself when he realized that he was recalling those expensive dinners with Isobel—back in the days when he had thought they were exclusively married to each other in every way.

He wondered how he could take Skye to those restaurants in Atlanta without recalling his days with Isobel. Perhaps it was best for him to move out of Atlanta and bury old memories, after all.

Skye touched his arm. "It's okay."

"I'm sorry. I want to move on with you." Diehl held her and kissed her forehead.

"Would you like to say grace before our food gets cold?" Skye asked softly.

Holding Skye in his arms, Diehl thanked God for the food. "And may our conversation be edifying to each other and glorifying to You. In Jesus' name, I pray. Amen."

"That's a good prayer." Skye held Diehl's hand and led him to the porch.

Diehl seated her and placed a cloth napkin on her lap.

"Thank you," she said.

Diehl prayed about how to talk with her about his past without pushing her away. He took his seat across the table from Skye. He felt nervous.

"Let's enjoy our dinner," Skye said. "And talk about our fears and failures later."

"Over dessert?" Diehl raised his eyebrows.

"I didn't get dessert materials at the grocery store."

"And you barely made a dent in the groceries you bought." Diehl remembered the many bags they hauled into the condo.

"Yeah. I'll work on them tomorrow. I don't feel like cooking all night tonight."

"Cooking all night?" Diehl asked.

"Sometimes I do that if I want to get things done." She told him about her tight schedule.

Diehl's eyes perked up. "When are you going to be in Atlanta?"

"Thursday."

Diehl checked his phone. "I have meetings all day Thursday and a business dinner. Are you staying through Friday?"

"No. I'm only going to Atlanta for one day. I'll fly in and fly out."

Diehl's heart sank. "I want to see you every day, but I don't know how."

"We will next year, won't we?" Skye asked. "You said that Riley will relocate to Atlanta after the school year, thus freeing you to move to St. Simon's."

"Right. But that's nine months away. Can we survive?" Diehl wasn't sure if he could.

"Soldiers do it all the time," Skye said.

"We're not soldiers."

"No? Ephesians 6:13-18 talk about the armor of God—thereby implying that we are soldiers of the cross."

"Every day I don't see you, my heart hurts," Diehl said.

"Mine too, but maybe the Lord would want us to grow spiritually apart from each other."

"You're practical." Diehl did not want to bring up any other men's names, but several potential suitors might sweep Skye off her feet before he could return to St. Simon's to claim her.

He put his hand on his side pocket. The small box was still there.

But this wasn't the time.

They finished their curry dinner, and Diehl was full. "That was so delicious I want a third helping, but I'll resist."

Skye pointed to the river. "The sun is going down. Do you want to watch the sunset from here or outdoors?"

Diehl looked in the direction she pointed. "How do we get there?"

"There's a path along the river, with benches to sit on."

"Let's go." Diehl stood up and helped Skye out of her chair.

"Thank you," she said. "We have a few minutes to put away these leftovers. I'll do the dishes later."

"When we get back, I'll help." Diehl meant it. He didn't have to do that in his own home, but here in Skye's house, he wanted to show how useful he could be.

They put away the leftover rice, curry, and vegetables in the refrigerator before they went downstairs and through the back of the condominium complex to the riverside.

The sun glowed and the sky turned a million shades of orange and red when Diehl took several photos with Skye and several selfies of themselves with the sunset in the backdrop.

They didn't say much to each other as they stood at the river's edge, watching the setting sun. Diehl enjoyed her company and felt completely at ease, as though he could tell her anything.

In the waning light, Diehl kissed Skye's neck as he held her while the sun slipped away into the horizon on yet another day's end, ushering in twilight across the river and over the marshes.

When the sun was gone, Diehl gently turned Skye toward him, whispering in her ear heartfelt words.

"I love you and I want to..."

His phone rang.

CHAPTER FIFTY-NINE

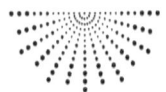

A big knot in his stomach accompanied Diehl to the beach on Saturday morning as he waited in his truck at Brinley's beach house for nine o'clock to arrive. He did not see Skye's car, so he assumed she was either late or had intended to park elsewhere on the public beach behind Brinley's house.

The radio was off, and in the quiet of his truck—save for the sounds of the ocean and morning birds—Diehl prayed and rehearsed what he was going to say.

He had almost done it the night before after the sun had set on the river, but Ethan's phone call broke his train of thought. When he heard Ethan's voice on the phone, crying and asking where Dad was, that killed his entire mood.

It caused Skye to send him home to Brooks Cottage, leaving her to clean up their dinner table and the kitchen by herself. He wished he could have stayed behind to help her do the dishes, but there would be other times, he hoped.

Perhaps every night in the future.

He had no idea why he enjoyed such a mundane task. Maybe it was the company. Skye had been so sweet to him all this time. They hardly had a heated argument—unlike his fourteen years with Isobel.

With Skye, their conversations were mature and quiet. No one yelled and screamed. No one cut off other people's sentences or assumed what others were thinking.

Skye waited for Diehl to speak his mind.

He hadn't realized how much he yearned for someone to listen to him without judging him. He felt that he could tell Skye everything.

At 8:45 a.m. Diehl made his way to the boardwalk behind the beach house. The wood was still damp from the overnight rain.

In the middle of the night at Brooks Cottage, he had woken up to the sound of thunder, and immediately recalled that night back in June when he had been stranded in Athens with Skye in her brother's off-campus apartment.

They felt at ease with each other, and Diehl knew he wanted to spend the rest of his life with her.

At the edge of the boardwalk, Diehl put on his sunglasses to scan the beach. No sign of Skye.

The ocean waves rolled on, their crashing sounds a reminder to Diehl that life went on no matter what.

Bittersweet life.

Tomorrow afternoon, he'd fly back to Atlanta with

his kids. The weekend was too short for him. He wanted more time with Skye.

"I don't know how I can wait another nine months, Lord," he whispered into the wind.

His voice blended into the crashing surf and the squawk of seabirds. Somewhere over the waters, a few brown pelicans glided in the wind.

Life goes on.

Unfinished conversations hung over his head. He had hoped to talk about his fears after dinner, but his time with Skye had been interrupted by his needy child who wanted him to tuck him in and read something to him before he slept.

Lately, Diehl had been reading the Bible to Ethan.

On Friday night, Dad was supposed to read to Ethan in Diehl's place—except Ethan had changed his mind about it at the last minute.

While Skye had agreed to meet Diehl this morning on the beach, he couldn't be sure she would show up.

Perhaps Diehl had expected too much?

How could they have a relationship with each other five hours of driving apart? Diehl wanted to be with her, hold her, hug her, kiss her every single day.

None of that could be done remotely via phone or video calls.

Even though he had lived that way before with Isobel living on a different continent, this time it felt different because Skye was a different type of woman.

She loved the Lord, wanted God's best, and seemed self-sacrificial. Still, would she wait for him?

He had tried to let her go many times so that she

could live free on the island and find a new boyfriend or marry another man. At the same time, he wanted to be with her.

Last night, he found out—and confirmed his own understanding—that Skye was on the same page with him in terms of their feelings for each other.

Now we have to make it work.

How do we make it work, Lord?

Diehl was sure that if Skye was meant to be together with him, they should not live so far apart.

It was past nine o'clock. Skye was late.

Diehl started to worry until he saw her coming up on the beach, walking along the shoreline in a pretty dress, her A-line skirt fluttering gently around her calves. Her long legs seemed to extend into the foam swirling around her ankles. She carried her sandals in one hand.

She wore a pair of sunglasses, and her hair was down, dancing on her shoulders in the morning wind.

Diehl thought she was prettier than she had been when she joined his family for a picnic at this same spot.

He pulled out his phone to snap a photograph of Skye walking on the beach, but ended up recording a video of her strolling toward him, the Atlantic Ocean providing background music and the sunshine providing perfect lighting.

This was how he wanted to remember her.

He was grinning sheepishly when she waved to him. She seemed to be aware that his phone was pointing at her. She smiled without a word, as if to say, "I want you to remember me this way."

Diehl nearly wept as his hands shook. He stopped recording.

He steeled himself.

"Caught in a moment." He could barely speak.

"What moment?" Skye asked.

"This." He pulled her gently toward his chest. Her hair smelled of fresh flowers and rain. Her dress was the softest silk. He closed his eyes and tried to remember everything about her, as if this was the last time he would see her in a long while. "I wish we could be here forever."

"You know, only heaven is forever," Skye said.

Diehl chuckled. "Reality check from my Sensible Skye."

"Is that your name for me?" Skye smiled. "What should I call you? Determined Diehl?"

More like Desperate Diehl.

"I don't want to lose you," Diehl said quietly.

"Is that what your fear is?" Skye's eyes seemed to be searching his.

Diehl couldn't speak.

"You haven't lost me," Skye whispered in his ear.

"Not yet?"

"Not ever." Skye's lips found his.

Diehl was enjoying her affection for him until a bird squawked overhead, and Skye pulled away.

"I don't want to be under a flying bird," Skye said. "You know what happened to my brother once, standing under a tree with a bird in it?"

"I don't want to know." Diehl chuckled. "Let's walk."

He led her along the shoreline. His feet were where the waves ended. Hers were on dry sand—most of the time.

"I was going to tell you something last night, but I had to go home because Ethan called," Diehl said. "I thought that maybe we could continue our conversation."

Skye nodded. "We were talking about fears. I wanted to tell you that I'm afraid too."

"What are you afraid of?" Diehl prayed he could handle what he would hear.

"You told me last night that you fear the past—at least that was the summary of what I heard."

"That's true. I look at my past and wonder how I could ever love you in the present and the future," Diehl said. "But my dad reminded me that I'm a Christian now. You reminded me that the past is gone. Pastor Fizz is helping me deal with all that. God makes all things new."

"And remember what you texted me that night in Athens?" Skye produced her phone. She scrolled up and read it. "Here it is, verbatim. 'With God's love, I can love you. I may be imperfect, but Christ is perfect. His love is what I give to you. Together we can help each other through the journey of life.' Do you recall?"

"Wow. I need to take my own advice." Diehl chuckled.

"Same here. I fear the future," Skye said.

"The future? It's not here yet."

"Isn't it irrational?"

"No." Diehl stopped walking. "What are you concerned about?"

"How do we go forward? We're stuck in two different cities. Your kids are in school in Atlanta. I don't like the idea that they change schools every year. They need stability, you know?"

"They'll be fine, I think."

"Besides, I don't want to communicate with you by video all month long and then see each other every now and then. What kind of relationship is that?" Skye's voice cracked. "I fear that we might not work out."

"In nine months, I'll be moving here."

"Can you wait nine months?" Skye asked.

"Even one day is agonizing." It was the truth.

"What if you don't move here in nine months?" Skye asked.

"What do you mean?"

"What if something changes and it takes longer?"

"I don't know."

"What if we're not supposed to live here?"

"What?" Now Diehl was baffled and confused. "What are you saying, Skye?"

"Do you like your job?" Skye asked.

Diehl nodded. "It comes with many personal sacrifices."

"I used to think so about mine, but it doesn't have to be that way." Skye wrapped her hand around Diehl's arm. "Olivia says we can have both."

"Pastor Gonzalez's wife?"

"Uh-huh. I talked to her about our dilemma. She said that we both may have to sacrifice something if we want to make our relationship work."

"Like a career?" Diehl wondered. "Just say the word, and I'll drop everything for you."

"I would do the same, but then I went and bought Watt's for Dinner. At first, I thought I made a mistake. Maybe I should have thought about it more before I made the commitment. But Watt wouldn't sell it to anyone else—and I had money from the sale of my Saffron shares."

"And it's in Alpharetta," Diehl said quietly. "In the same county as my office."

"Yeah, North Fulton. I don't want you to think that I bought it because of you. That was why I did not tell you about it. I had a feeling it would be in the papers, but I didn't think you would have time to read the news."

"I didn't at first. My assistant at work told me about it."

"I guess that's what they're there for."

They walked for a while as the sun rose above their heads. Bright umbrellas and weather-worn beach chairs spread across the public beach. Families with children surrounded them.

Diehl could see that Skye looked at the little kids longingly. Then she turned away as soon as she seemed to realize that Diehl was watching her.

"Between Pastor Fizz and Matt—well, and also Pastor Gonzalez's old sermons—I feel that God is showing me how to be the Christian man that I need to be so that someday, I could be a Christian husband for the one I love."

Skye went quiet.

Then she said, "I don't deserve you."

"Hey, wait a minute. That's my line." Diehl chuckled.

"We both don't deserve each other."

"We don't deserve anything but death, thanks to our sin nature. It is by the mercy and grace of God that we live day by day."

Skye nodded. "You're right. I forgot."

Diehl cupped her chin in his hand. "Neither of us has ever been married as Christians. A truly Christian marriage is a whole new ballgame, according to Pastor Fizz. As for kids, I have no idea if I will ever be able to have kids of my own."

"You don't know yet," Skye said.

"Bingo. Who holds the future?"

"God." Skye's answer was immediate.

"Who holds the past?"

"Also God."

"When we fear, we run to Christ." Diehl read a verse from his phone. "Romans 8:38-39 says, 'For I am persuaded that neither death nor life, nor angels nor principalities nor powers, nor things present nor things to come, nor height nor depth, nor any other created thing, shall be able to separate us from the love of God which is in Christ Jesus our Lord.' I know we believe that."

"Amen. And please read the verse before it."

"I like that verse too. 'Yet in all these things we are

more than conquerors through Him who loved us.' Romans 8:37," Diehl said, "I think I will memorize it."

"You're growing in your Christian faith," Skye said. "I truly believe God has brought you here into my life for such a time as this. I don't know when you will leave, but my life is richer because I met you."

Diehl tried to process what Skye just said. "Leave? I'm not going anywhere."

"I wore this dress because I wanted you to remember me this way, smiling and happy to be with you," Skye said. "Just in case you leave and find someone else in Atlanta when we are apart."

"Skye."

"I have thought about this for a while. I may not be the one for you. I'll always love you for the rest of my life but..." Her voice caught. "I've never been with anyone. What if you find me...?"

She couldn't get the word out.

"I find you beautiful." His lips brushed against her cheek before they reached her lips.

She was quiet.

"I find you lovely." He closed his eyes as they stood there in the warming sun, forehead to forehead.

"I..."

"Shhh." Diehl gently kissed the base of her ear, whispering, "I love you, Skye. Will you marry me?"

Looking stunned, Skye stepped back.

Uh-oh. Diehl waited.

"Did you just ask me... What did you say?"

CHAPTER SIXTY

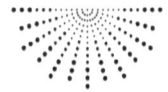

"*I* was going to ask you last night after sunset, but it didn't work out." Diehl was on one knee in the sand.

He prayed as he retrieved the small box from his pocket. It was the same box he had carried around all day on Friday. When he opened it, the blue diamond sparkled in the morning sun, its brilliant round cut reflecting the sun rays in every which way.

He cleared his throat. "I love you, Skye Blue Langston. Will you marry me?"

Skye began to sob.

"Ecclesiastes 3:4 says there is 'a time to weep, and a time to laugh, a time to mourn, and a time to dance.' Our time to weep and mourn is over, Skye. Our time to laugh and dance is here. This is our time to heal, to embrace, and to love." Diehl paused, his mind going blank. "I forget everything else I wanted to say. Will you marry me anyway?"

Skye smiled through her tears. She barely nodded.

"I can't hear you. The surf's too loud." Diehl reached for Skye's hand.

"I love you too, and yes, I'll marry you, Diehl Jeremiah Brooks." Skye extended her left hand toward Diehl.

"Ah, you know my middle name."

"Brinley told me you were named after the first Brooks who arrived in Savannah in the eighteenth century."

Diehl smiled. "Jeremiah Brooks bought his wife, Damaris, a Stradivarius violin. I bought you something smaller."

He placed the rare twelve-carat blue diamond on Skye's ring finger. It had been worth trading in his 1964 Ferrari 250 GTO for.

Technically, he had sold the sports car to Dad, who had room left in his garage for yet another vehicle he wouldn't have time to drive. Diehl then exchanged part of the forty-million-dollar profit for this blue diamond the color of the sky above St. Simon's Island. Other diamonds were more expensive, but they weren't blue.

Its previous owner—an Asian collector who had paid thirty-eight million for it at a London auction some years before—almost refused to sell it at less than what he had paid for it, until Diehl told him his love story. Diehl managed to negotiate seven million off the price because the diamond wasn't as deep a blue as the most expensive blue diamond ever sold. This one was sky blue, not lapis lazuli blue.

Diehl knew he had to have it. If the collector had stayed his position, Diehl would have paid for it because this was the diamond he wanted to give to Skye.

And it fit on a gold band.

Skye stared at the diamond. "It's my favorite blue."

"Is it?" He learned new things about her every day. "Perfect."

"Sky blue."

"Like your name." Diehl got off his knee and stepped toward Skye.

"No, like the sky above us and the sea in front of us." Skye touched the ring. "It fits perfectly. How did you know what size ring I wear?"

"I asked your brother, and his wife said you have the same jeweler as Brinley."

"Wait. You talked to my brother?"

"He gave me his blessing."

Skye's eyes widened. "When?"

"Last week."

"Last week?"

"As soon as my ring arrived." Diehl didn't say that he sent Malik to Tokyo to pick up the ring in person.

"You've been planning this."

"All month long." Diehl brushed strands of hair away from Skye's face. He glanced at her lips again. They were pink and smiling, beckoning him to—

A rush of air made Diehl turn toward the noise only to find a Frisbee flying past his head.

"Sorry!" someone said, running around the couple toward the Frisbee.

In an instant, he was tackled into the sand by a bigger man. Both of them splashed into the ocean waves.

"Whoa." Skye stepped away from the commotion.

Diehl stood in front of Skye to shield her.

The two guys in the water—one shirtless and the other in long sleeves—started standing up.

The shirtless man was furious as he watched his Frisbee float away into the ocean. "Look what you did! You're going to pay for the Frisbee."

The other man, hair matted to his head, trudged out of the water. Diehl laughed when he saw who it was.

"Malik?" Skye asked.

Some stranger went in the water to help Malik out. Malik waved him away, refusing any help. He came up to Diehl.

"Sir, are you okay?" Malik asked. "That was close."

Diehl glanced at Skye's hand. The diamond was still there. "We're okay."

"Wow," Skye said. "I've never had security detail before. This is new."

"He's not actually keeping an eye on us," Diehl said.

"Oh?"

"Nope. He's keeping an eye on your ring."

Skye stared at the ring. "Well... I suppose this means I shouldn't wear it when I do dishes."

Malik looked beyond alarmed. "No, ma'am. Never."

"Don't scare her." Diehl wrapped his arms around Skye.

"Carry on, sir." Malik walked away.

Skye eyed Malik shaking off water from his drenched clothes.

"Don't worry. We have privacy," Diehl said.

"Privacy on a public beach?" Skye laughed.

"Maybe we should consider a beach of our own. Know of any available oceanfront land?" Diehl asked as he held Skye's hand.

They walked along the water back toward Brinley's beach house.

"So you know about my property on Seaside Island." Skye smiled. "Every now and then, Brinley hints that Brooks Renovations might be willing to build me a cottage. Maybe we can talk to her about some ideas."

"Meanwhile, I wonder what God is doing in our lives." Diehl glanced at Skye to see if she knew what he meant.

"He's doing a lot, for sure. Which of the many things are you thinking of?"

"For example, we haven't talked about the fact that you now have an office in Alpharetta, forty-five minutes from my house—which I was going to sell in the spring before we move here."

"I want to downsize Watt's for Dinner," Skye said. "Look at me. I keep calling it Watt's for Dinner. By the time I'm done, it will be all signature STL."

"I know what you mean."

"Between you and me, I think Watt sold me his

company for a song because it's not worth that much the way it is now."

"Oh?" That, he didn't know. Then again, sometimes the news inflated the company's worth for public relation gains.

"Watt overextended his company, I think. He has personal chef plus corporate catering," Skye explained. "Catering is Seb's department. He's moving to Atlanta when Em finishes music school, so I don't want to mess with his restaurant's catering arm. I'd rather see us sticking to personal chef services—which might include cooking for dinner parties, but not in a way that might compete with my brother."

"Makes sense. In my case, I don't want my Brooks Properties to compete with Brin's Brooks Renovations either. I'm focusing on commercial properties henceforth, and she's focusing on residential and historic preservations—which could include commercial properties, but not in the areas I work in."

"So you know what I mean." Skye nodded. She lifted her left hand. "I can't believe you proposed."

"You said yes. Don't retract now," Diehl warned.

Skye placed her palm on his chest. "I think people usually kiss after a proposal. Did we forget?"

"We were busy figuring out how to manage our lives the next nine months when we're apart."

"Who says we need to be apart now that we're committed to each other?"

Diehl raised an eyebrow, then another. "What are you suggesting, my sweet and pure Christian fiancée?"

"Banish the thought, future husband."

"What thought? Us moving in together and thereby sinning against God, ruining our testimony, and showing a bad example to everyone?"

Skye ignored his tease. "I'm referring to the fact you pointed out earlier. After I restructure Watt's for Dinner in metro Atlanta to fit my STL concept, I was going to send Chef Joseph to run the Alpharetta office. He's single, doesn't care where he lives, and can move to a new town at a moment's notice. But now..."

"Now you're thinking you could switch places?" Diehl prayed it was the case.

"Joseph has been with me at STL for years. He'll have to duke it out with Gillian at the office on St. Simon's, but it's only for nine months. Then we'll be back, where we both want to be, and I can send Joseph to Atlanta next summer."

"That's exactly what I thought you were going to suggest." Diehl caressed the back of her hand. "On my part, I talked to my kids about moving to St. Simon's Island next year when Elisa starts high school and Ethan starts middle school, and they're open to the idea of a change of place. For me, it's a change of *pace*. I am looking forward to moving to someplace more laid-back."

"There's still work to be done every day, you know. It's not all hammock life on these islands," Skye said. "While we're in transition in Atlanta, we'll want to attend marital counseling, right? Could you check with Midtown Chapel about that?"

"I already did."

"Before or after you bought the ring?"

"Before the ring, but after I prayed about us."

"I'm glad you prayed first," Skye said. "What type of marital counseling does Midtown have?"

"I think it's a bootcamp." Diehl laughed. "Pastor Gonzalez at Seaside told me theirs is two months long. Not to be bested, Pastor Fizz has designed a marital counseling program that lasts six months."

"Six months!"

"Yes, it's all-encompassing, but we only meet with him twice a month, so we have time to do the homework."

"Did you say homework?"

"I know, right. I think they think that if you're not serious about marriage, you won't last six months and it will save the family from a future divorce—especially if kids are involved."

"Makes sense."

"He said that we could attend the sessions remotely on live video," Diehl added.

"That won't be necessary now that I'll work out of the Alpharetta office until the school year ends."

"So you've decided."

"Right here and now."

Diehl smiled. "Look at us making decisions on the fly."

"It's the right thing to do," Skye explained. "I prayed about it too, you know. I was waiting for an answer and it came today."

"Where will you stay? Near your office? Near my

house?" Diehl still held Skye's hands as they stepped on the boardwalk toward Brinley's beach house.

"I'll rent a place somewhere in between. I don't need a big place since Watt's for Dinner has test kitchens," Skye said. "I'll have to keep my St. Simon's stuff still in storage for another year until we build a house or..."

She stopped in her tracks.

So did Diehl.

There, in front of them, the whitewashed walls of Brinley's beach house shone in the morning sun. The French doors upstairs reminded Diehl of the first morning he woke up in the bedroom to the sound of a sparrow flying around in the room because he had left the door opened.

He started to hum "His Eye Is on the Sparrow."

Skye looked away, and then back to the house. "It's a cozy cottage."

"It is." Diehl remembered the grand piano in the house. "I have fond memories of the Treble Trio practices. How are you going to be here for practice when you're in Atlanta?"

"I'll fly here when the trio sings at church," Skye said. "I'm not giving it up."

"I'll come here with you. It's usually on Sundays, anyway. We can fly in for the weekend and then out again."

"We don't sing that often unless we're filling in for vacationing choir members—like we did in June."

"I enjoyed it. It's a nice break for me from work."

"It's fun work."

"Yep." Diehl held her as they stood there on the boardwalk staring at the beach house, backs facing the ocean.

"I wonder..." Skye's voice faded into the wind.

Diehl's chin was on the side of Skye's head. "Wonder what?"

"Could we...uh...live here?"

"Sure. Do we need to build a minimum-required big house on Seaside Island when we can just move in already?" Diehl warmed up to the idea.

"It has a kitchen that I helped Brinley design," Skye said softly.

"It is small."

"But cozy."

"Yes. If we need more room, we could expand it."

"What about security?" Skye asked. "The kids. I want them to be safe. We're so close to a public beach."

"I'll ask Malik to look into it. Lots of people live on St. Simon's Island, and we know it's one of the safest beach towns in the country."

"Maybe we can work with the local communities to make it even safer for families to raise their kids here." Skye paused. "I guess I'm just a bit concerned, though I am reminding myself now that Elisa was lured away by people she knew and trusted."

"Exactly. This beach town is not a hotbed of crime."

"I think Seaside Chapel has a community outreach arm for safety during the summertime when it runs summer camps for kids. We can ask Pastor Gonzalez if it extends to the rest of the year."

Diehl nodded. "So do you want to ask Brin if she's still selling this house?"

"Shall we pray about it first?"

"Of course. If this is where God wants us to be, then we can make Brin an offer." The rustling of trees made Diehl's eyes look to the side of the house where the yard was. "I wonder who has been filling the bird feeder and bath."

"I have." Skye pointed to the trees. "My car's parked across the street. I brought another bag of bird-seed today."

"I'll help you with it. We might need to scrub the bird bath."

Skye chuckled, apparently at a memory. "Remember that day you came to town? You drenched me with the hose, causing me to be late for a rehearsal."

Diehl cringed. "I'm sorry. It was really an accident."

"I know. It was also my fault that I didn't have spare clothes in the van and had to go home to change."

"Remember that spot on the grass where we all lay down and looked at the sky?" Diehl pointed toward the trees. "Thank you for talking to Elisa about her issues. She told me last week that she approves of you and wants to learn to play the guitar."

Skye sniffled. "She's a sweet kid."

"As for Ethan, he's easy to please. You won him over with cheesecake." Diehl faced Skye. "I thank God every day for you."

"I thank God for you too. I'm so glad He worked it all out for us and our children."

Our children.

Diehl felt his eyes sting.

He buried his face in Skye's hair and tried not to weep openly on a public beach.

CHAPTER SIXTY-ONE

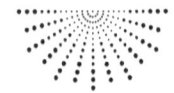

*S*kye liked routines, the certainty and steadiness of time and schedule. No surprises. No shocks. Just expected events for her to look forward to all year long.

Like the six months of marital counseling with Pastor "Fizz" Fitzpatrick at Midtown Chapel in Atlanta, where Skye attended church with the Brooks family—except for Rose Brooks, who slept in every Sunday morning and refused to listen to any conversation about God, Jesus, church, or anything halfway religious. Diehl had been praying with Skye about his mother's spiritual condition, and they left it at that.

By the time Diehl and Skye's marital counseling sessions wrapped up just before spring break in April, Skye could not believe how fast the months had rolled by between Diehl's beach proposal in August and her subsequent temporary move to metro Atlanta in September to spending Christmas on Seaside Island with Diehl and his kids, along with the children's bodyguards.

Ned and Rose Brooks were delighted to have everyone present at their family Christmas dinner. Chef Pierre and his new team did a lovely job feeding Riley Brooks and her two teenagers, Brinley and Ivan and their son, Sebastian and Emmeline with a baby on the way, plus Zoe and Quincy and their young ones who only spoke French.

Before Skye knew it, it was June, only one of the hottest months of the year on St. Simon's Island. One year after she and Diehl fell in love with each other and ten months after their engagement, they were finally going to be married.

Of course, it had to rain on this fine Saturday morning.

The weather wiped out their plans for a beach wedding behind the beach house they had bought from Brinley, and an outdoor reception under the trees by the bird feeders and birdbaths—where Rose Brooks had gifted them a small garden of flowers from Brooks Cottage.

Still, when the weather report came that God was going to pour showers of blessings on their wedding day, Skye and Diehl chose to thank Him instead.

Finally, brethren, whatever things are true, whatever things are noble, whatever things are just, whatever things are pure, whatever things are lovely, whatever things are of good report, if there is any virtue and if there is anything praiseworthy—meditate on these things.

As she stood in the bridal dressing room at Seaside Chapel, waiting for her brother to accompany her to the wedding chapel down the hall, Skye recalled the words that Diehl had read to her from Philippians 4:8.

She smiled at Avery Chung, who was busy adjusting the veil covering Skye's face and trying not to cry.

"I'm so happy for you," Avery kept saying between sniffles.

Brinley Brooks-McMillan walked into the dressing room. She shook her head at Avery. "You're going to ruin your makeup."

"Waterproof," Avery replied.

"Then by all means cry me a river." Brinley chuckled. Her gaze moved up and down Skye's pure white wedding gown. "You look lovely, Skye."

"Thank you," Skye said. "How's little Jovan doing?"

"Sleeping at the moment. Let's see how Ivan handles a ten-month-old at a wedding." Brinley gave a half-laugh. "He's sitting in the back row in case they need to sneak out."

Skye looked past her bridal party to a small window. Outside, rain continued to fall, drowning out the sounds of the ocean on the other side of the dunes and any music that would have floated out of the wedding chapel adjacent to this room.

Brinley lifted Skye's left hand and tilted her ring

finger toward the ceiling lights. "I can't get over how lovely that diamond is. My brother must really love you to trade his Ferrari for this ring."

"Did he even have to sell the car, though?" Avery asked.

"Actually, no," Brinley said. "However, it was a gesture on his part. He never does things half-heartedly. He wanted to show Skye that he meant it."

Yeah, when Skye had found out that the diamond had set Diehl back thirty-one million dollars, she almost passed out until Diehl told her that the most expensive blue diamond ever sold went for forty-eight million at auction.

He still had nine million dollars leftover from the sale of the Ferrari, and in honor of their nuptials, Diehl suggested that they tithe it to Seaside Chapel toward the new gymnasium they were planning to build for teenagers, a safe place for them to hang out after school. That had been in addition to the thirty thousand dollars that Diehl had given Seaside Chapel in June of the year before from the reward money that Skye earned helping to lead the police to the safe recovery of his daughter.

"Time to let me hold your engagement ring for you," Brinley said, palm out. "After the ring ceremony, I will give it to Diehl to put it back on your finger so that you don't have to fix the ring order."

Skye nodded. She knew that the wedding band was supposed to be at the base of her ring finger.

"Closer to your heart." Avery wiped her nose with a wad of tissue paper.

"I had no idea you're a romantic, Avery," Skye said.

"I'm just weeping and gnashing my teeth because y'all won't let me play my trumpet at the processional." Avery laughed through her tears.

"I gave the music program to Emmeline so that she and her brother, Claude, could arrange the processional medley for us," Skye reminded her.

Her sister-in-law was now three months pregnant with her first child, but she was more than happy to help. Claude even composed new music in the arrangement so that he and Emmeline could play double harp, accompanied by a small string ensemble from Sea Islands Symphony Orchestra that Emmeline used to be a part of.

The ensemble did not include Ivan, assigned to babysitting his son so that Brinley could be in the wedding party. Just as well because lately, Ivan had spent more time running the Yun McMillan Music Studio, named after his grandmother, than teaching violin lessons, so he had no time to rehearse for the wedding on top of everything else.

"Is Claude single?" Avery asked out of the blue.

"Focus, girl." Brinley took the engagement ring from Skye and put it on one of her fingers with the diamond turned under so that she could hold it in a fist.

"Thank you, dear friends." Skye smiled at Brinley and Avery. She tried not to cry on such a happy day. "You've been with me through life's trials, prayed with me, advised me, listened to my complaints."

"Complaints?" Avery asked. "You rarely complained. You're the one who thinks things through before doing them."

"I agree," Brinley said. "You're perfect for my brother. Diehl is like that too. He overthinks things sometimes."

"Let's pray before Sebastian gets here," Avery said.

Suddenly they were Treble Trio again, holding hands to pray as they did before every performance. One by one, they took turns to pray away Skye's nervousness and wedding jitters, as though they knew she would have them—and yes, she did.

They went around a second time as each prayed a sentence or two.

"Lord, help Skye not to trip on the way to the altar," Avery prayed.

"Help me not to lose this ring," Brinley pleaded. "But seriously, Lord, I pray that You will bless Diehl and Skye with only Your best. They love You and want Your perfect will to be done in their lives and the lives of their children, both now and in the future."

"Lord, I also pray for a forward-looking marriage for this new husband and wife in which they will let go of their past and walk forth together in the light of Christ and on the path that You will lead them," Avery concluded.

"Thank You, Jesus," Skye prayed. "Father God, may Your name be glorified not only in our marriage but also in the lives of everyone present at our wedding today, from family to friends, from church staff to the caterers, and everyone else. May You be honored, Your name be well spoken of, and may Jesus be lifted up so that He might draw all people to Himself. In His holy and precious name, I pray. Amen."

"Amen," a male voice said.

Skye opened her eyes. Sebastian was at the door.

"Ready?" he asked.

Skye nodded as her palm pressed against her stomach. She drew a deep breath.

"I've done this before," her matron of honor said. "Just focus on where you're going, one step at a time. At least you don't have to walk outside on gravel and on the boardwalk all the way to the pavilion. This is a very short walk between this room and the wedding chapel. Just down the hallway. You can do it."

Skye thanked Brinley for that piece of advice.

"Don't worry. It will be over soon." Avery gave her a serious look. "Just follow me."

Skye laughed and kept the smile on her face all the way down the hallway as Brinley led the processional, Avery behind her, and Skye behind her maid of honor, clinging onto her brother's arm as they entered the century-old wedding chapel.

The string ensemble led by two harps played a beautiful medley of some of the hymns that had impacted Skye and Diehl in their Christian lives, in lieu of the more traditional "Wedding March" or "Pachelbel Canon in D Major."

Diehl and Skye had both agreed that hymns would calm their nerves during the processional.

And they were right. Skye found herself humming to the hymns from her childhood and adult life, and to the hymns that Diehl had chosen in his first year of being a true believer of Jesus Christ.

As she walked slowly on the red carpet amidst a sea of smiling faces, Skye wished that her parents, and Aunt Irma and Uncle Miller could be here to share her happy day, but life on earth wasn't perfect. To be sure, her aunt and uncle had imparted much to Skye and her brother, and their legacy would live on through the next generation.

The most important thing was that God was with them today.

Perfect God in all His glory, who had chosen to rain them with showers of blessings from heaven today, to remind them of the seasons of life.

Glory be to God!

Perfect God who had been with Skye since she was saved as a child, through the turbulent times of a broken family, and who had delivered Skye and her brother through to adulthood unscathed.

Perfect God who had saved Diehl's soul one year ago in this very month of June and transformed his life from lost to found, pain to gain, and sorrow to joy.

And perfect God who had chosen Diehl to stand at the altar now, waiting for Skye to make it through the long red carpet so they could begin their wedded bliss as husband and wife in Christ.

Diehl stared at her with a smile on his face. He blinked.

Skye could tell he was nervous.

Sebastian patted her hand in the crook of his arm, as if to say, "You okay?"

Skye nodded slightly, her eyes never leaving Diehl, who was coming closer and closer to her view. Standing next to him was his dad, holding a cane, and ring-bearer Ethan in a spiffy tuxedo.

Skye was happy that Diehl had chosen his dad to be his best man. It had also been the right decision for Diehl to remain at their Atlanta office for the entire school year to help Brooks Investments to transition to their split company structure. His dad was grateful to have Diehl by his side when they sold Brooks Manufacturing to some company in Texas. And it gave them time to help Diehl's sister-in-law get back into corporate life as she slowly moved back to Atlanta.

An older sister Skye never had, Riley Brooks had become a friend. They had rapport and respect for each other as businesswomen and entrepreneurs. Riley also brought new clients for STL, and Skye was grateful.

Speaking of the personal chef company, after Skye moved to Atlanta from August to May to restructure Watt's for Dinner to fit more into her Skye's the Limit style of business—and to attend marital counseling with her fiancé—she found herself evolving into a CEO position rather than cooking every day as a personal chef. Her chefs needed a leader to guide them in menu planning, take care of their 401K and healthcare, and provide them with job security.

She enjoyed coming up with new menus in her test kitchen—with Diehl being daring enough to try dishes he had never tasted before.

Not cooking every day had freed up Skye to spend

more time with her future stepchildren whenever Diehl was tied up at work. Her flexibility with her schedule meant she could drop off and pick up Elisa and Ethan at school and attend all their school events in the entire school year, rain or shine, to the point that Ethan almost called her Mom.

She smiled at the thought.

Within arm's reach now, Diehl's eyelids fluttered ever so slightly, but Skye noticed.

When Sebastian handed Skye over to Diehl, she saw that his eyes were glistening with tears.

She gently squeezed his hand. He leaned toward her, and she whispered, "God makes all things new."

He nodded.

Pastor Gonzalez began the wedding ceremony with a prayer to Almighty God. The prayer, as well as the rest of the wedding ceremony, was peppered by rain all around the wedding chapel, and occasional distant thunder.

After the traditional wedding vows were exchanged, Pastor Gonzalez said, "Revelation 21:5a says, 'Then He who sat on the throne said, "Behold, I make all things new."' Now the bride and groom would like to say a few more words to each other before they exchange their wedding rings."

Skye and Diehl faced each other and held hands.

Diehl looked lovingly at Skye as he spoke. "Philippians 4:13 says, 'I can do all things through Christ who strengthens me.' I will love you with God's love for as long as we both shall live. Until my last days on earth, I will hold your hands and never let go."

His voice cracked and caused Skye to almost forget what she was to say next. "Romans 8:37 says, 'Yet in all these things we are more than conquerors through Him who loved us.' I will always be with you whether you are very well or very sick. We will go through it together. I will rejoice with you and suffer with you."

Diehl smiled. "Deuteronomy 31:8 says, 'And the Lord, He is the One who goes before you. He will be with you, He will not leave you nor forsake you; do not fear nor be dismayed.' We acknowledge that God is with us and He will never leave us. We pray for His protection over our marriage and our lives together as husband and wife, and parents to our children."

To which, a young man shouted, "Amen!"

Everyone laughed as Ethan grinned, standing next to his Grandpa Ned, who motioned for him to go forward. Ethan stepped very carefully to his dad, holding a cushion with two rings on it.

Diehl glided the gold wedding band onto Skye's ring finger. "With this ring, I thee wed."

Brinley handed him Skye's engagement ring. Diehl placed the blue diamond back on Skye's finger. He winked at Skye, causing her to chuckle and feel slightly giddy.

Skye picked up Diehl's wedding band. It was heavy. It had three square princess-cut diamonds embedded into the lustrous gold. When she put it on Diehl's finger, she rotated the band such that the three diamonds appeared precisely on top. "With this ring, I thee wed."

"By the power vested in me, and in the name of

Jesus Christ, our Lord and Savior, I pronounce you man and wife," Pastor Gonzalez declared. "You may kiss your bride."

Diehl lifted Skye's veil. They stared at each other through misty eyes. Slowly, he lowered his lips to hers.

Honey-flavored lip balm again. Skye savored his kiss as Diehl held her.

She didn't know how long the kiss was, but it must have been a bit too long because Pastor Gonzalez cleared his throat twice.

"Kiss later, Dad," Ethan said loudly. "Cheesecake awaits!"

The entire chapel erupted in laughter and applause.

When Diehl and Skye straightened up, Skye glanced over to find Ethan bowing to the crowd.

"You're welcome," the ten-year-old said.

Somewhere in the chapel, a baby cried. There was only one baby in attendance, so Skye knew who it was. Big lungs. Future singer, that Jovan McMillan.

Diehl held Skye's hand as they faced the wedding guests. From this vantage point, Skye could see the old wooden beams above the chapel, and the few chandeliers here and there. Surrounded by stained glass windows, she could not see the outside, but her ears told her that the rain might have subsided, at least a little bit.

"I now present to you Mr. and Mrs. Diehl and Skye Brooks," the pastor said.

Applause echoed off the walls and ceilings as

string music filled the air again with another hymn medley for their recessional.

Hand in hand, Skye and Diehl walked down the aisle to the cheers and whistles of family and friends.

Skye was too nervous to look at the faces of all in attendance, but she had seen the RSVPs that Avery and her cousin, Gillian, had sorted out for her.

Among the crowd would be members of their Sunday school classes at both Seaside Chapel on St. Simon's Island and Midtown Chapel in Atlanta.

Of course, all the men from the Monday morning men's Bible study group would be here too, as well as the ladies from the Tuesday night Bible study group, including Olivia, the pastor's wife, and their two daughters, home from college for the summer.

Somewhere in the crowd would be colleagues and executives from Brooks Investments, plus many of the chefs working at Skye's the Limit at their two locations.

And Watt Watanabe and his now wife, Anastasia. If not for them deciding to retire on St. Thomas and selling Watt's for Dinner to Skye at a price she could afford, she would not have been able to spend eleven months in Atlanta with Diehl. Their marital counseling would be somewhat incomplete. Much of their session assignments required both of them to demonstrate problem-solving skills and teamwork. They had to be together in person to do the activities to improve their odds of staying married after their honeymoon and the first four years of marriage.

Indeed, God had brought all these people together

to help Diehl and Skye prepare for their married life together, including Pastor "Bootcamp Fizz" Fitz-patrick, who had assigned them so much homework that Diehl asked for a diploma after their six months of marital counseling was over.

Instead, Pastor Fizz had arranged for several meet-ings with at least a dozen Christian couples who had been married to their spouses for over fifty years. They shared with Diehl and Skye their pitfalls and perils, as well as their secrets and successes.

Skye learned that those couples did not have a single method to a joyful marriage—except that they all had one thing in common: faith in the living God who created marriage in the first place.

Yes, the giver of all good things was none other than God Himself.

God alone had brought Diehl and Skye together. And God alone would keep them together.

As they crossed the rotunda at the back of the chapel, Diehl pecked Skye on her cheek. "I love you."

"I love you too," Skye said as the wooden double doors opened to a surprise burst of sunshine outside.

The rain had stopped, making way for glorious rays of sunshine that basked the wedding couple in its late-morning summer warmth. Nearby, the ocean waves crashed the shoreline in their usual time signa-ture. Sea birds returned, gliding in the winds that also swayed the sea oats that separated the wedding chapel grounds from the sandy beach.

A new day.

A brand-new start for Skye and Diehl, the beginning of the rest of their lives together in Christ.

"And God made all things new," her husband whispered in Skye's ear.

She nodded.

Indeed, God had made all things new.

DEAR READER:

Thank you for reading *His Morning Kiss*. Did you enjoy the story of Skye and Diehl? If so, you might like my next novel, *His Quiet Serenade,* the story of Skye's friend, trumpet teacher Avery Chung, and the novelist next door, Devon Hu. Do you remember Helen Hu from my Savannah Sweethearts and Protector Sweethearts collections? Devon is Helen's cousin, who moves to St. Simon's Island for some peace and quiet so he can write his novels. Unfortunately, his neighbor's brass studio is anything but quiet. Can he get her to move? Coming soon!

His Quiet Serenade (Seaside Chapel Book 4)
JanThompson.com/quiet

Sign up for Jan Thompson's mailing list to be notified when *His Quiet Serenade* is released:
JanThompson.com/newsletter

BRINLEY BROOKS-MCMILLAN IS IN HIS LONGING HEART

Diehl's younger sister, Brinley, kicks off the Seaside Chapel series when she returns to Seaside Island to spend the Christmas holidays with her wealthy family. There's her great-aunt Ella, whom Brinley is left to babysit. There's her trust-fund-baby sister, Zoe, who is in love with an erstwhile hairstylist, who happens to be the brother of Brinley's acquaintance, Ivan, first violin in the Sea Islands Symphony Orchestra. One thing leads to another, and Brinley ends up spending time with Ivan and his grandmother, Yun, both devout Christians who live in a rundown cottage.

His Longing Heart (Seaside Chapel Book 1)
JanThompson.com/longing

SEBASTIAN LANGSTON IS IN HIS WAKE-UP CALL

In trying to win back his ex-fiancée, Skye's older brother and restaurateur Sebastian cooks up an idea to rent a girlfriend. Who in the world would agree to help him? How about Emmeline, a desperately poor harpist who needs all the help she can get? After all, it's only for one summer. And she tells him they can't hold hands. That should take care of any issue, regardless of how attractive Sebastian is to Emmeline, right?

His Wake-Up Call (Seaside Chapel Book 2)

JanThompson.com/wakeup

EARL YOUNG IS IN NEVER A TRAITOR

Private Investigator Earl Young plays a supporting role in *His Morning Kiss*, as he does in *Once a Hero* (Protector Sweethearts Book 2). He finally gets to headline his own story when he goes undercover as the fake boyfriend of an informant and whistleblower in *Never a Traitor* (Defender Sweethearts Book 1). As they solve a white-collar crime in a corporate setting, they try not to fall in love with each other.

Never a Traitor (Defender Sweethearts Book 1)
JanThompson.com/traitor

Sign up for my mailing list to be notified when future Seaside Chapel novels are published. In addition to beach romance, I also write romantic suspense and near-future romantic thrillers.

Subscribe to Jan's book news:
JanThompson.com/newsletter

*C*ontinue reading for more information about the next Seaside Chapel novel, *His Quiet Serenade...*

THE NEXT NOVEL IS HIS QUIET SERENADE

SEASIDE CHAPEL BOOK 4

He is a novelist looking for a quiet place to write his next blockbuster book. She is the trumpet teacher next door who just started a new brass ensemble in her home studio. They say opposites attract, but will Avery's loud business venture shatter Devon's writing career in this beach romance?

A TRUMPET SOLOIST AND TEACHER...

When she is not playing in the Sea Islands Symphony Orchestra (SISO) or the Seaside Chapel Sanctuary Orchestra, Avery Chung teaches trumpet to local students in her Joyful Noise Brass Studio. She is overjoyed when she raises enough funds to form a brass ensemble that comprises trumpets, trombones, horns, and tubas. Her excitement is shattered when her closest neighbor shows up at her house to complain about the "noise" and proceeds to tell her what to do.

A TENSE WRITER AND NEIGHBOR...

International bestselling author Devon Hu arrives on St. Simon's Island, where no one cares about the worldwide success of his medieval fantasy saga. In the pursuit of continually satisfying his voracious and hungry readers, Devon has given up dating and his personal life, with the exception of caring for his paraplegic sister. He hopes to earn enough income to support her for the rest of her life. The last thing he needs is for his loud neighbor to make a racket every day but Sunday, robbing him of his concentration and distracting him from meeting his book deadlines.

A TRUCE BETWEEN THEM...

When Avery's students continue to make their joyful noise, Devon offers to rent her a music room at the Yun McMillan Music Studio on the other side of the island.

Avery accepts the gift on the condition that Devon will sit in on their ensemble practice sessions once a week and attend local SISO performances for a year. Devon agrees, only to find out that his season ticket affords him frequent and up-close contact with the otherwise charming Avery. Devon's heart begins to tune in to Avery's beats, and he knows he's in trouble when he spends way more time sitting in on orchestra rehearsals than writing his books. Will he be able to get away fast enough before his career is ruined?

His Quiet Serenade is the fourth novel in *USA Today* bestselling author Jan Thompson's **Seaside Chapel** small town Christian beach romance series. Devon and Avery's story takes us to the interior of St. Simon's Island, where these two neighbors live among spreading live oak trees near the marshes.

His Quiet Serenade (Seaside Chapel Book 4)
JanThompson.com/quiet

Seaside Chapel
JanThompson.com/seaside

Sign up for Jan Thompson's mailing list to be notified when *His Quiet Serenade* is released:
JanThompson.com/newsletter

ACKNOWLEDGMENTS

Many thanks to my Georgia Press publishing team for keeping up with my writing schedule.

I appreciate my copyeditors and proofreaders who worked on this novel: Lesley Ann McDaniel, Lenda Selph, and Judy DeVries. Their eye for detail is from the Lord.

A special thank you to my loyal readers who have been with me from the beginning. Your enthusiasm for every book I write is encouraging and inspiring.

Additionally, I would like to thank these helpful professionals who answered my research questions in the writing of this novel:

- Author and detective Dony Jay and retired detective Rich Frazier (and his lovely wife, Angie) for answering my many questions about kidnapping investigations. It was quite eye-opening to see the amount of work involved at the local and state levels. Those men and women who go out daily to find and rescue stolen children are heroes!

- Author and attorney Heather Ijames for explaining child custody law in various states in the USA. Very helpful to me, a non-lawyer novelist.

I am grateful to God for my husband and son for their support and encouragement. I also thank God for my parents and my three brothers for my happy and memorable childhood. I'll always remember my beloved mother and my late father for having instilled in me the love of reading and writing from a very early age. I miss my father here on earth, but I will see him again in heaven someday.

Most of all, I am eternally thankful to my Lord and Savior, Jesus Christ, who died on the cross to save me from my sins and rose again from the grave to give me eternal life. Without Him, I can write nothing (John 15:5).

Joyfully in Jesus,
Jan Thompson
John 3:16

READ A FREE EBOOK IN THE SAME STORY WORLD

Set in Georgia, South Carolina, and Tennessee, this clean and wholesome Christian romance tells the story of art gallery archivist Sheryl Breckenridge and world-famous sculptor Winton Pace. Read this ebook for free!

Time for Me (A Vacation Sweethearts Prequel)
JanThompson.com/time-free

BOOKS BY JAN THOMPSON

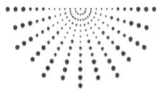

CONTEMPORARY CHRISTIAN COASTAL AND
BEACH ROMANCE

Seaside Chapel (7 Books)
JanThompson.com/seaside
Savannah Sweethearts (12 Books)
JanThompson.com/savannah
Vacation Sweethearts (8 Books)
JanThompson.com/vacation

CONTEMPORARY CHRISTIAN CITY ROMANCE

Midtown Christmas (4 Books)
JanThompson.com/christmas

CHRISTIAN ROMANTIC SUSPENSE

Protector Sweethearts (6 Books)
JanThompson.com/protector
Defender Sweethearts (6 Books)
JanThompson.com/defender

NEAR-FUTURE TEHNOTHRILLERS WITH
CHRISTIAN ROMANCE

Binary Hackers (4 Books)
JanThompson.com/binary

Subscribe to Jan Thompson's mailing list:
JanThompson.com/newsletter

SEASIDE CHAPEL

Welcome to *USA Today* bestselling author Jan Thompson's Seaside Chapel Christian beach romance series. These novels are set on real-life St. Simon's Island, Georgia—a beach town where history is all around and the future is a moment away—and the neighboring fictitious Seaside Island, where the rich and famous live.

Savor the small-town atmosphere and the warm southern beaches of St. Simon's Island and the idyllic Golden Isles along the Atlantic Ocean. Enjoy the music of the orchestra and hymns of the church, and hang out with our Christian friends who attend Seaside Chapel, a little church by the sea known for its beach weddings and fair share of love and life.

As these Christians grow in their knowledge and understanding of God, they are tested in their spiritual maturity, their love lives, and their relationships with others. Share their heartaches and healing, and cheer them on as they celebrate faith, family, and friends.

~

JanThompson.com/seaside

- Book 0 (Prequel): *His Surprise Proposal*
- Book 1: *His Longing Heart*
- Book 2: *His Wake-Up Call*
- Book 3: *His Morning Kiss*
- Book 4: *His Quiet Serenade*
- Book 5: *His Waiting Love*
- Book 6: *His Beach Retreat*

SAVANNAH SWEETHEARTS

Welcome to the new south! From *USA Today* bestselling author Jan Thompson come these clean and wholesome, sweet and inspirational Christian romances set on the romantic beaches of Tybee Island and in the coastal town of Savannah, Georgia. Meet a group of multiracial and multiethnic churchgoing Christians who love the Lord, work hard in their careers, and seek God's will for their love lives. Against a backdrop of ocean, sand, and sun, these inspirational romances showcase aspects of the human need for God and for one another. Have some tea, settle in a comfortable reading chair, and enjoy these sweet celebrations of faith, hope, and love in Jesus Christ.

JanThompson.com/savannah

- Book 1: *Ask You Later* (Artist Romance)

- Book 2: *Know You More* (Multiracial Romance)
- Book 3: *Tell You Soon* (Asian-American Romance with Suspense)
- Book 4: *Draw You Near* (International Romance)
- Book 5: *Cherish You So* (Wheelchair Billionaire Romance)
- Book 6: *Walk You There* (Old-Meets-New Tour Guide Romance)
- Book 7: *Love You Always* (Romance with Suspense)
- Book 8: *Kiss You Now* (Multiracial Romance)
- Book 9: *Find You Again* (Multiracial Romance)
- Book 10: *Wish You Joy* (Christmas-Themed Romance)
- Book 11: *Call You Home* (Deaf Chef Romance)
- Book 12: *Let You Go* (Asian-American Romance with Suspense)

∾

Read *Ask You Later* (Book 1) for free:
JanThompson.com/ask-free

VACATION SWEETHEARTS

Travel with our friends from Savannah, Georgia, to the coast and to the mountains. Cheer them on as they celebrate the immeasurable grace and undeserved mercy of God through Jesus Christ.

The Vacation Sweethearts novels are a spin-off of Jan's Savannah Sweethearts series, and fans will recognize familiar faces from Riverside Chapel, a church in the coastal city of Savannah, Georgia. In fact, we might even visit the beach town of Tybee Island from time to time to visit old friends and beloved families...

JanThompson.com/vacation

- Book 0 (Prequel): *Time for Me*
- Book 1: *Smile for Me* (Beach Romance in the Bahamas)

- Book 2: *Reach for Me* (Romance with Suspense in the Smoky Mountains)
- Book 3: *Wait for Me* (Romance with Suspense on a Cruise Ship)
- Book 4: *Look for Me* (Romance with Suspense in a Florida Beach Town)
- Book 5: *Pray for Me* (International Romance in the City of Atlanta)
- Book 6: *Care for Me* (Small Mountain Town Romance)
- Book 7: *Cheer for Me* (International Romance)

∼

Read *Time for Me* (Prequel) for free:
JanThompson.com/time-free

MIDTOWN CHRISTMAS

Big city romance, small town feel. Four Christian couples minister at Midtown Chapel in metro Atlanta, and Midtown Village, the community of tiny homes for needy families. From November to January every year, this place turns into a Christmas Village for a small-town feel right there in the metropolis of Atlanta, Georgia.

- Book 1: *Let Me Hold You* (Levi Theroux and Maggie Jacobs from *Pray for Me*)
- Book 2: *Let Me Adore You* (Erika Song from *Look for Me* and Hiroki Yamada from *Walk You There*)
- Book 3: *Let Me Honor You* (Forsythia McDevitt from *Call You Home* and Owen Grayson from *Find You Again*)
- Book 4: *Let Me Love You* (Leila Patel from *Find You Again*)

PROTECTOR SWEETHEARTS

Private investigator Helen Hu and her associates specialize in searching for missing persons and hunting for lost treasures. Join them in their adventure suspense around the world in *USA Today* bestselling author Jan Thompson's Protector Sweethearts, a series of Christian Romantic Suspense with a side of mystery.

Protector Sweethearts is a spin-off of Savannah Sweethearts and Vacation Sweethearts.

JanThompson.com/protector

- Book 1: *Once a Thief*
- Book 2: *Once a Hero*
- Book 3: *Once a Spy*

- Book 4: *Twice a Fighter*
- Book 5: *Twice a Convict*
- Book 6: *Twice a Soldier*

DEFENDER SWEETHEARTS

Defender Sweethearts is a sister series to the Protector Sweethearts Christian romantic suspense collection. While the heroes in Protector Sweethearts search for lost treasures and lost people, the Defender Sweethearts novels focus on protecting the helpless and hopeless. The main characters in Defender Sweethearts come from the supporting cast in Protector Sweethearts.

JanThompson.com/defender

- Book 1: *Never a Traitor*
- Book 2: *Never a Hostage*
- Book 3: *Never a Fugitive*
- Book 4: *Always a Maverick*

- Book 5: *Always a Champion*
- Book 6: *Always a Guardian*

BINARY HACKERS

Like more suspense with your Christian romance? Like to read suspense thrillers? If you're looking for clean near-future romantic suspense without compromising the Christian faith, these books are for you.

From *USA Today* bestselling author Jan Thompson come these inspirational near-future cyberthrillers combining technothriller and romance, starting with Binary Hackers that feature computer specialists living at the edge of cyberspace, where they have to juggle being law-abiding truth-telling Christians while carrying out their assignments by any and all means possible.

The Binary Hackers series is set in the same story world as Jan's other books, and characters from the other series may make cameo appearances in this series and vice versa.

JanThompson.com/binary

- Book 1: *Zero Sum*
- Book 2: *Zero Day*
- Book 3: *Zero Base*
- Book 4: *Zero Trust*

ABOUT JAN THOMPSON

USA Today bestselling author Jan Thompson writes clean and wholesome contemporary Christian romance with elements of women's fiction, Christian romantic suspense with an air of mystery, and inspirational international thrillers with threads of sweet Christian romance. Jan's books are for readers who love inspiring stories of faith, hope, and love in Jesus Christ.

Raised on a tropical island in the eastern hemisphere, Jan now lives and writes in the western hemisphere. Her international background gives her a unique multicultural and multiracial perspective to her novels and books. The island has never left her, and she reminisces about beach life in her beach romance novels.

When Jan is not busy writing small-town stories, she writes big-city romantic suspense and international technothrillers, a nod to her previous career in computer science. She weaves technology with human interests, reflecting the current and future digital world. And romance. There's always romance.

Beyond the printed page, Jan is a wife, mother,

avid reader, former quilter, erstwhile pianist, occasional artist, and chief of staff to the family cat.

Find out more about Jan Thompson:
JanThompson.com

Subscribe to Jan's book news mailing list:
JanThompson.com/newsletter

For God so loved the world
that He gave His only begotten Son,
that whoever believes in Him
should not perish
but have everlasting life.
—John 3:16